# Captain Easterday's Bargain

by

## Kathleen Buckley

**Captain Easterday's Bargain**

COPYRIGHT © 2019 by Kathleen Gail Buckley

Cover Art by *Abigail Owen*

The Wild Rose Press, Inc.
PO Box 708
Adams Basin, NY 14410-0708
Visit us at www.thewildrosepress.com

Publishing History
First Tea Rose Edition, 2019
Print ISBN 978-1-5092-2541-5
Digital ISBN 978-1-5092-2542-2


Published in the United States of America

"A lady in a domino the color of a ripe quince," a tall gentleman murmured as she brushed past and put a hand on her arm to detain her.

"Not for your plucking, sir." She laughed.

He spoke closer to her ear, lowering his voice yet more. "But when a quince ripens, it will drop into one's hand with only a little encouragement."

"Then perhaps I am not ripe." *Am I getting too much into the spirit of the thing?*

"Quinces harvested before they are quite ready will still ripen. In this cool climate, it's often necessary to gather them early."

It chanced that the orchestra had come to the end of its piece, and for that moment, conversation around them quieted and she heard the last part of his statement without distractions. She stared up into his eyes. In spite of being in shadow, she knew the speaker's identity and recoiled.

"Be easy, my dear. I have no intention of carrying you off from a masquerade ball, like some reenactment of the Romans' abduction of the Sabine women. Lord, it would cause a riot! Assuming anyone noticed."

# Acknowledgements

This novel resulted from research on shipping in the Pool of London for a previous novel, which brought to mind my own family connection to the shipping industry. My paternal grandfather worked for Railway Express throughout the Great Depression, until his retirement in the 1960s. My father worked for the Alaska Railroad from the end of World War II until he retired in the 1970s. I worked for two years as a security officer on Seattle's waterfront early in this century.

Most of us never think about how fruit gets to our supermarket in the winter, or that we can buy specialty items from half the world away and they arrive, sometimes now in a matter of days rather than months. But even with motor freight, shipping containers, and computerized tracking, some things haven't changed much since the days of sailing ships and freight wagons.

As one of the managers at the marine terminal put it, after a long, difficult day, "It just never f—ing stops, does it?"

Chapter 1

*July 1740*

The betrothal visit went well, after the first few days. Mariah chatted merrily with Captain Easterday's brother and his family and seemed delighted by the farm animals and the milking and cheese making. Her reaction to Lowfields Manor surprised him. He had feared she would find the country dull and his people unfashionable. Instead she played games with his nephews and niece, petted the lambs, and showed an unexpected interest in nature. The weather cooperated, sunny and dry.

He renewed his connection to his family, riding and walking around the manor with his brother, listening to his nephew Matthew's idea for exporting Scottish linen goods to the colonies, and joining in the family's lively conversation at meals. Hearing the familiar dialect and eating the traditional mutton, beef, onion, carrot, and turnip scouse, he felt London's docks and quays receding.

It never occurred to him that Mariah's newly acquired fondness for strolling by herself in the grounds was anything more than delight in nature, of which she could have seen little in London.

Geoffrey muttered to him once when they were out in the fields, "A good match. Even a country mouse knows that an alderman of the city is an important man. There's no saying he mightn't be elected Lord Mayor or be knighted. Rich, as well, I reckon, from what Mistress Mariah tells us. Not that I couldn't have guessed by his coach and the outriders. Glad you got over the other. You'll like being married."

"An old friend, too. Richard Saltstall encouraged me when I first went into business." It had seemed to make sense to agree to marry his daughter.

****

*Saturday, 19 July*

Two days before they were to start for London, Mariah did not come down to breakfast.

"Such a slugabed!" her aunt Henrietta remarked. "That maid of hers is not in the habit of waking her because of the late nights in Town, but after almost two weeks, she should know one rises earlier in the country. Even if the chit doesn't ring for her." When she sent Mariah's hatchet-faced maid to wake her, the woman returned precipitately to report that her bed was empty.

Mistress Easterday was a sensible lady and had four boys, ranging from newly come of age down to fifteen years, but she had only one daughter, a placid child of twelve. While the others were wondering where Mariah could be and Marcus Easterday frowned with a presentiment of trouble, his sister-in-law quietly instructed the maid to return to the bedchamber to see if she could find any clue to her whereabouts. Might she have dressed and gone out for an early walk? If her dressing gown and slippers were gone, mayhap she had wandered into some part of the rambling house which the maids had not yet visited.

Mariah's maid returned, white-faced. "Two of her

gowns and shifts are gone, ma'am. And her cloak, and some other things." At this point she was overcome and had to be revived with sal volatile. Mistress Easterday then sent her to lie down. "Wherever can she have gone?"

Little Sophie observed, "I expect she took them because she would need a change of clothing, wouldn't she?"

After a pregnant pause, Mistress Easterday asked, "Dear, are you suggesting that Mistress Mariah has run away? Why would you think such a thing?"

"Mariah likes Mr. Beresford."

Ellis Beresford was staying with the family of Sir Manfred Knott, a baronet with several daughters and a pimply son who had completed his first year at Oxford. The Easterdays had traded several visits with the Knotts and dined at each other's homes twice, with the second turning into an impromptu dance. New faces, rare in the neighborhood, always led to a spate of entertainments. Marcus Easterday had not paid much attention to Beresford, beyond noticing the blond youth possessed pleasing manners, if a little too lively. Still, a lad of one-and-twenty cannot be expected to be as serious as a man of six-and-thirty.

"What is that to the point, child?" her papa asked. He knew even less about young ladies than his wife.

Sophia wriggled. "He likes her, too. You can tell by how they look at each other." She cast an apologetic glance toward Marcus. "I know it sounds silly, Mama…but Mariah is rather like Alice, isn't she?"

"Oh, Alice." Mistress Easterday sniffed. "Sir Manfred's youngest daughter. I'm afraid she reads novels of the most foolish sort." The men at the table gazed at her, Geoffrey Easterday and his sons blankly, Marcus with growing disquiet.

"Sophia," he said quietly, "do you think Mariah may have gone away with Mr. Beresford?"

Nigel, seventeen, snorted. "She doesn't know anything. She's still in the schoolroom."

"I know Alice is always talking about how romantic it would be to go to Gretna Green with a gentleman who was handsome and titled. Mariah and Mr. Beresford talked together when Sir Manfred and his family came and we ate our supper down by the river. They stood looking at the river, and she sighed several times, and he patted her hand. I suppose it was very affecting, if one likes that kind of thing. It was like something out of one of Alice's books."

"Sickly stuff," the youngest boy said.

"But Beresford has no title." Mariah settle for a mere gentleman, when she had been determined to marry a duke?

At the same moment, his sister-in-law demanded, "Sophia Easterday, do you mean to tell me that you read Alice Knott's foolish novels?"

"Only when she will lend them to me, Mama," Sophie admitted in a small voice, "which is not very often."

Mistress Easterday frowned at her daughter, and returned to the main issue. "Marcus, the boy became Viscount Franley's heir a year or two since, when his brother died. We think of him as the boy who introduced frogs into the children's beds and who once tied walnut shells onto the cat's paws and released her into the uncarpeted hall in the middle of the night."

"I think I had best ride over to see Beresford."

Marcus stood up and inclined his head to his sister-in-law, and added, "Thank you, Sophie. What an observant girl you are."

"I wish it weren't so, Uncle Marcus. It's exciting to read of such things, but one wouldn't wish to actually do them."

He managed a wry smile at her, as his brother said, "I'll go with you."

The baronet's home, too, was in turmoil. Beresford had left a note on his unused bed. "Gone to visit a friend. Back in a week or so." He had taken a portmanteau but left most of his clothing. Ralph, the baronet's heir, could tell them little more than that Ellis liked to ride out by himself most days. The previous day he had taken his sketch pad and gone to draw some scenic vista or other and had not returned for hours. After finding his note, inquiry of the head groom revealed that Beresford's groom was gone, as well as their horses. "Seemin'ly they left in t'neet, wi'out mekkin' a sound."

Geoffrey Easterday drew Sir Manfred aside to apprise him of Mariah Saltstall's absence.

"Stap me!" Sir Manfred rapped out. "They'll not have gone far with Mistress Mariah riding pillion. They would hire a coach in Preston or take the stage. The border—and Gretna Green—is not much more than a hundred miles. Two days' coach travel, mayhap, unless there's rain. I've a speedy horse, Captain, which you are welcome to borrow. I will follow by coach, for I ride too heavy for such a race."

"Thank you, Sir Manfred. I accept your offer."

The baronet shouted to one of his grooms to saddle Lightning and be d—d quick about it. The groom ran to obey. Word would be through the stable and the house, too, without doubt. Next it would be the neighborhood.

Captain Marcus Easterday could not recall when he had last been so furious.

\*\*\*\*

*Sunday, 27 July*

He arrived in London and went straight to Saltstall, certain he would be home on the Sabbath afternoon.

Saltstall's library was scented with leather book bindings, and the furniture was old and masculine. Mistress Saltstall's taste for fashionable furniture had not been indulged here. The alderman nodded him to a chair and poured brandy without first asking. Both of them would be the better for a restorative. At least the news was not a complete surprise. Marcus had dispatched a short letter to Saltstall with a groom ordered to change horses as often as necessary. The letter had arrived two days before Easterday.

"Your account was necessarily brief," Saltstall said. "The news that all was well came as a relief, but as you did not explain, I do not quite understand…"

Richard Saltstall had made a fortune as a grocer from beginnings little different from Easterday's. He had not done so by indecision, but Easterday understood his hesitation. No elopement, even a thwarted one, could be said to turn out well. An elopement could lead to a duel, with all its notoriety, even if the outcome were not fatal. At best, scandal would attach to Mariah's name. More scandal.

"They had to ride to where a hired coach was waiting, and they could not ride fast, with Mariah perched up behind Beresford with no pillion saddle available. I was able to ride cross country. My older brother and I spent much of our free time as boys careering about the countryside. Then I had a stroke of luck. I came upon the coach by the side of the road, with a broken wheel. The coachman was there, but Mariah and Beresford and the groom had ridden to the next town to see about hiring another vehicle."

"But you caught them."

"The next town was no more than a village. It had a small inn, but the inn's stable kept no coach. They had a dogcart but had to send to the innkeeper's brother for it. While they were waiting, Beresford hired a chamber for Mariah and ordered a meal." Easterday paused. The next bit would be difficult.

"When I entered the inn and asked for them, the ale drawer told me that Beresford had been in the tap, pacing and waiting for their food to be ready until a few minutes before. Mistress Mariah, who the drawer claimed to believe was Beresford's sister, called down the stairs to Beresford very urgently, asking him to come up at once."

Saltstall looked away. "One might surmise that Mariah had seen you from the window."

"Very likely. I went upstairs immediately. When I found the door locked, I called for the landlord to bring his keys. I suppose he came as quickly as he could, but the door would not open. He apologized, saying he seldom had occasion to unlock the guest chamber doors. He tried all his other keys, which took a little time. None of them worked. He called for a servant to fetch a ladder and set it up against the room's window. However, we learned the door was barricaded when we heard some heavy object being shoved away. Of all the luck, it would be the one chamber with a great old-fashioned wardrobe, in which the innkeeper's wife stored the spare bed linens, blankets, and crockery."

"Did the young scoundrel rape my daughter to be sure of securing her hand in marriage when he realized you had caught up with them?" Saltstall grated.

Easterday cleared his throat. "I can acquit him of that charge." He blew out a breath. It was harder than he'd expected—and he had expected the worst, all the way from Lancashire. He went on, "Once the wardrobe was out of the way, Beresford flung open the door before I had a chance to kick it open. I believe he thought I might murder him out of hand. I give him credit; he stood there and declared that he and Mariah would marry, no matter what I—or you—wanted. And she clung to his arm and swore that no one could make her marry anyone but dear Ellis. Which is true, you must admit, Saltstall. Two hundred years ago, parents might have been willing to beat or starve a girl into agreeing to a marriage, but few today would consider it."

"No, of course not." He poured more brandy into Easterday's glass and his own. "I apologize for the intolerable insult my daughter has offered you. I understand how painful it must be. Her foolishness is its own punishment, for she has ruined herself this time."

Easterday raised one hand a little, brushing away the apology which he did not feel he was owed. Yet he did not quite see what he could have done differently, apart from not agreeing to the betrothal. Perhaps he should have spent more time courting her. Still, Mariah's maid and aunt should have been more alert, since supervising and chaperoning her had been their duty. "I am sorry for your sake, sir. But all is not lost."

"Mariah has shamed herself and her mother and me, although the latter is of little importance. Even if she has not lost her virtue, she is compromised. What can you call it but ruin?"

Easterday stared into the brandy. "I confess I felt a momentary urge to thrash the lad within an inch of his life. A few minutes' thought convinced me that it would resolve nothing. Recall if you will that Mariah called him upstairs. She was in a room facing the road. Young Beresford was downstairs in the tap, where he could not have seen me until I was at the door."

"Are you saying it was her idea to...?"

"She claimed it was, when the three of us spoke—after the first few awkward minutes. It may not have been the act of a gentleman to fall in with the suggestion, but they were both determined upon wedding, and, er, anticipating the event was the only thing they could do which would make it certain."

"I cannot like it. The insult to you, throwing herself away on a young good-for-naught when she might have married a man with sense..." He tossed off the rest of his brandy.

"Most girls prefer roses and moonlight and overblown compliments to sense," Easterday pointed out. " 'Tis not an improvident marriage. He is his father's heir, remember, and as far I can tell, he has no vices but the writing of poetry and an inclination to the romantic. I withdrew my claim but insisted that Mariah return to London as planned with her aunt and Abigail, with Beresford as an outrider. Beresford has written to his father to let him know that he has offered for your daughter and is going to apply to you for your permission."

"If my sister and that curst maid knew she had met the fellow, they should have been on the watch for mischief. They both knew she yearned after a title. That's why I sent Mariah out of London, so talk about her behavior in pursuing Guysbridge could die down."

"I believe they did not realize who Beresford's father was, for which we must blame the freer manners of the north. He was introduced to us merely as Ellis Beresford, their harum-scarum nephew."

"It's decent of you to try to smooth it over, under the circumstances. That my peagoose of a daughter should do this, when you'd been disappointed once before—"

"Not at all. Claudia Dean jilted me a dozen years ago because she was young and had romantical notions, and I had none. I should have learned from that mistake."

"You went to sea when you should have been at Eton. You had the maturity of a serious man in his thirties. Mistress Claudia was foolish to prefer a pup who'd never had two thoughts to rub together. As is my chit."

"Mariah is eighteen. Good God, I'm twice her age—I'm too old for her, and I ought to have known it. I am still not the man to appeal to a romantic-minded girl."

"And rather than simply saying she did not care for the match, Mariah needs must run off with that scapegrace. If I had caught them before—"

"If you had caught them, I think I must have withdrawn my offer anyway, Saltstall. What could be expected of a marriage to which the bride was forced—if you could induce her to say the words? Her husband-to-be is able to support her; he is young and he will have a title. It may not be the marriage you intended, but it's not an ineligible one."

"Ay, but will his father agree?"

Easterday smiled wryly. "It may not be the marriage he intended, but he will also see the advantages. Egad, it's not as if you're a costermonger! She's the great-granddaughter of an earl, and you're an alderman and can give her a good dowry. If that's not enough, throw in that Beresford unquestionably compromised her. The alternative to his marrying her would be a duel. I am sure the viscount would prefer to avoid such an outcome."

Saltstall sat silent, weighing the matter. At length he said, "It will do well enough, I suppose. Do I understand you were favorably impressed by Beresford?"

"It would be more correct to say that I was not unfavorably impressed. He's young and may become more serious-minded. He's not a fop, and he likes country life. That's how he came to spend so much time in the wilds of Lancashire with his maternal uncle's family."

Saltstall sighed. "I am sorry it came about for your sake, but I must thank you for arranging it without scandal. As I think on't, I realize it could have turned out worse."

"Very much worse. Imagine Mariah weeping or in hysterics while we waited for Sir Manfred's coach to arrive, and while she was dragged back to Lowfields. How could it fail to cause talk? Not to mention a duel with Beresford. I used to be competent with a cutlass or belaying pin, but he may be expert with a short sword."

11

"You were quite right to do as you did. Bless me, the talk it would have caused. Still, you need a wife. Perhaps my sister will have a suggestion."

"You need not trouble your sister." He had formed the opinion that Aunt Henrietta's ineffective assistance was worse than no help at all. "I will not marry now. I have no title nor family property which goes back hundreds of years. My niece and nephews may inherit from me with my goodwill."

Saltstall sighed. "Well, I am sorry that my suggestion turned out ill. And you are right—an imprudent match can be worse than none."

They both contemplated Saltstall's own marriage. Marianne Saltstall had been happy to marry a fortune but had never stopped regretting not having secured a titled husband. She had also been indiscreet before her marriage.

Saltstall went on, "I would not have blamed you for withdrawing your offer. Indeed, I honor you for agreeing to marry my daughter when you knew she was flighty and headstrong and had behaved improperly, and for not withdrawing when I had to reveal her mother's actions to you."

Marcus Easterday uttered a sympathetic "*Mmmm*." What could one say in reply? "Mistress Saltstall will be pleased with your daughter's match."

"That is something, too," Saltstall agreed.

"Let us drink to their happiness, then, before I go."

\*\*\*\*

As he walked to his lodgings, he felt very nearly as light-hearted as the people around him on the streets who were enjoying a sunny day of leisure. His relief at concluding the painful interview did not account for the sudden elevation of his mood. No, he rather thought he had been in a haze of melancholy for several weeks without being aware of it. He should have been looking forward to his marriage to Mariah Saltstall. She had much to recommend her. Didn't she? She would probably be as good a hostess as her mother—if she were not sulking. He had not been well acquainted with Mariah, of course. The times they had met, she had seemed reserved, though he had heard her prattling to other girls and young men. It had been a relief she had not chattered to him about hats or how she would decorate her boudoir and the drawing room when she was a married lady, or the last ball she had attended. Yet unless they found some subject of mutual interest, what could they talk about? He would be busy with his shipping company, and she would presumably have been taken up with managing their home. Children would have provided a bond. Though no doubt she would have spent most of her days planning and attending social events and shopping, as apparently Mistress Saltstall did.

He tossed a penny to a crossing sweeper. It was apparent to him that Saltstall was not altogether happy in his marriage. How much like Mariah had her mother been as a girl? Not that he would care for a wife like Marianne Saltstall, though until recently she had seemed to suit Saltstall well enough. For all her social skills, she seemed cold. Perhaps that was all one could expect of a well-bred lady. His brother Geoffrey and his wife were still affectionate with each other, even after decades of marriage. Some of his friends and acquaintances appeared happy with their wives, also, and one or two openly doted upon their mates. He would not trust such odds regarding a ship or cargo.

"Captain Easterday!" a lady's voice exclaimed. "Is it you, in truth?"

Sunk in his own musings, he had not noticed the elderly couple approaching. Recalled to his surroundings, he recognized a lady he had met at Saltstall's party at Vauxhall Gardens. Could it be less than two months ago?

"Good afternoon, Mistress Bradshaw. I hope I see you well?"

"Very well, sir." She twinkled merrily, a thing not usually seen in ladies in their sixth decade. She addressed her companion. "Mr. Hale, may I present Captain Marcus Easterday, a friend of Alderman Saltstall?"

After an exchange of civilities, Mr. Hale said, "My dear Mistress Bradshaw has not introduced me as completely as she might. She has agreed this very day to marry me."

"I wish you both the best, ma'am, sir."

"And you, Captain Easterday, I think you are betrothed to Mariah Saltstall."

"Ah…no. She found she had mistaken her feelings."

"Oh! I am so sorry." She pondered a moment while Mr. Hale fiddled with his cane in embarrassment. "Unless, of course, it is all for the best. Sometimes these things are."

"I am sure you are correct, ma'am."

What a relief to gain the sanctuary of his rooms. He owned a house in Queen's Square, bought in anticipation of his marriage but had not moved into it. In the normal course, Mariah would have chosen furniture and ornaments. At the moment, the only furnishings were those needed for the skeleton staff of servants present to maintain the house and prevent burglary.

Should he sell the house? His current lodgings were appropriate for a single gentleman. He might purchase a small house and install a mistress. It would give him the benefit of a woman's company and a sort of home life whenever he wanted it. Previously, when he had taken a mistress, he had supported her in rented lodgings.

He did not quite like illicit connections; his father and most of the neighboring gentry had practiced rather stricter morality than many of the aristocracy in London. But a man had needs, and a beddable woman was one of them. After turning thirty, the warmth and companionship of a home and the possibility of children had begun to seem desirable too. All those potential benefits had led to his betrothal to Saltstall's daughter. Envisioning Mariah sitting by the fire in the evening, sewing baby clothes or consoling a weeping little son or daughter…no, he could not imagine such a scene. The children would be confined to the nursery, their scrapes, bruises, and woes consoled by their nurse. Nor would Mariah be the sort of companion to him that his mother had been to his father, or his brother's wife was to Geoffrey. It had been foolish to expect it.

## Chapter 2

*Tuesday, 29 July*

Munns opened the door in his finicky way, admitting a gust of midsummer London smells and dust into the office. He passed through with a prim-lipped glance over his shoulder and pulled the door shut behind him very gently. Olivia found it more insulting than if he'd slammed it.

On pain of execution, she could not have told which emotion predominated in her soul at the moment: fury, humiliation, or anxiety. She should also be feeling grief over her father's unexpected death; who could have anticipated such a lean, active man would suffer an apoplexy when he had scarcely been sick a day in his life? Instead she felt—well, what did she feel?

Jonas Cantarell was not the kind of father who inspired deep affection. She regretted his loss chiefly because he had valued her talents and opinion. Unfortunately, he had never planned for what should be done upon his death. Apart from his will—that, thank God, had been taken care of years ago. Perhaps, like her, he had never anticipated the difficulties that might arise when she inherited. Certainly, he had assumed Munns would continue to work for her.

Jonas Cantarell had collapsed and died at his desk on Saturday. The office was closed on Sunday, of course, and the funeral had taken place on Monday, so the office was closed that day, too, though Munns had opened it for a few hours to have everything ready for today. She had come in to open the office to find Munns already at his desk. He had risen, greeted her, taken his hat from its peg, dropped his key on her desk, and informed her he was leaving the employ of Cantarell Shipping. She had not bothered to ask why; she should have expected his resignation. Fifteen years had not reconciled him to her presence.

She knew the names of everyone they shipped for, virtually every other shipping agent, and the faces of many. She knew the locations and capacities of the wharves, docks, and warehouses she could not visit. She knew the names and characters of shippers and agents in any port they had shipped to or from. She could figure the cost of shipping whatever cargo they were offered, the profit from it, and the tariff due, if any.

What she did not know was what she would do until she could find another clerk. Even then, Cantarell Shipping would not be fully staffed. She could hire an experienced clerk, as she was willing to pay more than the customary rate. She would still need a second clerk, even if she also hired a boy to run errands and carry messages. The fact was, in spite of being able to run all aspects of the company she now owned, she could not meet customers or captains to do business in an alehouse or ordinary, as her father had done. She could not visit Lloyd's Coffee House to hear the latest shipping news, though this was slightly offset by the delivery of *Lloyd's List*, for which Cantarell Shipping paid, and well worth the price. Such a lot of bother, merely because she was female.

One step at a time. Friday's edition of *Lloyd's List* was still on the front desk, other matters making its removal to the shelves in her father's office of low priority. It might as well remain for the moment; she had a use for it. Opening the desk drawer, she removed the Turkish dagger and slipped it out of its sheath. She stroked the ivory hilt, admiring its smoothness. The *Lloyd's List* concealed it on the right side of the desk.

Then she sat down to compose an advertisement for a clerk and to write a placard to place in the front window.

Chapter 3

*Tuesday, 29 July*

Easterday strode into the bleak little office, thinking of Matthew's idea. The front office was empty, which seemed odd, but perhaps the clerk was answering a call of nature, or was in the back, receiving instructions. The door to the passage leading to Cantarell's office stood open, although he heard no voices. He bit his lip, wondering again whether exporting Scotch linen made sense. Textiles were not something he had dealt with often. Brandy, wine, and port, raw silk from the Mediterranean for the Huguenot silk weavers, and German porcelain, certainly. Woods, both exotic and utilitarian. He should look into the price of linen in London, and—

A woman emerged from the back offices and stopped.

"I beg your pardon," she said, moving to stand behind the desk. "I hope you have not been waiting long, sir. How may I assist you?"

He was momentarily at a loss for words. Whatever was a woman doing here? He took in her plain gray dress, the crisp white kerchief filling in the square neckline, then her thin height and sand-pale hair worn close to her head, surmounted by a linen cap. The resemblance was unmistakable.

"Ah…You must be related to Cantarell, ma'am."

"Olivia Cantarell. His daughter."

Which still did not explain her presence. He bowed. "Marcus Easterday, at your service. Is your father in?"

She stood staring at him for a moment. "No, Captain Easterday. He died on Saturday and was buried yesterday."

"Good God!" Then, "I beg your pardon, Mistress Olivia. I only returned to town two days ago and have not yet heard all the news. I am heartily sorry for your loss. Forgive me for intruding at such a time. I will take my leave, ma'am."

"I assume you came to see my father on business, sir. Please be seated." She sat in the chair behind the desk. "How can I help you?"

He remained standing. "I intended to inquire about shipping, but…"

"My father is dead, but Cantarell Shipping is still in business. I am its new owner."

"But are you familiar with the business, Mistress Olivia?"

"I have been my father's assistant almost half my life, Captain."

She appeared to be about thirty years of age and certainly had the poise of a mature woman. A sketching pad lay on the desk, open to a detailed pencil drawing of a Turkish rug. A dot or swathe of watercolor indicated the color of each motif or border.

"Which no doubt explains the firm's reputation for importing the best Turkey carpets, but my visit has to do with shipping. Is the clerk in?"

"Thank you for the compliment. However, I have

kept the books as well. Munns is no longer employed here. He did not care to work for a woman."

"I suppose you will sell the business."

"No, I intend to continue operating it."

He stared at her. "But how can you possibly do so? It is no occupation for a female. How can you deal with—"

The door flew open. A gritty voice barked, "I'm overcharged for my shipment. Smedley says he'd have charged me only three-quarters as much. I'll have a rebate from you or know the reason why."

The speaker was now standing inches from the desk, a burly figure with fists clenched at his sides, leaning slightly forward, a stance meant to intimidate. Easterday thought he recognized George Noakes by his voice and manner, though he had not seen his face. Noakes had not noticed him standing to the left of the door.

Mistress Olivia had not reacted to the man's eruption into the room. "If Smedley would have charged you less than we did, you should have shipped with him. If you did not seek bids from other shippers before contracting with us, you have only yourself to blame." Her hand slid under a copy of *Lloyd's List* lying on the desk.

"I won't take that from a wench." Noakes started to lean across the desk.

Easterday cleared his throat, and Noakes spun to face him.

"You are interrupting my meeting with Mistress Olivia. As you well know, what she said is what any other shipper would tell you. I suggest you leave, after apologizing to the lady."

"Be damned to you, Easterday, and to her, too."

Easterday closed the door after Noakes stormed out.

"Thank you, sir." But she appeared perfectly unmoved. She might have been thanking him for handing her out of a carriage or passing her a cup of tea.

"Is Noakes the first to try that game?"

"No, two or three others have attempted something similar. "

"Attempted but not succeeded?"

She smiled. "Cantarell Shipping could not continue in business if I permitted myself to be bullied into giving back our very reasonable charges. He will not ship with us again, but he is no great loss. He has always been difficult."

"This must bear out what I was saying before he entered. You cannot take over your father's business. Men will not deal with you or will try to cheat you. Worse, you are not safe here alone, and you must also go back and forth to your residence. If I had not been here, Noakes might have harmed you."

"If you mean beaten or raped, Captain, you should say so."

Before he could respond, she went on, "I have thought of it, and it is a matter of concern to me. If you had not been present this afternoon, I might have had to harm Noakes. He would not have noticed that my paper knife is actually a dagger sharpened on both edges."

Her hand now gripped an ornate dagger.

"However, I agree it is best that I not deal directly with our customers. The problem with Noakes would not have occurred if Munns had not deserted me. I intend to hire two boys from the Whitechapel School. They can take turns running my errands and dealing with the public here, as Munns did, until I can get another clerk."

"But you yourself will still be coming and going each day. I admire your courage, ma'am, but the dock area is too dangerous for any woman."

"Except the whores and tavern wenches? If you will excuse my plain speaking, sir."

"It's dangerous for them, too, and for men as well."

She blew out a breath in an ungenteel manner. "I arrive and go home by hackney. Now, let us discuss your shipping needs, sir."

He sighed and gave up arguing. "I believe you ship out of Scotland?"

"We own a quarter interest in the schooner *Jean McPhee*, which regularly sails between the Tay ports, Leith, and London."

"But not to the American colonies?"

"No. Some ships at Kirkaldy sail to the Americas, Captain Easterday. I do not recommend them as their voyages are irregular. Sometimes they do not return for several years."

"I gather you do not own an interest in any of them, ma'am."

"That is true, sir. However, we would have more control if the goods were brought here and transferred to a vessel which regularly crosses to America. One in which we do have a share, or in one of yours, if you prefer."

She had a head for business, he granted her that much. "Do you have someone in Scotland with whom you deal? Who will continue to represent your interests there in the absence of your father?"

"Indeed, yes. He is unaware that the O. Cantarell who has written to him as Jonas Cantarell's assistant is female. I will be writing to inform him I have inherited, and that is all he needs to know."

"Very well. My nephew, who is showing an interest in business, has come up with a plan to export Scottish linen to the American colonies and the West Indies. The idea evolved from a visit to the Scottish Lowlands where he saw linen manufactured with stripes and checks in the Dutch manner, as well as plain cheap linen. He recalled a family friend saying that patterned linen goods were much admired in the colonies as an alternative to printed cotton. The well-to-do can buy printed India cotton, but poor folk will buy patterned linen when they can get it. To test the market, we would want to ship a small quantity. Say, fifteen hundred yards."

"I will have a price for you by tomorrow afternoon, if that is agreeable? I will send it by messenger, unless you chance to be in this area?"

"If you plan to be here tomorrow, I will call on you. In the morning, if I may?"

"Certainly."

"Now, is it not time you closed your office for the day? It's nigh upon six of the evening. I would be pleased to see you to your home."

She hesitated for a moment. "That is unnecessary, Captain. Though if you walked with me as far as Custom House Stairs, I would appreciate it."

Once out on the street, he offered his arm. She was so independent a female, he did not actually expect her to accept it, although she had agreed to his escort. But she twined her arm around his without hesitation.

Had he been strolling with a lady like Mariah Saltstall, he would have made some inconsequent comment about the weather or the scenery. It seemed inappropriate in this case—although Olivia Cantarell spoke like a gently bred female and her father had clearly been a product of the gentry, from his manners and speech.

"How did you come to work with your father?" Women of the lower classes worked in a number of trades, not only as seamstresses and milliners, but in family businesses of all sorts: coffee houses, bake shops, inns, public houses, and who knew what others? Not, however, in the shipping industry.

They crossed busy Thames Street carefully and passed into the narrow way by the west end of the Custom House. Easterday breathed in the familiar blended aromas of spice, tea, tobacco, coffee, and dank water reeking of sewers and rotting garbage.

"To understand requires some explanation. My father was no scholar in his school days and the active life appealed to him, so he went to sea as a young man, with an older cousin who owned a ship. Grandpapa bought him a share in it. He invested in cargo he thought would sell well and made money doing so— Ottoman silks, when they were still in fashion." She glanced up at him. "Later, he began trading in dye stuffs—cochineal, fustic, brazilwood, and madder, and in carpets, figs, and medicinals. Before he was thirty, he was able to give up sailing, open Cantarell Shipping, and marry my mother. He hired a clerk, and everything went well. When I was fifteen, the clerk fell ill after getting wet to the skin in a sudden shower.

"When the clerk had been gone from the office a day or two, Papa brought home the letters he had received and asked me to help him write replies. He said my handwriting was better than his, which was true. That was how I discovered he had difficulty reading. He said the letters shifted on the page. I suppose it was some trouble with his eyes. For several days, I read his correspondence to him and he dictated his answers to me in the evenings. He'd always had the clerk give him a verbal summary of each letter, you see, and then instructed him how to respond. When the clerk died of the chill he'd received, my father asked me to help him until he found a replacement. Mother had died earlier. My widowed aunt had only recently come to live with us and was too overcome with grief to object. He hired Munns." She paused.

"Who has now deserted you."

"Yes. Papa did not like to admit his trouble to Munns, who is extremely clever and well-educated but not obliging. He also has a very sharp manner. That is probably why he was not able to obtain a better position. So I continued to help my father at home—he had plenty to do with visiting the ships and wharves during the day, as that was not something he could delegate to Munns, who was too nice-minded to deal with the captains and warehousemen and other shippers."

"I see."

"A few years ago, I began to go to the office with him for part of the day. I had my own little room to work in, and he drilled a peephole in the wall of his office, up near the ceiling. I could climb onto a chair in my room and see who was calling upon him. The peephole is concealed on the wall above the top bookshelf. That was how I recognized you when you came in today."

"Dare I hazard a guess Munns was not pleased with the arrangement?"

She chuckled. "He wasn't. He never said so, but it was obvious. He may have thought I'd been brought in to check his work, thinking that Papa did not trust him. Though he was always absolutely honest, and my father made every effort to show that Munns had his full confidence. Or mayhap my presence simply did not suit his notions of gentility."

Easterday could not suppose they would suit anyone's notions. Instead he remarked, "Your work with Cantarell must have made your life a little awkward. Ladies have many calls on their time. Household matters, social engagements…" He realized abruptly that he was not actually sure what females did with their time, except for the poor, who had to shop for food, prepare meals, care for children, clean, wash clothes, and perhaps work as well.

"My aunt oversees the servants. I used to go to the office in the mornings and have the afternoons free, and my aunt and I would pay calls on friends then."

"I don't wish to pry, ma'am, but what did your father intend should happen at his death? Though I know some of us never think so far ahead," he added.

"By his will, I inherit the firm, with ten percent of the proceeds from the profits or the sale, if I chose to sell, to my brother. Julian never had any interest in shipping and wheedled a commission out of our father." She smiled wryly. "It enabled him to attract a baronet's daughter with a decent dowry, so he sold out and they

27

live in the country. Julian cannot challenge the will or demand the business be sold, as he signed an agreement to those terms years ago. Not that I think he would try to do any such thing; he has always been a kindly elder brother and used to express guilt about disappointing our father."

"But does he approve of your exposing yourself this way?"

"Neither of us anticipated that Munns would not remain, which will make things a little difficult until I secure another clerk."

She had evaded the question. Whatever Jonas Cantarell had supposed would be the outcome of his daughter inheriting the business, he must never have discussed it with his son. He could hardly have thought she would marry, at her age. Evidently Mistress Olivia had not raised the subject, either. Julian Cantarell should certainly have done so when he was asked to agree to the will's terms. But if he had never involved himself in the business, it might not have occurred to him how unsuitable it would be for a lady to work in a shipping firm. Or immersed in the life of a country gentleman far from the Thames and the Pool of London, he simply never thought about it.

"Who will visit the wharves and warehouses for you until then?" he asked.

Now that they were in the sun, stray wisps of hair escaping from under her cap and hat looked almost like a halo, though a less likely saint he had never encountered. No, he was mistaken. She was the very type of a martyred female saint: tall, thin, pale, and steering a course for utter destruction.

A faint vertical line appeared between her brows.

"It is not difficult to find an unemployed clerk. I will have a new one in a day or two."

"He is likely to be inexperienced," he pointed out. "Now, I have a proposal to make."

She flinched. Ah. Perhaps the word "proposal" had not been well chosen. He forged ahead.

"Let me lend you my head clerk's assistant." Seeing that she meant to refuse, he added, "You would pay his wages, giving you time to hire an experienced clerk. You would still need a boy or two to run errands."

She frowned for a moment before conceding. "Thank you, sir. I accept your offer."

"I will have him report to your office in the morning." They reached Custom House Quay, and both paused to admire the building and the activity between it and the water. A handsome piece of architecture, the esthetic effect was somewhat marred by the raised wooden sheds at the river's edge and the litter of barrels, bales, kegs, crates, and other cargo in the open before it. Still, the liveliness of the scene had its own fascination, similar to the foreign market places he had seen. In the mornings, the Long Room in the Custom House buzzed with those who had come to pay the fees on their dutiable imports and exports. Ah, London, the hub of the world. Mistress Olivia heaved a sigh, and they moved on.

No wherry waited at Custom House Stairs. If he had not been with her, she would have been standing here alone until one arrived. But the absence of transportation gave him a chance to speak further with her.

Thank God she was willing to accept help.

"Is this your usual way to go home?"

Her brows drew together, nonplussed rather than annoyed, he thought.

"No, Captain. When my father was alive, I would come into the office with him in the morning, and he would escort me to the hackney stand when he went to the ordinary for his midday meal. This morning I came by hackney and thought to leave with Munns. His way passes—passed—near a hackney stand. But when I arrived, he resigned. I decided the walk to Custom House Stairs was shorter—"

And less dangerous to a lone woman? Hardly.

"—and going by water to Hermitage Stairs and taking a hackney coach from there faster and pleasanter, as the streets are less busy."

But the walk to the place nearest the Hermitage Stairs where a hackney could be found would be no less dangerous than the one to Custom House Stairs. He did not know Mistress Olivia Cantarell well, but he felt sure it would be necessary to tread lightly here.

"I think going directly by hackney from your home to your office in the morning is a sensible plan. At the end of the day, Finley—the clerk I send you—will escort you to the hackney stand. It would be best to avoid being alone on the streets here. In some parts of town, it would present no risk beyond that of impropriety, but here—"

"I cannot let propriety interfere with my business, sir. I do not belong to the beau monde, after all."

"I agree that strict propriety would make it impossible for you to continue in business. On the other hand, will you not concede that Thames Street and Wapping are unnecessarily dangerous for an unescorted lady?"

A green-painted wherry knifed through the water toward them.

"I admit it," she said.

Her tone suggested the admission came only under protest. Of course, if she intended to run her father's shipping firm, she must fear making any concession to female weakness.

The waterman nosed his craft up against the stair.

"If you do not object, mistress, I will escort you down to Hermitage Stairs and see you into a hackney there."

"I am grateful for the offer, Captain. However, I will not give you the inconvenience."

"Ma'am, you have agreed the area is not safe. Why take the risk when I am ready to accompany you? I will even let you pay for my passage, if you wish," he added as a sop to her pride.

"In that case, I accept."

He detected amusement in her cool words. The waterman was grinning.

Chapter 4

Captain Easterday's offer of his clerk solved a problem that had perplexed her mightily, but she could not like having to accept his assistance. Perhaps she was being unreasonable; her father had concealed her part in the firm, and the only times she had gone down to the wharves or warehouses had been in his company.

She let herself into the house with her key and stood for a moment while her eyes grew accustomed to the change from sunlight to the dimness of the narrow hall. The blue-gray paneling in the entry hall (darker than when the paint was applied, about the time she was in leading strings, from the constant London soot) seemed to absorb light. Kitty would be in the kitchen helping prepare supper. Their footman/butler would be resting his arthritic bones. With any luck, her aunt would be in the kitchen fretting Cook. Alas, her aunt heard her and popped out of the parlor door before Olivia could escape up to her room to take off her hat and cape and gather her thoughts. For once, she was glad of the lack of illumination; Aunt Rachel could not have seen her expression before she forced her face into composure.

"I am glad you are home, Livvie. I worry when you go out with no maid. And to Jonas's office, too! I cannot like it. It was bad enough to go to that school to study drawing and painting."

If her aunt knew what she had really been doing instead of improving her drawing and watercolor technique at the Academy & Museum of Oriental Art, she would have fallen into a fit of the vapors. "You mustn't worry so, Aunt Rachel. I am surely old enough to go out by myself. And really, I could not take our maid to the office with me."

"Could you not sell the firm? How can you continue to go there, with your poor papa dead? Your occasional visits were bad enough when he was alive. All those rough men! And only old Mr. Munns to protect you."

"I mean to get two boys to help. Munns is retiring, but a clerk experienced in shipping will be replacing him tomorrow. Will dinner be ready soon?"

"Is the new man younger? However did you find him?—it must have happened very quickly. And yes, it will be ready soon. We are having the egg and onion dish, stewed celery, and some of the Portugal cakes."

She would have to steer a careful course around the facts. "A business acquaintance of Papa's, Captain Easterday, came by today to discuss shipping linen from Scotland and ended by lending me one of his clerks. I don't know his age. He will start tomorrow."

"Was Captain Easterday at the funeral? I do not recall the name. I suppose he is a grizzled former sailor."

"He did not hear of it, being out of town." Far better not to mention that he could not be more than five- or six-and-thirty, and tall, and well set up, with regular if undistinguished features.

"How obliging of him to let you have one of his clerks. Is he by any chance unmarried? An older man would not be a bad choice for an unmarried lady who is not too young. In a similar business, too, which would make it so convenient. Jonas's company would then be your dowry."

Fortunate that Aunt Rachel did not know that Captain Easterday had offered to escort her home! She made herself smile and said, "I shouldn't think he would be looking for a wife. I imagine he is married already."

"You should find out. His clerk would know and would tell you if you can introduce the subject casually."

"I will bear it in mind."

"You really should marry, dear. To spend your days among clerks and sailors and worse must be ruinous to any lady's reputation. It was bad enough when your father was alive, but now you simply cannot. I suppose you must wrap up the business, especially with Mr. Munns leaving, but you should be chaperoned. And we must devote ourselves to finding you a husband."

Olivia had not confessed that she meant to retain her father's business. She was also much like her father, practical and unsentimental.

"I don't think I am likely to marry, Aunt. Men prefer pretty, tender-minded females."

"But you could pretend to be those things, my love. It's often necessary to let gentlemen believe what they wish. We women do it all the time."

"I don't think I could, Aunt Rachel, any more than I could learn to sing."

"I believe it was because you did not choose to apply yourself. It is very odd, because you are exceedingly disciplined in all other ways. Most other ways, at least. You could perfectly well learn to encourage a man if you wished. It is merely to smile at him and ask him about himself—and not talk about tonnage and foreign exchange and dunnage—whatever that is! And while I am thinking on it, do not forget the assembly at the Moon and Stars Assembly Rooms on Friday evening. We must go in spite of being in mourning. Your green robe à l'Anglaise would do very well. I only wish you had a better pair of shoes to go with it. The old ones are terribly scuffed."

"I suppose we must attend, as my father thought it useful for business contacts. I will wear black ribbons with the green gown, and my pleated silk cap, but the ribbon on it must be changed to black. And I will wear my mourning ring and the black enamel pendant."

"I think that will do very well," Aunt Rachel agreed. "Do you recall the poulterer's family a year ago when his father died? Such a display would have been more suitable for mourning a royal death than a tradesman's. For the laboring classes and even families like ours, it would be ridiculous. Not that we are in any way in unmindful of our loss." She sniffed dolefully. Rachel, having far more sensibility than Olivia, had been distraught at her brother's death. Perhaps her grief contained an element of fear as well, her husband's death having precipitated her into poverty. "Your mama's family were gentry, and Jonas's and my father was Baron Lees."

She gave her aunt a little hug and kissed her cheek. "I know. I agree such a parade of grief shows a certain vulgarity. But I do not think black ribbons excessive, do you?"

"Not at all, especially with that pretty cap. Would you like me to see to changing the ribbon on it? If you will insist on taking your papa's place in that office, you will have little time to go out to buy ribbon or sew it on."

"Thank you, Aunt. And thank you for not mentioning the size and unevenness of my stitches."

"No thanks are due me. I enjoy needlework. And I want you to be looking your best for the assembly. The green silk is one of your most becoming gowns."

Olivia smiled again as they proceeded to the dining room. Rachel Williams cherished hopes that her niece would meet a suitable man at the assembly and form an affection for him, or at least be persuaded to accept an offer of marriage. It was too much to hope that one's female relatives would not feel they had to matchmake. Her aunt's urgent desire for her marriage was shown by the fact that she considered the assembly a husband-hunting ground. Ten years ago, she would have stigmatized such a gathering as ungenteel, fit only for tradesmen and their families.

While not over-proud herself, Olivia did not really enjoy the public assemblies. As they were by subscription only, the poorest were excluded, but the fee was low enough to ensure that many of those crowding the hall were decidedly common. She and her aunt would be conversing and dancing with their baker's and greengrocer's relations, the owner of the local livery stable, perhaps an officer or two, a confectioner, a silversmith, an attorney's clerk. Many would not be well bred, and their daughters and sons would be bumptious. There would probably be some Scandinavians involved in the timber trade, as a number of such lived in the Square; they at least tended to be serious and well behaved. At a private ball—a truly private ball, given by a family for its friends and relatives—one would meet gentlemen and ladies. But clearly Aunt Rachel had given up hoping for invitations from a better social circle.

In what company did she and her aunt belong? But for her desire to promote a marriage for Olivia, Aunt Rachel would likely not have attended the assembly. She had been accustomed to better society before her husband's death reduced her from gentility and a spacious house near Hanover Square to the need to live with her brother. Her social life now was limited to the exchange of calls with the most genteel of their neighbors and the occasional card party or musical evening. She had cut herself off from those she had known before she was widowed; they would not wish to continue an association with her now that her circumstances were so straitened, and she would not wish to be seen in gowns that were out of date and even shabby.

Baron Lees, Olivia's grandfather, had died before her own birth. Her uncle, his successor, had suffered poor health and held few entertainments, even when in London. Her cousin, the current Baron Lees, was unmarried and thus did not entertain and had in any case replied very coldly to their letters of condolence on the death of his father. Apparently, he preferred to distance himself from any commercial connection. His sisters lived in the country with their husbands and children much of the year, and during the times they visited London, were too busy to bother with distant relatives—especially poor relatives who did not belong to the beau monde.

Her maternal grandfather had been a squire in Gloucestershire; his wife had insisted on bringing their daughter to London, where somehow their path had crossed that of a rising young man named Jonas Cantarell, third son of a baron. One of Olivia's maternal uncles was now the owner of a modest manor. Of his two brothers, one was an attorney-at-law in Gloucester and the other was a gentleman farmer on land his wife had received as her dowry. None of them visited London often.

She anticipated both the following day and the assembly without enthusiasm. Would Captain Easterday's clerk be willing to work for her, even temporarily? If he did, would he be surly, like Munns? As for the assembly...well, she had agreed to go, mostly to please her aunt. She could well imagine an evening of boredom and humiliation: broad jests by the older men, undignified romping by girls and young men barely out of the schoolroom, attempts by a few of Aunt Rachel's female acquaintances to match her with some widower with children who needed a stepmama, or some impecunious cousin or nephew. Cantarell Shipping, while only a small concern, was still an inheritance which many in her circle would covet.

****

When she alighted from the hackney before the door of Cantarell Shipping the next morning, she found a man waiting for her. Not a threat, she decided. He was neatly but plainly dressed and looked like a gentleman. He bowed as she approached the door, key in hand.

"Jeremy Finley, at your service, ma'am. Captain Easterday sent me."

Voice and manner were pleasant; he was a few years younger than she. His only remarkable feature was a scar that ran diagonally across his forehead to the outer end of his left eyebrow.

"How do you do, Mr. Finley. It is good of Captain Easterday to let me borrow you, my own clerk having left without notice." She hoped to sound him out on his feelings about working for a woman, but it would become obvious soon enough.

"Not at all, Mistress Olivia. It will give us a chance to see how my assistant does in my absence."

They were in the front office.

"If I understood correctly, you plan to hire a boy to act as messenger," Finley said.

"Two boys, in fact. I hope at least one of them can be trained up to be the assistant to whomever I find to take over from Munns, so that you can return to the captain."

"You will still be shorthanded, ma'am. My employer told me you had Noakes here yesterday. I should be in the office at all times during the day to discourage further unpleasant visitors. Yet someone other than a messenger boy must visit a ship or warehouse. You cannot do so, and if I do, who will man the office?"

"One of the boys. It will be good experience."

"Do you think one—or both, for that matter—will be able to stand up to Noakes or his like?"

"Forgive me for asking this, Mr. Finley, but could you?"

He laughed. "I do look rather boyish, do I not? When I was fresh out of school, I wanted a life of adventure. After I made two voyages, I decided I did not care to make a career of the sea. But I did learn a great deal about shipping and trade, and I have a wide experience of dockside brawls. No, Noakes will not try to intimidate me. Or not a second time, anyway."

While the young man was not brawny, he did look athletic. Easterday did not appear heavily muscled, either, but certainly gave an impression of strength. More than that: grace. It was odd to think of a man as graceful, but it was the right word. The image of a leaping cat came to her. It would be interesting to see him dance. Or to dance with him. She gave her head a little shake to clear it of irrelevant thoughts.

"I suppose I had better advertise for…well, how would one phrase it, Mr. Finley? A clerk experienced in dockside brawls?"

"Captain Easterday and I came up with several candidates and after discussion, were left with one we believe would be suitable. He suggested you interview the man to see if you agree."

"Oh!" Was it a little high-handed of them? It did save her the trouble of interviewing a succession of men who might or might not be suitable, or if they were, might not wish to work for a woman. On consideration, she admired the practicality of the solution. "That was very well thought of," she said. "Can you arrange for him to come in so I may speak with him?"

Finley looked like a guilty schoolboy. "To save time, I told him—I know him—to come in at nine this morning."

"Admirably efficient, sir."

The morning's tasks were completed with time to spare. Indeed, more efficiently than when her father was alive, as she need not read correspondence or *Lloyd's List* or the *London Gazette* to Finley. Then she had stayed in her own little office, and Papa had had to go back to consult her.

Matthias Barlow, when he arrived, proved to be younger than Finley. Indeed, he seemed too young in face, if not in manner, to have sailed on a merchant ship for several years. There was the faintest suggestion of a Scottish burr in his voice.

"You have quit the sea?" Olivia inquired.

"Ay. I was needed at home after my mother died a year ago." Seeing her inquiring look, he went on. "My father died a little more than a year before her. I received word of his death and left my ship to come home. By the time I arrived, I found my mother in failing health. Soon after…" He ended with a shrug. "My sisters and brothers—two of each—are young. The oldest is seventeen. I had to stay home to make arrangements for them."

"There are no other relations able to take them in?"

"Not really. My mother was an orphan. My father had a brother," he added, as an afterthought, "but my parents did not want my sisters and brothers to live with him."

"I see." She had no right to inquire further, although she would certainly like to know the reason! The possibilities ranged from the uncle's being appallingly vulgar to spendthrift or dissolute or…well, imagination failed her. "They must keep you busy when you are not at work, then."

He looked somewhat disconcerted. "They live in Scotland, ma'am. My mother took them there not long before I returned. The exertion hastened her death, but she felt she must take the children to her old governess, who was willing to take charge of them. She could not be sure I would be home in time. When I arrived, we agreed that they should stay, even if it were necessary for me to come to London to find work. There are not many opportunities in Scotland."

"Can you support them and yourself on a clerk's pay?"

"My mother had some money of her own, which goes to pay for their room and board with my mother's friend, ma'am. It pays for the boys' school fees and for lessons in music and dance for my sisters. My mother's inheritance was not great, but it was in good English money, and it's a deal cheaper to live in Scotland."

"Better not to uproot them, I apprehend, since your mother had already settled them there."

"That was a consideration, with the boys being enrolled in a good school."

"Will you miss the sea and the excitement of seeing new ports? I have heard men say they loved that life, even while they complained about the food and the officers."

"After nearly being swept overboard in a gale, and tying knots in the dark with fingers stiff with cold? No. And while my siblings live hundreds of miles away, at least I'm not on the other side of the world. London suits me very well, Mistress Olivia, and in many ways, I find more of interest in arranging for the shipment of freight than in sailing to the most exotic ports."

"I apologize for seeming to pry into personal matters, Mr. Barlow. Perhaps a man would not ask such questions. But your answers have provided me insight into your character. The desire for interesting occupation is the reason I will continue to operate Cantarell Shipping, rather than selling it as one would ordinarily expect a woman to do."

"I do not make the mistake of supposing all women are the same, any more than all men are, ma'am. I once saw a great bruising fellow who was sure that no woman would fire a pistol. If he had obeyed her order to come no closer, he might still be alive."

"Then I take it you have no objection to being employed by me?"

"None at all. As you have not asked, ma'am, I should add that I write a fair hand, can add and subtract, and am punctual."

"Those abilities I assumed, based on Captain Easterday's and Mr. Finley's having suggested you." His appearance and speech were gentlemanly, he appeared to have a sense of humor, and he had come recommended by Captain Easterday and Mr. Finley. He would do very well, and she engaged his services on the spot.

Feeling the office was in competent hands, it seemed safe to visit the Whitechapel School. When she announced her plan, Barlow and Finley exchanged glances, and Barlow said, "I'll find a hackney coach for you, ma'am."

She was about to object that she could perfectly well find one herself, and then reflected that if she already had her charity boys, she would have sent one of them to summon a coach.

"Thank you, Mr. Barlow."

****

Her visit to the school founded by Ralph Davenant for the education of poor children in Whitechapel consumed much of the rest of the day. The school occupied the almost rural eastern end of Whitechapel Road, near an almshouse and burying ground. Soaring like a bird, the distance might not be far. Even threading one's way through the maze of streets around Tower Hill and north and east to Whitechapel would not be so time-consuming if not for the other coaches, carts, drays, riders, foot travelers, and street vendors. At least the journey gave her time to make plans and to hope that she would be able to get a useful pair of boys.

The school's appearance suggested a pleasant house; a walled garden fronted the building, which was supplied with large windows to light the ground floor with dormer windows upstairs.

The schoolmaster was surprised to be visited by a lady but set the students a task to perform while he spoke with her. He obviously expected that they would do it without his supervision, which was reassuring.

Explaining what she wanted took little time. Persuading the master to place boys with her was far more difficult than convincing Easterday that she meant to run the shipping business.

"I am very uneasy about entrusting two of our lads to a lady. A shipping office is no place for a female. How can you keep your father's business going? How can an unmarried lady manage a pair of boys? Now, if you had inherited an inn or a coffee house, it would be another matter. Innkeepers' wives do find themselves in possession of the family business sometimes, but the tapster, waiters, ostlers, and porters can oversee lads. We are always looking for positions or apprenticeships for our students who have reached the age of fourteen, but this is so irregular, I do not think we can oblige you, ma'am."

"I have two clerks, one of some six-and-twenty years and the other of about one-and-twenty who will be the boys' immediate superiors." She set Finley and Barlow's ages a little higher than perhaps they were, but she needed errand boys. "I am offering a wage of two shillings a week, and Mr. Finley and Mr. Barlow will teach them as much of the business as they care to learn. If Cantarell Shipping should fail to thrive, they will at least have the advantage of experience to offer another employer."

"It would be an excellent position, in many ways," he admitted. "If only a respectable man would testify to, er, the stability of Cantarell Shipping, my doubts would be put to rest. If you had a brother or uncle to whom I could apply for…"

"Reassurance? I have no uncles in London, and my brother lives in the country, and none of them ever had aught to do with the firm."

He heaved a sigh. "Mayhap you could supply me with the name of your banker and of men with whom you have done business? It may take some time to hear from all of them, however."

"There is Captain Marcus Easterday," Olivia said. The thought of asking him to give her a character galled her, though she had already accepted his help.

"Marcus Easterday, the ship owner? Will he vouch for you?"

"I believe so, sir. He helped me find a head clerk." By lending her one of his own, but why mention that fact?

"I will write to him, with your permission, then, Mistress Olivia."

"Why not send him a message now? Very likely we could settle this matter today. If you will supply me with pen and ink, I will write him. If you would be good enough to send for a messenger?"

Fortunately, Easterday was in his offices and replied immediately, but the matter still ate up the afternoon. But she was promised the two likely boys the governor had presented for her inspection would report the next morning. One was a bit small for his age but appeared intelligent. A blond boy with green eyes was larger, if perhaps somewhat shy, but stammered his gratitude for the chance. On the whole, she was well pleased.

When she returned, about two hours before their closing time, Barlow and Finley appeared visibly relieved. She apologized for her tardiness and explained the delay.

"I had to stop to buy a pair of shoes," she confessed, as she had the parcel under her arm. "I would not ordinarily take time out of the day to do such an errand, but I agreed to attend an assembly tomorrow night. I should not attend, with my father's death so recent, but my father considered assemblies a way of making contacts with men who might require our services. With one thing and another, I had no time to shop earlier. Not that such fripperies are important, but I do not wish to embarrass my aunt by appearing ill-dressed."

"It is important to present a good appearance," Finley said. "It reflects upon Cantarell Shipping. And as you are in business, you must be seen in public. If you were to stay home in full mourning, it might be thought that your hand was not on the reins here. Or the tiller, to use a more nautical term After all, men do not go into seclusion even for the death of a parent or wife. Where is it to be held?"

"The Moon and Stars. Do you know it? The hall is handsome, and the refreshments are good."

She might be quite reluctant to give Finley back to Easterday eventually. Then she inquired whether any problems or new business had come in, the discussion of which lasted until it was time to lock the door.

Chapter 5

It had been some years since Easterday had attended such an event, before his first betrothal, surely. Once he had become successful enough to be an eligible suitor, he had attended private parties and balls given by London's merchant class. There he had met pretty, blonde Claudia, daughter of a banker. At seventeen, she had been too young for his four-and-twenty years, three of them spent as a ship's captain.

When he was a junior officer, he had sometimes frequented public assemblies to dance with the daughters of middling tradesmen, lawyers, and such. He had forgotten what they were like. The entertainments of London's wealthy merchants and bankers tended to be more sedate than those of the upper reaches of society. The middling folk in the rooms of the Moon and Stars turned the assembly into a romp. One young man ogled a blushing girl and dispensed with the formality of an introduction, while her chaperone sat gossiping with friends. *I must have grown middle-aged. Did I ever enjoy such occasions?* But he'd come of gentry, not the lower commercial classes. He would not have come if Finley had not mentioned Olivia Cantarell meant to attend; he was curious to observe her when she was at leisure. He might have suggested that Finley take his place if he had not known that Finley was spending the evening with the family of a young lady he fancied. No, he could not have asked Finley to spy on her. He simply wanted to get a better idea of her character.

Then he saw her standing some distance away beside an older lady who was seated. She had not noticed him, so he took the time to study her.

Olivia Cantarell possessed an elegance not apparent when he saw her at Cantarell Shipping. The moss-green robe à l'Anglaise suited her pale complexion and the curls of pale hair visible under her cap. The cap was too matronly for her, even if she were not in the first flush of youth. But perhaps she wore it as one of her touches of mourning, like the black ribbon trimming her gown. She was really quite handsome when dressed for a social occasion and flushed from the exertion of dancing.

He was glad he had come, in spite of the status-grubbing lower-middle-class mamas and papas hoping to marry their children into better society. And why should they not? Baronets schemed to betroth their daughters to barons, and earls aspired to ally their sons with dukes' daughters. It was common prudence. His own origins were not so elevated that he could sneer at prosperous shopkeepers. Lowfields Manor yielded no more than one thousand pounds per year, though it was cheaper to live in the country, making his brother's family moderately well-to-do.

He was lucky they had had a family connection to a ship's officer, who had secured Easterday's first shipboard position. Lucky, too, that he had wanted a career at sea. By the time his younger brother was old enough to settle on a profession, Marcus had been able to contribute to the cost of sending him to Oxford and paying his fees at Lincoln's Inn. Harry was now a barrister and seemed in a fair way to prosper.

The Cantarells were well bred and Olivia had strength of character, but he doubted the income from Cantarell Shipping amounted to much more than five hundred pounds per annum, after expenses. It was enough for living comfortably, if one were careful, but it was not wealth. If the business should fail, or even simply decline, her situation might be dire. She needed to marry sensibly.

Several men approached her. She danced sets with two of them; the others evidently came only to talk to her. To offer their condolences? Possibly, but they lingered longer than mere courtesy required. Apparently, neither of them solicited her hand for a dance. It might be that they felt that a lady who had recently lost her parent would not dance, even if she attended an assembly, or felt she should not dance even if she were willing.

It was interesting that Mistress Olivia appeared somewhat flustered by the attention paid her by the men. She blushed and cast down her eyes, but she danced very prettily for such a tall and unfeminine lady. How surprising she should be put out of countenance, when he had seen her face down a blustering bully. The situations differed, of course. He would wager that she was not much accustomed to the interest of men. Had she realized word had got out that she was an heiress, if only in a small way?

He smiled wryly. In this company, Cantarell Shipping would not be considered an insignificant inheritance, particularly if she married quickly and her husband sold it before it lost value. She would hate losing her father's company—but lose it she would, as soon as she married, yet what else could she or her new husband do? A landlord or attorney or owner of a livery stable would not be able to run a shipping company, any more than Olivia Cantarell could. Less, for she at least was well versed in maritime shipping. The attorney who had claimed her for the third set would be the best choice for her. He appeared to be a gentleman, at least, though she would be wiser to make a push to find a husband connected to the shipping industry, if Cantarell Shipping were to continue and prosper. What a pity Finley's affections were already engaged; his marriage to Olivia Cantarell would benefit both of them. Even his being a few years younger would be to the good, given that men tended to die earlier than females, apart from deaths in childbed.

He continued to watch her even as he made conversation with the few men he knew: a ship's chandler who introduced his wife and son, a maker of nautical instruments, a few junior officers from merchant ships.

Easterday danced a set with the chandler's wife before deciding it was time to pay his respects to Mistress Olivia. To have sought her out too early might have appeared as if he had come for that purpose. As he made his way around the edge of the room, the master of ceremonies approached Olivia, accompanied by a man who was better dressed than most of those present. Easterday had not worn his best, not wishing to stand out from the men of business and professional men who were likely to attend. The gentleman now bowing to Olivia Cantarell wore a coat of peacock-blue silk laced with silver, and his waistcoat was embroidered with silver thread. His hair was powdered, but his profile was unmistakable.

Ambrose Hawkins. One would take him for a man of fashion, wandered into this unfashionable assembly by mistake, if it were not for his face. His features were aquiline; presumably most women would find him pleasing, and yet something about his expression set him apart from both gentlemen and the hard-headed tradesmen in this group. Or perhaps Easterday saw the ruthlessness because he knew something of the man.

Hawkins shipped and traded and had a hand in other maritime businesses, though his fine manicure could not conceal the traces of old calluses and scars. He had worked his way up from cabin boy on a merchantman without the benefit of a relative among the officers. Rumor claimed he bore the scars of at least one flogging on his back and that he had sailed with pirates.

Easterday forced his face to relax into what he had been told was its normal blandness as he neared the little group.

"Your servant, ma'am," he said, making his bow. He nodded to Hawkins, who favored him with an equally cool greeting.

"Captain." Clearly rattled, Olivia turned to the older lady. "Aunt, may I introduce Captain Easterday? He is an importer for whom we have sometimes shipped. Captain, this is my aunt, Mistress Williams."

"Why, Captain Easterday. How nice to meet you. I believe I recall Jonas mentioning your name."

He murmured his sympathy for the loss of her brother, and she murmured her thanks and hoped he was enjoying himself. She was eying his burgundy-red suit covertly. It was good cloth, and his waistcoat a creamy brocade, but he could not match Hawkins's splendor.

"I hope to, ma'am. Will you dance the next set with me, Mistress Olivia?"

"Thank you, Captain, but Mr. Hawkins has claimed it already."

"Then the one following, if you are not already engaged for it?"

"As it happens, I am not. I will reserve it for you."

He and Hawkins made light conversation with Olivia and her aunt until the set formed, and Hawkins led her onto the floor. What did she make of Hawkins, he wondered. Mistress Williams's gaze followed them complacently.

"Mr. Hawkins appears to be a gentleman of substance," Olivia's aunt remarked. "Though I know that even gentlemen who hardly have two shillings to rub together may dress as fine as lords." Her smile invited him to confide in her.

"Oh, he's well-to-do," Easterday assured her. "If he's not rich as Croesus, he's at least able to afford almost anything he wants."

She peered up at him. "I believe I hear a reservation, sir? Do you know aught to his discredit?"

"Most would say not, Mistress Williams. He is rich, his manners and birth are a gentleman's, but you must remember he made his money at sea."

"As my brother did the same, it does not seem to me a fault," she remarked, frowning a little.

"Not as such. I did the same. But a sailor's life at sea is not easy, and his was worse than mine, as I was fortunate to have a relation aboard as first mate, while

Hawkins ran away to sea. His experiences have hardened him somewhat, I fear."

She toyed with her fan, glancing back at the shifting pattern of dancers, where the vivid blue coat stood out. "One would prefer a man to be an oak rather than a reed. It is only charitable to give him the benefit of the doubt."

Mistress Williams favored Hawkins, it seemed, and must be hoping that he would form a partiality for Olivia. It would be a very good marriage for her.

Chapter 6

To her surprise, Olivia enjoyed the assembly. Several men she knew slightly from previous occasions approached her to offer their sympathy on the death of her father. A few more, or their wives, introduced brothers, uncles, sons, or cousins she had not met before, all of them unmarried. She could guess what that was about!

Then the assembly's master of ceremonies came up to her, trailing a richly dressed man behind him who gave poor Mr. Fordyce almost no time to request Olivia's permission to introduce him. If Mr. Fordyce had not been available, would Mr. Hawkins have ignored the formality of introduction entirely? A list of rules to be observed at the assemblies was conspicuously displayed at the entrance, though many of them were observed only on paper.

He spoke respectfully of her father's acumen and integrity, which pleased her, and recounted a humorous incident in which her father had been involved earlier in his career.

"I can't claim I saw it," Hawkins admitted. "I would have been a scrub of a schoolboy then. I've only heard of it from older fellows. I wish I'd seen the tarantulas come out of that crate!"

She had never heard the story. He must be six or eight years older than she, which would mean she had been a young child. Nor had her father been much for telling funny stories. His conversation tended to the dry and factual: when such-and-such a ship might be expected, or how many tons it carried, who could be trusted, who would try to cheat. He had never done business with Ambrose Hawkins that she could recall.

Hawkins had ships of his own. In London's busy port, his path might never cross that of Cantarell Shipping, though he might have met Jonas Cantarell in an ordinary or on the wharves. It was the more kind of him to seek her out to offer condolences.

Then he asked her to dance. How could she not be flattered? Everyone was watching him; he stood out like a battle flag in his rich, bright clothing. He was attractive, too, in a way at odds with his fashionable dress. He looked like a man who had visited exotic places under a hot sun and had adventures there. He had a nose like a bird of prey and thin lips. They were warm when he kissed her hand at the end of the set and asked if he might call upon her at home.

"Any friend of my father's is welcome," she said. "Though at the moment, I am spending most of my time at Cantarell Shipping's offices." Best not to explain why.

"Are you?" He did not sound surprised. "Mayhap I might call upon you?"

"Certainly, sir." Her heart had beaten faster the whole time they had danced. Now she wondered a little about their last exchange. One would not pay a social call at an office, and if it were not a social call, what was his purpose?

Returned to her aunt's side, she saw Hawkins make his way leisurely through the crowd. Her aunt asked her something, and Olivia lost sight of the figure in blue and so did not see whether he went into the card room or on toward the entrance. Possibly he was on his way to some private ball, for he was dressed exceeding fine for such an assembly as this. He had not been present long before securing an introduction to her; no one could have overlooked that peacock-blue coat. How odd that he should have bothered to come to the Moon and Stars at all. She hid a self-mocking smile behind her fan. He had not come to meet her, for how would he have known she would be here?

A momentary stir caught her attention, or rather, Aunt Rachel did, by whispering in her ear, "Look at that pert chit by the door! I wonder if Mr. Fordyce—"

Olivia looked. The girl was definitely wearing a gauzy, lace-trimmed apron, and Mr. Fordyce was bearing down upon her. He inclined his head toward her gravely and spoke. The girl blushed and said something. A stout matron rose from a chair nearby and joined them. She addressed Mr. Fordyce placatingly before saying a few words to her daughter. The latter pouted and turned around so her mama could untie the apron strings. She then folded it up neatly, and it vanished into a capacious reticule. A few more apologetic words from both the matron and the girl, and Mr. Fordyce smiled, bowed, and went on his way.

"Well!" Rachel Williams uttered. "She was monstrous proud of her pretty apron and wanted to show it off, though everyone knows ornamental aprons are for day wear, not for the ball room, even at an assembly. But young misses will try. The only wonder is why her mother let her."

Then her aunt turned her attention to a friend who

belonged to a committee which knitted and distributed stockings, mittens, hats, and infant jackets to the poor. The wife of a timber merchant living in one of the larger, newer houses on Well Close Square began to tell Olivia about her brother who had recently lost his wife. "… a gentlemanly man, a well-known clockmaker who has sold pocket watches and clocks to many noblemen. He has two pretty little children who need a mother." Before the doting sister could say more, Captain Easterday returned to claim Olivia for the next set.

The shifting figures of the country dance did not allow for much conversation. She did not know what she would have said if they had been able to converse. She felt awkward, though she had been comfortable with him before. Somehow, meeting Mr. Hawkins had made her self-conscious. He did dance very well, however, and such remarks as he made were those of a sensible man, not always the case with gentlemen.

When the set ended, the captain fetched wine for Aunt Rachel and herself. Several of their acquaintances came bustling up to be introduced by her aunt, while a few more claimed some acquaintance with Captain Easterday. Then they introduced their wives and their daughters, with whom he then danced. Marcus Easterday would be a very eligible match for someone. The younger men asked about his experiences at sea and the ports he had visited, to which he responded without showing boredom or condescension. He danced once with Aunt Rachel, too, who looked half amused and half flustered.

He had very good manners, she thought.

"It was a pleasure to meet you, Captain Easterday," Aunt Rachel said toward the end of the evening. "I hope we will see you again."

"If you are ready to leave, ma'am, let me escort you home."

Olivia began, "Thank you, Captain, but a servant will summon a hackney—"

Her aunt beamed at him, cutting across her words with "Why, thank you, sir. I feel so much safer with a gentleman's escort at night." So he took them home in a hackney and saw them safe into their house.

Olivia wondered what he thought of it. Most of the south side of the square was occupied by neat two-story houses with attics. But the courthouse on the corner with its small prison—mostly occupied by debtors—was not an attractive feature, though the building itself was impressive. The captain saw no more than the entrance hall of their own house, but its proportions were good, the paneling handsome, and the stair balusters were of the barley-twist pattern, which gave the stair a graceful touch.

"Captain Easterday lacks dash," Aunt Rachel observed after he had departed, shedding her cape. "I do not think he likes Mr. Hawkins, or mayhap he is envious of his success and polish. But the captain is a very courteous and kind gentleman. He endured Abraham Quesnel's foolish questions—mermaids, indeed! Though he could not know I overheard him—now, what have I said to make you laugh, and in such a hoydenish manner, too?"

"Young Mr. Quesnel believes in mermaids? Was that when he drew Captain Easterday aside?" Olivia gasped when she could stop laughing.

"He's a serious young man and was sincerely concerned for the sailors' moral welfare," her aunt said reprovingly. But she was overcome by a prolonged fit of coughing, causing her to press her handkerchief to her mouth, which set Olivia off again.

Eventually her aunt was able to continue. "But what I started out to say was that I very much appreciated Captain Easterday's offer to escort us home. I vow I am quite torn. Mr. Hawkins is very charming and clearly admired you, besides being so well dressed, but it was not quite good manners to ignore everyone else. And the captain is the better dancer."

Olivia did not think she was blushing noticeably. Likely her face was still flushed with laughter. Had others noticed Ambrose Hawkins paying her so much attention? She had hoped they would, at the time she was dancing with him. Now she felt somewhat embarrassed by it. To be sought out by a handsome, well-dressed gentleman was flattering, but would it make her an object of gossip and envy? Or pity for a plain spinster fluttering with excitement at being singled out by an attractive man? Insupportable!

Chapter 7

She was in the front office with Finley, reading the newly delivered *Lloyd's List* over his shoulder when Barlow burst in. He was winded and white around the lips. He had gone out to arrange delivery of cargo that had come in on the *Sarah R.*

"Are you all right?"

He waved off her concern but leaned on the straight chair in front of the desk and took a few deep breaths. "It's gone," he said at last. "From the warehouse."

Olivia and Finley both stared at him.

Barlow sank into the chair he'd been leaning on and took a deep breath.

Olivia bit her lips.

Finley spoke in a dangerously soft voice. "Damnation." He added, "I beg your pardon, ma'am."

She waved the apology aside. "Do you think I've not heard worse? But both consignments were accounted for yesterday when the cargo finally cleared the customs inspection! Are both gone?"

Barlow nodded mutely.

"So…," Finley muttered.

Theft from the lighters that ferried cargo from ship to wharf and pilferage on the wharves and in the warehouses was common. According to her father, a third of the lumpers who unloaded the cargo were part-

61

time thieves. Taking into account the river pirates, lumpers, and the cargo damaged while it waited to be transferred to the wharves, losses every year must be enormous. But for two small shipments to vanish, both of them hers, seemed too great a coincidence.

"What had Hart to say? Could he tell if he'd lost anything else?" Finley asked, still in that soft, level tone.

"He said he'd released both consignments yesterday, to an agent of Cantarell Shipping."

Silence reigned. Finley looked thunderous. Olivia suspected him of suppressing some vigorous dockside language. After a significant pause, he observed, " 'Tis odd. An occasional bale or chest gone missing is to be expected. Two shipments, however, and one of considerable size, seems excessive."

"It could not have come at a worse time, Mr. Finley." Had she been her father's son rather than his daughter, the loss of the cargo would have gone unremarked. As she was female, it would make her appear weak.

Barlow looked up and frowned. " 'Tis a test, Mistress Olivia. At school, boys will try to provoke another—a new student—to see if he can be bullied. What I should like to know is whether Hart knew."

From his expression, Finley was turning the matter over in his mind. When he did not speak immediately, she asked Barlow, "Whoever came for my cargo had bills of lading?"

"Oh, ay. And I showed Hart ours—which was written in your hand, ma'am—and examined his copy. Hart scarcely glanced at them, which seems strange. I would have wanted to see if I could note any differences. The listing of cargo was correct, but the handwriting was different."

"By now you have seen many examples of my former clerk's hand, I suppose?"

"Ay. 'Twasn't his, either."

"Who was the supposed agent?" Finley demanded.

"Hart said he didn't know the fellow, but he signed for it. Hart reckoned you'd got a new employee. It's no secret Munns has left your employ."

"You took note of the name of the agent, I trust?"

"I did. I misdoubt Ephraim Wallis is his own name as I can guess how he came by it. There is an alehouse in the next street with its proprietor's name, one E. Wallis, writ large on its sign, under a very...ah...pretty angel. It's Edward, not Ephraim, but if I were trying to make up a false name, it might spring to mind."

Finley said, "You use a printed bill with blanks to be filled in with the name of the ship, the ports of origin and destination, the cargo, date and so forth, but without your company name at the top. I have seen many like it; I suppose the printer uses the same form for all and sells them either blank, like yours, or imprints a company name if it's wanted."

"It is cheaper to buy them as they are stocked, rather than imprinted," Olivia explained. Her father had never felt the need to spend the additional money.

He continued, " 'Tis a few minutes' work to complete one. But as you say, Barlow, an honest man would examine the bill you brought, to see whether it differed or not."

"If he is not an innocent dupe, he conspired with someone who knew what the cargo consisted of." Olivia held up her hand, fingers spread. "My father, myself, Munns, the shipping agent in Turkey, the consignees—"

"Someone in the merchant's employ," Barlow added.

"We can eliminate the apothecary from suspicion. He has been our customer for a dozen years or more and never given any trouble, Mr. Barlow. He would know what his order was, but not the viscount's. I misdoubt he would know where to find a blank bill of lading, in any case. The agent in Turkey or a clerk in his office would have had access to the information and to blank bills, but he would have to have a confederate here in London to pick up the cargo. It's not a sufficiently valuable cargo to warrant such a conspiracy. And Viscount Bernis seems an unlikely suspect."

"Because he's a viscount?" Finley inquired with gentle humor.

"No. But based on my father's dealings with him, I conclude he's not clever enough to arrange for forged bills of lading. Besides, he wouldn't know of the medicaments."

Both young men were eying her with considerable respect, she saw, and she had had nothing to complain of in their manner to her before.

"I had not considered the value of the cargo," Barlow admitted. He looked down at the documents. "Senna, opium, gum tragacanth, gum Arabic, and coloquintida. Not much value. Even the Turkey rugs don't amount to much. Hardly worth stealing, given their bulk. Besides, barring pirates, aren't most losses thefts of opportunity? A keg of tobacco here, a chest of tea there, things easily sold or used by the thief. It is passing strange."

"I've heard an organized trade takes in stolen goods and sells them throughout London. But this theft is by a trick I believe I have not encountered before." Finley scowled. It made him look far less affable and more like a man who might have taken part in dockside brawls. "We are in agreement that the apothecary, the shipper, and Bernis are ruled out, as are you and your father. That leaves your clerk, Munns, who seems to me a very eligible suspect."

Olivia said, "I am sorry to think it might be Munns. But he would know the particulars of the shipments and could have taken blank bills of lading when he left. My father always found him honest, and I never saw any sign that he wasn't—and I would have, doing the accounts—but he heartily disapproved of me." She sighed. "I will write to Viscount Bernis's man of business and the apothecary, explaining why we cannot deliver their merchandise."

"Ma'am, may I suggest that you delay until I write to Captain Easterday, and have one of the boys deliver it."

"Why put it off, Mr. Finley? Disagreeable as the task is. And why trouble Captain Easterday?"

"He trusted me to serve you until you could hire an experienced clerk, and now this has occurred."

"It was certainly not your fault, or Barlow's."

"No. However, the captain may have an idea of the best way to proceed. Do you not think the theft must have been a spur-of-the-moment decision? You took Mr. Cantarell's place, and Munns had access to the details of the bills of lading and to the blank forms. It must have seemed like an easy, safe way to cause you trouble. If it was he, he will not necessarily have made any plan to dispose of the cargo. Sometimes one can recover stolen goods."

"For a price?"

"Sometimes."

Cantarell Shipping could not afford to make a habit of paying to ransom their shipments. What was to keep it from happening again, if she did pay? But it would be fatal to look beyond the current crisis. If she looked further ahead, she might lose heart to go on. Best to focus her thoughts on this problem and deal with it somehow. With, if she must, Easterday's assistance.

"Very well. I will be in my office."

He made a polite little bow of acquiescence, took out a sheet of paper, and uncapped the inkwell.

\*\*\*\*

The blond Whitechapel School boy, Hezekiah ("They mostly call me 'Ky,' ma'am and sirs."), had been dispatched with Finley's letter to Captain Easterday. Olivia had finished mentally composing the letters she would write to the apothecary and the viscount's representative when Ky came with Captain Easterday's reply. He must have run all the way, for he was flushed with exertion. He gave Barlow, who was at the desk a sort of half salute. Approaching Finley and Olivia at the table where the maps were kept, he made a little bow to Finley and a deeper bow to Olivia.

"You were very quick, Ky. I suppose Captain Easterday was away or busy and did not send a reply." Finley was staring hard at the boy. She hoped Ky had merely been extremely fleet-footed, rather than having forgotten to wait for the captain's letter, if he had been available to write one.

"Sir, ma'am, I went to Cap'n Easterday's office and put it in his hand. And I says I'm to wait for an answer." Ky paused, whether to catch his breath or to build suspense, she did not know.

"What did he say, boy?" Finley demanded.

"He read it, and it didn't take him long. Then he says I can take a message straight back here. He frowns something fierce."

"Where is it, then, Ky?"

"He told it me. Made me repeat it twice, he did." Ky straightened almost to attention and intoned, "I will call upon you at your office, by which time I may have useful in-for-ma-tion to bring you. Take no further action now."

She almost felt she had witnessed a young, blond simulacrum of Captain Easterday. Perhaps Ky belonged on the stage. She could imagine him portraying Puck in *A Midsummer Night's Dream*. Finley blew out a breath, and Barlow's pen stopped its scratching across paper.

"Very good, Ky. Here's a farthing as a reward for your speed and efficiency."

"Thanks, mistress. And the captain already give me tuppence that I'll give my mam tonight."

It was not easy to return to her instructions to Finley for arrangements regarding a shipment of dried figs and raisins consigned to a fashionable grocer. "As soon as you've expedited the inspection—by whatever means are necessary—get it delivered. The shipment is somewhat late already. Mr. Cole is anxious to get them."

## Chapter 8

Hart's office, up one creaking flight of stairs from the ground floor of the warehouse, had one window, from which it was possible to see a corner of the Custom House, and beyond it, the Tower. The warehouse owner greeted Easterday in his cluttered office with a cheerful "A good day to you, Captain. Sit down, sit down. May I offer you a glass of rum or brandy? The rum's good, the brandy…" He gave a little shrug.

"Thank you, no." Easterday remained standing, and Hart, who had begun to seat himself, arrested his descent. "My errand will not take long." He did not care to accept the man's hospitality.

"Then how can I serve you, Captain?" He leaned over his desk, hunched a little, like a crane peering at a frog, though with no appearance of predacious intent. Perhaps he had already swallowed a frog, for although Hart was tall and thin, he did possess a pot belly.

"I understand you gave up Viscount Bernis's rugs and a crate of medicaments and apothecary's materials to someone claiming to represent Cantarell Shipping."

Hart stared at him blankly. "Ah…ay. Some new clerk."

"One you'd never seen before, and you so careless that you did not think to verify his identity?"

"He had the bills of lading," Hart said, more

firmly.

Having once labored his way through Malynes's 1622 work on bills of lading and charterparties, and several later pieces as well, Easterday knew that possession of the bill had come to be considered proof of the bearer's right to the merchandise.

"Under ordinary circumstances, that might release you from responsibility. But the use of the bill as evidence of the right to cargo is custom, not law. Here I think a court might find you negligent. Cantarell Shipping had a new owner, and the man who presented the bill of lading was one you'd not seen before."

"Ah..."

"Had you seen him previously, or know him, perhaps?"

"No! Never saw him before in my life!"

"It never crossed your mind to wonder whether he actually worked for Cantarell or whether he had acquired the bill of lading in some illicit manner?"

Hart's Adam's apple bobbed in his throat, and his lips moved without forming words. How the devil did he survive in the cutthroat shipping business? Easterday had not raised his voice above the level suitable for speaking with ladies, and the man was all but collapsing before him.

"Yes, I believe a court would rule that you had a duty to assure yourself of his identity. Relative of Edward Wallis, was he?"

"I suppose—how would I know? I've never heard of Edward Wallis."

"When the court decides in Cantarell's favor, you will owe the new owner compensation for your mistake." Which might be true, or not. One never knew, when one went to law, and it could take years to get a decision. It might be too late to help Olivia Cantarell.

Hart stood frowning in thought. Likely he was wondering how to get himself out of his trouble. Not quick-witted, Timothy Hart. He did well enough day to day, but in an emergency, he floundered.

"To drag the law into it," he said finally, "would only waste everyone's time and money. If the Cantarell woman would accept some compensation…"

"Mistress Olivia Cantarell will probably be willing to consider it. However, the impact on the firm's reputation must be taken into account, not merely the loss of the goods."

The warehouse owner licked his lips. "If a mistake was made, I'm very sorry for it, and I'll do what I can to make it right, but I don't know what I *can* do. I can't afford to pay a great deal. There's never much profit, expenses are high—"

Several facts and things he had observed came together in his mind. Easterday interrupted, "You don't own this warehouse, do you? You pose as its owner, but you merely manage it."

The man dropped into the chair behind his desk. "Of course I own it. The sign says 'Hart's,' don't it?"

"Paint on a board. It could say 'Rose & Briar Public House,' but that wouldn't make it a public house."

Tim Hart pulled himself together. "Well…that's all beside the point. Do you know how much Mistress Olivia would want for the goods and inconvenience?"

"She will wish to take advice as to the damage to her firm's reputation, but you might minimize your liability by recovering the merchandise."

"Where would I look for it? Every second man, almost, is a thief. They'd steal your eyes if they wasn't fixed in place."

Easterday smiled. "I'd start with your brother-in-law, Noakes. Noakes has already tried to cheat Olivia Cantarell over some shipping charges."

"She'd say that," Hart began.

"Noakes didn't tell you I was present, did he? I suggest you get the shipment back, Hart." He added, "I take an interest in the fortunes of Cantarell Shipping. Also, I detest a thief." He added, "I'm not all you have to worry about, apart from legal proceedings. What will the real owner say when he learns that you aided Noakes in his gull. Or did he approve it?"

Hart swallowed and said nothing. Easterday had not expected him to answer. It would be pointless to ask who the owner was. It was probably not relevant. The diversion of the shipment was a minor matter and easily resolved. If Hart could not get the rugs and apothecary's shipment back, he would pay, with Noakes footing the cost.

He took the time to drop in at Lloyd's Coffee House to learn the latest news and stayed to discuss it with some of the men with whom he did business. As Cantarell's death and his daughter's inheriting the firm was still being talked of, it was easy to mention that he was taking an interest in Cantarell Shipping, as a favor to the late Cantarell. Some had already heard that one of his clerks was working there. They were clearly curious, though no one asked any questions. But the speculation would speed the word that Olivia Cantarell was not without an ally.

Chapter 9

"Your aunt's in the parlor, ma'am," Kitty said as Olivia entered the house.

Olivia sighed. She had hoped to slip in unnoticed and go to her chamber to collect herself before having to face Aunt Rachel. She nodded an acknowledgement, removed her hat and cape for Kitty to take upstairs, and betook herself to the parlor where her aunt sat embroidering. She prayed Aunt Rachel would not ask about the events of the day. It was too much to hope for.

"Livvie, dear, you look quite put out. Your day must have been vastly disagreeable, though I'd think any day in your papa's office would be horrid."

"A small shipment was delivered wrongly, Aunt. Finley and Barlow will locate it tomorrow."

"How vexing. Now I know you will wish to repair to your chamber to tidy yourself. When you come down, we might have a glass of ratafia. 'Twould soothe you before supper, and I will tell you what I heard about that son of Mr. Chalmers, which will make you laugh."

"That sounds very pleasant," she agreed and hastened up to wash London's grime from her hands and face.

She had only just returned to the parlor when their footman came to announce a visitor.

"Mr. Ambrose Hawkins, ma'am." He addressed the "ma'am" to the air halfway between them. William had grown old in their service and could never have been as smart, brisk, and socially adept as a footman in a fashionable household. Olivia ascribed to tact his reluctance to decide whether she or her aunt was the ranking lady in the house. Aunt Rachel was older and had certainly occupied that position when she first came to live with her brother and niece; on the other hand, Olivia was her father's heir and now owned the house. William found it a dilemma.

"Show him in," Aunt Rachel said, beaming. "How nice of him to call, even at such an odd time. And bring Mr. Cantarell's claret and a glass for our guest."

Hawkins was dressed less vividly than he had been at the assembly, in dark green. The cloth and cut were excellent, however, and his waistcoat was embroidered saffron silk. He bowed over Rachel Williams's hand, then over Olivia's, holding it a few seconds longer. He accepted a glass of claret and talked with her aunt, who had been trained in girlhood to make light conversation. Mr. Hawkins did not fail to include Olivia, but she had never caught the knack of chatting about nothing. At last, Aunt Rachel gave her a Look which she had no difficulty in interpreting: say something!

Before she could think of something, anything at all, to offer, Hawkins said, "It must be very trying, taking over your father's business."

Aunt Rachel said, "Only today, some problem occurred, and Olivia came home in low spirits. A matter of something lost or stolen, was it not, dear?"

"Misplaced only, I think, Aunt," she replied, giving her a quelling glance. "It was nothing of significance."

She would be damned if she would let Hawkins know that her cargo had been stolen, thus far with impunity. The thought of what her aunt and Hawkins and—oh, anyone!—would think to hear her use such language brought a smile to her lips.

"You take it very lightly, Mistress Olivia. Are you sure 'tis only 'misplaced'?"

"We have a very fair idea of how and where it went astray. I have no doubt it will be returned shortly." She could infuse conviction into her voice, since some of her statement was actually true. Showing weakness would be fatal.

"I'm glad to hear it." He seemed to find it convincing, as he continued, "You have the heart of a Joan of Arc—if I may compare you to a Popish saint—to attempt the challenge of managing a shipping agency, Mistress Olivia."

Aunt Rachel protested, "Joan of Arc was burned at the stake, Mr. Hawkins."

"Mistress Olivia does not face such a dire end. I have a suggestion to offer. I should apologize for calling upon you at this time of day, but it seemed best to speak with her before a suitable chaperone."

"Oh! Of course."

Olivia said dryly, "I hope Cantarell Shipping's clients do not all take the same notion."

Ambrose Hawkins smiled. His teeth were white and even. "This does not, strictly speaking, deal with shipping. I have a business proposal to place before you."

"Indeed, Mr. Hawkins?"

"You do not want to spend your days in a fusty office, dealing with rough men, always at risk of insult, if not worse. Sell me Cantarell Shipping. I'll pay you a fair price. What say you?"

"It would be a very good thing," Aunt Rachel said.

"I have not given any thought to selling," Olivia responded after a pause during which both her aunt and Hawkins watched her expectantly. Neither showed any sign of thinking she would refuse. An emphatic "No" had been her first thought, but she was not much in the habit of speaking without thinking.

"But Livvie—"

"Aunt, the estate has not yet been settled. Though my father's executor agrees I have the right to manage the company, I misdoubt I could sell it yet. By the time I have the legal right, I will have decided what's best to do."

"I would accept an assurance that when you decide to sell, you will permit me to purchase it," Hawkins said.

"Until the estate is 'proved,' as I believe is the term, I don't feel I can make even such a promise as that, sir."

"Ah, I see you are as cautious as your papa. I will hope that we may do business in the future, then. Ladies, I've trespassed too much on your evening." He rose and bowed, and they both accompanied him to the door.

When he had gone out, and the door was closed, Aunt Rachel murmured, "Did you note his coach? It was his own, for no hackney is so fine, and the horses, too! Do you know anyone with his own coach? I can think of no one we know, not since I moved from Hanover Square. My dear, you should have agreed to sell him the business. He's a man, he's connected to the shipping industry, it would be the perfect solution. Though not as perfect as…" She sighed and broke off.

Olivia guessed her unvoiced thought and also sighed. Rachel Williams was an unalloyed optimist. In spite of Mr. Hawkins's flattering attention to her at the assembly, his interest could not be romantic. She had allowed herself to bask in it that night, knowing she was looking her best and that he had paid no attention to any other lady. In view of his offer, he could only have been ingratiating himself to induce her to sell him her company. Ambrose Hawkins was a wealthy man. Everyone on Thames Street and on down the river to the estuary knew his name. Hawkins's name and his ships were known half the world away. "A dangerous, clever man," she recalled her father remarking once, which brought to mind something she had overheard, listening at her spyhole. The captain of a ship in which Cantarell owned a share had been speaking.

"For all he looks and talks like a gentleman, he has the heart of a pirate. There's men hanged at Execution Dock I'd've trusted sooner."

"There's a mort of men, gentlemen and nobility included, that are no more than unhanged rogues," Jonas Cantarell had replied, unmoved. "Before you trust a man, watch to see if he cheats others."

He had not been a warm or affectionate father, but he had more than common sense and was as honest as a churchman. Possibly more so, if one believed his rule of thumb that you could not assume anyone's honesty, based on their words or station in life. She would watch Hawkins.

"Livvie, why is Captain Easterday called captain and Mr. Hawkins is not?"

They had gone in to supper, a meal Olivia could well have dispensed with. Had she lived alone, she would have made do with cheese and an apple.

She looked up from the boiled fish she had been picking at. "Captain Easterday was captain of a merchantman for several years. Mr. Hawkins was at sea too but never rose beyond being first or second mate, I don't know which."

"Yet he went into business and made a great deal of money. He must be very hardworking and clever."

"He is said to have got his start by good trading instincts while he was yet a sailor."

"I do remember Jonas telling me that officers are permitted to ship a certain amount of freight. He himself made a tidy sum doing so."

"Indeed. Of course, he was part owner of the ship, too. Aunt Rachel, I've meant to mention this…if I increased the household allowance by two pounds a week, do you think we might have better breakfasts and dinners? With perhaps tea in the morning? And less fish at all times?"

Since she was now gone all day, she and her aunt had changed to dining in the early evening rather than at midday with only a light supper in the evening. Her father had taken his dinner at noon in an ordinary, and therefore needed no more than some cold meat and cheese and perhaps soup if the weather were cold. Olivia could not sit elbow to elbow on a bench with the men who ate the ordinary's cheap but hearty dinner. In any case, she had always favored an early and substantial breakfast and had little appetite for a heavy early afternoon meal, such as she and her aunt had taken when her father was alive.

"Can we afford it? Your father disapproved of unnecessary expenditures. I can't think where he acquired such Puritan ideas, for he wasn't like that as a young man. When I came to care for you I was quite shocked at how...frugal...he had grown."

"He became a skinflint as a result of the South Sea Bubble when I was a child, Mama told me, not that she said 'skinflint.' 'Excessively economical' was how she put it. He lost a great deal of money, and I suppose stringent economy was needed for a while. When I began assisting him, I realized that we were not in terribly straitened circumstances after all. But I could not mention it to him, when it worried him so to spend money. It can't worry him now, and really, our meals are not good, and it's not Mistress Grissom's fault."

"Livvie...," her aunt began. "I was glad to see you had bought new shoes before the assembly. Your old ones were quite worn out. It was no wonder at all that the two finest gentlemen there showed an interest. We wouldn't need as much as two pounds more per week. Another one pound a week would help, if it wouldn't run us into debt—and it would be so much more pleasant. I would dearly love a cup of chocolate on a cold morning."

"I think we can spend enough to have chocolate sometimes."

"If you were to sell out, we might have roast chicken occasionally, rather than only when we visit Vauxhall Gardens."

"What a daring suggestion! But even if I do not sell, we can have chicken. We are not really so badly off. Aunt, I cannot help but notice that your gown is frayed in places."

"I only wear it at home, where it does not matter."

"You must have a new one. That particular one is too worn even to pass on to Kitty."

"Is it wise to make any unnecessary purchase when our future is unsettled? If you sold the company—or married some man with an independence—we might order two or even three, for Mistress Wilkes could make them up quite economically."

"It will not bankrupt us to order them now, Aunt Rachel."

Chapter 10

Finley was before her at the office the next day. From his welcoming grin, she knew he had good news.

"The shipment's back, and I've put it upstairs. There was room."

"No damage? Everything is there?" She seated herself to conceal the weakness in her knees.

"All accounted for. And I've locked Hart's restitution payment—one hundred pounds—in the strongbox." His brow furrowed with worry. "You should have been consulted, but it was resolved after you'd left, and…mmm…Captain Easterday felt the amount was reasonable. He asked me to apologize on his behalf for taking the liberty of accepting Hart's offer. The captain thought it best that the matter be wrapped up as quickly as might be."

"I quite agree. I'm very grateful to both of you, and I will write him to say so."

"There's something you should know, ma'am. Hart is Noakes's brother-in-law."

"Is he? Well, we won't be using his warehouse again. We have, once or twice in the past, when our usual warehouses were full. From now on, these are the warehouses we use." She pulled a blank sheet of paper toward her side of the desk, dipped a quill in the standish and wrote three names, each one followed by its direction and the manager's name. "If we should have some small shipment, we can store it upstairs, as you did with the recovered goods. It must have been a challenge, getting the rugs upstairs, as narrow as the stairs are and with the right angle turn."

"Rugs bend, ma'am," Finley said with a grin, "and a good thing, too."

Barlow was writing out a bill of lading for the household goods of a newly married lady whose husband had been appointed to some colonial post. My lady did not intend to set up housekeeping among the savages with naught but rough-hewn bed frames, stools, benches, and planks laid over trestles for a table.

"But New York is not some uncouth frontier settlement," Finley protested. "I have been there and found it quite civilized, with handsome buildings and well-dressed inhabitants. How could it not be? The port accommodates even the largest vessels and ships a great quantity of goods."

Olivia levelled a look at him. "We know that, and you may be sure Sir Henry knows that. He also knows his lady will be happier with her own pretty furnishings around her. The freight charges are a small price to pay for marital felicity."

"I will remember that, ma'am."

They had already settled into a routine very different from what she had been accustomed to with her father and Munns. The changes went far beyond the lengthening of her day. Either Barlow or Finley arrived in the office before she did. The other began the day by visiting Lloyd's Coffee House in Lombard Street to hear the latest shipping news and gossip. The boys came in after her, playful as a pair of puppies. The greatest alteration in the office was the occasional laughter. Olivia had assumed any business setting required a somber demeanor. Neither Munns nor her father were given to laughter or even to smiling at some mild jest. Finley and Barlow bantered back and forth, trading quips that made her laugh in spite of herself. Barlow frequently displayed a dry wit—a pawky wit, the Scots called it, he said. Kit and Ky grinned, and yet Cantarell Shipping functioned smoothly.

Barlow and Ky had gone out for their midday meal at the ordinary nearby where the food was plain but good. Although her arrangement with the Whitechapel School had been to provide for Ky's and Kit's dinners, she and Finley had decided to do things differently. The lads still received the money intended for their food but instead of sending them out on their own, Finley would take one with him to eat at the ordinary one day, while Barlow would take the other to a public house once Finley had returned, as the ordinary served its meal only for an hour. The next day, Barlow and his charge would eat at the ordinary, and Finley and the other boy at the tavern.

There were numerous benefits to offset the additional cost. Within two days after his arrival, Olivia had guessed that Ky did not use his money to eat, or only something very small and cheap, preferring to save it for his mother. She was not sure about Kit but thought he probably bought something cheap but filling and shared it with Ky. Barlow pointed out that although they were willing, hardworking lads, they were still boys and needed good meals. "They would be the better for regular meals of meat," Olivia said, and so they ate in shifts, and the first pair to return brought back something for her. It was certainly preferable to

Munns's practice of bringing bread and cheese.

She was working on the account book in her father's office overlooking the tiny yard between their building and the one behind it, the door almost closed to shut out all but a murmur of voices from the front, when Kit tapped on the jamb and announced, "Cap'n Easterday to see you, ma'am. About a shipment, like. Ummmm…"

She glanced around. She was going to have to make some changes to the room. Like her father, it was austere and threadbare, if you could use the word of a space that contained not a wisp of textile. Bare board floor, no curtains over the window—which, now that she noticed, was grimy. The sill was coated with soot. The shelves contained dusty boxes holding over thirty years of business records, including every copy of *Lloyd's List* ever received. It might be time to dispose of some of those, past ship arrivals and sailings no longer having any current relevance. She was ashamed for the captain to see it, but she had no choice. Finley was dealing with a client in the front office already. Her own former little office was now Ky and Kit's waiting room. When Jonas Cantarell was alive, he would have invited a second visitor into his office.

"Show Captain Easterday in." It meant being alone with him in greater privacy than was appropriate, but she would not keep Kit with her as a chaperone. He was needed in the front anyway to deal with any messengers or other customers who came.

"Cap'n Easterday, ma'am."

"Good morning, sir. Please be seated."

He bowed and did so, without taking finicking care to the stiff skirts of his coat, as some men did. Dark

83

blue cloth, plain and good, with an almost equally plain waistcoat, shirt, and neckcloth.

"I came about the shipment of linen from Scotland," he said.

"I regret not having sent to you to let you know—" she began.

"We have both been busy, Mistress Olivia."

"I have the figures for you, Captain." She retrieved the sheet from the drawer and passed it to him.

A glance sufficed. He handed it back to her. "This will do very well. My nephew has entered his order for the goods. I will send you the details by messenger today."

"Very good. As the shipment is not coming from foreign parts, we need not worry about clearing customs, at least. That will save time." They completed arrangements for transfer of the linen to one of Easterday's ships, and Olivia rose, supposing their meeting was at an end.

"There is another matter I would like to discuss with you," he said.

She sank back into her chair. "Yes, Captain?"

"Have you had any replies to your advertisement for a clerk?"

"Well…one. But he came for his interview much the worse for drink. You must need Finley returned to you. I'm very grateful to you for lending him to me; he has been an entire army, all on his own. But I can do very well with Barlow, now I have Ky and Kit."

"There is no urgency about Finley returning to me. I am not quite easy in my mind about you."

"I beg your pardon?" Her back stiffened.

"The reason you have not been able to find another

clerk is that it's felt that you will not be able to keep Cantarell Shipping and that a clerk who takes a position with you will have difficulty finding a new place when you sell. There are wagers as to how long it will be before you give it up."

She saw no point in wasting energy on anger. From the first, she had known that running Cantarell Shipping would not be easy. Women were always at a disadvantage in a man's world. "As it happens, sir, I have already had an offer and turned it down."

It was plain from his face that he would like to ask who had offered, and equally plain that good manners would restrain him from asking. "Mayhap it's not significant," he admitted, shrugging. "As I mentioned, there's talk. Also I inquired about Munns, as it appears certain he assisted Hart and Noakes by providing the information for the bills of lading. He has not taken another position, and I was unable to locate him."

"He may not have found it necessary to work any longer. My father paid him well, and he was always thrifty."

"I visited his lodging house. The landlady was not certain of the day he moved away, but his rent was paid up, with several days remaining and he asked for no refund—which she would not have given in any case," he added. "As nearly as I can tell, he departed the day after he left your employ. The woman recalled two things of interest."

"It's odd he should leave after living there since before he came to work for my father. He might have found lodgings nearer, but he said his landlady's talents as a cook outweighed the inconvenience of the location."

"I believe he had good reason to remove himself. She mentioned he had a visitor only a day or two before he told her he was leaving. It was an uncommon thing for Munns, which impressed it upon her mind, as did a few words she overheard when Munns escorted the man to the door. It was the phrase 'as you are coming into some money, I trust you will leave London.' She was pleased for Munns, because he was a very quiet tenant and no trouble to her and at the same time she was sorry to think she might lose him as a boarder, but she did not feel she could ask him about it. Munns and his visitor did not see her when they came down the stairs, and she did not wish Munns to think she had been eavesdropping."

"Could she describe the man?" The implication would be obvious to the most trusting person on earth.

Easterday shook his head. "She only saw him swathed in a roquelaure. He was tall—but she is very short—and she noticed that he spoke like a gentleman, which she found reassuring. Otherwise, she would have hesitated to admit a man with his lower face concealed by a wrap-rascal." Here some peculiar expression passed over the captain's face. It almost looked like humor.

"Do you know, Captain, this almost makes me feel better about Munns's betrayal."

Easterday stared at her. "How so? If someone paid one of my employees to cheat, I would be exceeding angry."

"I can understand someone in his position giving way to greed; he is not much younger than my father, and however carefully he has saved, his means will be slight, for how much can one save on a salary of three pounds a week? I can't approve of it, but the alternative would be that he hated me enough to leave a remunerative position and commit the fraud."

"That's a point, ma'am. It makes it less of a personal betrayal and more of..." He paused. "More of a business opportunity, however dishonest. Also we must consider this: if the visitor was a gentleman, he was neither Noakes nor Hart."

"That being the case, his visitor must be unconnected with them. What they stole was simply not worth enough to justify bribing Munns, for it would have had to be a large bribe. Like my father, Munns was a cautious man, and he never betrayed my father's trust. Only mine."

"If the landlady is correct, Munns received his visitor before Noakes confronted you. It would be interesting to ask him what he was paid to do, and why. I will send someone to the nearest coaching inns to see if anyone recalls an elderly fellow departing on that day."

"He wears spectacles, and he is shorter than I am," Olivia contributed.

"That may be helpful. Though after this many days, with the coaching inns always busy, 'tis like to be impossible to trace him. Does he have any other identifying feature by which he might be recognized?"

"He is thin rather than fat, his hair is gray, and he does not wear a wig. It's too expensive to maintain one. His features are sharp. He is like a thousand other elderly clerks in London and anywhere else. He has nothing to distinguish him." She spread her hands. Then she exhaled abruptly. "Unless he took his books, which I suspect he would."

"How would that be of assistance?" the captain asked. "Surely he would have a trunk, and who's to know if it contained a volume or two?"

"If he spent money on anything, it was books. He was very well-read in the Latin authors, and he had a taste for natural philosophy as well. He spoke from time to time of this or that book he had found for a few pence after a long hunt at the bookstalls in the Strand. They will not have fitted into one trunk. More likely they would require a separate trunk or a crate. The landlady would know, I imagine."

"That may be helpful, Mistress Olivia. I will take my leave of you now. I have various matters to attend to, as do you, I'm sure."

"I could call upon Munns's landlady and see if he took his books and how many trunks he had," she suggested.

"I will do that, as she already knows me."

## Chapter 11

Munns said, "I was trying to do her a kindness, if the stupid woman had the wits to realize it."

He had reluctantly received Easterday in his lodgings in Cambridge. Tracking him through the carrier who had transported two crates of books to a lodging house in a pleasant part of the town had been easy.

A neat maid answered the door and requested Easterday to wait while she went up to see if Mr. Munns was in. She came back to tell him apologetically that Mr. Munns could not receive him.

"His room is on the first floor, I think?" The maid had gone up only one flight of stairs; Easterday had heard her tap at the door and heard the murmur of voices.

"Ay, sir, but he don't care to see anyone."

"He'll see me."

"Sir—!"

He ran up two steps at a time. There was only one door, and stairs that continued up to the next story. Munns occupied the entire floor, then. Pleasant, indeed. He knocked briskly and called out, "Munns! You had best admit me."

"I've no business with you nor you with me."

"Then Mistress Cantarell will lay a charge against you of theft. As your whereabouts are now known, your arrest will follow shortly thereafter. Or you could grant me a few minutes of your time."

The grizzled man who opened the door was very much as Olivia had described him, though she had not mentioned his long, sharp nose or the ill-tempered lines that ran from either side of it to the corners of his mouth. It was not the face of a happy man.

The room Munns used as a study overlooked a small, well-kept garden. He indicated an armchair and seated himself behind his desk. A wooden packing box was pushed against one wall; bookshelves against another wall were partially filled with well-used volumes.

"I do not know what you're talking about, but since you've threatened me with legal action, I suppose I must speak with you."

"Munns, you supplied the information to forge at least two bills of lading, enabling your confederates to divert Cantarell Shipping cargoes from Hart's warehouse. You may escape prosecution if you answer my questions."

"Are you assuming my guilt because I left Cantarell Shipping? As soon as I realized *she* meant to try to run the business, I decided to leave. Stubborn baggage! I don't know what Cantarell was thinking of, letting her involve herself. As for your unfounded allegation, quite a number of persons know what any given cargo is. The shipper, the captain, and one or more of his officers, the consignee, the—"

"All those possibilities have been considered, Munns. You had access to the information needed to complete the bills of lading, you dislike Olivia Cantarell, and you left without giving any notice. You have settled in extremely comfortable lodgings. Mistress Cantarell told me her father trusted you. She herself was certain you were honest. It must have been a substantial bribe to overcome your scruples."

"I had no need to accept a bribe, even assuming I would. I've lived very inexpensively for many years and saved my money, and I was not entirely destitute even though I had to take a position in a shipping company," Munns replied curtly. "I took my degree here. Having decided to retire, I returned to work I enjoy, as a tutor in the classics."

Too much explanation not to be partly a lie. "I might believe that—although the other circumstances are still damning—except for the gentleman who called at your lodgings. He told you to leave London with the money you'd 'come into,' didn't he? Was it Hawkins?" A palpable hit, judging from the way Munns stiffened. "Come, Munns. You might as well tell me. You may trust me not to let Hawkins know how I found out."

"Very well, then, it was Hawkins. You cannot claim it harmed the company, as that woman will not be able to keep it anyway. Cantarell Shipping can be sold while it's a profitable concern. If she tries to hold onto it, it will fail and no one will buy it. Hawkins meant only to make her realize the necessity of selling while she can still get a good price. She'd best do it and devote herself to whatever old maids do to occupy themselves. I was trying to do her a kindness, if the stupid woman had the wits to realize it. What harm was there in helping him convince her it's in her best interests to sell?"

"Ambrose Hawkins does not have a reputation for kindness. He'd be more likely to wait until he could buy at a bargain."

Munns primmed up his mouth. "Even Hawkins may feel some compunction about cheating a female."

"How could such a small company be of interest to him?"

There was an infinitesimal hesitation before Munns responded. "He likes owning things. Everyone knows that. Or mayhap he feels as the rest of us do, that a woman has no place in such a business. Selling would be the best thing for her. Can you deny it?"

"I don't like to see anyone, particularly a woman, tricked in a business transaction. Or any other, for that matter. Hawkins had Hart do the dirty work?"

Munns shrugged. "A connection of Hart's sailed with Hawkins years ago."

"Noakes."

The man took up a quill and studied its point. "May I ask why you concern yourself, Captain Easterday? Do you intend to try to buy Cantarell Shipping?"

"Good Lord, no. I don't need it. But some deeper game is going on, and I mean to find out what."

"On your head be it. Mind you do not involve me, sir. I will deny speaking with you."

## Chapter 12

Business was slower than it had been when her father was alive. It would rebound, as it was seen that Cantarell Shipping continued to be run as it had been for many years. No new problems arose, which was fortunate, as Olivia admitted to herself, because Captain Easterday had gone out of town in pursuit of Munns. Finley thought he would be gone three or four days.

Mr. Barlow was escorting her to the nearest hackney stand, both of the boys having been sent on errands. As he was handing her into the coach, a foppishly dressed young man hailed him.

"Ainslie! I say, Ainslie! I'd no idea you were in London." Beside her, Barlow started. Unquestionably, he was the one addressed. The vision in pale blue velvet with rather too much silver lace and red heels to his shoes minced toward them.

"Oh damn," Barlow breathed, and said aside to Olivia, "I'll explain tomorrow, ma'am. It's too complicated, and I can't let Choate know."

"I'll look forward to it. Good evening." Barlow shut the door and called up to the driver to be off. As they began to roll forward, Olivia heard the jovial remark, "Looks a bit elderly for you, old fellow. 'Less she's rich…" Then they were out of earshot. She smiled sourly.

\*\*\*\*

When she arrived in the morning, both Barlow—Ainslie?—and Finley were in the office already, the first looking guilty, the other grave. Both sprang to their feet with even more than normal haste. They reminded her irresistibly of Jack-in-the-box toys.

"Where are Kit and Ky?" she asked as she shed hat, gloves, and cape.

"I sent them out on errands. It seemed best."

Ordinarily, she took her wrap and hat back to her former little office immediately on arriving, but it seemed cruel to let Barlow stew longer. She sat in one of the chairs meant for clients. "You said you would explain, Mr. Barlow. Please do so. I see that Mr. Finley is already in your confidence."

"I apologize for the deception, ma'am," Finley said. "I did not think it would do any harm, and it seemed necessary. Umm, as Barlow—Ainslie—will explain."

Barlow, or Ainslie, picked up the tale. "You may recall I mentioned my mother moving my sisters and brothers to Scotland when her health was failing after my father's death."

"I do. She had a friend there with whom they could live."

"That was only part of it. The thing was, she knew that when she died, we would have to have a guardian."

"We?"

"I was still at sea, but even if I returned in time, I'm not of age yet. I'll be one-and-twenty in six months. When I returned, I found my family in a dilemma. I don't suppose you know much about Scots law—except as relates to shipping," he added hastily.

"I know it's often quite different from English

law."

"Ay, indeed. My mother feared that when she died, our guardianship would pass to my uncle—my father's brother. In England, the nearest male relative would be the usual choice. In Scotland, that would not necessarily be true. She took the children to Scotland and named as guardian and trustee under her will an old family friend in the legal profession. After my mother's death, my brothers and sisters and my mother's old governess moved to a cottage rented by the guardian for them." Barlow laced his fingers together. "My mother's fortune was not great, but it was English money rather than Scots. 'Tis adequate for the rent, food, and the children's education, but not much more. My father's manor and fortune is left to me—once I'm of age. I could not find work in Edinburgh or Glasgow, even with our guardian's assistance. I was sure I could get work in London, as I've a few friends here from my boyhood and sailing days." He and Finley exchanged grins.

Finley said, "We sailed together on the *Merrythought*—"

"And what a leaky bucket it was!" Barlow interjected.

Olivia could not help laughing. "The ship was named *Merrythought*?"

"Ay, ma'am, because the owner swore he'd won it after he'd wished on a chicken's merrythought to mend his fortune."

"He sold it after our voyage," Finley added.

"I beg your pardon for the divagation, Mistress Cantarell," Barlow said formally. Recently the clerks had taken to addressing her as if she were a married female, a courtesy sometimes used for a woman in a position of authority—or a cook.

"Granted. Continue, please."

"I came to London and found a temporary post as a clerk which ended several days before I came to work for you. It seemed best not to use my own name, lest I come to my uncle's attention somehow. Although my uncle, Horace Ainslie, lives near Hereford, at whiles he visits London. He is something of a gamester and loves fashionable life," Barlow said repressively.

"But your friend Mr....Choate, was it?...wasn't in on the secret?"

"No. His family lives in Cumberland, not far from my father's manor. Now he's left Oxford, he came here looking for low amusement and caught sight of me."

"Did you explain matters to him?"

He shook his head. "If Choate murdered someone, he couldn't hold his tongue. The best I could do was not tell him I was using another name. I haven't seen him for several years. It's less likely he'll gossip about seeing a boyhood friend if there's no story attached. I most sincerely apologize for deceiving you, ma'am, but I don't know what else I could have done."

"I gather your objection to being your uncle's ward for another few months has to do with your inheritance?" Olivia asked.

"There won't be an inheritance if he gets control of it, and I plan to use some of the money to send my brothers to university. The girls will need dowries."

"Very sensible. But you did not attend university?"

"I am good with figures and practical things, but I am not bookish. I like activity and wanted to see other countries. My father could never have afforded to send me on the Grand Tour. Going to sea appeared to be the answer. A friend of our family arranged for me to sail on a ship owned by his cousin."

"Mr. Finley, is Captain Easterday aware of this?"

"No, Mistress Cantarell."

"Why is that?"

"I am pretty sure 'twould not suit his notions of proper behavior. It seemed best not to put it to the test. When he was trying to find you a second clerk, I suggested Ainslie—well, Barlow—as I knew he could do the work."

"Hmmm." It would have been interesting to know the captain's thoughts on how to preserve Ainsley's secret. "As far as I am concerned, you remain Barlow."

"Thank you, ma'am. I am sensible of your kindness in not discharging me out of hand."

"Have you given any thought to how you will change back to your own name?" While it had nothing to do with his working as her clerk, she could not help but be interested. She had more in common with Finley and Barlow and liked them better than anyone else she knew except her aunt. She found Captain Easterday admirable without being quite sure whether she liked him. As for Hawkins…she was not sure how she felt about him.

"It will be the easiest thing in the world. When I come into my inheritance and am safe from my uncle, I shall give you my resignation—regretfully—and disappear. I will reappear in Cumberland as a country gentleman."

"What, and never come to London for your sisters' seasons?"

"Ay, I must do so. It will be my duty. But dressed

fashionably and escorting them to parties and the opera and plays, I won't encounter most of the people I see around the wharves and warehouses. If I do come upon someone who knows me, I'll raise my eyebrows and drawl that he must have mistaken me for my relation, Barlow, known to the family but not actually part of the family, an' ye know what I mean?"

Olivia laughed. "You do that very convincingly. It may answer. Only six months until your birthday, you said?"

"Ay. In January, which will be early enough to begin planning for the London season, as Julia, who is turned seventeen, does not let me forget."

"At least I will have a good assistant clerk until then." Assuming Cantarell Shipping continued in operation for half a year. Why should it not, no matter what anyone thought?

****

No one made any further attempts to cheat or bully her. Ambrose Hawkins came to the office once, to see how she went on and remained to chat for a half hour or so. She took him back to her office, leaving the door open for propriety.

"Cantarell Shipping has excellent connections in the Mediterranean, I know, Mistress Olivia."

"We do, sir. It was where my father got his start. Though we also ship to and from the Indies, and to the North American colonies."

"As do my ships. But as it happens, a business acquaintance of mine has a small cargo to send to Turkey. He asked my recommendation of a shipper and I thought, as you frequently serve that area…"

"In other words, Mr. Hawkins, the consignment is

too small to be worth your while." She said it with a slight, cynical smile.

He grinned. "In a word, ma'am, yes. Why not give Cantarell the benefit of it, I asked myself."

"It's not monkeys, is it? Or some other plaguey nuisance? I beg your pardon! I was used to hear my father talk, and sometimes one of his expressions pops out. He did try to mind his language when I was present."

"I'd wager that's not the worst you heard." He laughed. "No, it's not monkeys. It's only scientific equipment—microscopes and prospect glasses, reflecting quadrants, a camera obscura and such. No care or feeding required."

They discussed the details. Olivia thought their meeting was at an end when Hawkins said, as he rose to leave, "May I escort you—and your aunt, of course—to Chelsea on Sunday? The weather seems likely to hold, and the fields and gardens are pleasant, after the soot and smells of London."

She agreed, somewhat surprised. She had convinced herself that he had not really singled her out at the assembly, not for herself, at least. It could only have been because he had come to offer her his condolences, then felt obliged to ask her to dance. To invite her for a drive in the country argued that perhaps his interest was more personal, unless he still hoped she would sell him Cantarell Shipping.

Still, she found it almost as gratifying as his referring a customer to her, which could only help her business. Word would spread as it always did on Thames Street and in Wapping.

Aunt Rachel was pleased by the invitation. "I think

you must see about ordering a new gown and petticoat or two, if we have money enough, Livvie. It's too late to do anything now, but I will change the trim on your hat. Mr. Hawkins will not expect you to dress elaborately for an expedition to the country."

Chapter 13

Mr. Hawkins arrived in an open vehicle, the day being warm enough to be pleasant and the sky cloudless. Riding in the fresh air was pleasant, and with their parasols, they did not risk ruining their complexions. Mr. Hawkins's coachman took them by what seemed a rambling route though she was beyond the limits of her experience after they passed from the Strand to Charing Cross. She had never been so far west. As they drove down White Hall, Mr. Hawkins pointed out the Admiralty Office, the red brick mass of Horse Guards, its twin sentry boxes each large enough for a mounted trooper, and the site of the future Westminster Bridge, only recently begun.

" 'Twill be a great convenience when 'tis completed," Hawkins remarked. "Though we will not be crossing it any time soon."

Soon after Petty France became James Street, the way was bordered by fields and open ground. The road turned sharply at Buckingham House, and they passed the turnpike at the beginning of the Chelsea Road.

When they came to the Chelsea Bun House across from the burying ground, the coachman brought the team to a halt with the coach door even with steps up to the colonnade of the long, low building.

"Ladies, it would be a shame to pass without getting buns to make our fingers sticky."

And so they did. The light, square rolls spiraled around a sweet filling and were coated with a sugar syrup. Similar buns were sold elsewhere, but these were better. When they had finished, Hawkins brought out a closely stoppered pottery flask of water and napkins, so they could rinse their fingers.

She would have considered this by itself a delightful excursion, but it was not yet over. Turning back, they crossed the little Chelsea Bridge, past the Neat Houses market gardens and continued down to the Thames, by the Chelsea Waterworks. The low-lying ground might make for damp houses, but the fields of cauliflower, artichokes, celery, and other vegetables were a dozen shades of green.

"We could have walked among the limes and chestnut trees at the Chelsea College, or Don Saltero's coffeehouse is in Cheyne Walk and contains many curiosities—but of course one cannot take ladies to such a place." He smiled down at Olivia. "Coming here seemed particularly appropriate as both your business and mine depend upon the Thames."

"Curiosities are nothing compared to the countryside," Aunt Rachel murmured. "I miss the country. I came to London as a girl and married, and my husband did not care for country life, not having been bred to it."

"Perhaps your niece will marry a man with a country property."

Aunt Rachel sighed. "I'm sure I do not know how, living as she does."

Aunt Rachel meant well, but to have her prospects discussed as if she were not present was embarrassing.

"A man who earns his living by the water might

also have a home elsewhere." He glanced at Olivia. She was glad that sun and the breeze had whipped color into her cheeks to conceal what must be a blush. And she never blushed! Or not until recently. Mr. Hawkins could not be suggesting he had an interest in her. Could he? How ridiculous for a woman of thirty to be thinking like a schoolroom chit. She acquitted him of the suspicion he wanted to marry her for her company. It might make sense for him to buy Cantarell Shipping; as a dowry, it could not attract a man as rich as Hawkins.

They dined at the ancient Monster Tavern. Aunt Rachel pressed Mr. Hawkins for descriptions of the foreign ports he had visited. He obliged, with such vivid details that she could imagine the spice-scented breezes of Ceylon, the damp, heavy heat of India with its sun-drenched bazaars and exotic foods, the islands of the West Indies and the Spanish Main. He kept his account to amusing anecdotes suitable for ladies. Even an encounter with a pirate ship was mentioned only for its happy ending, when a cannonball felled the pirate's mainmast, making it impossible for them to pursue Hawkins's ship. Olivia hardly knew what she ate.

Fresh air and excitement were certainly exhausting. By the time they arrived at home, she was nearly as tired as her aunt. Though the hour was not late, they did no more than exchange a few commonplaces about how fine the day had been, and how enjoyable, before they went to their chambers. Olivia had not had much experience of the country, Vauxhall being the closest she had ever come to nature. Aunt Rachel claimed that Chelsea was no more the countryside than Vauxhall's lighted paths and scenic views were. They were pretty, however, and she could not help but wonder what the real country would be like. She could not imagine living surrounded by trees and fields that went on for miles.

At breakfast, after saying once again how much she had enjoyed the outing, and how attentive and gentlemanly Mr. Hawkins was, Aunt Rachel broached a subject which Olivia had hoped would not be mentioned.

"He is quite struck by you, Livvie. I almost think I understood him to hint he would purchase a country house, intending it to be an inducement to you."

"It might be an inducement to *you*, Aunt. I am a town creature." Her aunt would happily move to a country home. Aunt Rachel would become a fast friend of the vicar's wife, take part in parish activities and good works, enjoy planning a flower garden. She herself had always lived in London, and her business was here. If not for her business, would she still wish to live in town? It was not as if she had friends in London, but she would find no employment for her time. A married lady would have other things to do, perhaps more interesting ones. Caring for her children…the activity that led to those children (but that would not take up much of the day—ah, night)…running the household? No, because Aunt Rachel or a housekeeper would do a far better job.

"I don't suppose he would insist upon a house in the country, if you did not care for the idea." Aunt Rachel sighed. "But would it not be nice to live in a better part of town? Not that Well Close Square is bad. Yet I am sure Mr. Hawkins lives in a larger house, very likely with more servants than he needs, and fashionable furniture. While mere possessions cannot outweigh good character, pleasing manners and appearance are not to be despised. He is a gentleman, too, not a vulgar tradesman."

## Chapter 14

Captain Easterday came to the office late in the afternoon, some four days after their last meeting and requested a few minutes of her time.

"I've no doubt you are busy. However, I felt you should hear what I learned directly on my returning."

She invited him into her office and closed the door. She was becoming hardened to the necessary improprieties involved in running Cantarell Shipping.

"I spoke with Munns."

"You were able to find him, then!"

"Thanks to your information about his library. He is living in Cambridge and setting up as a tutor."

"Then he has merely changed professions, and only forged the bills of lading to make trouble for me, I suppose."

"He was not very forthcoming, but he was bribed, and quite handsomely, too. I discovered from another source he has purchased two properties, and I suspect he owns the house in which he is lodging. The rents will enable him to live comfortably."

"Could he not be using his savings to buy them?"

"I think it's unlikely he had so much saved. There's the conversation his landlady overheard, as well. Before I left town, I arranged for discreet inquiries to be made through a banker. I expect to have the result soon—today, possibly." He cleared his throat. "Munns should not have betrayed your trust. Yet a large bribe might have been an irresistible temptation."

She stared out the window at the trampled, barren little yard. Kit was trotting back from the privy. She really must get some curtains made to screen the window.

"Particularly as Munns disliked and resented me. If someone paid him to destroy Cantarell Shipping…the shipping trade can be ruthless."

"They may wish to force you to sell out."

"Noakes would be happy to put me out of business, but I cannot imagine him wanting to buy it." She groped for the words to explain. "He inherited his business, and he does things as he was taught to do them—although he has added bullying to the usual procedures. His clerks were hired by his father and are competent. Heaven help Noakes if he has to replace one, as he is not clever himself. I don't think he would know how to manage a larger business."

"That point had not occurred to me. What I did consider was that if the bribe was as large as I suspect, he could not have afforded to pay it. Which brings me to another question…"

She waited, watching Captain Easterday try to form it.

"To whom would your company be worth a large bribe?"

Ah, he had been hoping to phrase it inoffensively. He had failed, but the attempt did him no discredit in her eyes.

He went on. "It's been a going concern for many years and supports you. It might be worth a small bribe, but to make you sell at a low price, your business would have to be failing. Even to buy it cheaply, after paying a bribe, does not seem sensible."

"No. Unless the goal was to put Cantarell Shipping out of business, rather than to acquire it."

"Mayhap I have a devious mind, but I am sure I could think of cheaper ways of accomplishing that end."

A tap sounded at the door, simultaneous with Kit's "Ma'am? Someone asking for Cap'n Easterday."

"If you will excuse me for a moment?" He left the office door open behind him. Olivia heard a voice like a Cockney sparrow's, and Easterday's deeper, measured tones, then his brisk footfalls. He entered the office, breaking the seal on a letter.

"My friend's report on Munns's finances has arrived. Admirably terse, too," he said, scanning the sheet. "Ha!"

She found herself leaning forward.

He looked up, folded the paper, and tucked it away in his pocket. "Munns has a tidy nest egg, enough to live on in a modest way for the rest of his life, particularly if he earns something for tutoring. He has not used any of it. However, he established a relationship with another bank a day before he left Cantarell Shipping, and deposited a sum."

"He did take a bribe, then. I hope he found it worth his while," she added bitterly.

"Two hundred fifty pounds? That is either very adequate compensation for selling his soul, or else very little. But on the whole, he did well out of it, for the next day, he made a second deposit of the same amount."

"A total of five hundred pounds! That's a fortune."

"In a postscript, my informant adds that he has now drawn out part of the money. I would estimate it to be enough to buy two or three houses in Cambridge."

Olivia stared. "He may have sold information about other shipments, but it can't have been worth such a figure! However much someone wanted my business to fail, that's a very high price to pay for accomplishing it."

"Yes, too high, when they might simply start rumors, encourage the lumpers to pilfer your cargo as it was unloaded, attempt to frighten off any clerk who might come to work for you, or attempt to frighten you."

"I will not be intimidated into giving up Cantarell Shipping, sir."

"And Finley and Barlow won't be scared away."

"Then I think all will be well, as I have already informed the wharfingers and warehouses with whom we do business that they are to release Cantarell cargoes only when the bills of lading are presented by Finley or Barlow."

"A very wise precaution." He bowed and took his leave.

She smiled cynically. Captain Easterday would be wondering if it had occurred to her that her instructions might be ignored. Would he add his warning to hers? Finley would not hesitate to supply him with her list of usual warehouses, she guessed. But this was one time when a man's word would not be taken more seriously than hers.

****

Aunt Rachel met her at the door, clutching a thick, creamy sheet of paper covered with a sprawling, bold writing. "Only think, Livvie, Mr. Hawkins has invited us to join his party at Vauxhall Gardens the day after tomorrow!"

Visits to the Gardens were a rare treat in their lives. "How kind of him. It would be delightful…if you think we can go."

"Certainly we can go. Such lovely, romantic surroundings, and music and fireworks. I will send our acceptance immediately."

Chapter 15

Olivia felt reassured about the party by the time they entered Mr. Hawkins's own six-oared barge which would take them up the river. Hawkins had invited eminently respectable guests: Sir Benjamin and Lady Whitson, Mr. Brewster, a very fashionable silversmith, and his wife, and a man of about her aunt's age, Giles Nevis, who had lost an eye and part of his left hand as a young captain at the Battle of Malplaquet.

What a luxury not to have to share a boat with strangers! Ordinarily, the watermen set out for Vauxhall Gardens from the Westminster or Whitehall Stairs and would stop and pick up additional passengers if they had room. When the boat disembarked, gentry, tradesmen, aristocrats, merchants, and anyone else with the shilling admission price would flow into the Gardens. At the end of the evening, young men who had drunk too deeply sometimes tried to force their way into boats containing young women they admired. It could be quite alarming, if the men of one's own party were old or unathletic. It should not be a problem tonight.

They all strolled together for a time, until Nevis asked Aunt Rachel if she would care to sit at one of the tables outside the orchestra building to listen to the music in comfort. The suggestion found favor with Aunt Rachel, who went off on Nevis's arm. Aunt

Rachel's voice drifted back. "I remember hearing of Malplaquet and worrying for the older brother of a friend. He was in the 5th Regiment of Horse. My family knew several others who fought there, too, but I had rather a *tendre* for him though I was only a schoolroom miss…" The glamor of former military rank, an eye patch, chiseled features, and a roguish air, clearly combined to beguile Rachel.

The two other couples walked on with them until Mistress Brewster announced that she yearned to see the statue of Milton among the trees and shrubs of the Rural Downs, and her husband obligingly led her off.

It was growing dim under the trees. The orchestra had ceased playing for the moment, and the grounds were almost hushed in expectation. At a shrill whistle, the thousand oil lanterns throughout the gardens came to brilliant life, ignited by a fuse system. What could be prettier or more magical than this sudden illumination?

Sir Benjamin and Lady Whitson continued with Olivia and Hawkins, carrying on a lively conversation about the music they could hear distantly from the orchestra pavilion. When they came to a smaller walk which was less frequented, Hawkins suggested they turn into it, making their way back toward the Grove, where the supper shelters were located. "It will be the shortest way."

"How vexatious! I've turned my ankle," Lady Whitson exclaimed.

"There is a bench a few steps back, my dear. Let me carry you to it, and I will be your doctor and examine it to see what harm has been done."

"I am sure I will be able to proceed if you will rub it a little, as you did once before."

"Ay, and no doubt I will be rubbing it again, too. How do you ladies walk in such shoes? No need to wait upon us, Mistress Olivia, Hawkins. We will follow you in a few minutes."

Olivia felt a momentary doubt about the propriety of walking on by herself with Mr. Hawkins and dismissed it; she was a sensible woman, an old maid. And Sir Benjamin and his wife would be with them again shortly. But she found herself almost tongue-tied. When the others were with them, conversation bubbled along. She was not a ready conversationalist, having never gone about much in genteel company. One could not talk about shipping in such a setting. In desperation, she asked Hawkins if he had ever seen pleasure gardens in China.

"I saw little except the wharves and godowns. Godown means warehouse, as you may know. Europeans cannot easily travel in China. Their paper lanterns might interest you, however."

"Paper lanterns! How could that be?"

They sounded delightful as he described them, though she would have thought them a terrible fire hazard. She could imagine the softly glowing lanterns hanging and perhaps swaying a little, lighting a path such as this one. Hawkins drew her into a little clearing.

"Look, now we are not surrounded by trees, we have a fine view of the moon."

It was quite dark in the clearing apart from the moonlight which cast odd shadows.

"Is it not dangerous to wander so far from others here in the dark? They say that criminals lurk here to rob or...er, molest the unwary. Though the moonlight is lovely," she admitted.

"You're safe with me."

He spoke in the same tone he might have used to state their location or the tonnage of a vessel, which made it the more convincing. Thinking of their location—however had they wandered so far from the main path? She had been caught up in listening to Ambrose and had paid no attention to her surroundings.

"It's devilish hard to get a lady alone," Ambrose Hawkins said. "Always some chaperone or other around."

"There's sound reason for that, sir."

Even in the dim light, she saw him grin. "There is, of course, but sometimes a man has something on his mind instead of lovemaking. Or in addition to it." He took her hand and raised it to his lips.

She felt a tremor of…well, she didn't know what, but it was decidedly pleasant. No one had ever kissed her hand before. She had no idea what to say or whether it was necessary to say anything.

Apparently not, for he went on. "My dear, will you do me the honor of marrying me?"

She could only gaze blankly at him, like some ninny.

"Have I taken you by surprise? You cannot be unaware of my admiration of you."

Had she been unaware? She herself admired a number of people for business sense, or charitable work, or artistic ability, without having any romantic interest in them. Captain Easterday, for instance. As a young girl, her daydreams about marriage had centered on some vaguely imagined but handsome man who would love her.

When she was of an age to consider the matter

seriously, she realized it was impossible. She could not abandon her father, who needed her help. Any man would expect his wife to move to his house and tend to it; he would certainly not permit her to spend even part of her day in her father's office.

"I gave up thinking of marriage years ago, Mr. Hawkins—"

"Ambrose. Surely we are on first name terms by now."

"Ambrose. I am an old maid. It never occurred to me that you were attracted to me. No man has paid me any notice since I was a girl." *Or even then.* What a dispiriting admission to make. Did she sound wistful?

"If other men are fools, I am not. I once saw a medieval ivory carving of the Virgin Mary—Popish, but a thing of great beauty and value—from a Spanish ship. You remind me of that figure: pale as the moon, slender, calm. A man could be comfortable with you."

Then his arms were around her, and he bent to kiss her lips.

His lips were soft; his body was warm and hard. She felt an overwhelming urge to melt against it. She had neither breath nor will to pull away. Instead, her arms wrapped around him. Yearnings she had thought dead and buried were clawing their way out of the grave. To her utter humiliation, her hips...vibrated. The working portion of her mind prayed fervently her petticoats and hoop would conceal the involuntary reaction.

"My love." He finally released her. "May I take it you accept my proposal?"

She stood blinking, trying to gather her wits. Marriage to Ambrose Hawkins was an enticing prospect with all it entailed: more kisses and what would follow on their wedding night, children, other shared interests. As Aunt Rachel had pointed out, his business was similar to hers. He would not expect her to sell it.

Another thought followed. He would own it and everything she possessed, because that was what happened when a woman married. Her fortune and property were no longer hers. He would own her. She took a deep breath. "My thoughts are all upside down. I must have time to accustom myself to the idea before I can answer." She managed a shaky laugh which she hoped did not sound false. "It is as strange to me as the idea of flying to the moon on gossamer wings."

He laughed, too. "As strange as that! I cannot deny you the opportunity to consider it. Now we should find our way back to the Grove, before I am considered to have compromised you, which would necessitate our marriage."

"We should go back for the Whitsons, shouldn't we? What can have delayed them?" Her voice sounded odd to her, because she realized the dropping off of the rest of the party must have been arranged by Hawkins.

He smiled down at her, as if he knew her thoughts, and led her back to the walk.

They came upon Sir Benjamin and his lady at their supper pavilion in the Grove.

"I brought my dear Martha back by the way we had come," the baronet explained. "The paths at Vauxhall are carefully tended, but even leaning upon my arm, the dimness of the path you had taken made it difficult for her to walk, as even the slightest depression jarred her ankle."

"I am sure that by the time we are ready to leave, my foot will be much recovered," Lady Whitson murmured.

It must be the gentry's training in social deceit that made them such accomplished liars, Olivia thought, as she smiled and replied, "I do hope it will be better soon. We should have stayed on the main walks."

Chapter 16

Hawkins settled into the chair as if he were accustomed to visit Easterday's office, and looked around. "Not bad. You might almost be a successful green bag. Though their offices tend to be full of boxes of documents. Dustier, too."

"If you mistake me for an attorney, at least you admit 'tis a successful one. What brings you here, Hawkins?"

"Your business is more genteel than mine," Hawkins admitted. "Still, you sailed for years—"

"Longer than you did."

"True enough. I don't suppose you've forgotten how to fight, or that you don't have some fellows working for you who know the use of a cutlass."

"However my offices are furnished, my business is on the river. And ships."

Hawkins nodded thoughtfully. "Captain Wilkes's *Jolly Jane* is at anchor in the eastern end of the Lower Pool, newly arrived from Africa and as full of ostrich feathers, ivory, ambergris, and ebony as she could be."

"And waiting her turn at the Legal Quays? Ay." In spite of himself, Easterday's curiosity was piqued.

"River pirates will pay it a visit tonight."

"At the dark of the moon. How do you know this?"

"Last night, I chanced to see a man I recognized from my days in the Caribbean. Came ashore when he

118

lost a hand a few years since. He's a sneaking, nasty piece of work. I invited him to one of my warehouses for a chat. The subject of the *Jolly Jane* came up."

"And word of your 'chat' won't get back to the gang?"

Hawkins shook his head. "Ollie's only connection to them's through his aunt's husband. Their paths won't be crossing."

Easterday blew out a breath. He could guess what the "chat" had entailed. He wondered if Ollie had survived. "What's your interest in the *Jolly Jane*?"

"I mean to lead a party to take the river rats and save old Wilkes's cargo for him. We'll catch them where they gather to get in the boats and settle their accounts."

Easterday understood why Hawkins was feared on the river. "Better to take them in the act and let the law hang them."

"That would mean letting them board the *Jane*, Easterday. They'd have room to spread out and fight. At the boats, they'd be in a tight group, easy to surround."

"The *Jolly Jane*'s crew could swell your numbers once they were alerted."

"She's been sitting there near a week. The crew have been going off in shifts to drink and whore. Some will be ashore, some that are on board will be nursing their heads." He grinned evilly. "I was hoping you'd help."

"What do you get out of it? Wilkes is no friend of yours, is he?" From what he knew of Wilkes, Easterday could not imagine the two of them dealing well together. "Does he even know?"

"Wilkes being the next thing to a parson, we never did agree. His first notion in an emergency is to pray. The first mate's the one that keeps the ship from sinking. He's not much for flogging, either," Hawkins added with a tight smile. "I'd warn him—but he's on the *Jolly Jane*, and I don't think he'll come off until the freight's on the wharf, judging from when I knew him. I can't get word to him without chancing the pirates guess something's afoot. If I could, he'd still need help to fight them off. "

Easterday sat staring at his visitor, eyebrows raised, waiting for an answer to his original question. When none came, he asked, "Is this a scheme for you to seize the cargo?"

"No!" Hawkins snapped. "Hell, man, would I ask your help if it were? You'd see me hanged and feel you'd done a good day's work. You want to know why I want to stop them?" He took a few slow, deep breaths. "I hate pirates. You look down on my morals and methods, but I'm a saint compared to the decentest pirate that ever lived. Filthy and vicious as rats, every one of them. Go to the authorities and two things will happen: the pirates will hear about it and the arresting party, if they show up at all, will either break and run or be cut down. The naval patrol is no use. My men won't talk. Neither will yours, will they? Are you in?"

The most dashing thing he had ever done was to deliver Richard Saltstall's message to the Duke of Guysbridge before the duel caused by Mariah Saltstall's attempt to lure—or trap—the duke into marriage. Disguised in a roquelaure! No wonder a girl of eighteen thought him old and boring. Easterday began to think he had grown too staid. "By God, why not?"

\*\*\*\*

Easterday lay among the clumps of willows and brush that throve in the marshy ground, clad in a plain cloth suit his valet would have thrown away. His spirits rose ridiculously. If he did not feel young again, at least he no longer felt old. Had he been suffering from melancholia for years? How had he not realized it?

A barge laden with a few crates and barrels was moored nearby. Closer still, two wherries were tied up. According to Hawkins, the barge would be brought up to the *Jolly Jane* to receive her cargo once the raiders had secured the ship. Out in the river, even the *Jolly Jane*'s riding light was blurred by the fog. Easterday nudged Hawkins as he caught a mutter of low voices.

"… fog coming up, wouldn't'a needed to wait for moon dark."

"Shut your gob," someone hissed. "Sound carries."

"Joe?' The question came from the other direction. Concealed as they were, they could only track the speakers by their voices. The men stopped near the wherries. More waiting, then other voices. Eventually, a gruff "All here?" and grunts of assent.

"Let's be at 'er, then," Gruff Voice said. "Remember, we want the ivory and ambergris first."

Hawkins clapped Easterday's shoulder, giving the signal. Easterday did the same to the man next to him, and so it passed down the line, as it did on Hawkins's other side. Twenty men swept down in silence to surround the men by the wherries. Easterday's men were armed with cudgels as well as cutlasses; if a broken arm or broken head took a pirate out of the fight, so much the better. Hawkins's men favored the cutlass. It was safe to assume none of the pirates were armed with pistols as they were of little use in the sort of fight they'd be anticipating on the ship. A cutlass need not be reloaded.

The oaths, groans, and meaty thuds of cudgel on flesh and bone brought back to him half a hundred fights in his sailing days. His body remembered old reflexes with no need for thought. It was easier than the fencing most gentlemen were taught as boys: there were no rules, only cut and hack, and the broad, sturdy blade stood up to heavy use.

The man before him dropped his sword to clutch his left arm, which was spurting blood. Easterday heard Hawkins utter a short, explosive sound. Hawkins had one booted foot on a fallen pirate's chest in an attempt to free his sword from the man's skull, where it had lodged. But he released his grip on the hilt and pulled out a long knife, to bury it in the side of a bearded brute lurching toward Easterday with blade upraised.

Hawkins had bought him the chance to bring his own sword up to deflect the blow, the force of which was already weakened by the lunge that drove in Hawkins's dagger. The bearded man staggered and stumbled over the body of Hawkins's previous opponent. The man on the other side of Hawkins cut his throat as he fell.

Hawkins pulled his cutlass free while Easterday braced himself to fight off the next attacker. None came. Men stood panting or lay on the ground, some moaning or cursing. After a long moment, Hawkins called out, "Jemmy, get the lanterns and the rope."

They did not need as much rope as they'd brought. Only six of the river pirates needed binding; four were dead, the other survivors were too badly wounded to attempt escape. "The rest will be, too, soon enough," Hawkins said, grinning. "A good night's work; none of our own dead or hurt bad."

They left the bodies where they had fallen. Much of the rest of the night went to transporting their prisoners to a warehouse owned by Hawkins. "They'll keep until morning. Do you care to try to find a magistrate awake tonight? "

Easterday agreed. "There's no point. The Admiralty Court will try them." Some of their men would stand guard until morning. They each chose the steadiest.

"Meet me here at eight, and we'll deliver these vermin and give our statements—if it meets with your approval, Easterday?"

"Certainly. Did you invite me to join the party to lend respectability?"

"It crossed my mind. You have the reputation of a worthy gentleman. Though my testimony alone would suffice if necessary. Being rich is almost as good as being respectable. Sometimes better."

"I'll be here."

\*\*\*\*

There were questions, of course.

Not only "How did you come to hear of the attempted piracy?" to which Hawkins responded that he had heard a rumor. No, he would not reveal its source lest reprisals be taken. In any case, the fellow was now aboard a ship bound for the American colonies.

Easterday hoped the claim was true, even if Ollie had gone unwillingly.

"Why did you take it upon yourselves to thwart the gang?"

"I hate pirates," Hawkins had repeated, with the same stony expression he'd worn when Easterday had asked the same question.

"Every decent man does, yet most do not undertake to rid the seas—or Thames—of them."

Easterday thought it time to take a hand. "The losses to river pirates every year are enormous, sir, both in goods and loss of life. Hawkins and I knew of the planned attack, and we had men able to deal with pirates. No organized body exists to deal with these marauders. The watch? Hardly. The military?"

The Admiralty's representative snorted, then added, "There are naval patrols on the river."

"Too few and how can they be at hand when the crime is in progress?"

"Well...they cannot be everywhere. You say you heard of the raid, Hawkins, and you, Captain Easterday, agreed to take part. You both overheard their leader instructing them as to what cargo to take." The man brightened. "Several of your prisoners were being sought in connection with previous raids. Ay, a solid case. I believe we have reason to thank you for your assistance."

They breakfasted at the King's Arms, Leadenhall Street, where Easterday's growing curiosity about Hawkins went largely unrewarded. One could not ask personal questions of another, unless he were a very close friend. He did believe Hawkins bitterly hated pirates, which did not necessarily mean he had never been one himself. It did not mean his business practices ashore were not cutthroat. Metaphorically speaking, at least.

Most of their conversation was limited to

reminiscences of foreign parts and near-disasters at sea, although he picked up some clues. Hawkins spoke like a gentleman much of the time. Around his men, his speech had been rougher, though not as unpolished as theirs. It made sense for a man who had sailed before the mast. Upper-class diction and vocabulary would have earned him no favors. Surely his family could have helped him to a career, even at sea, more suited to a gentleman? Still, boys did run away to sea. Or he might have been left a penniless orphan.

He knew Hawkins had scraped acquaintance in the lower tiers of the aristocracy, with whom he did business and drank and gambled without being fully accepted. The ruthlessness not quite concealed under the veneer of gentility warned them off, Easterday supposed. Still, his money and genteel background should make him an acceptable catch for the daughter of some purse-pinched titled family. Aristocratic lineage without cash would not pay the servants or put coal in the grate.

A chance remark of Easterday's in passing elicited the fact he owned an extensive library. It included works on maritime law, Asia, navigation, history, medicine, and surgery. No Latin or Greek classics, but some Spanish—"I picked up a few words in the Caribbean, as sailors do." Among men whose tutors had whacked Latin and mayhap the basics of Greek into them, he would not be considered well-read but plenty of country gentlemen were not well educated. Whatever else he lacked, no one could doubt Ambrose Hawkins possessed a keen intelligence.

In reply to a remark about the China trade, Easterday mentioned an importer of Chinese porcelains with a shop near St. James's Square.

"Trash," Hawkins said curtly. "Did you see the pug-dog figure in his window? The platter enameled with an English couple dallying in a garden in the center, surrounded by an explosion of flowers and brocade designs in what the Chinamen call *yangcai*? It means 'foreign colors.' The tints themselves are handsome, but the mixture of European and Chinese styles in the same piece is jarring. I only buy pieces in the Chinese mode."

"You speak Chinese?"

"Ay, I learned some. Acquired a taste for their porcelain at the same time, if not for their food. Too many underdone vegetables and not enough good red beef."

"You have no difficulty getting the best, I suppose."

Hawkins grinned. "You'd think I might, but it's not easy. I've ships and a business to run, tying me to London. I send my orders for a celadon glaze dish or Kangxi *wucai*, five-color-ware from the reign of the emperor before last. What comes back in a year or two may or may not be what I wanted. If I like it, I keep it. If not, I sell it. I'll miss Jonas Cantarell. He often brought in very fine pieces, God knows how, without the assistance of the East India Company. I bought a number of them. I'm damned if I know how he always got the best. He wouldn't say."

Easterday remembered something Olivia Cantarell had said, when he had remarked on Cantarell's Turkey carpets, and the sketch pad he had noticed in her office. "Ah."

By the time they had finished breakfast, he

regarded Hawkins in a different light. Not as a friend, but not as a thorough scoundrel, either. Men were an odd collection of contradictions. Women, too, he supposed.

Their way lay together for a distance yet. In the hackney, shortly before they arrived at Easterday's premises, Hawkins offered, "Sorry to hear about your engagement. Its end, I mean."

"I was too old for her." Thank God! He had agreed to the match with Mariah because he was ready to marry and Richard Saltstall was a friend. Saltstall himself admitted she was headstrong and spoiled and had come near to ruining herself by a bird-witted attempt to win a titled husband.

"It might be a blessing in disguise. It would have been an acceptable match—but you could have a nobleman's daughter for the asking."

Easterday was startled into asking, "Which one?" which earned a laugh. Hawkins always knew whose business was in trouble, where to find the most desirable commodities, how to sail close to the wind without coming to ruin.

"Ha! Almost any but the haughtiest, I imagine. There's a fine selection from among the impoverished upper aristocracy. Expensive habits, sons to provide for, several daughters needing either a dowry or a rich husband who doesn't require one—an untitled gentleman who's wealthy is a prize."

"I have no mind to try again. Do you intend to marry some young lady of the aristocracy?"

"It's different for me. It's true I was born into what they'd call a good family." His face hardened. "I think a young lady of the beau monde might not suit me. I'd terrify a chit straight from the schoolroom. They're brought up sheltered and timid. Most young ladies, for all they stand ramrod straight, lack backbone. It's the difference between a lap dog and a lurcher. I need a female who can fit into the best society and yet not scorn a man like me. The best choice would be one not too young, perhaps a widow in straitened circumstances, who would be glad to make a marriage with any decent man who can support her in luxury. Society's not lacking in spendthrift men who die leaving their wives to live on a shilling."

When they parted company, he was no nearer to understanding why Hawkins had paid Munns such a large bribe. Hawkins was said to pay well for secrets. Yet two hundred fifty pounds was a great deal of money to a man employed as a clerk; five hundred pounds was ridiculous. What had Munns sold him? What had Hawkins wanted that he could not get cheaper?

## Chapter 17

Kit and Ky were in and out of the office, delivering messages or taking mail to the penny post. Finley dealt with customers. Barlow's day consisted of visiting the wharves and copying bills of lading. Both had work enough to fill their day, while Olivia spent part of her time studying the latest bills of entry to see what was being imported or exported, in what quantities and by what merchant, and the rest calculating duties on the goods they shipped or imported.

William Smithson, who had not darkened Cantarell Shipping's door since her father's death, came in to arrange for transport of a load of ironmongery to the West Indies. Olivia was surprised. She would not have thought Smithson willing to deal with a company owned by a female and said so when he was gone.

Kit piped up cheerfully, "I expects it's because ever'one knows that the Cap'n is your partner, like."

"I beg your pardon?"

Finley's head had snapped up. "Ah…"

"Ever'one says it," Kit repeated.

"Mr. Finley?"

"It has got round that Captain Easterday takes an interest in your business, ma'am. Some may have concluded that meant he'd become your partner."

"I see."

"I realize you mayn't like it, Mistress Cantarell, but

it would be unwise to contradict it. Eventually, it may become known that he has nothing to do with the running of your business, but until everyone is accustomed to doing business with you, it would be best to let it go."

"Cantarell Shipping has been in business for over thirty years," she retorted, although she knew what he meant.

"But they were dealing with your father. They did not know you took part in the business, did they?"

"No," she admitted. She had stayed out of sight, working with the ledgers and copying bills of lading. Munns would make out the first; then because he had no junior clerk (a fact he bitterly resented) and because his hands were somewhat arthritic, he permitted Olivia to write out whatever number of copies were needed. He always reviewed them for correctness. After the first thousand or so, she thought he might have given up the annoying habit; she reviewed them herself and never made a mistake, anyway. She also read the *London Gazette*, checking for legal announcements that might bear upon their business, a task her father could not perform and Munns was too busy to do, or said he was. To be fair, he probably really did not have time, as Jonas Cantarell left to him some of the functions he himself should have been doing, if not for his difficulty in reading and writing. Instead, he was the one to go to the Custom House, the warehouses and wharves, and to call upon their customers.

"I understand their concerns," she admitted at last.

"They will grow accustomed," Finley said.

Ky came in then, bringing a message from one of their best customers, a dyer who did not care who he bought his dyestuffs from, as long as they were of the best quality, which meant Cantarell Shipping. Decades of experience in the eastern end of the Mediterranean counted for a great deal in obtaining the best madder from Smyrna and the best mordanting galls from Syria. While she was reading the note, which appeared to have encountered yellow dye in the writing of it, Ky asked, "Mr. Finley, have you seen a cove as has been loitering in the street? A ferrety fellow that don't always look the same?"

"How do you mean, Ky?"

"Sometimes he's dressed one way and sometimes another. T'other day, he was in the cookshop, taking his time about eating. Last week, he was juggling three or four balls and had a dog that did tricks. Today, he was going up and down the street with a parcel, like he was looking to deliver it but couldn't find the place. Kit thought he saw him begging one day, with one o' his legs bandaged, leaning on a crutch."

Barlow returned in time to hear the last part of Ky's statement. "I've noticed that beggar. He's a fraud. I've seen him around without a crutch."

Olivia looked up from the dyer's query as to whether Cantarell had a stock of madder. "How very odd."

"I have not noticed such a person," Finley said, "but you may be sure I will take care to look for him in the future."

"Kit thought as how one of us might sit at the window upstairs—when we hadn't nothing else to do—and watch him."

Finley glanced at Olivia, who said, "As long as you keep up your lessons, I have no objection. If you are both busy, the ferrety fellow must go unobserved."

"Ay, ma'am. The thing we wondered about is, he's there pretty regular though not every day…but what if the days he's not there, some other cove is?"

"What, indeed?" Olivia echoed, and Finley pursed his lips.

****

One afternoon, Hawkins came to ask her opinion of a Chinese vase he had bought. He had never seen anything like it; perhaps with Cantarell's connections in the Orient, she might have seen something similar. It was a straight-sided cylinder with a very spare sketch of bamboo, plum, and pine and a column of Chinese characters.

"It's a brush pot for a scholar's writing brushes. I've heard the plum, bamboo, and pine are called the 'three companions of the deep cold,' and symbolize long life. Or so I'm told. One never knows whether one is being accurately informed. I wish I could learn to read Chinese, but I'm sure it's very difficult, their alphabet—if it is an alphabet—" she said doubtfully, "being so different. This isn't export porcelain, either; it conforms to Chinese rather than European taste."

"You're well informed," Hawkins said. "I knew Cantarell imported the finest Chinese wares. Did you acquire your knowledge from him?"

If she contemplated marriage with Ambrose Hawkins, they must get to know each other, as she had told him at Vauxhall Gardens.

"No, sir. My father did not have an eye for art. To him, it was all merely decoration. I learned what I know from a China trader after I first saw a shipment of Chinese goods my father had invested in. I was already in charge of dealing with the Turkish rug merchants." The term "China trader" came as close to the truth as she was willing to go with Hawkins until she knew him better.

"Cantarell had a valuable asset in you."

He tried to give her the brush pot, but she declined with thanks on the ground that it was inappropriate for a lady to accept an expensive gift from a gentleman who was not a relative. He accepted her refusal in good part; he knew the rules as well as she.

Then, as it was near time for the office to close, he offered to drive her home. He had arrived in his open chaise, making it permissible. It would also give them time to talk.

He knew a good deal about Chinese art, in spite of his ploy in asking her about the brush pot. But she knew things that were new to him, possibly because he had acquired his knowledge secondhand from East India Company supercargoes.

A day or two later, he arrived at Cantarell Shipping again to escort her home, this time in a closed carriage. It was raining heavily, and she had been hoping it would stop or at least moderate, as she did not like to send one of the boys out to fetch a hackney. He would be soaked, and still have to make his way home, where his mother might find it difficult to dry his clothing.

The following morning, Finley diffidently pointed out that to ride with a gentleman in a coach might be thought somewhat indiscreet.

"I know. Unconventional at the least. However, I'm not a young girl, and I am already thought extremely odd for taking charge of my father's company. Also, it was raining exceeding hard." None of these was an adequate excuse. She could hardly admit that she wished to become better acquainted with Ambrose Hawkins.

Finley looked a little worried but said nothing more.

Somehow, it became customary for Hawkins to come for her in his carriage at the hour she left the office and take her home. On a few occasions, his coach came for her anyway, his footman explaining that urgent business kept Hawkins from coming himself. She knew that both Finley and Barlow viewed it askance, though Barlow went so far as to admit that he had not quite liked to see her go home by herself in a hackney coach. He supposed there was no impropriety when Hawkins escorted her in the open chaise.

One sunny late afternoon, Hawkins suggested that they walk in Well Close Square. She would not be very late in getting home, as they could end their stroll at her house. After debating with herself briefly, she asked Finley to send one of the boys to tell her aunt she would be a little late. It chanced to be the day Aunt Rachel had arranged to have two women in to assist in taking down draperies and bed curtains to shake them and hang them outdoors, and she had said they would eat a simple, cold supper that night. A little delay would not matter.

Well Close Square was edged by trees, and the Danes' church at its center was also bordered by trees and a spacious lawn, making it a pleasant place to walk.

"Some other day we will walk in St. James's Park," Hawkins said, helping her down from the chaise.

St. James was the popular promenade, attracting the rich and fashionable and everyone else, too. One might see a duchess or a laundrywoman, the heir to an earldom or an apprentice dressed in rented or borrowed finery. If one wished to talk, a quiet churchyard would be preferable.

A lady accustomed to flirtation might be able to elicit the information she wanted smoothly. She herself was not adroit in such matters. Once they had exhausted the weather as a subject, she ventured, "You have quite a reputation in the Pool and on the seas, Mr. Hawkins."

"I was a wild lad. I ran away to sea, after all. And I've a reputation for being rough."

"If you were wild as a lad, I think you must have largely overcome the tendency," Olivia said. "It seems to me you are rather controlled."

"I've learned to focus on what I want—and get it." Two young boys ran by, laughing, on their way home to supper.

"What did you want when you ran away to sea?"

He shrugged. "What does any boy want? Adventure. To get on with my life."

"What of your family?

"What of them?"

"Did they not try to bring you back? Did they become reconciled to your going to sea?"

"I have no idea. I haven't seen or heard of them since I left the breakfast parlor one morning and made for the London road." Her eyes widened in surprise. How could one break so completely with one's family, even if one lacked a close relationship?

He chuckled ruefully. "I wanted to get away from my family as much as find excitement. There wasn't anything for me at home, as my older brother was the heir—not that it was a large property or that there would be anything left apart from the land with my stepfather dipping his hand into the cashbox. My mother doted on the blackguard. I liked my sister, but she'd married and moved away. "

"Was being a sailor an improvement?" From her father's tales and those she had overheard in the office, a common sailor's life sounded thoroughly disagreeable. She would not want a son of hers sailing on a merchantman or even on a naval vessel, unless he were an officer. Possibly not even then.

"Ay! The food and discipline were often bad, but I saw foreign parts I could never have visited otherwise and I learned to be a man." He added, "The prospect of making money also appealed."

She did not pursue that subject. Hawkins was known to be rich, and his business instincts were sound, unlike some aristocratic families who appeared wealthy but were deeply in debt.

He chose to expand on the subject. "I was fortunate and made enough to set up my company while I was still a junior officer. There was no point in waiting to be made captain."

"You must have been clever as well as lucky," she said.

"Well…I had paid attention to what others were importing. I took some chances, and they paid off. Now I've a mind to live like a gentleman."

"Give up your business?"

"No—why should I? The gentry and aristocracy sneer at men in trade but not at money—not when they need it at all events. Young ladies of birth marry men of vulgar origins who have amassed fortunes in coal or ironmongery or the like. Young gentlemen marry girls who would be serving in shops or milking cows if their papas had not grown rich somehow or other. I see no reason I should not be accepted, even if I spend part of my day overseeing my commercial interests. Gentlemen of society have nothing to do with their time but drink and frequent clubs and gaming hells. Why should I idle away my time when I have something better to do? I can keep the reins firmly in hand with a few hours' effort each day. For the rest, I have men I can trust to manage for me, who know me well enough not to cheat me. All I need is a suitable house and a ladylike wife." He looked at her very directly.

"I wish you good fortune," she replied with a smile she hoped was not too encouraging.

Chapter 18

Easterday stared at the Parliament-issued book of rates. Why had Hawkins made the second payment to Munns? The first must have been for the forged bills of lading. The bribe had been enormous, but perhaps Munns would not turn traitor for less. If it had encouraged Mistress Olivia to sell Cantarell Shipping, Hawkins might have felt it worth the price—and he could certainly afford it. What had the second payment bought? Two hundred fifty pounds! *A man who knew where to look could hire a skilled assassin for a fraction of that amount.*

A friend whose office was near Cantarell Shipping claimed Hawkins's coach could be seen outside Cantarell Shipping almost any late afternoon. According to his informant, Hawkins often escorted Olivia Cantarell at the end of the day.

He put the book aside; Yates or one of the other clerks could calculate the duty on a load of Swedish iron. The Cantarell problem was distracting him from his own legitimate business. Hawkins had a reputation for knowing everything that happened on the Thames, and much of what happened in the City, by the use of paid informants. Easterday had always relied upon the talk in Lloyd's Coffeehouse and other places frequented by shippers and businessmen. Using a network of paid intelligencers seemed to suggest less legal dealings. Not quite gentlemanly conduct.

Then he remembered Markham.

Easterday had met the man but did not know him well, except for what everyone knew: Markham was a gentleman of sterling reputation who had been engaged in importing until recently—indeed, still dabbled in it a little—and was commonly believed to be exceedingly well informed about all sorts of things. He was not likely to be an associate of Hawkins. Marcus did not quite like to ask a man who was almost a stranger for information, but Olivia Cantarell's situation worried him. She should sell the business, of course. Or marry. She was exposing herself to all kinds of unpleasantness and even danger, but he could not stand by to see her cheated by Hawkins.

Roger Markham had given up his office, but it was easy to find someone who knew his direction. "Wych Street, that's where you'll find him. South side, a well-maintained house. Anyone in the neighborhood will know. He used to have wharfingers and sailors and I don't know what calling on him in the middle o' the night."

Wych Street, between St. Clement Danes and Drury Lane, was not the sort of address Easterday would have expected a successful businessman to occupy. A suite of rooms in lodgings would have been more usual, if Markham was unmarried or a widower. Yet if he had late night visitors, and those of the less genteel sort, mayhap it made sense.

It proved unnecessary to ask which house was Markham's. The other houses (*Good God! They must date to Queen Elizabeth's day!*) appeared given over to the sale of used furniture, the upholstery trade, and other menial occupations. Markham's house, for all its age, remained well kept in its outmoded style, and the door was freshly painted and very glossy.

A butler admitted him. There was no entrance hall; one was immediately in a reception area the width of the narrow house, with armchairs, a cabinet, bookcase, and table. The butler, having asked him to wait, proceeded through a door at the far side of the room and closed it behind him.

Easterday had time to do little more than observe the furnishings and note that the table held yesterday's issue of *Lloyd's List* and the current *London Gazette*, before the butler returned.

"If you would follow me, sir."

Through the door and up a narrow dark staircase to the first floor and back along a corridor to a room lined with bookcases. It was well lit by windows in two walls. One window must overlook a yard, the other a passage between this house and the next, and very lucky to have it, when most of these houses were built cheek by jowl with adjoining side walls. Markham stood to greet him and gestured him to a comfortable chair. His host was a strong-looking man, no more than fifty, surely, with an air of both competence and humor.

After the usual civilities, Easterday asked, "Do you not find retirement rather boring? I have sometimes wondered what I would do with my time if I ever gave up business."

"Oh, I am managing to keep myself occupied with one thing and another," his host murmured. "It's important to have an interest in something beyond one's work."

It was an odd situation, neither social nor business

and therefore uncharted territory. It felt too abrupt to say baldly that he had come for information. "I suppose you heard of Jonas Cantarell's death?"

"And of his daughter keeping Cantarell Shipping. I have, indeed."

"I am concerned on Mistress Olivia Cantarell's behalf," Easterday began.

"Why?"

"Why…because she is a woman in a sphere in which she cannot succeed and may come to harm."

Markham grinned. He had very white, strong-looking teeth. "I'll trade you answer for answer, if it's information you want."

"So this is how you keep yourself notably well informed."

"It is. Tell me your connection to Mistress Cantrell."

Easterday described their first meeting. "I have no right to meddle in her business, but if I knew more, I could at least drop a discreet word of warning."

Markham nodded, evidently satisfied. "What is your question?"

"Do you have any idea why Ambrose Hawkins would be interested in the company?"

"Are you sure Cantarell Shipping is the object of his interest?"

"Sir, that is a question rather than an answer." Then Easterday realized he was mistaken. "You are suggesting that he is interested in the lady herself?"

"Is it impossible? Admittedly, I've heard Cantarell's daughter called plain, but plainness, like beauty, is in the eye of the beholder. My own dear wife was not famed for her face."

"I don't think they ever met until after Hawkins's first attempt to frighten her into selling." He found himself describing the bills of lading bamboozle, how he had traced Munns and his financial dealings, and his suspicion that the bribe had come from Hawkins because of Hart's connection to him.

"Ay, I dare swear you're right. Noakes sailed with Hawkins," Markham volunteered. "Yet there have been no more attempts to put the lady out of business? I have heard of none, at least. Though 'tis supposed you have become her partner."

"I have not, but no one has asked me, making it unnecessary to deny it, which affords her some protection."

"Between the two of you, Mistress Olivia would seem to be well protected."

"Between—you mean, Hawkins and myself?"

Markham tented his fingers. "Captain, you evidently pay considerably less attention to society and social matters than to shipping and business."

"I am primarily a man of business, not of society."

"Sometimes the way a young man about town gambles signals the coming decline of a family. The way a young lady wields her fan can foretell the joining of two families. You should not ignore such hints. You went to sea early and missed some opportunities of observing society. And then you became a protégé of Richard Saltstall."

Easterday stiffened. "The alderman is part of the reason I have had some success in business."

"Indeed. He is a very astute businessman. However, he is not particularly adept in navigating social currents, and therefore could not teach you to do so. Were you aware that Hawkins drove Mistress Olivia and her aunt out of town one Sunday? I think to Chelsea, judging from where they were seen."

"No. I wasn't." Did Finley know and not tell him? Or was the expedition arranged without his knowledge?

"It's known that she often travels home in his carriage, too. This sounds to me like a courtship, if an indiscreet one. You should listen to gossip, as I have, for many years."

"I must have missed a great deal by not doing so." Hawkins courting Olivia? *What an appalling thought.*

"I have put you out, I fear, Captain. Bear with me. I enjoy the Socratic method. If Hawkins is courting the lady, is he head over heels in love with Mistress Olivia?"

"I suppose it must be love, strange as it seems, for he would not seek to marry her for her shipping company."

Markham was watching with a glint of— something—in his eyes. Mayhap amusement.

Easterday felt obliged to continue, "Not that I suppose it's impossible for a man to find her admirable. She's intelligent, full of character, and brave. Why, she meant to run a dagger into Noakes if he had tried to assault her that day in her office. It was a wicked-looking thing, with a blade of at least six inches, razor sharp on both edges. But a man like Hawkins could hardly value those attributes."

"Do most men value them?"

Easterday winced inwardly. As he knew full well, gentlemen usually chose pretty, sheltered girls fresh from the schoolroom, whose only accomplishments were embroidery, the ability to dance prettily, and flirt.

"Perhaps not."

Markham continued, "A man like Hawkins, who is little concerned with the conventions, might find Olivia Cantarell's virtues more compelling than talent on the harpsichord or with the sketch pad."

"She actually draws very well. Almost like a draftsman." He realized it would not be considered a compliment by most young ladies. However, for a lady involved in importing luxury goods, it was probably more useful to sketch in detail the pattern of an oriental carpet or a Chinese vase than a sentimentalized landscape.

Markham grinned at his rush to establish Olivia's ladylike accomplishment.

"While I don't say Hawkins is a complete scoundrel," Easterday forged on, "he's no sort of husband for a decent lady. How could she even consider him? She might easily find a husband who was respectable."

"Now there, I must take leave to disagree. I shouldn't like the connection for my own niece, but she's only twenty. Hawkins is no more dishonest than many City men, and he's more honest about his ruthlessness than most of our aristocracy. His mistresses speak well of him."

"He's dissolute, then."

"Come, Easterday! Have you never had a mistress or visited a brothel?"

"Well…of course." He felt beleaguered. Damn it all to hell, he was no Puritan. Of course he had had mistresses (though he had parted from the last on his betrothal to Mariah and it was now damnably inconvenient); most men did or used whores occasionally.

"If Mistress Olivia were to marry him, he would doubtless be as faithful to her as many men are to their wives. He is not known to gamble or drink to excess—which sets him apart from many husbands—and he would surely not mismanage her business. In addition, I am told he has humor and a sort of gaiety which are attractive to many ladies. A sensible woman might do far worse. What is there to object to in that?"

He took his time answering, considering the question. He admired Olivia Cantarell, without having any romantic interest in her. She was utterly unlike Claudia Dean and Mariah Saltstall. Both had been young and lovely and pattern cards of female virtue. Except for the elopements. Did they have any interest in serious matters? Was it possible to tell, with girls who were well brought up? The sort of contact they were permitted with men left little time to discuss matters of importance, when they were supposed to be attracting a future husband. Or it might be that their mothers warned them to keep to topics of general interest, avoiding controversy. If Mariah had voiced an opinion on the exportation of grain when it was in short supply, how would he have reacted? Being Mariah, she would never have done so. If she had spoken of it, would he have turned the conversation to some unexceptionable subject? Very likely.

Olivia Cantarell might not hesitate to discuss how wheat shortages in England led to hunger among the poor, riots, and subsequent hangings. Olivia did not suffer from missishness. It was possible that a man with as little concern for convention as Hawkins might listen to her opinion. He would be right to do it; she was a sensible female, apart from her determination to engage in business. Marcus wondered whether she would favor exporting wheat to be sold at a higher price abroad or would feel the poor had a right to object.

Finally, he laughed ruefully. "To save my soul, I cannot tell you. Hawkins is admirable in business, even if his reputation is not spotless. I admit I am judging by rumor. It does trouble me he began his courtship so suddenly. I am not a believer in love at first sight." Easterday paused. "As I told you, Munns sold him information about the two cargoes, which was used to steal them, and afterward he sold someone, almost certainly Hawkins, something else. Yet the attempts to ruin the business or persuade Mistress Olivia to sell it came to an end. I can't prove that money came from Hawkins, but Munns was frightened, and who else could it be?"

Markham sighed. "You have all the terms of the equation. You have not combined them. What are the things everyone in our business—from shippers to those who insure cargoes to the warehousemen, lumpers, and lightermen—knows about Hawkins?"

"He's successful in business, he's ruthless…He has excellent sources of information."

Markham leaned back in his chair. "Now, what does everyone know about Jonas Cantarell?"

"He was successful enough to make a living from shipping and importing goods on his own. He was no competition to you or me or Hawkins. A cautious man. Parsimonious. He had to be, I suppose. I don't know what will become of Olivia if she is unable to keep the company in business, unless she marries."

"Oh, I expect Cantarell Shipping will survive,

given that you and Hawkins, like Gog and Magog, are thought to be protecting her. Would it surprise you to know, Captain, that my niece's family believes me to be in straitened circumstances and that Jane—my niece, you know—cannot hope to inherit more than a pittance from me?"

"What nonsense! Everyone knows you did very well for yourself."

"Everyone in shipping and in the City knows it. My niece's father has no connections to those circles. His reasoning runs that if I could afford a manor in the country or a house on St. James Square, I would buy one."

"Are you suggesting that Cantarell Shipping was more successful than it appeared to be? His volume of business does not support that possibility. Would he have worn threadbare coats if he could afford better? And his sister and daughter are near as poorly dressed as he was."

"He lost a great deal of money in the South Sea Bubble."

"Twenty years ago? I had gone to sea not long before. I did not take an interest in investments until I began to trade in foreign goods myself."

"He lost much, but not all, and it made him wary. I think he became afraid to spend a farthing more than necessary. He seems not to have liked it known he had more than enough money to live quietly."

"But if he made investments, it must be known."

"It's not impossible to set matters up to conceal, or at least to make it very difficult to find out, who the owner of properties is."

"Even so, it must show up in his account books."

"And who kept those?"

Easterday said slowly, "If he were concealing his income, he would, surely." *His daughter claims he had difficulty reading and writing.*

"In that situation, I would certainly be my own clerk," Markham agreed. "But I wonder if somehow Munns found out. If Cantarell's assets were substantially more than was commonly known, that information might be worth a substantial bribe."

He stared at Markham. "By a fortune hunter? I suppose it's possible if Mistress Olivia is in possession of a fortune. Does she know?"

"I have no idea."

"It is hard to believe Hawkins would marry for a fortune, when his own is so large. If she doesn't know, she should be warned."

"Her inheritance would be better in his hands than in the control of a more outwardly respectable man who might gamble it away. Marriage to Cantarell's daughter would have at least two benefits for him: he would get control of another part of the Pool's trade, if not a large one, and Olivia Cantarell is sufficiently well-bred and well-connected to be an ambitious man's hostess. With a large enough fortune behind them and no vulgar connections on either side, their children would not find it hard to marry into the beau monde in twenty years' time."

"Damnation!" Then he wondered why he was outraged. Markham was correct. Easterday could not even claim to believe Ambrose Hawkins would be a bad husband; Markham was quite right that many men would be worse. He was certainly not impecunious or profligate.

"Her father's attorney may have informed her. If not, the warning might best come from someone she knows."

"I've tried not to intrude upon her business. Yet I think I should say something to her. Or sound her out, at least."

"It would be a kindness, one way or the other," Markham said.

Chapter 19

She had repeatedly told Hawkins he need not take her home every day. He protested he did not like to think of her taking a hackney and enjoyed seeing her. She liked talking with him, but at the same time, his persistence bothered her. He wished to further a relationship with her and was pushing it inexorably, while she was not quite sure what she wanted. Clearly, her body had carnal appetites clamoring for satisfaction, but her rational mind was not willing to gratify them without being quite sure of what kind of man Ambrose Hawkins was. Women gave up their freedom in marriage, mostly for financial security and children. She had as much of the former as she needed, and she did not know how she felt about babies. True, she was becoming fond of Ky and Kit, and one hardly needed to see one's children until they were of an age to converse. Or even then, of course, if what she heard of the beau monde was correct. By marrying, she would be giving up a great deal for a very uncertain return. She must be sure it was worth it.

"Do not come for me tomorrow," she said. "I must stop at a dressmaker's shop on my way home, and no man enjoys such an errand."

"Ah, but dressmakers have assistants and seamstresses, and many of them are pretty and flirtatious. A man need not be bored while waiting for his lady." He was looking remarkably fine in dark blue velvet with gold embroidery, and a waistcoat the same ripe wheat color as his hair. Girls and women too might well be tempted to flirt with him.

She wondered if he were implying that he considered her his lady and decided not to make an issue of it. "I will be leaving the office early, as it will take some time to try on three gowns. My aunt has already gone in for her last fitting, so hers are ready. I am hopeful that no adjustments will be required to mine." Three gowns for her aunt, and three for herself. They were more elaborate than the ones she wore to go to the office, but Aunt Rachel had cited their recent flurry of social engagements—a flurry by their standards, anyway!—and argued that if they were not as purse-pinched as they had always believed, they could replace some of their most worn or outmoded clothing.

"At least, if we can afford it?" Rachel added. "Even if there is money for only one thing, you must have a pretty new gown."

Olivia felt near to drowning in a wave of shame. Her aunt assumed she had only learned at Jonas Cantarell's death that their circumstances were easier than he had disclosed. Olivia had never realized how grindingly poor her aunt had felt them to be. Having grown up with her father's frugal ways, she herself had thought them unremarkable. Guilt led her to take her aunt to a mantua-maker rather than the seamstress they had patronized when it became necessary to replace a garment worn almost to rags. Mistress Deaver did good work, but while her customers might sigh wistfully over the extremes of fashion and fine silks, they ordered durable gowns, jackets, and petticoats. Claire, on the other hand, was preferred by ladies in the neighborhood whose families could afford to buy them several outfits each year, complete with accessories to match. They might not possess jewels, but they would seldom be at a loss for a handsome gown to wear to any given event.

Olivia made a mental note that she must have Mistress Deaver make them both new smocks and bed gowns, for those need not be fashionable or ornate, and the poor woman needed the money.

"I will give myself the pleasure of escorting you. My coachman will not object to waiting while a hackney man might."

Having no way of discouraging him short of rudeness, Olivia agreed that he might call for her the next day.

**** 

She did not like to leave work early, but as it was unavoidable, she told Finley and Barlow where she would be, and at what time she expected to reach home in case of emergency. They were probably able to deal with anything likely to arise, but she was the head of Cantarell Shipping.

Madame Claire's bow-windowed establishment was located in High Holborn, but it might have been a world away. It took them some time to get there, in spite of the coachman's aggressive driving. Poor streets with ramshackle houses teemed with wagons, street sellers, and barrows, and people on foot dodging between them, and streets with fine houses and manicured squares were clogged with coaches, wagons, sedan chairs, and riders.

There was no need for adjustment to any of the

gowns, and Olivia admitted to herself that they were all surprisingly becoming. She regretted changing back into her plain blue petticoat and *casaquin* when the assistant helped her out of the last gown, a rose mantua.

"I regret not having been permitted to see you in your new raiment," Hawkins said when she emerged from the back of the shop.

"It is not the practice for ladies to parade themselves in the front of the shop when they come in for fitting," she said. Indeed, it would be considered quite indecent, although the chief problem would be that one was usually surrounded by the dressmaker's assistants, tweaking folds of fabric and pinning them for a better fit. Two of the assistants came bustling out behind her, laden with the wrapped gowns.

"All yours?" Hawkins inquired.

"Mine and my aunt's."

"One moment," he said to the shop girls, and strode to the door. On the step, he whistled shrilly and beckoned his footman to load the packages.

Olivia settled the bill on the spot, startling Madame Claire, who seemed hardly to know whether to eye her with contempt or with respect. Olivia preferred to pay for expensive purchases as she went, rather than waiting for a bill to be sent.

The coach was a few steps down the street, there having been no place for it to wait nearer the shop. Hawkins was asking whether she had any other errands to do, when the boy pelted up to Olivia, panting, and reached out a hand to stay her.

Before he touched her, Hawkins cuffed him hard enough to knock him to the flags. "Keep your hands off the lady, you young limb of Satan," he snarled.

Kit gaped at him, speechless, as Olivia exclaimed, "Mr. Hawkins! This is one of my messengers. Are you much hurt, Kit?"

"No, ma'am." He scrambled to his feet, though one hand was pressed to the side of his head, which Olivia suspected was still ringing. "From Mr. Finley. But..." His eyes slid toward Hawkins.

She nodded briskly. "Mr. Hawkins, Kit and I will walk a little way apart. I'm sure you understand." She said it without apology and without a smile. This was business, after all. She was also bothered by Hawkins's reaction to Kit's approaching her. If he had been ragged and dirty, she could have understood it, though she would not have approved of the blow. But Kit and Ky both wore neat dark suits supplied by Cantarell Shipping, and while neither was ever point-device for more than an hour or two in the morning, they did look respectable.

Some yards away, with their backs toward Hawkins (whose annoyance Olivia sensed), Kit muttered, "You know Mr. Finley thought as we should watch any coves that's watching the office, ma'am. To see what they was about, like, thinking they was coves as don't like our business, and—"

The possessive "our" gave her a moment's amusement.

"—me and Ky been keeping an eye on them out o' the upstairs window where they couldn't see us. Ky would watch while I run an errand and then me while Ky was out."

"Has Mr. Finley deduced their intentions?"

"Don't know what he's 'duced, but today it appeared there was two of 'em. I saw one follow Mr.

Barlow when he left to go home, and Mr. Finley sent me after him with a message." Kit's mud-colored eyes gleamed at the memory. "Cock and pie, Mr. Finley's mortal clever. He tells me to whisper to Mr. Barlow what the trouble was as I gave it him, and to go to the Marsh Yard warehouse to lose the cove. *And* to meet Mr. Finley at seven in the morning at the pastry-cook's where the red-polled girl works. Thought of it all quick as a cat on a mouse, he did."

"Did Mr. Finley say why?" she asked. She had no notion what Finley might have told the boys to account for it.

Kit shrugged. "No, ma'am. But if they was following Mr. Barlow, it can't have been for good, can it? So Mr. Barlow was to go, like he had business at the warehouse, and he could either stay the night or slip out the back, that being one where it's easy to do, and the warehouseman being obliging—to us," Kit added. "I reckon he's got a kindness for our company, Mr. Cantarell having got him the job at the warehouse after he lost his leg."

Meakin had been as close to a friend as her father had. They'd sailed on the same ship for several years. She'd visited the warehouse with her father many times, and Meakin treated her like a favorite niece. He was good-natured, loyal to Cantarell Shipping, and maybe a bit obvious about it. Anyone would assume his friendship with Jonas Cantarell accounted for it.

"Good, Kit. But what does Finley propose to do tomorrow? We cannot succeed with the same ruse tomorrow evening."

"Mr. Finley told me to tell Mr. Barlow that he figured to have spoke with you tonight to ask instructions and would pass them on to Mr. Barlow at the pastry-cook's shop."

"Does he want me to return to the office?"

"No, ma'am. He said as he'd give himself the pleasure of calling upon you this evening."

She nodded. "That will do very well. Thank you, Kit." She started to turn back toward Hawkins.

"Ma'am? Ky thought as the watching cove we're talking about might be a thieftaker. He's got to be wrong about that, Mr. Barlow being no thief, but Mr. Finley said you should know."

"I see." One would hire a thieftaker to catch a thief, certainly—but one might equally hire one to find a runaway, if it were important enough. "Kit...what of the second watcher? But I suppose you cannot know whether he continued to observe the office or followed you."

"He didn't do neither, ma'am. He was already gone. Sometimes both Ky and me is gone at the same time, if we're busy. The second man was gone when I got back from my meal. As near as Ky and I could figure, it must have been around the time you left. Right after which Ky was out to take a message down the street, but he wasn't gone but half an hour, if as much, and the cove was gone when he got back."

*How peculiar.* "You've done well, Kit. Are you off for home now?"

"Ay, mistress." He made an awkward little bow and ran off. When she turned to walk back to Hawkins, she glimpsed a coldness in his face before he smiled and came forward to reclaim her arm.

"It troubles me to see you burdened by business matters, my dear. There need be no necessity for you to be troubled at all hours, when you could be living the life to which you are entitled."

"I do not consider myself burdened, Mr. Hawkins. I assisted my father with his business from the time I was still in the schoolroom." Or would have been in the schoolroom if she had had a governess. Instead, first her mother and then her aunt had instructed her thoroughly in reading, writing, and genteel manners and patchily in others, like music and history. Arithmetic and geography she learned from her father. "I never had any turn for embroidery or the usual ladylike pursuits. The only aspects of the shipping business I have not experienced firsthand are visiting Lloyd's Coffeehouse to hear and discuss the news, dining with other agents and shippers at an ordinary, and going down the hold of a ship. And I have two very competent clerks to handle those duties."

Glancing up at him, she saw an odd, impassive expression she had noted several times before. In spite of it, she thought he was surprised, and his next words confirmed it.

"Did you?" After a pause, he continued, "I had heard that you sometimes accompanied him to warehouses and even to a ship on one occasion. Some said he hoped to find you a husband by taking you about with him—a captain or importer who would be able to take over Cantarell Shipping in due course. After making your acquaintance, I was surprised you had not been snapped up."

"By some ambitious man who hoped to get control of my father's business? Hardly. My father was not a trusting man, and I was never likely to be taken in by a suitor who courted me only for what I might inherit.

And, of course, there's my brother."

"I heard Cantarell settled an amount on him that he might purchase a manor, having no turn for business, and that he has no expectations from the company."

"Oh…my brother came into some money from a relative," Olivia said vaguely. "Papa did give him a bit more, and he has inherited a ten percent interest in Cantarell Shipping."

"A ten percent interest in a small company seems no great expectation."

"No, indeed not," she agreed.

****

At home, she mentioned to her aunt that Finley might call upon her that evening on a matter of business, to give Aunt Rachel time to grow accustomed to the idea. She also hoped that the parcels of new gowns would distract Aunt Rachel.

"Coming here? Goodness! What will the neighbors think? What can it possibly be that won't wait until tomorrow? I vow—"

" 'Tis something we must arrange before morning, but the information we needed had not come in when I left to go to the dressmaker's."

"Oh!" After a longish pause, she inquired, "I recall your mentioning Mr. Finley. Is he a young man, dear?"

"Some six-and-twenty, I would guess."

"And of a good appearance?"

"He's well enough." She could see where Aunt Rachel's thoughts were straying. "More to the point, he is a very efficient and obliging clerk, far better than Munns."

"But Mr. Munns was older, and so respectable and steady. No one could think anything of his calling upon us in the evening, any more than if he had been an elderly male relation of ours."

Olivia sighed, realizing she had been guilty of the same foolish behavior she deplored in men: keeping a truth from a female merely because it was unpleasant.

"Aunt, I should have told you the truth about Munns leaving the firm. He provided information that enabled someone to steal two of our cargoes. No doubt it was partly out of spite, because he hated the idea of working for me, and—"

"The poor man! To lose his employment at his time of life! I wish you had not dismissed him, though to be sure it was very naughty of him if you are correct that he was indiscreet. I would never have suspected him of disloyalty. Certainly Jonas never thought him dishonest."

"I did not dismiss him as I did not discover his perfidy until after he resigned. Fortunately, the cargoes were recovered and his accomplice has paid for the inconvenience, nor has word of the attempted theft leaked out."

"I am glad, Livvie, dear. I hope he may find another position that is more to his taste, and will not starve or have to go upon the parish."

"I misdoubt he will not have to do so. He has been traced to Cambridge, where he is living very comfortably, and has bought a property or two with the money he was given for his assistance to the thief."

"I can scarce believe such a shocking thing of Munns. He must have been tried beyond endurance by your papa's death."

Olivia restrained the *Damnation!* she felt rising to her lips.

Hawkins's footman had deposited the packages with their new finery on the settee in the drawing room at Olivia's direction. Kitty, busy helping the cook prepare dinner, would take them upstairs later. She almost suggested that she and her aunt carry them up to their chambers, then dismissed the idea. They might serve as a distraction for Rachel while Finley and she talked.

She suppressed her annoyance. "I have noticed that men who will behave honorably with other men do not always feel constrained to deal with women in the same way."

"Well…but…"

"Dear Aunt, you are not—I hope!—going to say that a man may cheat a female but not a man?"

Rachel opened her mouth to reply, closed it, and then stammered, "N-n-no, but…" Evidently realizing that she must either agree with Olivia or seek to defend the indefensible, she tacked before the wind. "I fear Mr. Hawkins will wonder at your clerk visiting us in the evening, if he learns of it. Unless you have told him your Mr. Finley was coming on a matter of business?"

"Certainly not. The workings of Cantarell Shipping are no concern of Mr. Hawkins's. I would appreciate it, Aunt Rachel, if you did not mention Munns's dishonesty to anyone—anyone! We are still attempting to determine who paid him, and if that person comes to hear of how much we know, it will be the harder."

"But it will be his concern if you marry him, Livvie, as surely you must mean to do. Why, he brings you home every evening, and his intentions are unmistakable. He is eligible in every way. He does not have a title," she admitted, "but we could never expect a titled suitor, given Jonas's business and your lack of significant dowry. Even if you were well dowered, I dare say a nobleman or even an untitled gentleman of the beau monde would consider that your running your papa's business would make you ineligible."

Olivia smiled. "I think that would not be the only point which disqualified me." Enter the beau monde? Good God, what a terrifying thought. She would hang herself from sheer boredom within a month.

As it fell out, both their maid and Aunt Rachel were upstairs putting away the gowns when Finley arrived. Having heard a coach in the street, Olivia had gone to the window and thus was able to open the door to him before he lifted the knocker.

In the parlor but with the door left ajar for decency, she waved him to a chair as she seated herself. One consideration was at the forefront of her mind. "If someone followed Ainslie—Barlow, I should say—to the warehouse, even if he slipped out the back, will that not alert the watcher that Barlow knows he is followed?"

"It will. But there was no time to think of anything beyond getting the fellow off his trail." He flashed an unexpectedly boyish grin for such a responsible young man. "I recalled Kit saying once, when he went there with a message and was kept kicking his heels, he noticed that an agile fellow could leave by the first floor window at the back, cross an adjoining yard, go through an alley and come out in the next street. Young imp that he is. I would not have thought of it otherwise."

"I hope it may have served."

"We'll know in the morning. In any case, it means we—you—have lost your junior clerk. I will set about finding a replacement, by your leave. I'm very sorry that my bringing my friend into your employ should have occasioned—"

"Don't be foolish, Mr. Finley. I agree we must get a clerk to replace Barlow, but that is by no means the end of the matter. I must also see to Barlow's safety." She smiled at him. "I say 'I' though it will be necessary to involve you, if you are willing. Do you think Ky's suspicion that the man was a thieftaker was correct, or was it merely a boy's love of excitement?"

After a moment, he replied, "I don't know. I misdoubt I've ever seen a thieftaker. Were I trying to find someone, I'd hire a thieftaker—if I could afford it! It would make sense to employ someone familiar with London and with rogues, which would be a thieftaker, wouldn't it?"

"That was my reasoning," she agreed.

"I am willing to do anything I can to help. Matt is my younger brother's best friend and like a second little brother to me. But what can we do?"

"It depends upon circumstances as they unroll tomorrow. If he has been taken up, I must find out where he is and hire an attorney for him. It must be possible to keep his guardian from dissipating his inheritance. If he is still free, he must be got away."

"He would have to use another name. His current nom de guerre must now be known to his pursuers. And to find another position…I suppose he will have to sign onto a ship. Once it's sailed, he will be beyond his uncle's reach. By the time he returns, he'll have attained his majority."

"I don't think we have to send him to sea." She drummed her fingertips on the chair's arm. She hated to part with a secret which had been useful for many years, especially to a man whose allegiance must be divided between Easterday and herself. She could avoid it by asking Hawkins to help her. He would know how to spirit Barlow away, she had no doubt. Unlike the scrupulous Captain Easterday, he would have no qualms about keeping her clerk out of his uncle's clutches—if she requested his help. But accepting his help would place her under an obligation to Hawkins in a way that accepting his escort home each night did not. She was not ready to commit herself to him. What a pity Captain Easterday was not a little more like Ambrose Hawkins.

To ask assistance of either would be to appear weak. Had there been no other way, she might have— no, really, she could not. It would be best for Barlow to lie hidden until the searchers gave up. They would be expecting him to run for Scotland. When the hunt was abandoned, she could write him a letter of reference— in a new name—and send him to Willis in Bristol, or Reed in Portsmouth. Cantarell Shipping had good business connections with both, and she would trust either to give him a place or help him to a position in some other company.

"I know a place where Barlow may be concealed until he can go elsewhere. At that time, I will supply him a reference and possible employers in other ports."

She wrote out brief instructions and an address and sealed it with wax and a seal bearing the image of a ship and "CS" for Cantarell Shipping before passing it to Finley. "When you meet him in the morning, give him this and have him read it immediately."

"His pursuers will be watching to see if he comes

here or will follow us to see if we lead them to him."

"They may follow you to the wharves and warehouses or wherever else your work takes you tomorrow, with my good will. You will not lead them to Barlow, nor will I. You must both trust me."

"Ma'am, may I take the liberty of saying I had no notion there were ladies of such resolve and decisiveness. Except, I suppose, Queen Elizabeth, but by all accounts, she must have been something of a flibbertigibbet compared to you."

That drew a laugh from her, if a wry one. "I had some advantages, Mr. Finley." *And some disadvantages, too.* "What will you tell Captain Easterday about Ainslie—Barlow, that is—leaving?" she asked.

"I don't report your business to the captain, ma'am. Except, ummm, ah…"

"We will discuss that 'ummm, ah…' another time. My aunt may come downstairs at any moment. But if he hears that we are looking for another clerk…"

"He will ask you, Mistress Cantarell, not me. Having lent me to you, he would feel it inappropriate to question me about Cantarell business."

"I suppose he would. I will tell him as much of the truth as necessary—that a family emergency necessitated his leaving. Which has the advantage of being true."

"Thank you, Mistress Cantarell."

She closed the door behind him as footsteps pattered down the stairs.

"Livvie, did I hear the door? Has your clerk come?"

"He has come and gone."

"To receive a man by yourself is most improper. You should have sent for me to come down."

Aunt Rachel still forgot at times that their staff consisted of their cook, Mistress Grissom, Kitty, who was upstairs putting away their new finery, and their elderly footman, who was off duty in the evenings except by previous arrangement, in exchange for which freedom he worked for lower wages than footmen in similar posts. In Baron Lees's household, a number of footmen made certain the family seldom had to open a door for themselves. Her aunt's home during her marriage kept a full staff, too. *I could have gone upstairs to fetch her or shouted from the bottom of the stairs if I had wanted a chaperone. Which I did not.*

"Our business was quickly done, Aunt. Merely a matter of sending off a letter."

Chapter 20

When she left home in the morning, Olivia carried a covered basket containing meat, cheese, bread, pickled onions, and even a bottle of wine, telling the cook that her clerks might have no time to go out to the ordinary or tavern for their midday meal. Neither Mistress Grissom nor Aunt Rachel found anything suspicious in the matter, being ignorant of the office routine. Today, she would make different arrangements for the future.

Finley, Kit, and Ky were all in the front office when she arrived and responded to her greetings like schoolboys anticipating a scold. Could something have gone wrong? "Did you meet him, Mr. Finley?"

"Ay, ma'am, and he said as he'd do as you bade."

"Are there watchers this morning?"

"Ay, ma'am," Ky answered. "Two of 'em."

"Kit and Ky, I suspect you boys have lessons to do."

"Shouldn't one of us watch?"

"We won't worry about them for a while. Go study while it's quiet." Though the boys read, wrote, and ciphered satisfactorily, Finley had suggested that it would do them no harm to learn more about other countries and ports, and what cargoes were shipped from each. "They'd pick it up, but they may as well study it in a methodical manner and use any time they aren't needed for errands."

They bobbed their heads in agreement and retreated to the little office in which they waited to be sent on errands. No doubt they had discovered the spy hole, so she murmured, "Come over by the map table and keep your voice low." She did not want them overhearing her talk with Finley. He nodded and moved two chairs to the side of the table facing away from the back offices. He, too, must now know of the spy hole.

"Did Barlow tell you if he had any plan for escaping London?" she asked when they were seated.

"No, ma'am. Neither of us considered that the loiterers the boys noticed had anything to do with him. He thought it was someone wanting to frighten you into selling, and I thought it might be someone Ambrose Hawkins sent." He looked uncomfortable.

"Really? Why would he do such a thing?"

Finley did not meet her eyes. "Mayhap to protect you. He's made it known he takes an interest."

She was not going to pursue that topic, which made her as uncomfortable as it evidently made Finley. "Then when I see Barlow, we will discuss what plans should be made."

She spent a few minutes organizing her thoughts and jotting notes on a scrap of paper. Then she picked up her basket and told Finley, "I'm going upstairs for a while. I won't be very long, and I have every confidence that you will handle any question that arises."

"If I feel I should consult you, ma'am, I will defer an answer until your return."

"Very good."

She hooked one arm through the basket's handle

and used the other hand to raise her petticoat a little to climb the narrow stairs. Finley would assume she was going up to use the room her father had constructed when she began to spend time in the office with him. She had improved it over the years, but its basic function was as a private area for a washstand and chamberpot. The men used the necessary house in the narrow yard behind the building, and she suspected they employed the alley as a urinal when in a hurry. Why should they differ from thousands of other men in London?

The rest of the space was used to store small cargoes they chose not to send to a warehouse and for their own imports. She continued up to the top floor.

Half the width of the building overlooked the yard. The other half extended farther, to meet the extended back half of the building behind. A dozen crates, trunks, and enough furniture to equip a cottage, all belonging to Aunt Rachel, filled the room. She had brought them with her when she moved in with them in Well Close Square, but there had been no place to store them in the attic, which contained the servants' rooms.

One of the trunks was uncorded. Two years ago, Olivia had retrieved some sheets and pillowcases at her aunt's direction to replace worn ones at home. She took out a quilt and a blanket and decided it was quite unnecessary to bother with sheets for this purpose. She stacked them on a small table. There was an armchair which would do. Several featherbeds were rolled up, each wrapped in a holland cover. She carried the top one over to the left back corner of the room and set it down. The quilt and blankets were easy to move, and they soon joined the featherbed and her basket.

The door her father had added in the back wall where it joined the building behind was stout, and the lock a very good one. He had not pinched pennies on such precautions. On the other side was an empty passage lit by a small window overlooking the yard, with a door at the other end. She made sure to keep as far from the window as she could in case someone in the yard should look up.

When she unlocked the second door, she beheld Barlow standing rigid a few feet away, an expression of alarm on his face.

"Mistress Cantarell!"

"Indeed. I gather Ah Fong did not explain I would come this way."

Barlow laughed, from sheer relief, probably. "He's very close-mouthed. Doesn't speak much English, I apprehend. Though he understood when I said you had sent me to him to be kept out of sight."

"Oh, he's fluent enough—when he wants to be. But English people don't expect it, which makes it easy for him to ignore any question he doesn't care to answer."

The chamber was the rear third of the top floor of the building behind Cantarell Shipping, lighted by a pair of windows facing the yard, the shutters half open. By their light, she saw Ah Fong had provided their guest with a chamberpot, a straight chair, a jug of water and a cup, and a plain cabinet in the Chinese style. It would keep mice out of Barlow's food supply.

"We will have to be quiet while we move some furniture into your quarters here."

Barlow shifted the heavier things. When the room was furnished with a washstand, bowl and pitcher, the

169

featherbed and bedding, armchair, table, and two candlesticks, it was tolerably comfortable. It was also secure. Barlow's room was separated from the main section of the upper floor by another door, locked from Barlow's side. *What a fortunate thing for Barlow that Father was a worrier!*

"If the day is warm, you may open the windows. Ah Fong does so ordinarily and leaves the top stair door open. It makes the shop cooler. At dark, you will have to shutter the windows, and see—he has provided you with a pretty lacquer screen, which we will position to prevent any light from leaking out through the shutters."

"Can we trust him?"

"We can." There was no need for him to know that she owned the building Ah Fong used for his shop and home and that he and her father were longtime associates. She had dealt with Ah Fong ever since she became involved in the importation of Chinese goods. Ah Fong passed her orders on, with his own, through two or three sailors on East Indiamen for small merchandise and one East India Company supercargo for larger items. They handed the orders on to contacts in Canton. Ah Fong's shop sold less expensive Chinese wares; the best quality porcelain and jade and ivory carvings went to fashionable shops.

Having settled him in his lodging and arranged with Ah Fong to provide Barlow's meals in the future, she started back down, remembering to bring her basket with her. On the first floor, however, she paused to peer out the front window. A man idled in front of a chandler's shop, appearing to read a newspaper. Another man walked back and forth with a tray of thin, cheaply printed books suspended from a strap around his neck. He cried his wares (*Ballads! Humor! Rogues, heroes, martyrs! Verse and history!*) less frequently than one might expect. They might well be watching Cantarell Shipping.

Chapter 21

Easterday did not enjoy the prospect of speaking with Olivia Cantarell about matters which clearly were no concern of his. On the other hand, to abandon her to Hawkins's wiles did not suit his notions of decency. He had involved himself in her life already to the extent of providing her with a clerk and letting it be seen that he took an interest in Cantarell Shipping. However awkward, he must make sure she knew her father's estate might be larger than she thought, so she could be wary of men who might want to secure it for themselves. One man: Hawkins. If she actually had a sizable fortune, it was not common knowledge. If she were unaware—and how could she not be, to judge by the way she and her aunt dressed—he could help her discover the extent of her holdings. He did not have either Hawkins's or Markham's sources of information, but he did have a banker friend who could advise him how to proceed.

After transacting business not far from the Custom House, he walked to Cantarell Shipping. On entering, it was clear he had come at a bad time; Finley looked harried, and Olivia stood at his shoulder, peering at a sheet on the desk.

"I'll prepare the first three," she said decidedly. "They're the longest."

"Quite so. They'll take as much time as the other

six—"

They looked up as he came in. Interesting! Finley's face was a picture of guilt. Olivia merely looked worried.

"Have I come at an inconvenient time?"

"No, no, of course not, Captain Easterday," she said. "Come into my office. What can we do for you today?"

He saw her exchange a glance with Finley. *Something most peculiar going on there.* First things first, however.

"I hope I see you well," he said when she had led him into old Cantarell's office. No, her office, now. It had acquired curtains since his last visit and several pieces of Chinese porcelain had replaced moldering stacks of papers and documents on the shelves. A small watercolor depicted with exquisite detail a ship at dock with a crane hoisting a netted cargo. The background faded into mist or fog, with only glimpses of the rough wooden buildings that lined the river in the Pool of London.

"Very well, thank you. You will have heard, of course, that the *Devon Maid* has sailed. With luck—meaning good winds and currents," she added with a smile, "your nephew's linen yardage should reach Boston in sixty or seventy days. I beg your pardon! You know that, of course. I recently had to deal with someone who had never shipped before. He was a gentleman's secretary whose employer had instructed him to ship a harpsichord to Philadelphia. He asked if it wouldn't be quicker to 'go 'round the other way.' "

"I've dealt with such questions myself. All shippers have." They exchanged conspiratorial glances.

He cleared his throat. "There is something I must discuss with you which is no business of mine, but as it explains that second payment to Munns I feel I must bring it to your attention, in case…errr, in case it should have an impact upon your business decisions."

"You found out what it was for! I confess I had almost forgotten about it in the press of other matters. How kind of you to look into it further, Captain Easterday. Thank you. How did you find out?"

"I asked someone who has very good sources of information. Even he was not certain, but he suggested something that I had not considered. The matter is rather delicate."

She raised her sand-pale brows inquiringly.

"Have you ever seen any indication that your father might have more assets than Cantarell Shipping? It was suggested to me that the second payment to Munns might have been for information about money or properties he owned beyond this firm. Munns might have had access to records…" He shrugged.

"Or a pirate map to a chest of doubloons?" she asked with gentle irony after gazing at him for what seemed far longer than it probably was.

"Ridiculous as it sounds, if he did have hidden assets and your old clerk knew of them, it would explain much."

"I hope that whoever suggested this idea to you is not spreading it up and down the City and the river, sir."

"No, certainly not. He is discreet and questioned me about my interest in your affairs. I believe he would not have hinted at his suspicions if I did not have a good reputation. Nor do I necessarily believe him to be correct about the possibility of hidden monies or property. Few secrets that involve two or more persons can be kept entirely secret, and business dealings typically do—the parties themselves, at least one attorney, a banker perhaps." He remembered Markham's example of his niece's father not knowing that Markham was wealthy. Perhaps if Cantarell's other holdings were outside London, or not connected with shipping, word would not have spread. "And I don't believe your father would...ah, would have failed to lavish every material advantage upon you if he had had the resources to do so."

Her eyes crinkled at the corners. "You can't have known my father well. I loved him, but he was as thrifty as a Scot. Thriftier. My aunt claims that when he was young, he took a less bleak view of life. I remember he used to laugh and joke with us when I was a child. He started to change after he lost money in an unwise investment."

He made a sympathetic "Mmmm," not knowing what else to say. Having mentioned the idea to her, there was no reason for him to stay longer. After she had thought it over, she could investigate it if she found it credible.

"You have a very good reputation, Captain, not only for honest dealing, but for kindness. I've heard about the porter you continued to pay while his broken leg mended, and that you paid the doctor, too. That is why I will tell you. It is possible that Munns saw my father's other set of account books. Ordinarily, they were—and are—kept at home. Last autumn, it was necessary to have builders in to repair a leak in the roof that caused some damage to the wall in our library—

our office. The repairs took several days, so my father brought the ledgers here, and I stayed later than usual, working on them." She sighed. "You know what the business is like, captain. It's not impossible he left the ledgers unattended at some point after I departed, and that Munns might have seen them. He would not have had to pore over them, only to see that each was labelled with the name of a property. Munns had—has—an extremely good memory, better than Father's, even. He could routinely recall quite insignificant details of transactions from five or six years ago, sometimes more than that. It made him very useful."

"He sold the information to someone."

"It seems he must have done."

Easterday did not broach the subject of the purchaser's identity. If Hawkins was indeed courting her, as it appeared, she might resist the idea that he was doing so for her property. She was able to figure it out herself, if she were not blinded by the man's attentions. "I wonder if Munns knew you were aware of the other properties, Mistress Olivia."

"I cannot think he would be, sir. He knew I worked with my father on the Cantarell Shipping ledger and resented it bitterly. I am sure he did not see me with the other ledgers because he avoided me whenever he could—which was usually. When I was in the small office behind the front office, the door was closed in case a visitor going back to my father's office should be scandalized by the presence of a female."

Here he must tread very carefully. "If your clerk did not know you were aware of Cantarell's other holdings, the purchaser would not know. Is it possible that by buying Cantarell Shipping, he might get the other properties as well?"

"No," she replied decidedly. "They are separate entities." She gave him a very thoughtful look, however. He might have succeeded in planting a seed of caution in her mind. Not that she was impulsive. Olivia Cantarell was the most level-headed woman he had ever met. What he did not understand was why she insisted on running Cantarell Shipping. Whatever the other properties or businesses were, they evidently did not require her personal attention. They might be rents, or commercial ventures run by competent, honest managers.

"May I ask you a rather personal question, ma'am?"

"You may ask. I may not answer."

"That's fair. Given the difficulties and even hostility you encounter here, why not sell Cantarell Shipping? I assume that the other income would support you with fewer problems. Or if you wish to retain the company, which I would understand, why not leave it in the care of a good manager? I'd cede you Finley. You would still go over the accounts, as you do the others."

She bit her lips, making them even thinner than usual. She looked rather like a young girl posed a difficult lesson.

"I don't think you will understand, sir. Reviewing the ledgers takes comparatively little time, not enough to fill a day. Cantarell Shipping is…it's what I do. I have no turn for music or needlework or endless calls on friends who do nothing else."

"You might buy a house with a garden and…ah…"

"Music, needlework, or calls upon neighbors. I

have never had a garden, and while I enjoy flowers and trees, I dare say I should not have any turn for planning or tending a garden. Gentlemen have so many more interesting things to do with their time than ladies."

"Only if they have an occupation."

"My point exactly, captain. They are able to pursue a career."

"For most ladies, marriage is a career."

"Which consists of overseeing the servants and children, needlework, visiting, and perhaps parish activities. All of which would bore me. It is no use to say, as my aunt does, that I would find I liked those activities if I tried. Even if I did, I would be giving up my freedom and giving up control of my businesses to a husband. I think I would find it irksome. Would you like to turn over your company to your spouse?"

"Damn my eyes, I would not!"

"That's honest." She laughed. It was an unexpectedly pretty laugh, and he found himself joining in.

"I beg your pardon. I'm not in the habit of using such language to a lady."

"My dear sir, it's a trifle compared to what I have often heard in this office."

"Still, it was inappropriate. I do take your point, however. Only recently I found myself wondering what I would do with my time if I ever retired."

"Did you decide to take up gardening or watercolors or parish activities?"

He laughed again. "No, I concluded that I would not be well suited to them. I suppose both of us must resign ourselves to continuing to work, if neither of us will settle to leisure."

As they passed out of her office, he ventured, "I believe someone has been calling for you in the afternoons, which is probably safer even than sending one of your boys for a hackney."

"Mr. Ambrose Hawkins has been very insistent about sending his coach for me at the end of the day."

It was surprising she had not given him a sharp rebuke. If she had romantic feelings for Hawkins, she should have shown some defensiveness or at least colored. Was it possible she was simply accepting Hawkins's assistance as she had accepted his? She had done so more easily than a man in her position would—but a man would probably not be in her position in the first place, and if he were, he would seek advice from friends. "That should afford you adequate protection. Very few men would risk angering Hawkins. I suppose in the mornings, you send a servant to fetch a hackney?"

"Mr. Finley felt it would be best if I were escorted, and as Mr. Barlow's lodging is not far from my home, he has been coming with a hackney coach in the morning."

By then they were in the outer office, where Finley still appeared beset. Two things were apparent: the slight hesitation before Olivia's reply and a tensing of Finley's shoulders as his pen stopped scritching across the paper.

"A very good idea," Easterday agreed. "Where is Barlow this morning? I had hoped to meet him."

"Ahhhh…" He saw Finley look to Olivia Cantarell for instructions.

She said, "Mr. Barlow has been called away upon a family matter."

"His family is in the north, isn't it?"

"Scotland."

"Then he will be gone some considerable time, and you will be in need of another clerk."

"Very true," she agreed, without losing one whit of her composure. "I intend to advertise the position. His family's situation unfortunately did not admit of any delay in his departure."

"I am sorry to hear it. May I lend you one of my junior clerks?"

She appeared to weigh his offer. A slight elevation of her chin suggested she was about to refuse. Olivia would think that two Easterday employees in her office constituted an invasion, and in her place, he would think the same. Although it looked as if Finley's allegiance was now to Cantarell Shipping. As indeed he himself had meant it to be; it had not been his intention to place a spy in her office. He went on, "Although your business is recovering, it's still possible clerks with any experience will be hesitant to apply to you. Do you expect Barlow to return and mean to re-employ him? If you do, it might be unfair to hire a man and then let him go in a month or two. There is also the risk that an experienced clerk who applied might supply information to one of your competitors."

"All of those points are valid," she admitted. "Very well, I accept. Thank you."

"I'll send Edmond Davant, I think. He's young and has not been with me long, but he learns quickly and will be the best for your purposes." Davant was adaptable and unlikely to have qualms about working for a female.

"Davant, ay, he'd be a good choice," Finley

agreed.

"Unfortunately, I sent Davant to Ipswich to call upon a customer. I expect him back late the day after tomorrow, but he could not begin here until the following day. In the interim, I'll send you a fellow of mine who's no clerk, but he's used to the shipping trade. He'll be an additional presence here in the office when Finley has to go out to a warehouse or ship. He's rough looking, but I've known him for years."

"Thank you, Captain. I think I must accept." Her thanks sounded sincere, but at the same time he read vexation in her face. He supposed she felt humiliated that she had little choice but to accept his aid.

"Thank you, sir," Finley echoed.

Easterday gazed thoughtfully at him for a moment. He wondered what had become of Barlow, for he did not believe in a family crisis, whatever it was. Olivia had been momentarily nonplussed when he asked about Barlow, and Finley looked nervous—and guilty. He wished Mistress Olivia would trust him more than halfway.

Chapter 22

To Olivia's relief, the next morning progressed almost in normal fashion, until Kit tapped on her door and came in. He closed it behind him. The reassuringly big porter the captain had sent was stowed in the little office with the door ajar to hear if he was needed.

"Ma'am, there's a fellow come asking for a clerk's position."

"Is there, indeed? But we have not advertised for a clerk."

"No, ma'am, and that's an odd thing. If I was you, mistress, I'd see the cove in the front, not here. He's not like Mr. Finley and Mr. Barlow."

"I quite agree." She stood, gave her petticoats a twitch, checked that her fichu was decently in place and followed Kit to the outer office. A neatly dressed young man stood before Finley's desk and bowed to her when she came in. She saw what Kit had meant; he was not quite a gentleman, and he had sharp, knowing eyes.

"Mistress Cantarell, may I present Thaddeus Williams, who thought you might need another clerk."

"Williams," she acknowledged. "How did you hear we might need a clerk?"

"I wasn't sure you did, but I recollected seeing Cantarell Shipping advertise for one and thought it worth trying."

"None of the other places you applied having had

an opening?"

"I've been that unlucky, ma'am." He smiled. "It's having no local references, you see, my having moved here from Liverpool. The young lady I was courting left when her widowed ma married a London man."

"And the steppapa doesn't favor your suit or he'd have found you work."

He flashed the ready, meaningless smile again. "That he don't, thinking Susan can do better than me, which is true enough. I hope to change his mind."

Finley had gone over to make an entry on one of the small slates mounted on the wall behind Williams. Finley glanced over his shoulder, shook his head, and grimaced. She thoroughly agreed, and said, "I'm sorry, but we do not at present need another clerk. I trust your endeavors will prosper, both business and personal."

"Thank you, Mistress Cantarell. It seems I must continue my search." Williams bowed to her again, then turned and walked out.

Kit, who had quietly carried a sheaf of papers upstairs came galloping back down, still with the papers. How duplicitous they had all become!

"He's off down the street, jaunty as you please."

"I apologize for making faces at you, ma'am," Finley said, "but there was something wrong about him."

"I thought as much. It was too great a coincidence that he happened to think of us today, when it happens we are so recently deprived of Barlow. He is not a bad actor, but his smile lacked sincerity. Are we agreed someone tried to place him here as a spy?"

"Mr. Barlow's uncle!" Kit exclaimed.

They gazed at him, and he wriggled in

embarrassment. "Thought I'd mention it, ma'am, sir."

Finley erased the entry he had made on the slate. It had only been a pretext to get behind their visitor. "You may be correct. The uncle or his agent would be aware that Barlow had fled."

"The thing that argues against it, Finley, is that the uncle or his thieftaker would have to find a man who was able and willing to act as his intelligencer and had some experience in shipping. A clerk who knew nothing of marine shipping would expose himself in an hour."

"Unless he thought he could accomplish his mission within that time by discovering that Barlow was hidden on the premises, or by overhearing some incautious word."

"Or unless whoever sent him did not realize that the work would be different from other clerks' work, and that either you or I would be likely to test his knowledge before taking him on. On the other hand, he knew enough to claim to be from Liverpool, where he might have been employed in shipping."

"That's another thing, ma'am; he didn't sound like a Lancashire man. Captain Easterday's from there and has no trace of it in his speech, but he's a gentleman and had it trained out of him. Williams isn't and didn't sound like a native of those parts."

"Well, at least we know someone is trying to…er, breach our defenses. I confess I suspected Williams only because it was suspicious that he came so pat upon Barlow's departure, and you distrusted him. I might not have noticed the inconsistencies in his story otherwise."

"Nor I. I merely felt that there was something about him that was not quite right."

"Well, we need only hold out for another day or so before Captain Easterday's clerk arrives."

Ky came into the office and dug a wad of documents out of his coat pocket. It was not an elegant way to carry messages and documents to and from their customers. On the other hand, if he'd had a satchel in which to carry them, it might be snatched from him by some fleet-footed felon.

"Mr. Hawkins going to ship with us?" Ky asked, handing over the papers after he unfolded them.

"Not that I have heard. Why do you ask?"

"On account of the cove as come out as I was coming up the street. Clerks for Mr. Hawkins, he does. I saw him there once when you sent him a message about them scientifical tools we shipped, and another time he come out of Hawkins's building when I was passing on my way to Sampson's warehouse."

Kit paused in sharpening a quill. "He asked for work and didn't mention having work here already."

"Are you certain it's the same man?" Finley asked. "You say you've only seen him twice."

"Ay, for he reminds me of my cousin Aaron. Same kind of funny ears, bigger at the bottom than the top. 'Cept for that, he looks a knowing one, don't he? I wonder if Mr. Hawkins turned him off."

Olivia and Finley exchanged a glance. "Very curious indeed," Olivia offered.

Chapter 23

Olivia liked Edmond Davant, a serious young man of Huguenot extraction. He lacked the sense of humor she enjoyed in Finley and which Barlow had also possessed, though she could not fault his competence and willingness. Cantarell Shipping accommodated itself.

On his return from dinner, Kit was sent to deliver a message to the consignee of a newly arrived cargo. When he did not return in two hours' time from a distance of no more than half a mile, Olivia began to be concerned. Not worried, precisely. Kit was a boy, after all, and might have become distracted, though he had never dawdled before.

"Mayhap Purtill was away and Kit had to wait for his return, or else went to find him at some public house or other." Finley did not sound as if he were convinced of it, which made Olivia worry the more.

Ky, who should have been writing out lists of spices and where they came from, emerged from the little office. He had been eavesdropping, for he offered, " 'Tisn't like Kit not to come back, 'less he couldn't. They wouldn't 'a pressed him, would they?"

"Into the navy, you mean, Ky? They press men of seafaring habits. They'd not want a mere lad, and Kit looks less than his age. Both of you are safe, I think. Something has delayed him, that's all."

"It's just..." Ky's eyes slid toward Edmond Davant, writing out the third copy of an unusually long and detailed bill of lading.

"I know just how you feel." Someone had to fill in the thought, and Mr. Finley was evidently having trouble thinking just what it was. "There have been a great many disruptions recently, have there not? Mr. Barlow having to leave us is merely the most recent, and therefore anything out of the ordinary is worrisome."

"That's it, ma'am. That's it, right enough." In spite of his words, which seemed to agree, his sunburnt forehead was furrowed.

A lesson would distract him. "Now, let us see how you are doing with the spices. Where does cinnamon come from?"

"Two places, mistress. There's some comes from Ceylon, and there's some comes from those islands near China."

"The Dutch East Indies."

"Ay, ma'am. They're not the same, the cinnamons, I mean. The taste's a mite different. That's what the book says, leastways."

"Very good." She sent him back to his lists.

She returned to her own office and her task, reviewing the previous week's accounts. Could Kit have been injured? Accidents were not uncommon on London's busy streets. He would tell someone to send a message to Cantarell Shipping, if he could. If he could not...what was the nearest hospital?

In the front, Finley exclaimed, "Kit! Where have you been?" Hurrying out, she saw Kit, face red and damp with sweat, disheveled as to hair and clothing.

"I'm sorry to be late," he squeaked, his voice higher pitched than usual.

"Come back to my office," she said and nodded very slightly at Finley, who raised inquiring brows. Hearing Kit's trudging steps and panting breath behind her, and Finley's slower tread as he followed, she hurried into her office to pour a mug of lemonade from the flask she had brought from home and gave it to Kit. "Take a drink, and sit, both of you. What's happened, Kit?" She took her place behind the desk and folded her hands.

Finley pulled the door shut behind them.

Kit drank the lemonade off in two swallows before dropping onto the nearest chair. "I was on my way to Purtill's when a cove grabs me and throws me into a coach that's come up behind me. I gives a yell, and a woman that's wheeling a barrow o' fish cries out, 'Ho there, what be you a-doing with that lad?' The cove calls back that I'm his boy that's run away from school and to mind yer own business, woman. I tried to shout it was a lie, but he'd clapped his hand over my mouth. Then the rattler-cove touches up the horses, and we're off."

"Good God!"

"Are you hurt, Kit? In any way?" Finley asked very softly. His face was grim.

"I got me some bruises, that's all, 'cause I tried to fight when he tied my hands. Once we was moving and past the fish woman, no one could have heard me, I don't think, but he gagged me, too. After a bit we're in the country, like, I guess, as there's stuff growing. Cabbages and such. The coach pulls over where there's nothing else. I couldn't see a house or anything but some trees in rows. Fruit trees, maybe. The cully asks me why I was sent after Mr. Barlow t'other day and what the paper I give him said.

" 'Oh ho,' I thinks. Belike Ky's right about a thieftaker looking for Mr. Barlow. I says I don't know naught, but there was some errand you wanted him to do on his way home."

" 'Didn't you have a look at the paper? Boys being curious creatures?' he wants to know. 'What, me?' says I. 'I wanted to be done and get home to me mam. She promised we'd have a meat pie.' He keeps on asking things, like what Barlow talks about, and what you talks about, Mr. Finley. I said, it's all tonnage and dunnage and charterparts, nothing but shipping talk."

"Charterparties," Olivia corrected.

"A charterparty is an indenture between merchants or owners and the ship's master, spelling out their agreements regarding the cargo and its transport," Finley added.

Kit nodded impatiently. "He laughs at that and says, 'Nothing about females? I never knew a young man—or an older one, neither—that didn't talk of morts.' I told him, very stiff, that you and Barlow wouldn't speak of such things where Mistress Cantarell might hear, she being our governor, like."

" 'A woman!' he says, mighty surprised. 'What's a woman—nay, never mind. A woman is always gossiping and asking about families. She'll have asked about her clerks' kin and homes.' I say, she asks if I've washed my hands and behind my ears, but she's not one for chatter. He laughs, but he keeps wanting to know this and that. Do I know where Mr. Barlow lodges? Does he have friends in London? I tells him, I don't know, as I figured as it was better to let him think the clerks don't talk to us boys except to tell us to do this or that. He asks the same questions different ways, like he expects the answer to be different. Huh!" Kit ended, scornfully.

"He let you go?"

"He has the coachman drive us to where there's some houses and a mort o' fields and gardens and he give me a purse full of coin and warns me not to say I've talked to him, and I should go buy some sweetmeats or whatever I want and pretend tomorrow that I run into a friend and went off with him. I let on as I would, for fear he wouldn't let me go if I told him to—"

"Yes, yes, we understand," Finley interrupted hurriedly.

"But when he let me out of the rattler, I didn't know where I was. I thinks to myself that we didn't cross the bridge, so if I walk south, I'll come to the river and then maybe I'll know where I am. Before I get there, I come to Shadwell and see a man loading a cart of greens and ask him whereabouts I am. Just short of Ratcliff Highway, he tells me, and he's going that way if I want to ride with him. Which I do. He was bound for Tower Hill and when we get there, I thanks him and runs like the wind. I went off to old Purtill's and then come straight back here. I took a roundabout way after Purtill's, which is why I'm so late, because..." Kit shuffled his feet. "Seemed like the cully could be downright ugly if he was crossed. I didn't want him to know I'd come back here."

"That is very interesting," Olivia said. "Kit, you may go back to the little office. Unless you have any questions, Mr. Finley?"

"No…"

"Thank you for telling us. I'm sorry you had such an unpleasant experience, but you did very well. We won't send you out again today."

Kit bobbed a sort of bow and mumbled thanks.

"And you may count your coins before resuming your studies," Olivia added. "If you haven't done it already."

"Oh, no, ma'am. I was in a bother to get back here."

Kit fled. At her gesture, Finley closed the door again, despite the impropriety. She preferred that Davant not hear. He was still Easterday's man, after all. "Thieftaker or not, that man is after Barlow. I am very uneasy that he abducted Kit to question him. It seems an act of desperation."

"I agree. Ma'am, I think we must take steps to deal with the matter."

"If you have a suggestion, Mr. Finley, I would be glad of it."

"Advise Captain Easterday of this development." Strain etched lines around his mouth and eyes.

"That would require telling him Barlow's secret. It would be difficult, if not impossible, to avoid telling him you have known Barlow for years and knew his circumstances and real name."

"I must simply admit that I lied. He will not wish to take me back when he knows, but we need help; what if this fellow abducts you next, hoping to learn more?"

"Or you, Mr. Finley, or Ky. And I am willing to employ you as long as you wish to stay. I was not looking forward to losing your services."

"I'm very grateful to you, ma'am. I will write out my confession, then, and send it by the penny post on my way home. I'm not likely to be abducted successfully, and I cannot but worry that Ky might be the next, even though he is larger than Kit, and will be forewarned now. "

"It will be better if I write, merely requesting Captain Easterday to call upon me here at his earliest opportunity, regarding a question of cargo. If it should fall into the wrong hands, they will learn nothing."

## Chapter 24

What a great deal of tumult Mistress Olivia Cantarell had brought into his life of late, Easterday reflected, listening to the duet of disclosures by that lady and Finley. He was not sure he enjoyed it. Importing and exporting should provide enough excitement for any reasonable man, after a youth spent at sea.

*Then why have I been feeling like such an old, dull dog?*

He had been brought up to behave correctly and responsibly. He certainly could not regret it. Otherwise, one would be a man like Hawkins. No. To be fair, Hawkins was not irresponsible. Hard and dishonest, but he did have a reputation for keeping his word. Roger Markham did not disapprove of him, which carried some weight. How could Hawkins live as he did and appear lighthearted, when he himself, often called "respectable" or "worthy"—*egad, what a horrid term! Another word for "dull"!*—derived very little satisfaction from life.

He often heard parsons praise sober demeanor. Taken to its logical conclusion, Cromwell's Parliamentarians would be considered admirable. Not that he would prefer the profligacy of the court of Charles II, far from it. Should there not be some happy medium?

"… and I am a little worried," Olivia concluded.

"As well you might be," he agreed. "I am extremely sorry that it was through my doing that a cuckoo was introduced into your nest." He levelled a stern glance at Finley, who looked suitably apologetic.

As he was wondering whether the metaphor was indelicate, Olivia gave a little chuckle. "Better a cuckoo than a sparrow. Nor was it your doing, and I do not blame Finley at all. Any blame belongs to Barlow's uncle. I am only sorry to lose Barlow, who was both efficient and pleasant."

"It is generous of you to overlook the deception practiced upon you by my clerk and Barl—Ainslie, Mistress Olivia." In spite of her unconventionality in insisting on keeping her father's business, she was a sensible woman who would surely disapprove of deceit.

She sat very straight in the chair behind her father's desk. Odd to see a woman occupying the position of authority!

"Captain Easterday, by my sex, I belong to a group which is subject to domination by men. It's true even when the woman is capable of managing her own affairs and the man is a fool or a spendthrift. I therefore have some sympathy for a young man of steady disposition, only months short of his majority, whose proposed guardian covets his inheritance."

"I see." Everyone knew that ladies were at the mercy of husbands who were dissolute. He was willing to dismiss all religious claims that the man should govern the family, as it was self-evident that some could not or should not, by reason of foolishness, incompetence, or evil propensities. The idea of women being their husbands' property he also rejected, for the same reason he would not take part in the slave trade; it seemed to him to encourage bad behavior on the part of the owner. As a practical matter, women were subject to their husbands, as children were to their parents, because they could not earn their own living. Except that some did; women owned and operated dressmaking and millinery shops, taverns, hostelries, and other establishments. White's Chocolate House was brought so much into fashion by its founder's widow, she had gone from being known as the Widow White to Madam White. Those were women of the lower or middling classes, however, who often had more freedom than ladies. There was food for thought here, but he did not have time to digest it at the moment.

"How may I serve you in this, ma'am?"

"I hardly know, Captain. I do not wish to risk Mr. Finley being waylaid as Kit was, or Ky, either. Or Mr. Davant, though he is less likely to be a target, having only come to work here after Barlow was gone. I am responsible for their safety, and I admit I do not know how to secure it."

"Are you not concerned for your own safety?"

Her eyes twinkled with...mischief? "No, sir. For once, being disregarded because of my sex works to my advantage. By Kit's account, his kidnapper was surprised to hear of me and shared the prejudices of the rest of mankind. It's not likely he will think I knew anything of Barlow's imposture."

"Not all of mankind, Mistress Olivia."

She smiled slightly. "Perhaps a few exceptions exist."

She really was an admirable woman. Not every businessman was concerned about the welfare of his employees. If one were injured or fell sick, many—most!—would hire a replacement. He remembered thinking her cold and unfeminine at their first meeting. Yet there was more to her than met the eye on brief acquaintance. It was true she had no feminine wiles or traits, if one took Claudia Dean and Mariah Saltstall as exemplars of female behavior. *Thank God they both jilted me!* Neither had a brain in her head, or any interest but in shopping and entertainments. Such things might be well enough in the wife of an idle aristocrat. He would find it tedious in the extreme.

He had helped her at first because he did not wish to see her put out of business by some cheat. Now he would help her in any way he could because she deserved to keep her business.

"What is your immediate goal?"

"To persuade whoever is watching for Barlow to go away."

"Ay, you don't want his pursuers underfoot in the hope one of you will lead them to him. We should provide some false scent for them to follow."

"Is it possible to lure them away?"

"It should be, if it can be managed the right way. But if his uncle is determined to get possession of him in order to loot his inheritance, even for a few months, he will not give up easily. If he's set on a false trail and then loses it, he—or his hireling—will come back, casting about for a new one."

Finley suggested hesitantly, "If he were believed to have signed onto a ship bound for the Far East…"

"That is a possibility. It should either lead the hunt away, in the hope of catching up with him at some port they'd put into along the way or end it. It would at least afford us some time to make other arrangements."

"It would work only if his uncle actually believed it, Captain."

"Very true. The information must come to the pursuers' ears from some source unconnected to you or Cantarell Shipping."

"Can it be done?"

He grinned at her. She must know as well as he how rumors travelled the Thames as freely as its ships, wherries, and lighters. "I think it can, though I believe I will have to enlist some help. Will you leave the matter in my hands, ma'am?"

Her lips compressed; she must find it frustrating to admit she could not spread the word herself by mentioning it casually in a coffee house, ordinary, or public house. Then they relaxed into a wry smile.

"I am very happy to do so, sir. Thank you."

Chapter 25

They went to the parlor after supper, Rachel to embroider the tops of a pair of slippers, Olivia (who was not skilled with a needle) to read aloud to her and wonder how the captain was arranging matters. She had chosen *The Rape of the Lock* from their library, which though quite extensive, contained few volumes later than 1720, when her father's fortunes had suffered such a calamitous decline. She should buy some recent works, if only secondhand. There were quite a number of novels and plays she would like to read.

Aunt Rachel had risen to fetch another candlestick from the mantel, saying, "How comfortable it is to be able to work by two candles. We could never have done so when poor Jonas was alive," when someone pounded upon the door. "I'll see who it is, Livvie."

Olivia rose and followed her, alarmed by the violence of the knocking.

"Mr. Hawkins!" Before Rachel could say more, Hawkins was in the hall. Olivia stopped in the parlor's doorway, surprised to see him. He was breathing rapidly and seemed discomposed.

"Mistress Williams, I beg your pardon for intruding, but there is a problem which urgently requires Mistress Olivia's attention. I'll take you in my coach, Mistress Olivia."

She set the book on the console table and went

forward. "What's happened?"

"Your clerk—Barlow?—is injured at one of your warehouses. A surgeon has been sent for, but there's more to it than his injury. He asked for you. There's no time to be wasted. It's serious, or I should not have felt it necessary to trouble you."

"Livvie, you are pale as death. Pray, sit down again for a moment and consider. You cannot mean to go out at night—" her aunt protested.

"Yes, I can." She crossed the drawing room to Hawkins in two strides. "Which warehouse?" *What happened at Ah Fong's to cause him to leave?*

"Livvie, if you must go, I will accompany you. Let me but change my gown to a warmer one."

"There is no time," Hawkins said, speaking very softly.

"I cannot wait, Aunt."

"At least take your cloak!"

She blew out an exasperated breath. "I'll be with you in a trice, Mr. Hawkins." She hurried past him into the hall and up the stairs.

"Less than a trice." He smiled when she came down, cloak over her arm.

Aunt Rachel had come out into the hall with Mr. Hawkins, still murmuring distressfully. "But what can you do, dear? If your clerk is being cared for, need you go?"

"He asked for me. My father would have gone. Don't wait up for me, Aunt Rachel." By then she was out the door.

As he helped her into the coach, Hawkins said, "I'm glad you felt able to come."

"If I had not, everyone would have claimed it

proved that a woman could not run a shipping firm. What happened?"

"I don't know the details. I happened to be passing on my way home when someone burst out of a building by Marsh Yard, shouting for a surgeon to be sent for. The fellow said your clerk was wounded, and I dispatched my coach for a surgeon. I went in to see what the matter was. As soon as my coachman returned, I came to tell you."

"How was Barlow?"

The coach turned into Neptune Street and then left into the Ratcliff Highway.

"I'm no doctor, but I've seen a fair number of injuries. This was a head wound, and he was conscious. At least, intermittently," he added. "His speech was rambling. All I could make out was your name, and 'my family.' He repeated it several times, though if he wanted them notified, he was not able to tell me where to find them."

"They live in the north. I do not know their direction. Once I've arranged for his care, I will send a messenger to my head clerk. I'm sure he knows."

Olivia interrupted Hawkins as he started to speak. "We have not turned into Virginia Street. Your driver has mistaken the way." She had been to the warehouse with her father many times. The most direct route was down Virginia to Artichoak Lane and then by Little Hermitage Street into Wapping.

"No, we must take another route. The narrow part of Little Hermitage was blocked by an overturned dray when we came. My man's familiar with this part of town. It will take a little longer, but not as long as waiting for the wagon and the barrels it spilled to be cleared away."

The coach rattled along the Ratcliff Highway at a good pace. She would arrange for Barlow to be moved to her house, if he could be moved. If the doctor advised against moving him…a bed would have to be brought in and suitable women hired to care for him. A warehouse was not a convenient place for an injured man to recuperate, yet it would somehow have to be made to work.

Hawkins did not disturb her meditations, except to rest his hand on hers where it lay on the seat between them. The coach turned. Good! They had not gone far out of their way; possibly a half mile. They would still have to go south and heaven knew through how many small streets, alleys, and yards their route might turn and twist.

The coach turned again, into a rutted street or lane, and she could not see a vestige of light. She hoped the coachman really did know where they were going. Most streets were at least dimly lighted by an occasional lamp standard. Besides, it was still early enough for homes and alehouses to be showing lights.

They pulled up suddenly, and Hawkins sprang out and let down the steps.

She moved to the door before realizing they could not have come far enough. The air was wrong; she smelled damp earth and the green scent of plants. The windows of a house glowed before her, the only lights visible. "Where are we?"

"Did I not mention I instructed the doctor to have Barlow moved to a house I own? He could hardly be nursed back to health in a warehouse. Here we are surrounded by market gardens and orchards."

"I thought to bring him to my house. My aunt could oversee a hired woman, and he is my responsibility."

"It would not be suitable to have him in your house. That you run a shipping company causes talk enough. I keep several servants here, so it will be no scandal or inconvenience to anyone."

She took his hand to let him assist her down, and froze, recalling something he had said when he came to the house. *Your clerk—Barlow?—is injured at one of your warehouses.*

"Mr. Hawkins, how did you know I had a warehouse?"

"Why, the fellow that was shouting for help mentioned it was yours—your warehouse, your clerk." He put his hands on either side of her waist and lifted her down.

But Hawkins had said "warehouses." Heart beating faster, she glanced around, hoping to see some other house. She descried a faint glow far off, most likely a candlelit room with a thinly curtained window. She could not judge its distance in the darkness, although she thought it was beyond a row of trees. Even if it had been closer, she could not run fast enough over unlit ground to escape. She could not outdistance Hawkins on even ground in broad daylight. A passerby might come to her rescue, but in one of the tracts of agricultural land that dotted the outskirts of London, there would be little traffic at night. If someone should happen by, it would most probably be one of the small farmers who lived in the area, and unwilling to confront a gentleman. Her best course was to comply—for now. Besides, the story might be true, except for how he had learned of its being her warehouse. Hawkins might well have been the one who had paid Munns for information about the Cantarell assets, if Captain Easterday was correct about that second transaction.

He kept an arm around her as he shepherded her to the door, which opened at their approach. A wooden-faced manservant said, "The medical gentleman's still upstairs, sir. In the yellow room."

"Good." He tossed his hat and gloves onto a side table before sweeping her cloak off and passing it to the man. "Come, let us see how the poor fellow is faring."

Engrossed in her thoughts, she formed no opinion of the entrance hall. He took her arm to escort her up the stair. The boards of the steps were well polished, the walls newly painted. The first floor passage confirmed her impression of excellent housekeeping. The hall runner was a good Oushak in madder red and indigo. She had seen dozens of similar carpets, though not all as fine. The doors of the half-dozen rooms were closed.

He opened the door on the left and ushered her into a bedchamber. A branch of candles cast enough light to show heavy golden yellow draperies and bed curtains and dark wood furniture, polished to a satin shine. The scents of rose potpourri and beeswax blended in the air.

Her first thought was how pleasant a sickroom it was, far better than the spare bedroom in her Well Close Square house. Then she realized the bed was empty. Even as she turned to face Hawkins, she heard the door close.

"Where is my clerk, Mr. Hawkins?" she asked, pleased to hear that her voice was level and did not shake.

"I have no idea, except that he must still be in

London, or you would never have believed my pretext for bringing you here."

"Then why have you brought me here under false pretenses?"

There was a decanter of wine and two glasses on a small table by a settee.

"You must know I love you, Olivia. But courting a lady is difficult when she seldom attends events where she can be enticed away from the crowd to further one's acquaintance. If the lady's papa were alive, an eligible suitor could apply to him for her hand in marriage. At your house, your aunt is always present, and at your offices, it would be awkward to conduct my courtship under the eyes of your clerks and boys."

"This is improper, Mr. Hawkins. It's…it's indecent. What would anyone say if they knew you had brought me here?" She knew, of course. It would be illuminating to hear how he responded.

"They would say I had compromised you and must marry you immediately. Which I am perfectly willing to do, and I don't think you are unwilling."

He stepped close and pulled her into his arms. She was too startled to resist. He smelled of spices and sweat and soap. "You can't deny that you liked it when I kissed you at Vauxhall Gardens. You wanted more. You're ripe for a man." He tilted her chin up and kissed her. His lips tasted of brandy. Her arms went around his neck of their own volition.

The trouble was, she was ready. As a young girl, she had had yearnings which she had never acknowledged. Later, she had ruthlessly suppressed them until they died, when she knew she could not abandon her father. Those desires had never had anything to feed upon until Hawkins invaded her life. She wanted…

No. She pulled back from the kiss, unwrapped her arms, and tried to push him away. He laughed softly and did not release her. "My sweet, I have a special license in my pocket. We'll marry tomorrow. Don't you think it's time for bed now?"

If it were not for what she now guessed of him, she would be tempted.

"I am not a loose woman," she said.

"You are a delightful woman."

Her usual businesslike manner would not serve. She hated to sound weak. *Think of it as a ruse de guerre, as the French call it.*

"I'm…I need some time to accustom myself. A woman's wedding and wedding night is precious. I suppose no man can understand how differently we regard these matters. Please take me home." She prayed she had chosen the right appeal.

He gazed down at her. She found it hard to meet his eyes and wished she did not feel like a small creature of the fields cowering before a hawk.

"I did not expect such conventionality from so daring a lady. Not one woman in a thousand would ever think of doing as you have done."

"Not one in a thousand is brought up in a shipping business. However, in spite of having assisted my father, I was reared to believe that a decent woman does not…does not…" Her voice shook a little. The limits of plain speaking had been reached here.

"Offer her virginity before her wedding night?" His voice sounded amused.

She nodded silently.

"I know you are a lady, Olivia, and you're passionate as well. You will make the perfect wife for a man like me. I can wait a little longer to please you. Shall we drink to our future?"

"If you wish, sir. Then will you take me home?"

"Ambrose."

"Ambrose." Had he noticed that she had not actually committed herself to anything?

He poured the wine. "You'll stay here tonight, my love. In the morning, we will go to a church I know, where the parson will oblige us."

"My aunt will be frantic with worry for me tonight," she protested.

"By now, she has received my message informing her that you feel it necessary to remain with Barlow to oversee his nursing by a poor but respectable family, and will return in the morning."

They sat together on the settee with their wine. Hawkins put his arm around her, which she permitted, as he showed no sign of renewing his attempt at seduction. She did not allow herself to lean against him; she was sure he would renew his dishonorable intentions at any encouragement. He seemed as willing to talk as to make love to her.

"I'll buy a house on one of the better squares. Your grandfather was a nobleman, and my people were gentry. Our birth forms no bar to moving in good society, and my fortune gives us the ability to do it. We will host a series of dinners, balls, and other entertainments. Organizing them will be child's play for you. You may wish to oversee our donations to a worthy charity or two. I give to a seamen's relief society, but ladies often interest themselves in the charities favored by the beau monde. Involvement in such charitable activities has a good appearance, and the charities appreciate the personal touch. You would be better at it than I."

He finished his wine; she had drunk only half of hers, fearful of lowering her inhibitions yet more. When he rose to leave, he said, "There is a key in the door if you feel inclined to use it. I'll send a maid up with water and to help you…ah, prepare for the night." She thought he had intentionally discarded another phrase, perhaps "prepare for bed"? Or "disrobe"? Nevertheless, she could see him thinking those words.

"Thank you." He bent to kiss her once more, putting his hands on her shoulders and kneading gently, and she was glad she had only sipped at the wine. She needed her inhibitions, which were fighting a desperate war with her body. As soon as he was out the door, she jumped up and turned the key in the lock, sighing with relief. Knowing what she did, she could not trust to his word.

She let the maid in when she tapped at the door and accepted her help in removing her stays, the only garment she could not manage unassisted. She had no nightgown but could sleep in her shift. She locked the door again after the girl left. Now there was only the morning to be faced.

****

"We might go direct to the church to be married." His tone was caressing.

She took her place in the coach and smoothed her skirts. "I must have my aunt at my wedding. She is all the family I have now."

"Well Close Square," he called up to the

coachman, sounding not the least put out.

Aunt Rachel's greeting was all that Olivia could have desired. She exclaimed, reproached, hugged Olivia, fluttered, and fussed. Before Rachel calmed enough for Hawkins to announce their forthcoming marriage, Olivia interrupted, "I must change my gown. I wish to look my best today." And she picked up her skirts and hurried upstairs.

"Livvie, dear, how unmannerly of you to leave Mr. Hawkins standing here…" her aunt called after her.

The sound of his voice carried up the stairway. "We might further our acquaintance while Mistress Olivia prinks, Mistress Williams."

A few minutes later, as she trod softly down the stairs, she heard fragments of speech in Rachel Williams's voice. "…so happy…I feared she would never…and so suitable, too!"

She was through the parlor door before they became aware of her. She stepped away from it and moved to the side of the room farthest from Hawkins. He sat in her father's armchair, and her aunt was seated on the rather spindly settee, as she had expected. She had not supposed Hawkins would trust himself to the settee.

"We are not going to be wed, Aunt."

"Not…? But—"

Hawkins rose. "My dear, you spent last night in my house. Mistress Williams, I beg your pardon, but I must say it. Olivia, the liberties you allowed me make it impossible for you to change your mind now."

"I have not changed my mind. If you will recall, sir, I never agreed to marry you. You assumed my agreement, and I let you do so, as I feared that if I did not, you would force yourself upon me."

"It wouldn't have taken much force," he murmured. Olivia trusted that her aunt, weeping into her handkerchief, had failed to hear his comment.

"Please leave now."

He took a step toward her, smiling, then froze in midstride as her right hand, previously concealed behind a fold of her petticoat, came up holding a pistol. Hawkins laughed ruefully. "I see you have my measure. But you can't carry a flintlock pointing downward without the powder leaking out. I assume you did load it."

"As you can see, Mr. Hawkins, this is a pocket pistol. It would be no use against footpads if the powder did not remain in place when carried in a pocket. And I did indeed load it."

He laughed with real enjoyment.

"Olivia, you are the first woman I have ever wanted to marry. In my eagerness to win you, I acted too hastily. A lady wants more courtship, I suppose, but you are a sensible woman, too. We have much in common. I am convinced that we'll deal exceeding well together."

"Please leave now." She thought of saying, "It's my property you want, not me," so that he would understand that she was not deceived about his motive for courtship. She rejected the idea as it occurred to her: her aunt was present and might hear—the sight of the pistol had stunned her into silence and immobility. Also, Jonas Cantarell had not been in the habit of giving out information unless it was necessary. Let Hawkins think he still had a chance of winning her hand. It would keep him from taking some other action to force her into marriage.

But oh, it would have been pleasant to think he valued her for herself alone. Even now, she could not help thinking of his arms around her, his kisses, and what they might have done in that very comfortable bed.

Hawkins bowed to her and to her aunt. "Ladies, if you will excuse me I had better take my leave."

Keeping a safe distance, she followed him to the door.

"You will understand, Mr. Hawkins, that I have no desire to see you again. Should we meet at some social event, I will be civil."

"Is that not a somewhat harsh punishment for a suitor who was swept away on the tide of his passion?" He smiled, inviting her to be amused at the overblown sentiment.

"It might be, for a stolen kiss. For abduction with the intent to force me into marriage? I think not. I no longer trust you, though I do give you some credit for not having actually raped me."

"Please accept my apologies. My only excuse, apart from my eagerness to make you my own, is that I have had little experience of the conventions of polite society since I ran away from home as a boy. I've become coarsened by my business and associates. I think I could be civilized by the right lady."

Truth and an appeal to her sympathy were so entwined in his speech that Olivia could not guess whether he were sincere or only attempting to manipulate her. "What you say may be true, sir, but I am not the lady."

"Yet I will continue to hope that you will forgive

me." He bowed and opened the door. When it had closed, Olivia threw the bolt with her free hand. She drew a deep breath. She had liked Hawkins. His kisses...she would not think of them. To toss away her independence, her inheritance, and worse, her real self, for physical gratification would be foolish. She really could not live with nothing better to do than act as her husband's hostess and the mother of his children. There was nothing wrong with such a life, but it was not for her. If it were possible to be a wife and mother and run her business, it would be different. After all, the wives of tradesmen and small merchants often took part in the family business. If it were possible with Hawkins, she would be tempted to accept his offer. The problem was, it wouldn't be possible. She could not trust him. She would never know whether he had courted her for herself or her fortune though she would like to believe he found her attractive.

"Oh, Livvie, how could you?"

"He abducted me. The story about Barlow being hurt was a lie."

"It was very naughty of him, but you like him, dear, and he is rich and almost handsome and a gentleman, and you could have a lovely house and children, and he would take all your cares upon himself. How could you refuse? To point a pistol at him, too! It was very wrong of you."

"He may appear to be a gentleman, but it seemed quite possible that he would simply pick me up and carry me out of the house. If he ravished me..." Would she feel obligated to marry him? Conventional wisdom would insist upon it. If she found herself with child as a result...she did not know. It would be unfair to the innocent child to raise it a bastard. It would be unfair to her to bind herself to a man lacking in character and decency, however charming. And she had no experience of babies and small children. Would she put its interests before her own? For that matter, would its interests be served by being raised as the child of a man like Hawkins? The words of her father's acquaintance came back to her. "For all he looks and talks like a gentleman, he has the heart of a pirate. There's been men hanged at Execution Dock I'd've trusted sooner."

She sighed. Aunt Rachel was correct; she had liked Hawkins, and she was powerfully attracted to him. But she would not marry if she could not trust. If he loved her...but there was no way to know. *Be honest with yourself. Munns sold information twice, only days apart. The second time was certainly to Hawkins, or he would not have known I owned warehouses. The first time almost certainly was, too, given that he was connected to Hart and Noakes, if only tenuously. But the real proof is that while Hawkins knows about my other holdings, it's not common knowledge, because if it were, there would be other men courting me. That is the way of the world.*

In his favor, he had taken her refusal well. What would he do next? That bore careful thought and additional precautions.

## Chapter 26

It cost him a battle with his conscience, or at least some part of himself, to go to Hawkins, but it was better than Olivia herself applying to the man for help.

He took a deep breath of Wapping's pitch- and tar-scented air. The weathered wooden building was what he had expected. It contrasted strangely with the freshly painted sign with "Hawkins & Co." picked out in gilt. The outer office contained half a dozen desks and stools occupied by clerks, and a straight chair on which a burly, crop-headed fellow lounged, bored. Easterday was escorted up to Hawkins's office without argument.

When the clerk tapped on a door and announced him, there was a noticeable pause before Hawkins called, "Come in."

Easterday found him standing beside his desk, his face unreadable. "Easterday."

"Hawkins. I felt a need to repay your visit."

"Oh?" Warily. "Be seated."

Easterday took the armchair in front of the desk, and Hawkins dropped into his desk chair.

There was no ostentation here. It was nearly as bleak as the clerks' room, except that the walls that did not contain windows or bookshelves held what must be mementos of travels or interests: an ornate curved dagger, a carved and brightly painted mask of some sort of demon, a scroll painting of an unnaturally precipitous mountain. The latter, he thought, was Chinese. Did China really possess such features or was it artistic license?

"Is this a social call?" Amused disbelief.

"No."

"What, then?"

"I need advice, and it seemed to me that you might have resources I lack."

Hawkins said, "If you need my resources, you must have a plaguey difficult problem."

"I believe it's not difficult, as much as simply out of my usual sphere."

"Tell me."

"There is a young man, not yet one-and-twenty, who stands to inherit a manor and a small fortune if his uncle does not become his guardian. I have made inquiries about his uncle—discreet ones. The man is in need of funds. The usual trouble—living beyond his means."

Hawkins shrugged. "If the uncle was named as his guardian—"

"He wasn't. An attorney in Scotland is. Unfortunately, the young man is here—"

"And if the uncle hauls him before a friendly magistrate or one willing to accept a gift in return for a favorable decision—as some do—he would find it easy enough to gain the guardianship? Very likely. Is there no other relative at hand to contest it?"

"No."

"How do you come into it, Easterday?"

"One of my clerks is a friend of his."

Hawkins had been toying with a small stone block with an odd-looking dog carved on its top. Easterday recognized it as a Chinese stamp seal. This one looked like jade.

His hand stilled, and he set the seal down. "It's only for the boy to ship out on a long voyage. Surely your clerk could manage that much."

"There are complications, Hawkins. The heir has younger siblings in Scotland for whom he feels responsible, though they are living with a family friend. However, the main problem is that an agent or agents of the uncle have been keeping the place where the heir was working under surveillance. A runner for the company was snatched off the street and questioned. I would like to provide a trail for the watcher to follow that will lead him away. It must be convincing enough to keep him from coming back. I don't have the expertise or connections to make it persuasive. I think you do."

"The easiest way to solve the problem would be to kill the uncle." Hawkins smiled thinly.

"I don't regard murder as an option."

"No, I agree. I prefer to avoid that kind of risk. Why have you come to me? I suppose the owner of whatever company he worked for dismissed him. Dismissing the fellow would solve the problem instantly—for the company." Hawkins was playing with the seal again.

Easterday was aware that his answer had not come quickly enough when Hawkins laughed softly. "It's Barlow, isn't it? He sounded like a Scot, the time I visited the Cantarell office. And your clerk is Finley, and both of them employed by Olivia Cantarell."

"Yes."

"I'll put an end to the problem before it comes to

Mistress Olivia's attention. Or—rot my guts!—before the uncle's man approaches her."

"Mistress Olivia already knows."

"How did she find out?" Hawkins demanded.

"Finley told her. One of the boys saw the watcher following Barlow when he left for the day, and Finley sent the messenger after him, directing him to do an errand on his way, and use a different exit when he left."

"Your clerk takes a great deal upon himself."

"He reported the matter immediately to Mistress Olivia. She did not disapprove of his action and made arrangements for Barlow to lie concealed."

"Where?"

"I don't know. Before you ask, neither does Finley. She sent a message to Barlow with instructions."

Hawkins growled deep in his throat. "She shouldn't be involved." Then he laughed again. "It's a farce." He did not explain but went on, "What of Barlow? He'll need to be sent away."

"Once the hunt is diverted, I can arrange for Barlow's passage to Scotland. And I've lent her another clerk."

"Running a shipping company is no work for a woman," Hawkins said.

"I agree. Yet if she were a man, I believe she would be better at it than old Cantarell was. She knows the business. Her decisiveness and quickness of mind are impressive. You've spent some time with her—haven't you seen it?"

Hawkins grinned savagely. He was in an odd humor. "I've seen she is a lady. We have not discussed the shipping industry."

"Perhaps you should."

Hawkins waved this away. "If we need only to divert the search long enough for Barlow to be packed off to Scotland—are we agreed his uncle will not try to drag him back to England from there?"

"It seems unlikely."

"Then why the devil didn't he stay there?"

"The family's finances are awkwardly left. His younger brothers and sisters are living on the interest from investments that were left them by their mother. Barlow inherits the small manor, but it has been ill managed and what income it produces must either go to needed expenses there or to the siblings, to augment their income. He could not find a position in Scotland. He thought it safe to find work here under an assumed name, not realizing how desperate his uncle's situation had become."

"Bad, is it?"

"His property is on the brink of foreclosure, and there are other debts."

Hawkins poured two glasses of claret from the decanter on his desk and offered one to Easterday. "I can draw off the uncle's hirelings. If he needs work in Scotland...that may be more difficult. I have no contacts there."

"Mistress Cantarell has business connections in Scotland. She can find him a post in Leith or Glasgow, or one of the other ports."

Hawkins raised his glass in an ironic salute, which Easterday returned. They drank.

"I do not like Olivia being involved in this," Hawkins said.

Easterday raised his brows at the familiarity.

Seeing it, his host said, "I have hopes that she will accept my offer of marriage."

"Really?"

"You need not look surprised. I'm not ineligible, and the marriage would benefit both of us. She needs a husband to manage her business. I want a well-bred wife who can be my hostess when I entertain. I could probably get a girl from some titled family. You know the sort: blue blood back to the Conqueror, but no money. The thing is, her family would likely expect me to pay their debts and support them and look down on me while I did it. I'll not be preyed upon." He tossed off the last of his claret and said, "I should get on with planting a false trail for Barlow."

"How will you do it?"

Hawkins frowned at him. "If you're interested, you might come along. You're not dressed so fine you'll look out of place. And you'll be with me."

Neither was Hawkins dressed richly, he noted. Evidently he saved his fashionable clothing for social events. Today, he looked suited to his shabby office, for his coat and waistcoat were subdued in color and cut. It made sense to wear something plain and serviceable if one meant to visit a ship or warehouse. He wore his hair in a short plait, which seemed odd. On the other hand, if one often went aboard ship, a wig was inconvenient and one's own hair blew around in the wind, unless heavily pomaded.

They went downriver by wherry, disembarking at Shadwell Dock Stairs. The tavern on Labour in Vain Street had a damnably unwholesome air, and if the men lounging outside practiced any lawful trade, Easterday was Archbishop of Canterbury. The group parted for

Hawkins, and one of them muttered something.

Hawkins responded with something that sounded like "Bean light man," whatever that meant.

"Bean light?" Some sort of password, mayhap. The door closed behind them.

"Bene lightmans. It means 'good day.' Criminal cant."

While it was not reassuring to find Hawkins familiar with criminals and their jargon, it was not surprising. What else was to be expected of a man reputed to have been a pirate? Hawkins stalked through the dim room, past tables and benches wreathed in smoke from many pipes, the reek of spilled drink, and the sour smell of sweat and unwashed clothes. Easterday had visited many similar taverns in his seafaring days. Hawkins gave a jerk of his head toward a door at the back, a gesture evidently intended for the man drawing pints of ale. The dash nodded.

Beyond the door were three other doors, one to the right, likely to an alley or yard, an open one to the left, revealing a kitchen, and one straight ahead, which was closed. A ruffian leaned against the wall beside it. He gave a brief nod to Hawkins and stared flatly at Easterday.

"I'll vouch for him."

The bully knocked on the door: three quick, then two slow raps. A harsh voice called out something indistinguishable to Easterday's ears, and Hawkins pushed open the door and entered.

*It feels like the first time I set foot in a foreign port.* The nervous tension, the need to observe without being obvious about it. The language he couldn't understand. The foreign customs. The crawling sense of potential danger.

The room was little larger than his brother's dressing room at Lowfields Manor but contained only an old desk and two straight chairs. A thin man sat behind the desk and dominated the space. He had sharp hazel eyes and russet hair that hung loose. His appearance might have been sinister, but the effect was rather spoiled by his canary-yellow silk coat and grass-green watered-silk waistcoat. Though obviously expensive originally, both had seen hard use, and the plentiful gold lacing on the coat was tarnished. Purchased at second- or third-hand, no doubt. His neckcloth was clean, the plain cuffs of his shirt no more than slightly soiled. The ruffles at the cuffs worn by gentlemen of leisure required a valet's constant care and were a disadvantage if one needed to draw a sword or knife quickly.

"It's been a long time, Hawkins. Who's your friend?"

"Captain Easterday. You'll have heard of him. Easterday, this is John Barlicorn."

Barlicorn saw something in his face, for he laughed, revealing slightly crooked teeth. "My father never heard a song but in church. He'd like to have stopped his ears before passing a ballad singer in the street, like one of the old Greeks avoiding the Sirens' song. I cap downright he'd'a burned any broadside ballad that came his way. Snares o' the Black-Spy, like anything else that might give pleasure. Sit, both of you. What brings you here?"

Hawkins explained, briefly and unemotionally.

"To make it work, you need a body. No use passing word that the cove has signed aboard 'less someone goes aboard and stays there."

"When you say 'a body,' Barlicorn…"

"Rot me, I don't mean backed."

"Dead," Hawkins translated.

"Nay, where's the profit in that? You want a cull that needs to get away from these fair shores under a new name and will pay for the privilege. Or who can't pay but has someone who'll buy his passage for him. He had best look like yours and dress like him, too. He'll go aboard as close to sailing as possible but make sure to be seen doing it. If there's a thieftaker or anyone else looking for him, they'll come 'round asking and learn he's away." Barlicorn opened a drawer and sorted through it, until he found half a sheet of dog-eared, grubby paper and a pencil. He pushed them across the desk to Easterday. "Write out his features. Color of hair, whether he's ruddy, pale, or swarthy, how high he stands, is he fat or a starveling. How does he dress? Ah, and how does he speak? Like a cockney or a rum-cove? West Country yokel? Gentleman?"

Easterday paused in noting Barlow's description. "He has a slight Scots burr."

"Better if our cove says little before sailing, then, and tries to disguise his voice, to make it seem he's hiding his way of speaking."

Easterday passed him the description he had written. John Barlicorn looked it over, nodded, and said, "Fifty pounds and I'll have no trouble filling your order."

"You charge both sides of the transaction?"

"No. There's only one side, 'less I stumble on someone who's the right appearance for your purpose and has got money. Like as not, the right man won't be able to afford to pay, as most men who need to flee seldom have fat purses. Someone must pay for the passage and here, it'll have to be you."

Hawkins reached into the deep pocket of his coat, drew out two pouches, and set them on the desk. Barlicorn dropped them into his own pocket. "Thank'ee."

"It's my place to pay, Hawkins." He had not come provided with so much money, not having realized the task would be accomplished in one visit. "I will repay you."

"The fellow's no more your man than mine, and I am glad to do a service for a…friend." Olivia Cantarell, in other words. "Besides, I still owe you something for the favor you did me."

They both noticed at the same time that Barlicorn was looking on in amusement. He said, "I'll send word when I've got someone and the right ship ready to sail. Best if I send to you, Hawkins, meaning no offense to you, Captain, but my messenger would stand out more at your office."

The man was right, Easterday admitted. A ruffianly looking fellow would be far less conspicuous at Hawkins's office. He already had a pack of them hanging around.

"An interesting fellow," Easterday remarked, as they waited on Shadwell Dock Stairs. "At times, he speaks like a gentleman."

"All sorts are drawn to London, hoping to thrive."

"You trust him."

"I've had dealings with him before. He's never choused me."

"He didn't bother to count your money."

"I've never choused him." They dodged around a pair of copulating dogs. "Neither of us wants a fight with the other. Why would we? We're not in the same trade."

Hawkins left the wherry at King Edward's Stairs, the nearest to his offices in Cinnamon Street. Easterday continued upriver. At Cantarell Shipping, he found both Finley and Olivia in the front office. When he came in, she looked up from the document she had been studying. Her face was composed, but a tightness around her mouth betokened anxiety.

"Have you had any success, Captain Easterday?"

"There is a distraction set in motion to decoy the search to sea. It should then be possible to get Barlow back to his native ground. It's now merely a question of waiting to hear that the fellow who will impersonate him has sailed." He smiled to reassure her the matter was no great thing and taken care of. He should mention Hawkins's involvement. To let her think he had managed it all himself was to be guilty of a lie, and Olivia Cantarell was the last person in the world he wanted to deceive. He opened his mouth to admit that it was Hawkins's doing.

No, by God! He was willing to agree that Markham's opinion of Hawkins was reasonable, and that Hawkins might even be a suitable husband for Olivia, but he was damned if he would further his suit. She could do better in choosing a husband than a man who would not value her for her real worth. Whatever Olivia's inheritance actually was, Hawkins didn't need it. To give Hawkins his due, Easterday thought Olivia's elegance, her family connections, and artistic taste were what had captivated Hawkins. Two out of three of those factors could be found elsewhere, in some lady of the beau monde who wanted nothing more than marriage to a rich man.

Instead he said, "Either you or I can probably find him work in Scotland."

Chapter 27

"Thank goodness. And thank you, Captain." She savored the relief for a moment before saying, "There must be costs involved in this. The man who is arranging it cannot be doing it without pay. Not in the Pool of London."

Easterday glanced around the office, coming to rest on Finley, who was writing out a bill of lading, the first time he had looked away from her more than momentarily. "He charges fifty pounds to a man who needs to leave the country, though in this case, we'll be paying it. 'Twould be a great expense to a poor man, but no great matter to you or me. Time enough then to discuss the details when he finds a suitable imposter."

How oddly unbusinesslike. "I wish...no matter, I accept that I could not have been present for a number of reasons. The thieftaker might have followed me, and I suppose your friend who is arranging it, who sounds as if he must be a criminal of some sort, would not have dealt with me."

"Not a friend, ma'am. Merely someone I was told could arrange matters."

"I beg your pardon, Captain. I did not mean to imply you associate with criminals." Of course he wouldn't. Everyone knew Marcus Easterday was a man of unbending honesty. Unlike Ambrose Hawkins. "I'm sorry you should have had to deal with this."

He laughed wryly. "No offense taken, ma'am. If he's not an unhanged felon, he must at least be on the fringes of that world. And no, he would not have dealt with you, I suspect, and you certainly could not have gone to the place he conducts business. You'd have found him amusing, however."

"Would I?"

"I did. He was a very engaging rogue, who seemed almost a gentleman, except for his taste in coats and waistcoats. Not that canary yellow and bright green are worse than the purple and turquoise blue I encountered in St. James Square a few days ago. "

"Oh, dear! Yellow and green would definitely be preferable. Well, I'm particularly grateful to you, as it can't have been the sort of business you are accustomed to."

"It wasn't, but I found it very interesting and learned a great deal."

"Such as?"

"I now know that the verb 'chouse' means 'to cheat.' "

"Is there any risk of that?"

"I've been told Barlicorn is reliable. I'd trust him before Noakes. Or before one or two of my customers."

"Or Barlow's uncle. Very well. While we await word, there is a minor detail to attend to. Barlow needs clothing, as he came away from his lodgings with no more than a spare handkerchief, neckcloth, pair of stockings, and a razor in his pockets. Both for whatever period he must hide and his return to Scotland, he must have changes of linen and another suit or two."

"It would be unwise to try to get his belongings from his lodging."

"I don't intend to try. But he might write a letter to his landlady that he was likely to be away for a month on business, promising to have rent delivered for the weeks not yet paid for."

"Or perhaps asking her to store his belongings, mentioning he expected to be absent for several months and would send someone to collect them. He could send a coin under the seal for her trouble. If someone came asking for him she might divulge his plans, which would direct any pursuer's attention to the coaching inns, livery stables, and port. That might be useful."

"Oh, very clever! Would you see to getting some second-hand clothing for him?" And she would supply a coin to secure the lodging keeper's cooperation.

"Is it wise to risk visiting him? You might be followed. It would be better to have someone unrelated to you or Cantarell Shipping manage it."

"Then that someone would know where he is concealed. No, Captain, I can do it in such a way that there will be nothing to lead the wicked uncle to my clerk. Do you wish to consult with your estimable rogue about the wisdom of Barlow's writing to the landlady? Lest it should attract the thieftaker's attention too early?"

"A very good idea. Timing will be important."

"We should also think how we are to get Barlow back to Scotland. He is safe and reasonably comfortable where he is, but the confinement will soon grow wearisome for an active young man."

"I agree, and I have given it some thought. I own two colliers that bring coal from Newcastle. My first notion was having him go aboard dressed as a common seaman. One usually carries a crew of sixteen, the other of twenty, so an extra man would not stand out."

"It sounds like a sensible plan."

"Except for the risk that the Impress Service would take him up. The press gangs often take men from the colliers. Barlow would not want to make a career of the Royal Navy."

"I should think not!"

"They've never impressed a gentleman, so far as I am aware. The Impress Service is supposed to take men of seafaring habits—or who at least seem likely to know one end of a boat from the other and don't have powerful friends. If he goes aboard dressed as a gentleman for the purpose of delivering bills of exchange to one of my commercial associates in Newcastle, he would be safe."

"But travelling aboard a coal-hauling vessel? Surely it would seem odd to anyone who heard of it."

"Ah, but you have not considered the risks of travel, Mistress Olivia. Going by coach with its potential for accidents, highwaymen, and loss of the documents by theft or fire at an inn would be far more hazardous. Colliers may be filthy, uncomfortable vessels, but they are also sturdy and stable, as they have to be. They travel in convoys for protection against pirates and privateers…though that's more of a danger when they're full of coal."

She laughed at his whimsical tone. "There would be little gain in capturing an empty collier. The only problem I see is that Newcastle, not being in Scotland, would mean Barlow would still have to reach the border by another means."

"I'll send him to my agent in Newcastle with a letter of instructions. He will see to getting Barlow into

Scotland. On a fishing boat, or disguised as a wagonload of neeps or a vicar. Some method will present itself."

How comfortable it was to deal with Marcus Easterday. He was a gentleman as well as a man of business, and he dealt with her as if she were the same. Or not exactly that, but as if a woman had the right to conduct her own business. If more men were like him, marriage would be an attractive prospect, though she would still be an old maid. Unfortunately, Easterday was unique in her experience.

Enough of that! The necessary arrangements were made, or at least planned for. Should she have mentioned the problem with Hawkins? She bit her lip. It had crossed her mind, but the severance of her relationship with Hawkins—whatever that had been!— had nothing to do with Easterday. Now she was glad she had instinctively kept silent. First, the incident made her sound like a weak woman, pleading for protection. Unthinkable! Second, confiding in Easterday might make trouble between him and Hawkins, which would be awkward if they did business together. Third, what if Easterday felt impelled to challenge Hawkins to a duel? Easterday might be killed or seriously wounded. Nor did she like the idea of Hawkins injured or dying for his ill-fated attempt. Keeping her own counsel was definitely the wisest choice. Though surely a sensible man like Easterday would not involve himself in such a foolish activity as dueling.

Chapter 28

He penetrated to Barlicorn's office in the Saracen Queen, though he thought the men eyed him suspiciously. The guard at the office door gave a different knock this time, and the voice called, "Who?"

"Capting Easterday."

"He's welcome in."

All that had changed, to Easterday's eye, was Barlicorn's dress, which today consisted of a coat and breeches of crimson velvet with a waistcoat of purple brocade. The man waved him to a chair.

"I did not expect to see you again, Captain. Thought you were fair struck speechless to find yourself in such a place."

"I've been in worse, when I was sailing."

"Ah, I suppose you have, at that. What can I do for you?"

"There are some arrangements to be made to secure Barlow's belongings until they can be sent on to his new home. I thought to ask the keeper of his lodging to store them as he is going to be gone for months, making a voyage. It might be unwise to send such a message until the decoy's ready to sail, however, to avoid attracting his pursuer's attention too soon to vessels bound for distant ports."

"That's well thought on but send a day or two after sailing." Barlicorn's crooked-toothed grin flashed. He had all of his visible teeth, and they were white, not yellow or dark with rot. "It depends on whether his rent comes due before that date, in which case, the landlady might sell it all the next day, or whether someone's approached her already, offering her money if she passes on anything she hears of her tenant."

"He paid the rent a month in advance the very morning he went into hiding. There's no saying if the woman would keep mum about the message."

"Foolish to expect it. A cove or mort might not peach on a family member or friend, but chances are, he's no one to her. Nothing but a chance to earn a shilling when life's hard for most. Wait until after sailing. I'll send word to Hawkins."

Easterday cleared his throat. "Would you send me a message as well, for a consideration? My employees will survive seeing a rough fellow in the office."

Barlicorn stared at him, sharp-eyed. "You don't trust Hawkins?"

"I do. But he's a busy man, and the matter is closer to my interests than to his."

"I'll send to both of you, then. No additional fee."

"Thank you."

Barlicorn stared at the scarred surface of the desk. "Hawkins would never worry about his possessions if he had to shab off, excepting whatever pieces of art he was able to take with him. I'm told he has some very fine jade and porcelain. Clothing and the like, he'd replace. Someone who'd likely not have the gelt to buy another suit or neckcloth may be glad of a friend to think of saving his things. Most especially if there's anything of sentimental value."

Easterday supposed his expression revealed

surprise. He would not expect a man like Barlicorn to think of such things.

The rogue made a wry face. "It's easy to keep your possessions if you live in Hanover Square. In lodgings, sleeping in the open, or hunted like a fox, you lose things. A favorite book or an heirloom or some cherished trinket."

Was he seeing Barlicorn as the man actually was, underneath the tawdry clothing and the rabble's vocabulary, which he had forgotten to use? "You are not a London man, I think?"

"No. Like thousands of others, I came here to make my fortune. London's been good to me, but sometimes I wish—well, never mind! I believe I've a lad that will do to act Barlow's part, the more since he's of decent birth and looks it. Got himself into some trouble and wants to be away 'til it's forgotten. It's an extreme remedy, but a better choice than he realizes yet. Shipping out as a common sailor will either kill him or make a man of him."

"Thank you, Barlicorn." He rose to go.

The archrogue stood and followed him out of the office. As they came to the door, Barlicorn clapped him on the shoulder and said loud enough for the drinkers nearby to hear, "I'm to be found at Job's Coffee House in St. Clement's Lane, Lombard Street, at the sign of the Grieving Man, on Tuesdays and Thursdays. Some find it more convenient to meet with me there."

It was a signal of some sort. He wondered what, until the hulking fellow at the door growled, "Bene lightmans."

Easterday found himself returning the greeting and concluded that he was now an accepted acquaintance of

Barlicorn. *Flattering!*

\*\*\*\*

"Ah…Captain?" his most junior clerk murmured, around the edge of the door.

"What is it, Yates?"

"There's a fellow here demanding to see you."

Easterday raised his eyebrows. This might be the message he had been awaiting. "What sort of fellow?"

"Rough, sir. He looks a proper scurvy sailor—on a pirate ship, mayhap."

"Show him in."

"Meaning no disrespect, Captain, but are you sure it's safe?"

"I've been expecting a message. I knew the man bringing it was like to be somewhat unpolished."

Yates suppressed a snort.

The man who shambled in did indeed look the veriest wharf rat, in spite of having obviously tidied himself, for he was almost freshly shaven. Although his loose breeches were ragged at the lower ends, his short jacket was open over a shirt which could not have been worn above a day or two.

"Capting," he said, ducking his head. But he said nothing further until Yates closed the door.

"You come from—"

"Ay, Capting, from his lordship." The man gave a gap-toothed grin. The last words had been spoken with respect. A nickname for Barlicorn; possibly to his men he seemed like an aristocrat, with his secondhand finery and sometimes refined speech.

"And?"

"The ship sails the day after tomorrow. The cove'll board tomorrow night."

"Very good. My compliments to…his lordship." He fished a coin out of his pocket and tossed it to the man, who caught it one-handed, grinning, and was out the door a second later.

Olivia would be pleased.

Chapter 29

At day's end, Olivia was pleased. One of their own shipments had finally landed, consisting of fine Chinese porcelain dishes and vases and jade exquisitely carved into desk accoutrements: little bowls for brush washing, flat plates to hold ink, brush holders, stamp seals in various shapes, and snuff bottles. Lovely things. More important, Captain Easterday had called on her with news of their decoy sailing. Tomorrow would be soon enough to write the landlady about Barlow's possessions.

Aunt Rachel called to her from the parlor as she was removing her cape and hat in the entry.

"Olivia, Mr. Nevis has paid us a call. Do come in."

Her aunt's roguish admirer from their visit to Vauxhall Gardens was indeed present. While Olivia made her curtsey and inquired after his health, Rachel poured her a cup of tea and put a piece of gingerbread, a Savoy biscuit, and several ratafia drops on a plate for her. The bohea was no longer quite hot, which mattered little, as she had learned from Ah Fong to drink tea without milk.

"I know you are always famished when you return from your...er...errands, dear." She offered more treats to Nevis, who accepted gingerbread with a smile and a word of thanks. *How much better the food is, on an increased household budget. How much younger and more sprightly my aunt is, entertaining a gentleman.* What else had she overlooked in the last ten or fifteen years?

"Mistress Olivia, I came today to invite you and Mistress Williams to accompany me to a masquerade ball at the Opera House at the Haymarket on Saturday week. Only a domino and mask are necessary. But your aunt would not agree without your acceptance, of course."

At Aunt Rachel's age, no one would accuse her of impropriety if she attended a social event with an equally elderly gentleman—Elderly? Rachel Williams had lost her husband early, and she had been much younger than her brother, half a dozen brothers and sisters having come between their births. She was no more than fifteen years older than Olivia, if as much. Giles Nevis was probably not above fifty. *Lud!*

Given the events orchestrated by Ambrose Hawkins at Vauxhall Gardens, she did not want to trust herself to one of Hawkins's minions. Seeing her aunt's hopeful expression, however, she could not refuse to go. Hawkins could hardly carry her off from a Haymarket assembly. Besides, Nevis might be cultivating Rachel on his own account.

"How delightful! We must certainly go." She put as much sincerity into her voice as she could, though it sounded a little forced to her own ears. Her aunt and Nevis seemed not to notice.

Soon after, Mr. Nevis excused himself.

"I wish we might have invited him to stay to supper tonight, or better yet, before leaving for the masquerade, if it were not thoroughly improper to entertain a single gentleman with no host present."

"We might invite three other guests to dinner some time," Olivia ventured, thinking how much her aunt would enjoy it.

"We could invite Mr. Hawkins and Captain Easterday, but what other lady could we include? Too, we would still not have a host, which makes it impossible."

"We could not invite Mr. Hawkins, Aunt. Have you forgotten that he tried to compromise me?"

"One must make some allowance for a suitor's ardor, Livvie, as he was urgent to marry you. It sounded quite romantic."

"Nevertheless, Mr. Hawkins and I are no longer on visiting terms." She added, "I am perfectly ready to further Mr. Nevis's courtship, if you wish." Though it might be advisable to inquire into the former captain's finances, morals, and general behavior before Rachel became too fond of him. Mayhap Captain Easterday could learn something of his history. Better yet, she could make sure her aunt's swain knew that Rachel Williams was all but penniless. That knowledge would separate the sheep from the goats. Was that the saying? Frowning a little, she wondered what the sheep and goats would be doing together in the first place. Surely they would not be in the same field?

"Is something wrong, dear?"

"No, not at all. I was simply thinking that we must obtain dominos and masks."

"If you will trust me to choose one for you, I will get them. What will you wear? The color of the gown and domino should not fight."

"Even though the domino will cover it? I suppose I will wear the green."

"Not again, Livvie! You wore that old thing to the assembly."

"But if it's covered…"

"Even so. What of the amber sacque gown? It is years out of date, but 'twill be concealed by the domino except for a little of the skirt. I suppose the trimming might be changed to make it more à la mode."

"Very well, I rely upon you to take care of it." She laughed.

"May I draw upon the housekeeping money?"

"Have the bill sent. Go to that milliner you like in the Long Walk. It's likely we need a few other things as well."

"Stockings." Aunt Rachel sighed blissfully. "With embroidered clocks, for both of us. I will see if she has any pretty caps, as well. "

****

Captain Easterday brought with him a sea chest and reported that the ship bearing Barlow's impostor had sailed.

"I'm sure you can arrange for this to be shipped." The corners of his mouth barely turned up, but he was teasing her. "To Barlow," he added softly. "Two decent suits of clothing with shirts, neckcloths, and accessories. I'll send word when it's time to take him to my collier. Bring him to me, and I'll get him aboard."

"Thank you, Captain. That will do very well."

"Now, you'll have somewhere to store this until it's ready to go?"

Davant, emerging from the back where he had been giving Kit and Ky a lesson, offered, "I will carry it upstairs, sir."

"No, don't interrupt your work. I'm not so old I

can't carry it."

She led him upstairs, past the first floor, to the upper story. "If you will set it here, I'll see to their disposition."

He lowered it to the floor where she had indicated. She would have Barlow fetch the chest through the connecting door later, as she was tolerably sure she did not want to try lifting it herself. Marcus Easterday possessed an appearance of strength without being brawny. He was a very graceful dancer, too.

Instead of turning back to the stairway at once, Easterday said, "It is not often one can speak privately with a lady unless she is a family member or one's wife. Sometimes one wishes to say something that could not be uttered before a third party."

"Oh!" Considerably disconcerted, she could not think how to respond. She was not a girl straight from the schoolroom to flee from...well, from whatever Captain Easterday meant to say.

"I don't wish to embarrass or frighten you, ma'am, and it will only take a moment, if you will but hear me out."

"I am neither, sir. After all, we have been fellow conspirators."

"Here, then. You must know that Ambrose Hawkins is attracted to you. He speaks of you with the greatest admiration..."

"Captain, you cannot mean to further Mr. Hawkins's cause?"

"No! No, on the contrary, though I mean to be fair. He does have much to recommend him. He is successful, well-read in the subjects that interest him, he has an appreciation of the arts, a sense of humor, and

I suppose a lady would find him attractive."

"I was unaware you were so well acquainted. In fact, I thought you did not get along."

"I only recently came to know Hawkins better. Previously, I judged him by his business practices and the rumor that he had been a pirate. I've since heard that he was taken from a merchantman after its capture and forced into service on a pirate vessel. It's said he made his escape the first time it made landfall, taking his fellow conscripts with him, after damaging the ship enough to prevent its sailing. Before the crew could complete repairs, Hawkins led a party from the nearest village—this took place in the West Indies—back to capture the crew and ship." Easterday paused. "Forgive me for trespassing on personal matters, but in spite of being an admirable fellow in his way, he is not the right man for you. I hope I do not give offense."

"Not at all. I have already stopped his sending his coach. May I ask the reason you think him unsuitable?" It would be interesting to see if their reasons were the same. Although Captain Easterday could hardly be aware of her abduction.

"He does not admire you for your business sense and courage in pursuing a career most would consider unthinkable for a lady."

"Most? I doubt anyone but myself thinks it suitable."

He smiled. "I may not think it precisely appropriate, but it would certainly be a pity to waste your talents. Hawkins wants a wife who will earn him acceptance in good society."

"I know. That is one of the reasons I have broken off contact with Mr. Hawkins. May I ask you how you came to be on friendly terms with him?"

Easterday did not blush. Even after years ashore in England, he had not lost all of the sun bronze he must have gained on shipboard. He did look as if he might be blushing, however.

"It's hardly something I like to tell a lady— although it's nothing indecent," he added hurriedly. "He asked my help in preventing a raid by river pirates."

"Really? I imagine you would both be capable of doing so. More capable than the authorities, certainly. What ship? How did you manage it?"

He laughed a little. "I keep forgetting how much you know about affairs on the river. 'Twas the *Jolly Jane*. Hawkins discovered the scheme and where they were to assemble on the Isle of Dogs. We brought men and surrounded them."

"They cannot have given up easily, Captain."

"There was some skirmishing with cutlass and cudgel. There were more of us. We overcame them with no deaths among our men, though several among the pirates. Then we took the survivors to the Admiralty to be dealt with."

"Well done!" She felt the blood rise in her cheeks and feared her eyes were shining. The thought of Captain Easterday, small sword in hand, stripped perhaps to shirt and breeches for the fight, was exciting in a way she preferred not to examine too closely. She eyed him speculatively. He was such a quiet gentleman, one forgot that he had once lived the harsh life of a sailor. The businesses of importing and shipping were not for the timid, either.

He was gazing at her intently, with a very faint

smile, exactly mirroring her own expression, she suspected.

"Mistress Olivia, I know you can seldom be at home to receive calls, and I seldom make them for the same reason, but may I call upon you and your aunt on Sunday? Or if you have plans this Sunday, perhaps the following Sunday?"

"We would both be pleased to see you and to hear about your experiences at sea. Come this Sunday, if you will."

Chapter 30

"Ma'am, ma'am!" Ky erupted into the back office, causing Olivia to blot a line in the account book and Finley, with whom she had been discussing expenses, to start from his seat.

"Mind your manners," Finley said.

"Whatever is wrong?" Ky was generally quiet and tapped at the door when she was needed.

He did not have to explain. Now that the door was open, she could hear the problem.

"...the woman? By God, I'll speak to her and find out what she knows of my nephew."

Finley stood up and strode out, and Olivia followed. "I'll handle it," he muttered over his shoulder.

She followed him. "I won't hide. This is my business and my problem."

Davant stood at the end of the passage, blocking entry by a stocky, red-faced man who was trying to bull his way past. Davant stood aside as Finley came up behind him. Olivia edged around Finley.

"I am 'the woman' here. My name is Olivia Cantarell. Who are you and what is it you want, sir?"

The visitor was expensively dressed, with a good deal of fine lace at his throat and wrists and a heavy sapphire signet ring on one finger. "I, madam, am Horace Ainslie and my nephew, who has been calling himself Barlow, though his name is actually Ainslie, is employed here. Where is he?" He rapped out the words with his chin thrust forward. It might have intimidated his usual cronies. Having dealt with men who could frighten Horace Ainslie speechless by looking at him, she was unimpressed.

"Barlow did work here for a time. However, he left without giving notice. I cannot help you."

"I don't believe you," he snapped. "The man I hired to find my nephew, who's underage and is my ward, is sure you or mayhap your clerk and boys know where he is."

"I cannot imagine why. Barlow was sent on an errand late one day, fulfilled it, and did not come in the following day or any day since. I had to employ a new clerk, at some inconvenience to myself." She frowned at Ainslie. "If some accident befell him, I should feel quite guilty. I assumed he had simply gone off, as young men sometimes do."

"Gone off, ay," Ainslie snarled, "to avoid my catching him. He cannot have done it without help, as he could not have had enough money by him to go far."

"Have you inquired at his lodgings, Mr. Ainslie?"

"Of course I have. Or rather, my agent has. Matthias left in the morning, as if he were going to his work. The owner of the house has not seen him since, nor have any of the other lodgers. The woman says someone may have paid him a call the evening before he disappeared. She herself was occupied in the kitchen and the maid of all work is weak in her wits and could not describe the visitor or even remember who he asked for. No one else in the house knew anything," he added sourly.

Or chose not to admit it. The other inmates of Barlow's lodging house were probably also employed on the river or in shipping, and unlikely to have anything to say to a stranger who asked about one of their own, most particularly if they thought the inquirer was trying to collect a debt. Ainslie's thieftaker had no familiarity with the port and its ways, if he were the one who had abducted Kit, and would be an object of suspicion.

"How very peculiar. I do hope nothing has befallen him."

"I am not deceived, mistress. I'll not have the ungrateful pup defying me. I make a bad enemy." With that, Ainslie turned on his heel and marched out.

Davant trod delicately to the door Ainslie had left open and closed it.

Olivia compressed her lips to keep from snickering.

"I nearly laughed aloud when he proclaimed himself a bad enemy," Finley remarked.

"Ay, Mr. Hawkins or Captain Easterday would have him for breakfast with eggs boiled soft and a cup o' chocolate. All heat and no fire," Ky smirked. "Kit will be sorry he missed seeing it."

Olivia smiled to cover her unease.

"I will report Ainslie's coming here to Captain Easterday, by your leave," Finley said later, when he found her alone.

"I think you should not," she replied. "At least…no one from Cantarell Shipping should go to him. If that man has someone watching, we do not want to draw his attention to the captain. I will write to him by the penny post."

During a lull later in the day, Olivia told Finley she was going upstairs for a while. She wished to warn Barlow of continued surveillance and had brought a newspaper and a book for him as well.

"We'll handle matters until your return, ma'am." Finley was blushing; naturally he assumed she was going on some female business.

Barlow was glad to see her and both relieved to hear of the collier's anticipated departure and worried by his uncle's visit.

After thanking her for the book and paper, he went on, "I am more grateful than I can say for your arranging to hide me. You have gone to a great deal of trouble on my account, and now my uncle Ainslie is haunting you. I'm glad to hear I'll be relieving you of my presence."

"I dare say you'll be happy to be home and see your brothers and sisters."

"That I will. I missed them sorely when I was at sea, and then when I returned, I did not stay long before I came to London to find work. I look forward to some rambles in the countryside, too."

"You are tired of being shut up here."

"It's true I'm used to more fresh air and activity."

"At least on the collier, you'll be able to walk on deck and perhaps the sea breeze will not stir up the coal dust too much." She went on, "We must be particularly careful now, as your uncle seems not to have heard that you have already sailed for the Far East. As he suspects Cantarell Shipping, I fear he will keep the office under surveillance. I had hoped he would learn of our decoy and draw off."

"My uncle Ainslie is not a clever man, and he is

perennially purse-pinched. He will not have hired the best agent to find me. A less skilled one may not have learned that I am supposed to have gone to sea."

"We will not worry yet." Time enough to do that when Captain Easterday informed her he was ready to take Barlow aboard the collier.

****

The captain's Sunday afternoon call went far to reconciling Aunt Rachel to Olivia's refusal to forgive Ambrose Hawkins. Unsurprisingly, she had insisted on providing Shrewsbury cakes and claret to entertain Captain Easterday. He was, after all, almost the first guest they had entertained since before Jonas Canterell's death. Except for Hawkins and Mr. Nevis, whose call on Aunt Rachel must have been unannounced, for surely she would not have invited him at a time when she knew Olivia would not be at home. Unless, of course, she had done so for that very reason. Now that she thought on it, the tea tray had been unusually well supplied with treats that day. Rachel's color was prettier and her eyes brighter than Olivia remembered them. In fact, she was looking younger.

Aunt Rachel set herself to draw their guest out and prattled happily.

"Mr. Nevis, who was one of Mr. Hawkins's guests at his Vauxhall Gardens party, has invited us to the ridotto at the Opera House on Saturday, and we are looking forward to it with the greatest pleasure..."

"Perhaps not the *greatest* pleasure," Olivia said under her breath. Her cheeks grew warm when Easterday cast her an amused glance. Faith, what had she meant by her unplanned comment? She remembered how it felt when Hawkins embraced her and hoped she had not turned fiery red. By way of diversion, she said, "Poor Mr. Nevis lost an eye at the battle of Malplaquet. He was a captain in the 37th Foot, though he must have been quite young."

"Part of his hand, too. Such a pity, for he is quite handsome otherwise. Do you enjoy masquerade balls, Captain?" her aunt continued, having missed both Olivia's interpolation and any telltale blush.

"I have not attended one recently, but I used to do so. Have you chosen costumes? I think Mistress Olivia would make a splendid Queen Elizabeth."

"Mr. Nevis has assured her that no costume is necessary. A mask and a domino will suffice."

"Then perhaps some future masquerade will see you in ruff and farthingale, Mistress Olivia. What color will your domino be?"

He could only be asking for one reason; he must intend to seek her out at the ball. "A golden yellow," she said casually. But her heart was racing. Rachel was looking on complacently, which caused the blood to surge into her cheeks again.

After he departed, she wondered why he had come. In a moment when her aunt was telling Kitty to bring more hot water, he had murmured, "I received your message about Horace Ainslie. Perhaps I can do something to direct his attention elsewhere." Then he went on to remark upon Aunt Rachel's cherished *famille rose* ginger jar on the mantel. But he could not have come only in response to her letter, as he had requested permission to call before Ainslie's assault on her office.

"He is very good company," Rachel admitted after

he departed. "I had not realized from meeting him at the assembly that he possesses a lively sense of humor, which is an attractive trait. In spite of it, he is clearly a steady, reliable man as well."

"Steady, reliable men not being known for humor?"

"Many of them do not possess a lively humor, anyway, Livvie. Prosy men tend to make rather ponderous jokes. I was very glad my father chose Mr. Williams for me rather than some other; my dear husband was never at a loss for a witty remark or bon mot. How we did laugh together!"

Olivia was reflecting on how enjoyable the visit had been and wished it might have been possible to speak with him alone, when her aunt remarked, "It's such a pity he's not as *exciting* as Mr. Hawkins."

"I, for one, think it a good thing," Olivia replied primly. The visit had yielded one other benefit; her aunt's newfound approval of the captain had eased her concern over Olivia's rejection of Ambrose Hawkins.

Chapter 31

Yates cleared his throat and offered Easterday a sealed letter.

"I did not open this one, sir, as it is marked for you only."

Easterday took it, surprised. The direction was indeed to "Captain Marcus Easterday, Easterday & Co., Leaden Hall Street, by East India House, to be opened only by Capt. Easterday." He did not recognize the hand, though it was distinctive, being bold and without flourishes. At least his clerk would not have mistaken it for a love letter.

He broke the seal and spread open the sheet upon his desk.

*Captain,*

*Having undertaken to inform Hawkins and yourself whether anyone inquired after the sailor you know of, I have sent a messenger to Hawkins and write to you, Believing you would prefer to be discreet. None of my sources report anyone sniffing around for news of the said Sailor, which means that there was no way to drop a word in his ear. However, as a curious man, and recalling the name you had mentioned in connection with the tar, I made a few Inquiries of mine own.*

*Jack Tar's uncle is known in my end of town, though only recently, when he began to gamble at the Cantwells' hell at the sign of the Parson, Heydon*

*Square. I learned of it from Ned Brown, the Cantwell sharper, who believed the uncle was no longer welcome at White's or other such places. I was able to confirm the same from someone who gambles there. The uncle does not Now owe money to the Cantwells, Ned having made it clear to him that the Consequences for chousing Them were more serious than losing one's Reputation as a gentleman. He made good his debt by borrowing from Solomon, Old Jury, Cheapside, at the Sign of the Scales. Should you wish to interview Solomon, write to me at Job's Coffee House, St. Clement's Lane, or call upon me there on Tuesday or Thursday. Solomon keeps his—and his clients'—secrets very Close, but he owes me a favor. Whether this will be of Use to you, I do not know.*

    *Yr Most Ob't,*

    *J. Barlicorn*

Well. Here was confirmation that Ainslie's skulker had not learned of their imposter. Several interesting possibilities occurred to him, and one or two other considerations. Barlicorn had connections among the better sort; the riffraff would not be permitted in the fashionable White's, where men wagered and lost fortunes.

Why had Barlicorn suggested that Easterday might want to interview the moneylender? A nod's as good as a wink to a blind horse; he must believe Solomon possessed helpful information. He would take the man up on his offer of assistance.

Interestingly, while it had no bearing on the matter of Ainslie, John Barlicorn wrote like a man of some education. But then, he spoke like gentleman, too—part of the time.

\*\*\*\*

Solomon was a youngish man, plainly dressed like a tradesman of the better sort, in a plain office that might have belonged to any middling businessman. Easterday and Barlicorn sat in comfortable armchairs facing him.

"I will tell you, since my friend Barlicorn asks it of me." He smiled slightly. "I assure you, I am not in the habit of revealing my clients' business dealings in ordinary circumstances."

"I appreciate your assistance, and the delicacy of your situation. No one will hear of it from me."

"Thank you." Solomon—Barlicorn had introduced him by the single name—opened a drawer and took out a battered book. Colored ribbons marked various sections. He opened it at the last, a repellently purple one. "This is not my ledger, only a sort of aide-mémoire. But I can supply the information you want from my notes." He flipped through several pages.

"How much did you lend Ainslie?"

"Nine hundred pounds, on the tenth of last month."

"Only nine hundred?"

Solomon looked up and smiled satirically. "It's not a great deal compared to the amounts I sometimes lend, but folk who live on a hundred a year would consider it a fortune."

"Well," Easterday admitted, "I don't think it a trifle myself. I am surprised that Ainslie was not in need of more money."

"Oh, he was. This loan was to pay a gambling debt of—" Solomon's finger moved down the page. "—£893, owed to H. Cantwell's gambling establishment in Heydon Square. The extra seven pounds was simply to round the number off. Pocket change for Ainslie. His debts are actually about three thousand, unless he's incurred more in the last few weeks. But I declined to lend a greater sum."

"His prospects are that bad?" Barlicorn inquired.

"In my opinion, based on those of my informants, yes. He owes the greater part to gentlemen with whom he has gambled, but those are not pressing, in spite of the convention that requires gentlemen to pay gaming debts immediately. You see, they will do no more than cut his acquaintance and make it impossible for him to play with them. He will have promised to make his vowels good as soon as his investments make a profit. The Cantwell debt was urgent, as they would do him bodily harm if he failed to pay."

"According to my informants, he has no investments. Or none that are known," Easterday objected.

"I do not think he does. He does claim guardianship of a young man who is heir to an unentailed manor in Cumberland and a small fortune. The manor is mortgaged; the amount owing now is a bit under seven hundred pounds. I contemplate buying that mortgage, although the property is being ill managed."

"Given what you have told me, I wonder you lent him any money."

"I would not have done so if he had not secured the loan with jewelry. He will never redeem it if I am any judge, and when I sell it to a goldsmith, it will cover at least the principal amount and the interest."

"Good God!" Barlicorn murmured.

"In that case, why did he not sell it outright, realize a greater amount, and avoid the interest?"

Solomon's grave demeanor broke, and he grinned, looking very boyish. "Ainslie is a fool about business, but he is not an idiot. I give you two reasons: one, if he sold the pieces to a jeweler, the sale would be known…and I suspect the pieces were not his to sell. If they belonged to his ward, they will have been mentioned in the inventory taken when his father died. Ainslie might claim the boy had taken them, as he is not under Ainslie's control at the moment. That defense would be useful only if no one knew Ainslie himself had sold them, as of course the jeweler would. Two, he cannot have known how much they were worth. Have I said it was a pair of very old-fashioned hair ornaments? Ugly, too. Not the sort of thing modern ladies wear. They are set with large, rather roughly cut emeralds in a circle around a balas ruby, and one is missing a stone. I can sell them and they will be recut and reset, and make my cousin, the goldsmith, a very happy man."

"Sol…," Barlicorn began. "About the balas rubies…are you sure they're genuine?"

"Ah, you are thinking of that man years ago who made imitations of balas rubies so good the East India Company was deceived and bought from him?"

"I wondered, when you said the ornaments were of an old style."

"It was a good thought, but no, these are the true stones. I learned about gems and jewelry from my uncle. It's a useful skill in my work."

"How did he counterfeit them?" Easterday asked. It was not relevant to his business with Solomon, but he could not resist.

"He had rock crystal cut like balas rubies, heated them very hot, and dropped them into a red dye bath,

Captain. The heat made tiny cracks open to take in the dye, and then they closed tight when the stone cooled quickly in the liquid. My uncle owned one, which is now my cousin's."

Solomon leaned forward. "I will tell you something that is my speculation only, as you have an interest in Ainslie's activities. The ornaments may not have been listed in the inventory. I suspect it because the widow and her children moved away from the manor. She would take her personal jewelry and the family heirlooms with her, where they would be out of reach of her brother-in-law. How then would he have got hold of them? I would guess that they may have been hidden somewhere in the manor house, and Ainslie found them."

"Mayhap they belonged to his branch of the family?"

Solomon shook his head. "Ainslie's father was a younger son, and sold off everything he could, most of which came as his bride's dowry, or so my grandfather says. You could say we are hereditary moneylenders to the Ainslie family."

"Solomon, would you consider giving me first right of refusal for the ornaments?"

"If Ainslie has not redeemed them in…ah, three months and eight days, certainly. You believe they are the ward's family heirlooms?"

"It's likely, is it not? If they are, he may wish to keep them or sell them. I would like to buy the mortgage, as well, though I would rather my identity not be known."

Barlicorn made a tiny movement, reminding Easterday of a cat, crouched, its hindquarters twitching before it pounced upon some hapless small creature.

The pause seemed portentous and longer than it could have been in reality. Probably they both wondered why he wanted to buy either mortgage or jewels. He wondered the same thing himself.

The silence was broken when Solomon remarked, "Sometimes jewelry is made as a set: necklace, earrings, a brooch, a bracelet. If the hair gauds were part of a set, and Ainslie found it, I would expect him to pledge those, as well, to get a larger loan. I think the existence of a treasure trove in the house is unlikely. The manor itself is worth substantially more than the amount owing on the mortgage, despite its current neglected state. If you still wish to buy the mortgage, Captain, I will buy it and resell it to you for a small handling fee. Five percent?"

"Done. You don't make much profit on it at that rate."

"I do a good business because my rates are not extortionate. Interest on loans is naturally higher," he added apologetically. "It has to be, given the risk in lending to men who mismanage their finances. Having them confined to debtors' prison will not get me my money when they have no remaining assets, including rich relatives or friends. I will have the mortgage for you in a few days. It should prove a good investment, one way or another. If you have no further questions, may I offer you brandy?"

Before they parted outside Solomon's office, Easterday said, "Barlicorn, could you make inquiries about someone for me?"

"Probably. It may depend upon what circles he moves in. My connections to the highest levels of society are limited," he admitted, grinning.

"I'm curious about a Giles Nevis, a captain in the 37th Foot, who lost an eye at Malplaquet and subsequently sold out. He is acquainted with Hawkins."

Barlicorn gave him a very straight look. "And you would prefer not to ask Hawkins about him?"

"There are reasons," Easterday replied vaguely.

"Very well. There will be some expenses involved, but they will be moderate. I will have to tip some of my sources. That's if anyone knows anything about him."

"Agreed. He is paying attention to a lady of my acquaintance. I want to know if there's anything about him that the lady's family should know."

"I am often asked to advise on similar matters. I'll write."

## Chapter 32

Olivia had never attended one of the Venetian-style ridottos put on by Mr. Heidegger, the Swiss opera manager, though they enjoyed great popularity. The opera house was beautifully appointed, the orchestra was excellent, and the tone of the gathering vastly superior to the assemblies at the Moon and Stars Assembly Rooms. The other attendees were at least mostly genteel, or even of the beau monde and aristocracy, to judge by their voices. If she were a young girl, she would be dreaming that some titled gentleman would be captivated by her beauty and become an ardent suitor for her hand. Which was nonsense for a purely practical reason: shrouded in a hooded domino, face concealed, the only attributes by which one could judge would be grace of movement, voice, and charm, until the midnight unmasking.

Manners were less formal at such a masquerade, as introductions were impossible when the object was to conceal one's identity. You might recognize a friend by his or her voice or some mannerism, but otherwise one mingled and flirted freely with someone who might be...anyone. Romantical-minded girls would naturally hope for the handsome heir to a dukedom. The anonymity could be a great advantage for someone whose face lacked obvious beauty—if only she were vivacious enough to engage in banter with whatever gentlemen addressed her.

Alack, repartee was foreign to her, though as the event went on, she began to find it easier to respond with a quip and a laugh, as though she were no longer herself. She would never meet these people again, making it unnecessary to fear embarrassing herself. She parted from her aunt and Mr. Nevis as they appeared to find each other's company pleasant and to need no other.

"A lady in a domino the color of a ripe quince," a tall gentleman murmured as she brushed past and put a hand on her arm to detain her.

"Not for your plucking, sir." She laughed.

He spoke closer to her ear, lowering his voice yet more. "But when a quince ripens, it will drop into one's hand with only a little encouragement."

"Then perhaps I am not ripe." *Am I getting too much into the spirit of the thing?*

"Quinces harvested before they are quite ready will still ripen. In this cool climate, it's often necessary to gather them early."

It chanced that the orchestra had come to the end of its piece, and for that moment, conversation around them quieted and she heard the last part of his statement without distractions. She stared up into his eyes. In spite of being in shadow, she knew the speaker's identity and recoiled.

"Be easy, my dear. I have no intention of carrying you off from a masquerade ball, like some reenactment of the Romans' abduction of the Sabine women. Lord, it would cause a riot! Assuming anyone noticed."

"I have no desire to continue this conversation or our acquaintance, Mr. Hawkins."

"You said as much when we parted. I understood that you were distressed and needed time. Rather like a green quince. I could not let our friendship lapse without assuring you again that I am heartily sorry for offending you and beg you will forgive me."

"I fear you are less sorry for your offense than for failing in your attempt to secure my property."

He was silent for several heartbeats. "Admittedly, it was learning you were a considerable heiress that first captured my attention."

At least he did not pretend ignorance.

"Once I knew you, your wealth faded into insignificance. Your elegance, your quick wits, and your beauty became everything to me."

"My beauty? Do you expect me to believe you find me beautiful?"

"Some can only see beauty in a Meissen figurine with its detail and bright colors. Some of us can see it in the severe lines of celadonware. You, my love, are the latter."

She swallowed. She preferred the pale green or gray porcelain, undecorated except perhaps for restrained molding, to the exuberance of famille rose china. As for the highly colored, oversentimentalized shepherds and shepherdesses of Meissen—faugh! To be compared to celadon china was by far the best compliment she had ever received.

And she could not forget the sensations she had experienced when Hawkins kissed her. This moment, if he embraced her, she would respond. No wonder men were ruled by their lusts! Fortunately, females had more self-control. Nearby, a lady in a purple domino laughed too loudly as the gentleman beside her groped under her domino at bosom height. The moralists were quite right to condemn masquerade balls and ridottos—their anonymity encouraged wanton behavior. Sometimes courtesans attended. At least in the opera house, it would be impossible to find the privacy for greater lapses of morality, unlike Vauxhall Gardens, where it was easy to steal off into a grove.

"I've never dealt with a woman like you, so I've made mistakes. Forgive me?" His voice caressed her.

Her heart pounded. How could she be so attracted to a man she did not trust?

"I...I..." She was stammering like a chit new released from the schoolroom. How humiliating! Worse, she really did not know how to answer. It was Christian to forgive. Her aunt considered Hawkins's attempt to compromise her of little importance, easily excused by his ardor. She wanted his embraces. To be honest, she wanted him to bed her. She could not have the marriage bed without marriage and his vision of what he wanted from her as his wife—apart from the bedding—did not appeal. To have nothing to do but be his hostess, to make and receive calls on friends, to manage his household, and be a patroness of some suitable charity? She would go mad from boredom. Worse, she did not trust him, given his reputation on the river.

"I need time."

"You shall have it, my cautious little love. I have your best interests at heart. Did I not arrange for Barlow to appear to have sailed for the Far East, even though you did not ask my help?"

She stared at him. He had arranged it? "It was very good of you. Thank you." Her voice sounded unnatural in her ears.

"Easterday did not mention he'd come to me for help, did he? I suppose he thought you would object, given our recent misunderstanding."

But she had not told him of the abduction. Why had he concealed Hawkins's involvement? It might be only from vanity, for men often were vain, though Captain Easterday had never seemed to suffer from that fault. Had he omitted mention of Hawkins's assistance because he thought Hawkins an unsuitable match for her? "I suppose he must have."

"He would not have known how to do it on his own."

No, Captain Easterday was a sedate, well-behaved businessman, even if he had spent years at sea. He would lack the sort of connections possessed by Hawkins, who had sailed on a pirate ship, however briefly and unwillingly.

They had been drifting with the crowd. She wanted to detach herself from him; she could not be perfectly certain that there were no nooks where the amorous might dally. She would not trust herself with Hawkins in a secluded spot. Both morality and common sense told her that granting him any liberties would be a mistake, but her body cared nothing for decency or reason. Some claimed that old maids became crazed for lack of...of...well, of male attention. She had not believed it until now.

"If you will excuse me, Mr. Hawkins, I must find my aunt," she said, seizing an opportunity as an inebriated young man following a vulgarly laughing female in a pink domino blundered into Hawkins, and Olivia slipped her arm free. A second reveler pushed between them. She slid into the crowd at right angles to the direction in which they had been moving. She wished now she had ordered a domino in black; there were plenty of those in the crowd.

Aunt Rachel's domino was periwinkle blue, a color of which she was inordinately fond. As most dominos were black and the colored ones tended to more vivid hues, she should be easy to find. But it was not so; the long room used for assemblies swirled with a black sea, dotted with red, green, purple, blue, orange, and every other color in many shades. Her aunt was short and might easily be lost among those taller than she. The sound of multiple conversations, interspersed by laughter, and the ebb and flow of the crowd were overwhelming. She kept being distracted by the beauty of the room with its many chandeliers and sconces illuminating the elaborately painted walls and ceiling. She moved around the periphery until she had made a complete circuit without catching sight of a periwinkle domino.

Supper would be served later in one of the other rooms, but she had not gone into the theater itself, where those inclined were dancing. She had seldom seen Aunt Rachel dance, but on the other hand, tonight she was being squired by Nevis. If he asked her to dance, she might do it. She seemed very taken with him. She edged into the hall, its size and suitability for dancing having been increased by flooring over the pit. It, too, teemed with people, some dancing, others watching, a few passing food or drink up to friends in the spectators' gallery. If she did not find Aunt Rachel here, there were still the rooms where one could refresh oneself with tea or coffee, a card room, and a room where ladies could withdraw to repair damage to their gowns or use a close stool.

Even if she espied her aunt, reaching her in the dense crowd might be difficult. She forged through the throng, allowing less opportunity for gentlemen to accost her in search of dalliance. Remembering how she had bandied words with masked strangers earlier made her hot with embarrassment. What had come over her?

It must be the safety of being masked, the absence of consequences...until the unmasking at midnight, when a gentleman might find that the willowy lady he had pursued was a pale spinster, long past marriageable age. How humiliating it would be, to see his surprise and disappointment or, Heaven help her, revulsion! Yet Ambrose Hawkins seemed to find her attractive, and not only for her wealth. While gaining possession of her property might be his primary goal, some of the compliments he paid her sounded genuine. No one had ever praised her eyes, hair, lips, and grace, but she knew that those were common objects of admiration. A lady's features might indeed be lovely, but a man's homage to her sweetly curved lips or brilliant eyes always sounded to her like the examples of correct correspondence to be found in letter writing guides, stiff and formulaic. But to be compared to celadon china by a man with exquisite taste in Chinese porcelain was convincing—and thrilling. Almost more thrilling than feeling his arms around her, his lips on hers, his body...He might really find her desirable. Her heart beat faster, imagining it.

And made her pay less attention to her surroundings. When she passed a man in a black domino who inclined his head toward hers and whispered, "Mistress Olivia?" she shied like a startled horse.

"I beg your pardon, ma'am. Err…you are Mistress Olivia, are you not?"

"Oh! Yes, indeed, Captain. I was looking for my aunt. I fear my wits were wandering."

"Perhaps I can see her. What color is her domino?"

"Periwinkle blue—but it doesn't matter. I merely wished to assure myself she was enjoying herself." Dominos flowed around them, as though they were boulders in a streambed. "I am glad we met here, as I wanted to speak with you about the arrangements."

"I have news for you also." He glanced around. "We cannot speak here. It's too noisy, and we would not want to risk being overheard."

"Where, then?"

"There are places, though I confess they are not usually employed for consultation."

The twinkle in his eyes was nigh irresistible. "You mean places where people go for dalliance?" She had observed several costumed females who could not by any means be called ladies or even decent, presumably courtesans. Hence the popularity of such events, perhaps.

"I assure you, ma'am, you will be safe with me. We only need a quiet place to talk."

"What a pity," she was horrified to hear herself say.

He laughed. "The effects of the masquerade make themselves felt even by the well-behaved."

"I've never attended a ridotto before. I had no idea how…how…"

"How liberating a mask and domino can be? It's shocking, isn't it? Here, take my arm if you can trust me, and we'll find a secluded corner in which to converse."

"You've been here before."

"A few times. It's enjoyable to dance and talk with ladies without the pressures that attend a private ball."

Where an eligible man would be prey to husband-hunting young ladies and their mamas. She had often observed it at assemblies.

She lost her sense of direction as Captain Easterday guided her through the theater. They came to a small stair leading up, to what she did not know. There was a little light at the top but no sound of voices. Captain Easterday stopped about halfway up.

"No one should be using this stair—except for dalliance—and if someone does approach, we will have warning." He kept his voice low. "I'll be ready to take our friend away the day after tomorrow, at midmorning."

"That is what I need to discuss with you. I intended to bring him to you, but I think I must tell you where to find him, in case his uncle still has someone watching my office." She could not help glancing both up and down the stairs and leaned closer to him to whisper in his ear, "He is at Ah Fong's Academy & Museum of Oriental Art in the street behind my office, at the sign of the Chinaman. I will inform him to expect you."

"Very good. Now, I must tell you that Nevis is known to be a good friend of Hawkins. They have been acquainted for many years, though I could not learn how. Nevis lives in lodgings here on rents from a manor he inherited in Cheshire. He is not known to drink to excess or gamble except for small amounts, and he is not in debt. Any trifling amounts owing to his wine merchant, tailor, or what-have-ye are paid within a month or two. He is known as a pleasant companion. I would not object to a relative of mine spending time with him."

"But if he is friendly with Mr. Hawkins, that explains…"

"What does it explain?"

"Why he might do him a favor by telling him the color of my domino…and keeping my aunt occupied when we visited Vauxhall Gardens," she admitted. She had not intended to mention that her real concern about Nevis stemmed from the Vauxhall Gardens incident. Had her aunt met Nevis at an assembly or in church, she would have thought nothing of his visiting Aunt Rachel.

The captain bent his head closer. "Vauxhall Gardens? The color of your domino? What, has Hawkins been persecuting you here—"

Feet pounded up the stairs, followed by the harsh demand "How dare you lure this lady away? My dear, let me escort you back to the dancing or to the long room." By then, Hawkins was one step below them, holding out his arm to her.

"Mr. Hawkins, I do not require rescue."

Easterday spoke at the same time. "I assure you, Hawkins, Mistress Olivia is perfectly safe with me." She heard faint amusement creep into his voice halfway through this statement.

Hawkins evidently heard it, too. Although she could not see his features in the dimness, she heard his breath hiss out.

"There is no reason for a gentleman to take a lady apart from the company unless he has dishonorable intentions."

"That is certainly the pot calling the kettle black, sir," Olivia observed.

After a moment of taut silence, Hawkins said, "Easterday, you will hear from me. Your servant, ma'am."

Before she realized what he must mean, he had turned and thudded back down the stairs.

"Captain, I cannot permit you to fight a duel with Mr. Hawkins, if that was his meaning. Pray consider how ridiculous it would be for sensible men to engage in violence over a mature female over whom neither has any rights. Good God, I am not the prize at some barbaric medieval tournament."

"But you are a prize."

Whatever could he mean?

He went on, "Though not, I agree, to be claimed by the winner of a contest. However, a man who feels an attachment to a lady also feels a responsibility to protect her—"

"Mr. Hawkins abducted me and attempted to force me to marry him by compromising me. He is the one I need protection from."

He breathed in sharply. "By God, I will meet him. You are engaged to marry Hawkins, then. No wonder he thinks he has a right to guard you." His voice was low and furious.

"No, I refused to marry him. That is why I severed the acquaintance. Please forget I mentioned that foolish episode; I did not mean to say anything about it." *Lud!* What was wrong with her? She never spoke unguardedly, or not since she was a green girl.

"But if he compromised you—"

Her cheeks burned. "Not like that!"

A diplomatic silence reigned, while she remembered that being compromised did not necessarily mean anything more than being found alone with a man. As she had been found with Captain Easterday moments ago. *Oh dear.* She must explain, lest he think the worst of her.

"He came to let me know he had found Barlow injured. I went with him, naturally, to arrange for Barlow to be moved, and when we arrived at a house surrounded by market gardens off Old Gravel Lane, I realized something was wrong. He said he would keep me there overnight, which would make it necessary for me to wed him. He didn't—I wasn't—In the morning, when he took me home, thinking we would marry by special license, I told him I refused to marry him."

"I confess to some surprise you felt you could turn down his offer at that point. Most young ladies would see no alternative. "

"A young lady with family to concern themselves would most likely be forced into marriage. But I was not actually assaulted, and I am not a young lady with a male guardian to insist upon my marrying my abductor to preserve my reputation, merely because I had passed a night under his roof. If he had…I mean…if I found myself with child, it might have been a different matter. If I make myself clear?" What an excruciatingly awkward conversation.

With the ghost of a chuckle, Easterday said, "I believe I take your meaning."

"So you see, a duel with Hawkins is quite

unnecessary."

He sighed. "I'm not a hot-headed young fool to seek out a duel. However, if Hawkins challenges me, as he seems to intend, I have no choice but to meet him. To refuse would make it appear I was afraid. It's impossible for a fearful person, man or woman, to survive in business in the port. In any port."

"I had not considered the consequences," she admitted, "beyond the possibility of your being injured." Or killed. She could not contemplate the thought of Easterday dying in a duel for her sake. She did not want Hawkins harmed, either, though she was thoroughly annoyed with him. "There must be some way of preventing such a dangerous, useless encounter."

He drew in a breath. "Mistress Olivia…Hawkins was correct about one thing. I should not have taken you away from the others. Most would consider that I have now compromised you. It's my fault for failing to think of you as a lady as well as a sensible woman of business."

She opened her mouth to point out that they had needed to speak privately and that she was a mature woman. Easterday might agree with her, indeed, obviously had agreed, or he would not have taken her apart to speak with her. The truth was, however, that no one else would see it the same way. When she considered it, she realized that her behavior had been unwise. Conferring together in the middle of a lawn in daylight would have been acceptable. Doing so on a dim stair at a masquerade ball was loose behavior, if not compromising. Not even being unquestionably a spinster freed her from the restrictions imposed on girls.

At fifty rather than thirty, or as a widow, she would have had more freedom.

"Not having been brought up in society, I am not a sheltered lady and tend not to think of such things, Captain."

"I understand. Nevertheless, even in Thames Street and Wapping, my behavior in taking you aside would be talked of and harm your reputation."

She gave a short, rueful laugh. "It might be thought odd of you, but it would be my conduct they censured."

"It does occur to me that there is one way to prevent both damage to your name and a duel. If we were engaged, no one would regard our stealing a few moments in private as dishonorable. It would remove Hawkins's reason for issuing me a challenge and also relieve you of his intentions."

"Why—but I...but you..." Heavens! Two proposals within a month, and she could not reject the second as easily as the first, because she could not bear the thought of Easterday risking himself for her. While she paid little heed to the intricate rules governing polite society, she was not unaware of them, thanks to her mother and Aunt Rachel. Marriage, either to Easterday or Hawkins, would make all right. If she accepted Easterday, Hawkins would have no choice but to give up the idea of a duel and his pretensions to her. Accepting Hawkins on the condition that he not challenge Easterday would accomplish almost the same end. Except that she did not quite trust Hawkins. Nor did she want to marry either man. Preventing a duel which she feared Easterday would lose fatally, however, must be her first concern. Hawkins impressed her as a man who had seen a good deal of violence; she doubted he would hesitate to kill.

"It's true we are not well acquainted, and I know you are reluctant to marry and give up your comparative freedom."

Yes, Captain Easterday understood her as Hawkins did not.

He continued, "I would be honored to marry you, but if you are reluctant, think of this: marriage need not inevitably follow a betrothal. You might choose to break it off in a month or two. Mayhap by then he will have come to accept your refusal."

Or mayhap not. Still, Easterday was correct; affiancing herself to him would prevent injury to both men and at least make it less likely Hawkins would renew his addresses.

"I would have to jilt you, sir. It would be a humiliation for you, as no one else would know our betrothal was only a fiction."

He laughed without much humor. "It would not be the first time."

Did he mean that remark as a general statement? Or had he been jilted before?

He continued, "It might be an embarrassment to you, if you later decided you wanted to marry."

"I do not expect to marry." She sighed.

"Primarily because you do not want to lose control of your businesses and fortune? But you could retain your place in your company without being obviously involved in it. It would require agreement by your husband-to-be. Whatever Church and State may dictate, what matters most is what is agreed between the parties."

If Ambrose Hawkins had been willing—but he

wanted a different sort of wife. To cover her moment of pensive reflection, she said briskly, "I accept your most obliging offer of a sham betrothal. It should serve very well."

"I will send the notice to the papers tomorrow. And now we really must return to the public areas."

She danced twice with Captain Easterday, drank a glass of wine with him, and eventually located Aunt Rachel and Mr. Nevis not long before unmasking. They all sat together when supper was served.

"I had heard that the suppers here were delightful," Aunt Rachel remarked. "Such a variety of dishes, and everything of the best quality. Thank you for inviting us, Mr. Nevis."

He murmured something that Olivia did not hear, but it caused her aunt to laugh softly and gaze down at the cold chicken on her plate. At least Nevis seemed to be respectable, even if he had passed on the color of her domino to Hawkins.

She did not mention the betrothal; neither did Easterday. They had agreed she must tell her aunt before the announcement appeared in the newspaper, but doing so here would attract unnecessary attention. It was not to be expected that Aunt Rachel would receive the news without exclamations of surprise and joy. She might break the news after they left the Opera House when Mr. Nevis saw them home in a hackney. He would likely tell Hawkins at the first opportunity, before the newspapers came out, which should prevent Hawkins from sending his second to call upon the captain.

Captain Easterday escorted them to the hackney and kissed her hands when he took his leave, making her heart beat faster, as if the lover-like gesture were sincere. Aunt Rachel noticed though she gave no sign, whatever she might have made of it.

Olivia was grateful for the concealment of the darkness in the coach. It was proving surprisingly difficult to find the words to mention her betrothal. She was not an accomplished actress. Finally, as they clattered through the early morning streets, she took a deep breath and mumbled, "Captain Easterday asked me to marry him."

"Olivia! Why, what wonderful news...You did accept, didn't you?"

"Yes."

"My dear, I am so happy for you. I can scarce believe it. You must not worry about planning the wedding and wedding breakfast, for you are always busy, and I will see to all. When is it to take place?"

"We have not yet discussed it. Because of all the noise and activity around us, you know. And my surprise. I suppose the announcement will appear in Monday's newspaper."

"Please accept my felicitations," Nevis said. He sounded sincere. "I hope I may expect to be invited?"

"Certainly, sir," Olivia responded at the same instant Aunt Rachel replied vigorously, "Of course!"

Chapter 33

Why had she not expected that the announcement would entail consequences? Her aunt was already composing a guest list at breakfast, and asking Olivia's opinion as to what dishes she would like at the wedding breakfast.

"We might hire the Moon and Stars assembly rooms, but should we have them prepare the meal or have it brought in from a good cookshop or inn?"

"Whatever is easiest, I think."

"I will think about it and make a decision. Next we must consider your bride clothes. You will have to come to the modiste with me in the next day or two."

"Can I not simply wear one of my new gowns?"

"Niece, you have the three gowns you bought recently, but that is not enough to be entering married life. You must have several more, and pretty bedgowns, and all manner of things. He is a wealthy gentleman and will expect his bride to be well dressed. Monday will not be too soon to begin the project."

"I must spend Monday in the office, Aunt. Tuesday, I will be at your service." Olivia could not refuse the expedition without explaining that there would be no wedding, and really, as she could easily afford new clothing, why not order it as part of the pretense? She kept forgetting that she was able to afford to replace all her garments, and Aunt Rachel's, and buy jewels, too, if she wished. That, however, would be ridiculous, as her social life did not call for such things. She did not really need them, when she would not be marrying Captain Easterday or anyone else. Nevertheless, the prospect of more new clothing was irresistible. Some of them might be practical to wear in the office.

"I am so happy for you, Livvie, and I am glad that you and Captain Easterday did not ape the beau monde by not publishing an announcement. I want everyone to know."

"Thank you, Aunt Rachel." Regret for the deception made her voice sound thin in her ears.

"I have always wished to plan a wedding. You cannot imagine how much I will enjoy it."

*Oh, dear.* She almost dreaded the prospect of ending the engagement, with the necessity of spoiling her aunt's innocent pleasure.

"Perhaps we will be planning your wedding soon?" she asked to get over the awkward moment.

Her aunt blushed like a girl, which was answer enough.

Throughout the rest of Sunday, Rachel's questions and suggestions and her own guilt kept Olivia in a fidget. She worried about Easterday's removal of Barlow, as well. The first thing on Monday morning, she pattered upstairs to the door into the Academy & Museum of Oriental Art.

Barlow was delighted to hear he was to leave and set about organizing his few belongings. She went down to see Ah Fong and tell him that Captain Easterday would come for his guest.

Ah Fong nodded. "A fine man. I have heard him

praised for honesty, courage, and propriety. The last is very important."

Which made the captain sound duller than he was. Add intelligence, humor, and kindness and the description would be more accurate.

Upstairs she paused long enough to give Barlow five guineas.

"Mistress Cantarell, I can't accept this! I thank you, but…"

"Don't be foolishly proud, Mr. Ainslie. You can't arrive in Newcastle with naught but a shilling or two in your pockets. Remember, you will need food and lodging, and you will have other minor expenses which will add up. And you will need to present a good appearance when you go to your new position. Further, part is owed you in wages."

"In that case, I thank you. I swear I will pay you back."

"Very well, if you insist, though I can afford it." She smiled. "Cantarell Shipping will miss you. Good luck." Turning to go, she paused. "When you return as a landed gentleman, I hope you will call upon us in Well Close Square."

"I will, ma'am. I am not likely to forget I could not have got away from my uncle without your aid."

"And that of Captain Easterday and Mr. Hawkins, and, I am told, a very fine rogue who arranged for someone to impersonate you."

That drew a laugh, making him look like the carefree young man she remembered from her office.

Chapter 34

Despite having been out late at the Opera House, Easterday rose early on Sunday. Hawkins must have left the masquerade after their confrontation; search as he would, Easterday had failed to locate a tall figure in a purple domino. He might well be up betimes, either to visit Easterday himself or to send a second. If the latter, it would mean he had gone direct from Haymarket to seek out a friend to act for him. Which meant Easterday should put his mind to thinking who he might ask to be his own second. Dueling! Foolishness, except in rare instances. It would not come to that pass, however, given his and Olivia's betrothal.

However, midday arrived before Hawkins was announced by the former valet who owned Easterday's lodgings. How fortunate he had not yet sold the house purchased in expectation of his marriage to Mariah Saltstall; he would certainly need it to support the tale of his new espousals.

"I believe I may owe you an apology, Easterday." The words sounded forced out past gritted teeth.

"Won't you sit and have a glass of claret? Or would you prefer tea or coffee?"

After a visible debate with himself, Hawkins did drop into the other armchair by the fireplace. "Coffee. Thank you."

Easterday opened the door to the corridor and

called down to the servant on duty to send up coffee. "My landlord's wife makes excellent coffee. She worked in a coffee house before she married him."

Hawkins growled or perhaps cleared his throat. "I understand you have proposed to Olivia Cantarell and been accepted."

"You must have seen Nevis."

"I encountered him this morning, yes, on my way to visit a friend. Did you offer marriage because you had compromised her or did I interrupt the proposal?"

Easterday did not believe he had met Nevis by accident. Hawkins meant to conceal the man's role as his intelligencer. "It was a bit of both."

"Both? How could it be both?"

"We had been discussing marriage without having resolved upon it. The matter was under negotiation, as you might say. Your coming upon us precipitated our decision, as you were quite right. My meeting with Mistress Olivia was improper, though it did not occur to either of us at the time. It's devilish hard to discuss such a thing with a lady while observing the conventions."

A crack of laughter. "How well I know it! Congratulations. I have never suffered a setback in business that grieved me half as much. You have secured a treasure. I hope you appreciate her."

"I do. Who could fail to admire her courage, her business sense, and her care of those dependent upon her?"

"Are you not overlooking her beauty, her exquisite taste, and—? Never mind, I have forgotten what I meant to say."

"Her beauty? She has a pleasing face and a graceful bearing…" Was Olivia beautiful? She was rather thin, or slender might be a better word. Her face was pale and composed except when she laughed or blushed. Which latter she did readily, given her alabaster-fair complexion. When her eyes sparkled with humor, she fairly glowed.

"Easterday, if you can't see how lovely she is, she's wasted on you."

Good God! On reflection, he supposed she was lovely, though utterly unlike the softly pretty girls who had jilted him. "She is indeed, if not in the common way. I first noticed her intelligence and determination. Mayhap they've blinded me to her other attractions."

"She is to our Nonpareils as a Damascus blade is to a trumpery dress sword that's all paste gems and gilt."

Easterday nodded gravely. Hawkins besotted even unto poetry was a nine days' wonder. He must love her. And he was correct. Olivia might be the Greek goddess Athena come to life. By right of her character alone, she was worth a hundred Mariah Saltstalls.

"Be damned sure you cherish her," Hawkins grated.

"I will."

The coffee arrived then. They enjoyed it in near silence except for Hawkins asking, "When will the marriage take place?"

"That's still under negotiation. Olivia needed to discuss it with her aunt. The banns must be read, anyway. That will allow time for her to order bride-clothes and to select furniture for my house. I meant to show Mariah Saltstall through it on her return from my family's home, but as you know, our betrothal was broken off before we returned from Lancashire."

When Hawkins left, their uneasy friendship had

been restored. Easterday discovered he was glad of it and also glad that Hawkins had not courted Olivia solely for her wealth. His feelings for her obviously ran deep. *What a pity that he values her for the wrong things.*

Their supposed betrothal had accomplished its purpose: staving off the duel and preserving Olivia's reputation. Not that he thought Hawkins would talk. The man's obvious feelings for her would prevent his spreading gossip about their meeting at the ridotto. By the time Olivia ended it, Hawkins should have calmed. He might see it as a second chance to win her hand. Or he might issue his challenge after all, to avenge either the original wrong or whatever he believed Easterday had done to cause Olivia to break off the engagement.

He would deal with the consequences when they occurred.

\*\*\*\*

"Do I really need such a pile of clothing?" They had already visited the linen draper's establishment to choose printed chintzes and were now at the silk mercer's, which visit she expected to take most of the afternoon. The wool draper where she would select wools for autumn and winter garments would await another day.

"Yes," Aunt Rachel replied. "Captain Easterday is accepted in the highest company—well, not the *highest*, perhaps, but by most of polite society. Lud! He's not a tradesman. His family are gentlefolk, and he is friendly with the Lord Mayor and Alderman Saltstall and I don't know how many others, as well as any number of bankers, scientific gentlemen, and no doubt many other worthy folk."

"Are you sure I need a riding habit, Aunt?"

"He will expect his wife to dress like a lady. Ladies ride."

"I don't."

"I'm sure he will teach you."

Olivia regarded the array of samples of thin silks, brocades, shimmering moiré, and velvets she could not resist stroking.

"Once you have chosen the fabrics, we will go to the modiste and decide upon the styles and trimming. And for you to be measured."

"But the seamstress already has my measurements."

"For these, we will be going to a more fashionable modiste. Plan to be available for several hours."

"Really, I can't see the need—"

"Let me be your guide in this. Before I was widowed, I moved in the circle in which you will find yourself. Captain Easterday purchased a house in Queen's Square not long since."

"Did he?" Bachelors more commonly lived in rooms ranging from a single chamber in a boarding house to suites of rooms.

"Indeed he did. He was betrothed to the daughter of Alderman Saltstall, a miss straight out of the schoolroom, half his age."

"What happened?"

"The most appalling scandal, my dear! Hushed up, naturally, but a thing cannot be concealed if more than two people know of it. No one would wish to embarrass the alderman, who is well liked, but the girl is a willful, scheming chit, I understand. She ran off with some sprig of the nobility—I cannot for my life recall his name at the moment—from the country house where she was visiting and was caught too late. Not but what the captain managed the matter wonderfully, for he sent the minx back to her papa so her marriage to her debaucher could be arranged in a seemly fashion. Still, her betrothal to Captain Easterday was known in June, and a month ago, news of her marriage to her seducer was published, so…" Rachel shrugged.

"Good heavens! Where did you come by this story?"

"Madame Harfleur was my modiste during my marriage. Or I should say, she was the chief assistant to my modiste, Madame Desmarets. She bought the shop when Madame retired. She hears all the gossip from her customers. She would not ordinarily pass it on, except to an old, valued customer"—here Rachel preened a little—"particularly as I mentioned the occasion for outfitting you with a new wardrobe was your engagement to the captain."

He had been jilted. She hardly knew whether he was more to be pitied or congratulated. If the girl was as flighty and wanton as it sounded, the latter. Still, it must be a blow to his self-esteem. Now he had suggested this false betrothal, knowing that he would appear to be jilted yet again. *Oh, no.* She would never have agreed to this deception if she had known. The knowledge quite took the pleasure out of planning her new clothes. Aunt Rachel interrupted her reverie. "What day will be convenient for you to spend the morning or the afternoon at Madame Harfleur's? We will need to look at *poupées de mode* and—"

"What, Aunt?"

"Fashion dolls, Livvie. They are dressed in the

latest styles. She has some from France, and drawings as well, not more than a year old. I prefer not to know how she acquired them, as I am sure that all French imports are under embargo. We must decide on trimmings at the same time."

"We may as well do it the day after tomorrow."

"Once you are there, you will enjoy it, I promise you, however reluctant you are to leave that horrid office."

Considering how pleasant she found it to study the fabric samples, Olivia admitted Aunt Rachel might be correct. It did seem much harder work than arranging shipping, however.

**** 

Cantarell Shipping was now busier than at its best under her father. She wished she might consider it her own doing, but the improvement was partly due to having two clerks now—and neither of them Munns, thank God!—allowing them to handle more work efficiently. Davant's connections in the Huguenot community brought in some new work, too. Lastly, she suspected Captain Easterday played a part in it, either steering shippers to her or simply because she was known to be engaged to marry him. Galling, but true; one's connections sometimes mattered more than one's own abilities.

Finley returned from Lloyd's Coffee House with good news. The *Rose of Ireland*, long overdue, had dropped anchor. "I don't know all the details, but word is her voyage rivalled Odysseus's return from the Trojan War. First they suffered a delay in getting their cargo, then they were becalmed. After they were underway again, they escaped capture by a privateer, and finally were damaged by a storm, requiring them to make lengthy repairs."

Easterday entered the office. How neat he looked in his dark green coat and breeches—why had she never noticed the breadth of his shoulders before?—not that his shoulders and well-muscled legs had anything to do with his neatness.

He greeted them all and kissed her hand, which seemed oddly improper in an office, whereas she would have thought little of it in a ballroom.

"Is there something we can ship for you, Captain?" she asked to cover the awkward moment.

"Not today. I hope I am not taking an unwarranted liberty—"

They were supposed to be betrothed, she recalled. Presumably, one's pretended future husband could call upon one without an appointment. Finley and Davant appeared to find nothing amiss. Finley took the liberty of smiling benignly at them.

"—but I wondered if you might have time to inspect the house with me today?"

"The house?"

"Our future home. You will wish to decide if you want any of the rooms repainted or perhaps papered. It is not furnished, except for the servants' areas. Choosing furniture is best left to the bride."

For some reason, she felt herself blushing. Really, Captain Easterday was uncommon thorough in carrying out their mock engagement. "Oh. I had forgotten."

"I am devastated." His eyes twinkled charmingly.

Her face must be scarlet. "I mean...this is all so new to me that, that..." *Please rescue me!*

"You have not yet thought of all the changes

285

marriage will bring," he responded as if he had heard her thought.

"Exactly, sir." What must she do? Should she ask to defer the visit to some other day or at least after the end of the business day?

"I do not think anyone could find fault with a newly betrothed couple sharing a carriage with the lady's aunt. Mistress Williams agreed to come with me. She is waiting in the carriage."

Her clerks had returned to their tasks, evidently seeing nothing remarkable in the captain's suggestion.

"I realize it may seem I have taken your agreement for granted, but she understands you may not be free to come today. It made sense to collect her first rather than returning to Well Close Square and having to double back."

"Of course. Certainly I can accompany you."

Finley murmured, "If you have not returned by closing time, ma'am, I will make sure that all is secure."

"Thank you, Finley."

Captain Easterday ushered her out the door.

****

"I look forward to seeing your house, Captain." Aunt Rachel fairly fizzed with delight.

"I hope you both may like it, ma'am."

They went by carriage to the Old Swan Stairs, west of London Bridge, where Captain Easterday's barge awaited and upriver to the Somerset House Stairs. From there, they took a hackney which wove through a maze of streets until they crossed what Olivia recognized as High Holborn. "So this is where we are! I had lost any sense of direction."

They emerged into the open area before the church of St. George the Martyr. The opposite end of the square—really, a long rectangle—having been left open, only the east and west sides contained houses. Rachel remarked, "I often visited friends in Queen's Square during my marriage. I always thought it very pretty. The view of Highgate and Hampstead hills gives such a feeling of spaciousness."

"I inspected half a dozen other houses, but I chose this house for its view." The coach pulled up before a double-fronted brick house twice as wide as their own home and a story taller.

Easterday instructed the coachman to wait and assisted them to descend to the pavement, as a footman opened the double doors. The first thing she noticed upon entering was the glazed double doors leading to a garden at the back of the house. Even on a gray day, they would brighten the ground floor hall. On the left, a graceful right-angled staircase led up from the marble-paved entry hall.

"The drawing rooms are here," Easterday said, opening a door to the right. "When the double doors between the two are thrown open, one might easily hold a small dancing party or a soiree."

The rooms were well lighted by two windows each in the front and the back. The dining room was across the corridor from the back drawing room, with a service area and stair connecting to the kitchen in the basement.

Aunt Rachel exclaimed over the simplicity of the mantel pieces and moldings. "How elegant! Nothing is heavy or stately. I like the paneling throughout better than the modern taste for papering the walls, which is fussy and hard to keep clean."

Three rooms occupied the front of the first floor, overlooking the square. Two more overlooked the garden at the back. The first three might serve as the man's bookroom, the lady's boudoir, and as for the third, who knew what? The ones at the rear would be their bedchambers with dressing rooms. Olivia particularly liked the built-in cabinets on either side of the fireplaces. The smaller rooms on the second story would be bedrooms for the children, and the servants would occupy the attic.

"It's a lovely house," she said, when they ended the tour in the domestic offices in the lower ground floor. The kitchen and servants' hall would receive light during the day from windows on the areaway.

"I had a copy of the floor plans made for you to assist in planning what furniture you would wish to buy." Easterday drew several folded sheets out of his pocket. "If you think it necessary, some alterations to the rooms are not out of the question."

"I will study them with great interest, Captain." She could buy a similar house. How nice it would be to live in such an airy home, with a garden to sit in when the weather was warm.

"You might call me Marcus. It's unexceptionable for a betrothed couple to use each other's given names."

This felt a trifle uncomfortable. Easterday was behaving as if their espousal was real rather than pretense. He was thorough in all things, as she knew from his business practices. The trait commanded her respect, as she was scrupulous about details herself. Indeed, what could any lady object to in the captain? His manners pleased, he was steady and careful, with regular features. She distrusted men who were too handsome; they tended to have an unnecessarily high opinion of themselves. The captain's children would inherit no bad features from him. The chit who had jilted him in favor of a younger, more exciting gentleman was a fool. In her experience (admittedly limited), exciting men were unreliable, gambled away more than they could afford to lose, had mistresses...Ambrose Hawkins was reliable in business and was not known as a gambler. No doubt both he and Easterday had mistresses, but what else could one expect of an unmarried man? Hawkins would have expected her to give up Cantarell Shipping, or at least her role in it. Easterday, for all he appeared more conventional than Hawkins, seemed to have less objection to her interest in business.

"Mistress Olivia?"

Her mind had wandered far afield from his original question.

Her aunt replied before she herself could gather her wits. "Despite her unfeminine interest in business, my niece is maidenly shy, Captain Easterday."

*I am not*, was her first thought. Since she could not say it, she murmured, "If I am to call you Marcus, you should call me Olivia."

"Olivia."

Gazing up at him, she suspected that he knew very well that her reluctance was not shyness. He looked amused.

All things considered, she was glad when they left Queen's Square. The betrothal was feeling worrisomely real. Also, she lusted for the Queen's Square house.

The barge's cruise downriver, enjoyable enough on its own, was further improved by Easterday's having provided a basket of fruit, cheese, crusty bread, little cakes, and wine. Finley had been correct; by the time Easterday's barge reached the Old Swan Stairs, Finley would be preparing to lock the door. Aunt Rachel pointed out they should go directly home, and Olivia admitted the truth of the suggestion.

Captain Easterday urged neither one course nor the other. She gazed at him a little resentfully, suspecting he would have gone to his office in the same situation. He said with a half smile, "I am permitting my head clerk to close the office for me today. I mean to think what furnishings I will want for my bookroom."

She found herself laughing with appreciation at the adroit way he made it seem no dereliction of hers to go home rather return to her business.

"What fun you will have deciding on colors and furniture, Livvie. You have such good taste. I did not much care for the arsenical green paint in the drawing rooms, did you? I always think it rather bilious, however fashionable it may be."

"It's a horrid color. I am not partial to blue-grey either. I would like a straw color and perhaps a creamy white for the dining room, Aunt."

She would never be called upon to decide the paint colors for the house. She sighed; it really was a charming residence. If she were furnishing it, she would ask Marcus if he objected to Chinese furniture. Ah Fong had some, goodness knew why, as he did not display it, so how could he sell it? One would not use Chinese pieces throughout, but a few, as focal points, would be appealing. A walnut and lacquer armoire she coveted—over six feet tall and nearly five feet wide— would provide a good deal of storage. It would need a large apartment.

She had also seen a charming bed upstairs at the Academy & Museum of Oriental Art when visiting Ainslie, a "moon bed," Ah Fong called it. From the foot and head, the canopy curved in an arc of some three-quarters of a circle. The wood was simply carved, relying on elegant lines for its beauty. Olivia had sighed over it, but it would be too large for her chamber in Well Close Square, besides looking out of place with the other furniture. Ah Fong assured her he would come with a crew of several men to set it up. "Everything go together just so in one order only." Seeing her hesitation, he had added brightly, "Long enough for tall English man."

She had colored at that and told him she would think about it. Although she was growing accustomed to having money, she had not quite come to think it permissible to buy a house merely because she wanted a particular bed. Would Captain Easterday—Marcus— like a Chinese bed? She suppressed the thought.

She went up to her own chamber earlier than usual, then spent an hour or more daydreaming over the Queen's Square floor plans. The moon bed would fit easily in one of the bedrooms. The Chinese armoire could go...well, somewhere. One always needed storage. A Chinese altar table might be useful against the wall in the drawing room as a place for a pair of candlesticks and a vase. Or in the entrance hall.

As for the garden, while she knew nothing about plants, she did like flowers. That lovely space behind the house, walled for privacy, contained only two trees and several rose bushes. If she lived there, she would add crimson peonies, hellebore, lavender, and bergamot. She knew those would grow, Rachel having pointed them out to her in a friend's garden. Perhaps the gardener would recommend other flowers, too. Herbs, of course, for the kitchen. She fell asleep to dream of lacquered cabinets and peonies the color of sang de boeuf porcelain.

Chapter 35

Really, she had scarcely enough time in a day! After several visits to Madame Harfleur's shop, first to study and choose from the latest designs, decide on trim, and be measured, then for fitting to ensure that each garment fitted exactly as it should, her new clothing had arrived. Her aunt had gone over every item, before storing them temporarily in the bedchamber formerly occupied by Jonas Cantarell. Olivia's did not have room enough for all of it. It was not merely the mantuas, petticoats, robes à la this and that, capes, and shifts. The hoops, corsets, shoes, hats, gloves, stockings, caps, fichus, and all the other accessories occupied boxes stacked on the bed. *That tall Chinese armoire would have held most of it.*

" 'Tis inconvenient, but 'tis not for long, Niece."

"Not really. I don't need these for every day. I could hardly wear any of these to go to the shipping office."

Rachel Williams sighed, audibly. "You must hire a lady's maid."

"Good God!"

"My dear! You will need one to take care of your clothing and arrange your hair. You have been doing it yourself and wearing it the same way since you were a girl. I can interview them first to select several who are suitable. Then you can interview them to choose the

293

one you prefer."

"I will be wearing my usual clothes until my marriage. I will not need a maid sooner."

Aunt Rachel tittered. "Certainly you will. It is only because Captain Easterday has no family living nearby, and our family has not mixed in more elevated circles, that there have been no invitations to dinner, the theater, soirees, and balls. The captain should take us to call upon some of his acquaintances, at least the ones most likely to hold entertainments. Most of the beau monde, of course, is out of town now."

*Thank God!* In any case, Easterday was hardly likely to have many dealings with the fashionable and aristocratic set. He did know a great many wealthy businessmen, but did they ape the habits of the upper reaches of society?

"Which reminds me, Livvie, when is the wedding to be?"

"We have not discussed the matter yet."

"You should. Ordinarily the betrothal is not long, for what would be the point? You have had time to order and get your clothes, which is already a longer period than would have been usual in my day. Life is uncertain. Best to marry quickly and get a child in case..." Her aunt stopped and took a deep breath. "Of course, most young ladies have adequate wardrobes to begin their marriage, as they have been recently introduced to society and gowned and decked out to attract suitors. A little delay is understandable when you really had so few appropriate garments. Now we should be setting a date and making up a list of those to invite. Does Captain Easterday's family mean to attend? They live in Lancashire, I believe?"

"I don't know."

"Gracious heaven, you and the captain must give such things some thought! If they intend to come, the journey would best be done before autumn, while the roads are not axle-deep in mud. Then there is the need to get furnishings for the house before the wedding…"

The conversation having taken place at the breakfast table, Olivia said, "Davant should be here shortly. I must get my hat and cape."

"Please write to your betrothed about these things. I know they are not near as fascinating as tonnage and dunnage and the *Lloyd's List*," Aunt Rachel said with gentle irony, "but they are quite as important."

"I will." *I will speak with Ah Fong about the bed and armoire, too. I will have them, even if I must buy a larger house.*

As it fell out, she had no need to write to Easterday, who stopped in at Cantarell Shipping late in the morning. She had become accustomed to seeing him in the office every few days and was not surprised when Ky came to her room to announce him.

Admitted to her sanctum sanctorum and invited to sit down, he began with a few fresh tidbits of shipping news which could only have reached Lloyd's Coffee House within the last hour or two. They were far more useful than the society and court news which her aunt passed on to her.

"I am glad you came in today," she said when they had chewed over the peculiar account of the fist fight between two well-regarded business partners on Custom House Quay, suspected to have been over the relationship of one with the wife of the other, and what it would mean for their business relationship.

295

"I hope I am always welcome." He wondered why he had said something almost flirtatious. She blushed very prettily, making it worthwhile, even if it struck both of them momentarily speechless.

"Our betrothal seems to be having a great many more consequences than simply preventing a duel between you and Hawkins."

"I suppose it has. We could not tell him we were engaged without making some effort to support the claim. He would not believe it without seeing it announced. Even then, if we did not act our parts, Hawkins has a sufficiently devious brain to guess we were shamming it."

"I agree. He would be quite angry if he suspected the betrothal was all hocus-pocus—anyone would! The problem is, my aunt wishes to know when the wedding is to be and whether your relations will attend."

He opened his mouth to reply that of course they would come to the wedding, stopping himself only just in time. *There will not be a wedding.* Which was why he had not troubled to write to his brothers about it. *Zounds, what if Geoffrey's seen it in the newspaper?* Unlikely. The only London newspaper Easterday could recall seeing at Lowfields Manor was the *London Gazette*, which Geoffrey read for its legal and business news when it eventually reached Preston. It did not, thank God, print social announcements. Harry might see an announcement; he would certainly receive the London papers.

"My brothers will not hear of it. You may tell Mistress Williams my older brother's family cannot easily leave the manor, Geoffrey having no steward to manage it in his absence. Harry is a barrister in

Nottingham and may not be able to get away."

"How fortunate that he does not live nearer to London. If he were a day's travel away, that excuse would not work."

"Yes, I chose my ancestors wisely," he admitted cheerfully.

"You showed great good sense. My aunt also expects you to provide a list of those you wish to invite and thinks you should accompany us to the furniture warehouses to select furnishings. Ah Fong—at the Academy and Museum of Oriental Art where you picked up Ainslie?—has a Chinese bed and an armoire I mean to buy." Her face took on a startled expression as she said this. She hurried on. "I mean to purchase those pieces, even though I suppose I shall have to buy a larger house to hold them."

"When you break off our engagement, I will make you a good price on the Queen's Square House." *I won't need it if I do not marry.*

"I don't really need such a large house though I confess I am half in love with it."

*And I am half in love with you.* He realized he was leaning forward and half smiling. He managed to say, "I believe I saw a set of chinaware in his shop. Though you will want to visit the shops near St. James to see if there is anything you like better. I am no expert."

"His will probably be more to my taste. Of course, if you do not care for it, there are still the other china shops."

"I have no doubt I will like it." His tongue followed his unruly mind before he could stop it. "Will the bed be big enough?—for you, I mean. You are taller than the Chinese I saw in Asia."

297

"Oh, yes. According to Ah Fong, it's long enough even for a tall Englishman. Not that…that is…"

"We aren't going to marry."

Her lips turned up a fraction. "No, we are not, are we? I keep forgetting."

"So do I." He cleared his throat. "Ah Fong's shop is full of contrasts. China and jade to rival the best to be found in London and gewgaws fit for children. How does he come by them? And how does he come here? He must be the only Chinaman in England."

"It is probably better not to inquire into his sources of supply, which I misdoubt include the East India Company. I have no idea if there are Celestials elsewhere in England, though I think not. He came here with my father when he was still sailing, I don't know under what circumstances. I think they did each other a good turn, and that Ah Fong needed to get away from China."

"I am only surprised he is not an object of wonder, as the Cherokee Indians were, who visited London ten years ago."

"Ah Fong having been here since before my birth, the novelty has worn off, I imagine, and his shop is in a neighborhood where sailors, importers, and a good many foreigners are to be found."

"We should pay him a visit. Will your aunt be shocked if she accompanies us?"

"We should probably go by ourselves. She is somewhat conventional."

"Very well. When shall we shop for conventional furnishings?"

"We need not hurry about it. After all, any painting and papering must be done before bringing in furniture, which is an excellent excuse for putting it off."

"And why bring in furniture until any carpets you choose are in place, which cannot be done until after painting. This works out excellently well."

"I do want to buy the bed and armoire before— heaven forbid!—someone else does."

"If you want to go today, you could have one of your lads summon a hackney. I would enjoy visiting the shop."

She seemed to be debating with herself; her eyes had that inward look signifying concentration to the exclusion of anything external. "We needn't go by coach. Come."

She rose from her chair and walked—strode, actually—into the front office.

"Mr. Davant, I am going upstairs to show some goods to Captain Easterday. It may take us some time. I don't want to be disturbed."

"Ay, ma'am."

The clerk's face was wooden. Perhaps the idea of Olivia Cantarell going upstairs unchaperoned with a male was too unorthodox even for a man who was willing to work for a female shipping agent. Easterday gave him a reproving glance.

They went up to the top floor, as they had the day he'd brought the sea chest with clothing for Ainslie. She paused at a small table against one wall. It held a candle lantern and tinder box.

"We'll need light," she said. "Will you carry the lantern, please?"

He lit the candle, wondering why they needed it when the space was well lighted by two windows in the front wall, and one in the back wall despite all three being grimy. She led him toward a head-high stack of crates. Instead of butting up against the wall, the packing cases stopped short of it, leaving a narrow passage that led around behind them. Olivia stopped at a door they had concealed in the back wall. With the crates blocking the daylight from the windows, he did not think it would be noticeable without the lantern. She brought a ring of keys out of the pocket under her petticoat.

"This leads to the extension on the west side of the yard. I suppose the boys know the door is here, if they've come up to this floor. Boys will explore. They probably think it's used for secure storage of small shipments."

He followed her through, and she locked the door behind them. They were in a cramped space, no more than a wide corridor. It was about ten feet long, with another door in the far end. She unlocked it, too, and they emerged into a similar hallway, with another door at the end. Beyond was a room the width of the Cantarell building.

"You may blow out the candle. We will not need it until we come back."

From a lacquered cabinet and one or two other signs, he guessed the truth. "I did not realize when I came to collect Ainslie that Ah Fong's backs up to Cantarell Shipping."

"Only three people, apart from Ah Fong, are aware of it now. You, myself, and Ainslie. I swore him to secrecy, and I trust you not to reveal it."

"You have my word."

She glided across the room and through another door that led to a storeroom and down the stairs. He followed, taking care not to step heavily, in case Ah Fong had customers. A few steps up from the last landing before the ground floor, she paused to listen, then touched a long string of bells hanging from the ceiling. Their chiming was surprisingly loud.

When another chime answered, she continued down the stairway.

Ah Fong spoke much better English than he had during Easterday's brief visit earlier. He also had amazing merchandise—when he chose to show it. Olivia was correct; the bed was a handsome one, unquestionably long enough for her, or for a tall Englishman. *Or both.* Olivia languidly mentioned she might—only might—consider relieving Ah Fong of the odd, bulky bed, making room for merchandise which would actually sell. She turned vivacious before his eyes when she and Ah Fong settled into a spirited bargaining session that was more a game to both of them than a commercial transaction. Easterday leaned against the wall and enjoyed the sight. They reached agreement on a price not much higher than one would expect to pay for a bedstead of excellent quality but low indeed for an exotic Chinese bed. Like Ah Fong, it must be unique in England. They began the process all over again for a tall cabinet with lacquered panels. When they were done, Ah Fong agreed to hold them until she could have them moved.

"It may be two or three months," she said.

He nodded gravely. "You will want silk for the bed. Come see." He went to a large, battered crate standing on end against one wall, untied a cord around it, and pulled open what had once been its lid and was now a door. The inside was lined with a smooth veneer and fitted with shelves holding flat rectangular packages about twenty-eight inches wide. Each was wrapped tightly in coarse linen marked with a few Chinese characters. The merchant glanced down the shelves, muttering to himself, until he exclaimed, "Ah!" and pulled out one of the parcels. He placed it almost reverently on a table nearby.

Unwrapped, the contents were a length of crimson damask. Its brilliant hue must come from cochineal, supplied by the East India Company. Silk dyed with the available Chinese vegetable dyes was more subdued, not a clear, true red.

Olivia ran her hand gently over the fabric. "Soft and clingy. I believe you can always tell a Chinese silk by that one characteristic, even without the contrasting selvedge."

"Very good quality," Ah Fong said. "Not packed damp like some, to increase weight and price. No mildew. A very good color for marriage bed."

She raised her eyebrows. "What marriage?"

"The captain is here. Why bring a man who will not be sleeping in the bed?"

"The circumstances are difficult to explain," Olivia said.

Ah Fong murmured something Easterday suspected meant, "English people…tcha!"

"What is the length? Thirty-eight *chih* or forty-five?"

Lord, she could be an East India Company supercargo, if she weren't a female. He himself knew just enough to know a *chih* was about fourteen inches. Thirty-eight *chih* was a standard length for Chinese silk.

"Thirty-eight. But I have two lengths. Plenty for bed." *And likely a coverlet, too.*

Another lively bargaining session ensued, at the end of which Olivia owned both lengths at a price low by the standards of the East India Company silk sales, where the buyers would then have been required to re-export the silk to Europe or the colonies, to protect the English silk weavers. Surreptitious sales and re-importation by smugglers were not uncommon, however. Easterday misdoubted the English silk industry could meet the demand for silks for clothing and furnishing fabrics. Further, the Company had—or was supposed to have—a monopoly on the China trade. Easterday found himself guiltily unshocked. He glanced at Olivia, who misread his look.

"I hope you are not offended at this irregularity," she murmured.

"Olivia, I will take offense when members of the House of Lords stop drinking run brandy."

"Ha!" she blurted.

"Just so."

"I have *gorgoroon*, *goshee*, paduasoy, *poisee*, and taffeta if you wish," Ah Fong continued after their exchange.

"I will come back another day to look at those, Ah Fong."

The Chinese nodded. "I will put bed damask with the cabinet."

They returned to Olivia's office, where Davant was still wooden-faced. They had been upstairs and unchaperoned for well over an hour which would be scandalous if it had been true. Most parents would not permit even a betrothed couple to be alone longer than half an hour. On the other hand, they were mature adults and could be expected to be past the age of yielding to overwhelming passionate impulses...Or perhaps not. Olivia Cantarell's intensity while bargaining with Ah Fong made her glow. Her passion might not be limited to commercial matters. The thought of that exotic bed (*long enough for a tall Englishman*) draped with crimson silk gave rise to fascinating images.

Working in the maritime trade's free and brutal world, Davant's punctiliousness was surprising. Well, Davant was young, new to shipping, and came of Calvinist Huguenot stock. He would get used to it. Wouldn't he? It occurred to Easterday that his own reaction would ordinarily be much like Davant's, his own upbringing having been fairly strict.

Men behaved one way with ladies and another with women outside polite society. He would never have taken Mariah Saltstall off to an isolated area at the Haymarket ridotto or at Cantarell Shipping. Unless she were Olivia's age?

He thought not. Mariah, like Claudia Dean, was part of the genteel world. Behavior and expectations were rigidly defined. Ladies might flirt; they might not practice a profession. Gentlemen might keep mistresses for pleasure and spend time with other men for friendship. The lady's sphere was the home and child-bearing. No wonder many men found the company of their wives boring, when they often had no more in common than their children. God knew he had seldom paid attention to Mariah's chatter and silliness, or Claudia's, either. Though Claudia had usually simply listened to him. Her attention had flattered him, egotistical young idiot he'd been.

Once married, he and Claudia—or Mariah—would have spent less time together than they had during their engagement—and that had been little enough. They would have dined together in the evening and possibly gone out to some social affair where they would spend time with others, not with each other. They would have had separate bedrooms, and he thought he would have felt it unsuitable to impose his male lust upon his tender young wife too often.

Yet Olivia was a lady and also involved in a demanding business. Since they had become friends, he had overcome his initial disapproval while wishing he could do something to ease her way. For Olivia's intelligence to be wasted in ladylike pursuits would be like hitching a race horse to a cart.

He managed to chat for a few minutes with Olivia, Davant, and Finley, who had returned from a visit to one of the wharves. When he took his leave of her, he kissed her hand without thinking how odd a thing it was to do in a commercial setting.

Chapter 36

Aunt Rachel was busy with the cook when Olivia arrived, dealing with who knew what domestic disaster. She put away her cape, hat, and gloves, washed her face and hands, and spent an hour in the small bedchamber her father had outfitted as an office. The figures from the managers' reports of her warehouses and rental properties were overdue to be entered in the ledgers, a chore for which she never seemed to have enough time now. She might have taken them to the shipping office where she could have worked on them during any lull in the day's business. This she refused to do because of Munns's betrayal. She was sure she would not forget to lock the books away if she left the office, but likely her father had believed the same.

She did not see her aunt until dinner, on emerging from her lair with the warehouse ledgers completed. The rental ledgers must wait until tomorrow.

"Livvie, the most delightful thing," Rachel bubbled as she entered the dining room. "Dear Julian has written that he and his wife intend to come for the wedding. You and the captain must fix a date to allow them time to make arrangements."

"Julian is coming?"

"Yes, of course. He was very pleased to hear of it and wanted to know why neither you nor I had mentioned you were courting. He did complain that you had not written of late, you naughty girl. You have been busy, I know, but one must keep up one's correspondence."

"But how did he hear of it?"

Aunt Rachel stared at her. "Why, from my letter, naturally. I write at least once a month, though when you and Captain Easterday became betrothed, I fired off the news to him immediately. He does not always reply. You and Julian have much in common in that regard. On this occasion, he wrote at once."

"I see." Improvising quickly, Olivia said, "We have discussed marrying sometime in the spring. Autumn is coming on, the house in Queen's Square is not likely to be ready until the weather has turned cold and wet, and then early spring is often wet and makes travelling difficult. If we are to have any guests coming from a greater distance than my brother, we must take the weather into account." *And if Marcus agrees to set the date so far out, we can postpone breaking off the betrothal.* A long engagement would let Hawkins get over his ire, put off any renewal of his claim on her, and give her months to enjoy being affianced to Marcus Easterday.

"Do we anticipate anyone coming from a distance?" Aunt Rachel inquired dubiously.

"Captain Easterday's brothers may be able to attend if the roads are fit for a coach. One lives in Lancashire and the other in Nottingham, you know."

"I confess I had forgotten, if I ever did know. It would be wonderful if they could be here. I am not in favor of long engagements, but there are a number of preparations to make. You will need silver, linens, dishes, glassware, and draperies as well as furniture.

Nor is it too soon to begin shopping. I don't suppose the captain owns a set of good silver? Or if he does, living in a bachelor establishment, he will not have enough for a dinner party of more than half a dozen guests. You should inquire. Carpets, too—"

"Aunt…" What could she say to distract her aunt? She could not tell her there was really no need for furnishings or planning a wedding because they had no intention of marrying.

"I know it must seem overwhelming, but with organization and a long betrothal, it need not be. We will manage it one step at a time. I do think we should hold a series of little dinner parties to celebrate. We can only seat twelve comfortably, but there are not hundreds of people who have to be invited. Only Captain Easterday's particular friends and their wives, and our friends. Should we invite Baron Lees? As your cousin and my nephew, he is too close a relation to ignore. He might come, given that the captain is a man of some substance."

"It would be very improper to have male dinner guests without a host."

Aunt Rachel laughed gaily. "I am amazed to hear you voice such a conventional objection. It would be improper, of course, but I thought we might ask Mr. Nevis to act as host."

"You like him, don't you, Aunt? But would he do it? It would be very pushing to ask of a casual acquaintance."

"Nevis is a friend, not merely someone with whom I am on nodding terms."

"After only three meetings?"

Rachel's pale skin turned rose-petal pink. "We

have seen each other oftener than that. We have gone on little outings together during the day. While you are away at that office, he has taken me to Chelsea and to market days around town, which are very amusing, and to lectures and entertainments."

"Mayhap we should be planning your wedding, Aunt. He appears to be a pleasant, worthy man. Doesn't he own a little manor somewhere?"

Her aunt became flustered and admitted that there was a manor though Nevis had chosen to live in London since his wife's death because he found himself lonely living alone—except for the servants, of course—and the nearest village did not provide much interest. He would like to live in the country again if he need not live by himself, but they had not discussed...she was not sure if his daughters would object, but they were married and lived in Cornwall and Manchester, and his son was a naval officer and seldom in England...

"By all means, ask him to be the host at your dinner parties, if we must have them. It will give you more opportunity to get to know him." If Rachel and Nevis decided to marry, her aunt might lose interest in Olivia's supposed marriage, and the end of the betrothal would be less of a blow.

"If you wouldn't object, Livvie..."

"I think it a wonderful idea."

"I feared your annoyance with Mr. Hawkins might color your attitude to Mr. Nevis."

She would not mention that Nevis was willing to aid and abet Hawkins and pass on tidbits of information to him. "Not at all, Aunt Rachel."

"He has known Mr. Hawkins for many years, you

know, and although he did not say so, I believe he helped him with introductions when Mr. Hawkins first started in business, after he left the sea. I suppose he thinks of him as a sort of nephew."

As she ate her veal cutlet and spinach, it occurred to her that if Ambrose Hawkins made no secret of his courtship, his friends would see nothing wrong with giving him an opportunity to evade chaperonage or revealing the color of a domino. Nevis had not, after all, taken part in her abduction.

For once, Rachel did not question her about her day's activities. Just as well! Instead, she talked of Nevis. Clearly, she was smitten with him.

"...and his manor in Cheshire produces a great deal of cheese, the grass there being peculiarly good for the production of milk. You know there is no cheese more popular here than Cheshire cheese. I wish I might see it sometime..."

Aunt Rachel must mean the Nevis manor, as they had a fine wedge of Cheshire cheese in their pantry.

If Nevis were as taken with Aunt Rachel as she was with him, it behooved Olivia to promote their courtship by way of distracting her aunt from Olivia's affairs. Though if Aunt Rachel married, it would be necessary to acquire some indigent lady or retired governess as a chaperone. Whoever she employed would doubtless be more concerned for propriety even than Aunt Rachel, who was accustomed to her niece's activities.

**** 

Easterday attempted to mask his unease when he arrived at Cantarell Shipping, but when he was shown into Olivia's office, either she was not pleased to see him or else some trouble weighed upon her, for her eyes were not sparkling.

She motioned him to sit. "I was going to write to you, Marcus. I learned something from my aunt last night that gives me cause for concern."

"What a coincidence," he said hollowly. "I have also received unwelcome news."

"Business or personal?"

"Personal, I fear."

"Mine too," she sighed. "Will you go first, or shall I?"

"Ladies first, by all means."

"I am not a good correspondent, except regarding business matters. My aunt is. I foolishly forgot that fact, or I would have foreseen she would write to my brother about my betrothal. He and his family mean to come for the wedding."

"My news is much the same. I did not write to my brothers, on the theory they would not hear of it. Some friend of Geoffrey's who lives in London wrote to him about the announcement, and he tells me he has written to Harry."

"A false betrothal seemed such a sensible way of avoiding trouble between you and Hawkins, and now it has turned into a farce."

Easterday found himself laughing. "I can visualize it on stage at Drury Lane. It's like a pebble tossed into a pool, generating ripples."

" 'Twould be funny if 'twere happening to someone else," she admitted, with a hint of amusement. "The mischief is, how are we to stop it? The more people are concerned in it, the more difficult it becomes."

"I had noticed that fact."

"My aunt wants to hold several dinners to celebrate. Our dining room is not large enough to invite all our friends and well-wishers at once," she explained. "She thinks we must also shop for furniture—"

"More than merely the bed and armoire?" The thought of Olivia in that bed kept returning to him. He should engage a mistress…but that would be one complication too many at the moment, for such things always became known among one's male acquaintances. The best one could hope was that one's wife and female relatives remained ignorant of one's liaisons. Not that he would be likely to keep a mistress if he were married, unless his wife disliked marital relations. Some women did, he understood, but how dismal such a marriage would be.

She turned pink, and her lips curled up in spite of herself. After an apparent struggle to control her amusement, she said, "She naturally assumes we will—would!—need other furniture. A dining table and chairs, sideboard, small tables, carpets…everything. I did not mention the bed and armoire."

"Very wise. It might have shocked Mistress Williams to think we had shopped together for a bed. Oh, the indecency of it!"

She crowed in a most unladylike way which Easterday found charming in so controlled a female. "The situation is really not much worse," she admitted finally. "It merely affects more people. I told my aunt that by the time the rooms have been redecorated and the draperies made up, winter would be upon us and we must wait for spring so that travel will be easier as your brothers might be able to come. I have one piece of good news. Aunt Rachel and Mr. Nevis have spent time together, and he will be acting as host at my aunt's dinner parties. I hope this will lead to their marrying, and therefore to taking her mind off anyone else's nuptials."

"We can also hope that some scandal or startling occurrence diverts attention from our ending our betrothal."

"We had best hope that our announcement is not the scandal. Though it's not as if either of us moves in the circles where such a thing really would be cause for scandal."

"Yes, the merchant class worries less about gossip. We'll weather the storm." Though he could not imagine how.

Chapter 37

On returning to his offices, he found two letters waiting for him, one from Richard Saltstall— *Damnation! To become betrothed so soon after my betrothal to Mariah ended must seem an intolerable insult*—and the other from John Barlicorn.

"Elliott, I may have to go out again. Is there anything pressing that needs my attention?"

"No, sir, barring several letters that need your signature." Elliott's voice reproved him for thinking any important matter would have gone unmentioned. His head clerk did not approve of problems and did not permit them to arise, so only acts of God and other unpreventable catastrophes required Easterday's intervention. *I should put him in charge of my personal life.*

He glanced over the letters awaiting his signature, all of which were perfect, as he had known they would be, and signed them, before opening Saltstall's and Barlicorn's.

Saltstall merely requested that he call upon him at his Earliest Convenience. The wording gave no hint whether the meeting concerned a business or a personal matter. Zounds, what now? Barlicorn's message was also a request that he call:

*I have learned something of the greatest urgency regarding Mistress O. C. I will be at Job's until late afternoon and at the Queen thereafter.*

    *Yr most Obedient,*

    *J. Barlicorn*

From a man like Barlicorn, the words "greatest urgency" took on worrisome significance. What would he consider urgent, other than an imminent appointment with the hangman? A cold hand closed around his heart at the reference to Olivia.

Moments later, Easterday was striding toward Job's Coffee House in St. Clement's Lane, off Lombard Street. He had passed within hailing distance of Job's every time he made his way to or from Lloyd's. Did Barlicorn's favored coffee house function as a gathering place for men doing nefarious business, as Lloyd's did for shippers, captains, and merchants? Why else would Barlicorn regularly spend a substantial portion of his day there?

The unpretentious exterior would not attract a passerby. Its sign showed a dejected gentleman, head resting in one hand, bowl of coffee in the other, and "Job's" writ large above. The burnt-toast aroma of roasted coffee beans hung in the air outside. Inside, the furnishings consisted of long tables and benches and a rack of newspapers. In one corner, a woman was preparing coffee, surrounded by a counter covered with coffee grinders, pots, and bowls. A boy tended a coffee roaster over a small coal brazier on the hearth nearby. A pleasant scent of pipe smoke mingled with the smell of coffee and chocolate.

One of the serving boys nodded pleasantly and wished him a good afternoon and invited him to be seated. Easterday scanned the room until he sighted John Barlicorn at an isolated table in a far corner. But when he approached, an older waiter approached and asked deferentially if he would not prefer to be seated at a different table.

"I've come to see Mr. Barlicorn."

"In that case, sir, I do beg your pardon. I did not recognize you."

"I haven't been here before."

"Will you want coffee, sir? Or tea or chocolate is available."

"Coffee will do."

Barlicorn beckoned him over as the waiter hastened away.

"Good day, Captain. Ah…I see you have noticed my magnificence."

Easterday forced his eyes to focus on Barlicorn's face, rather than the coral silk coat with its many-colored embroidery of flowers and birds on the broad cuffs and down the front edges, worn over a waistcoat of bright blue.

"In truth, it strikes the eye."

Barlicorn laughed. "Fair puts it out, I'd think. My people and those who usually come to talk to me expect me to dress richly and in bright colors. Sober garb would not impress them, no matter how costly. Please be seated."

Easterday sat on the bench opposite Barlicorn and waited.

Barlicorn wasted no breath on civilities. "A cully came nosing around t'other day and learned that our man sailed for the Far East on the *Morning Star*. I never heard a whisper of anyone asking questions until then; either the hound and his master are remarkable slow to catch the scent or this is a new fellow with some intelligence." Barlicorn raised his coffee bowl, and gazed at Easterday over the edge before taking a swallow. "He kept on asking up and down Wapping and heard you and a similar young man were seen going aboard a collier."

"Did he? But as it's sailed and docked at Newcastle by now…"

A boy approached with Easterday's coffee, silencing him.

When he was again out of earshot, Barlicorn replied, "You might apprehend he can do nothing, and that's true enough, if you mean directly. But an informant of mine mentioned today that someone approached him to arrange for several huffs to carry out a kidnapping. The intended victim is Mistress Cantarell of Cantarell Shipping."

"Damn his eyes!"

"I thought you might be interested."

"The lady and I intend to marry."

"I had heard that same. I told my informant I would take it as a favor if he delayed for a day. He agreed but asked that if the project is to be prevented, his four lads not be injured or arrested. He will advise them to make some display of resistance, then flee. This they would do anyway if they met with serious opposition, but I told him I did not approve any threat to Mistress Cantarell and did not wish to chance injury to her defenders."

"Did he know why she was to be abducted?"

"The cove didn't tell Alfred, which isn't his name—when you hire out to do mischief, you don't want your own name in the business! But as he was the one inquiring for Barlow, it must be connected. There's only two reasons I can think of that a lady's snatched up. One is to marry her—"

Easterday sat bolt upright.

Barlicorn went on. "—and t'other is to extort money from her friends. It can't be to force Barlow to come back; that'd take too long. What your lad's wicked uncle wants is money, Barlow's or anyone else's, and if he believes Mistress Cantarell helped him escape, the more reason to take her money. Gelt in the hand is more convenient than getting control of a ward who has nothing but some little property in the wilds of Cumberland. Now, about how it's to be done."

"You know the details?"

"When I realized who was involved, I asked. Alfred wants my friendship more than that of the Turk that hired him. A hard, dangerous man, I mean, not literally a Turk. It will be the day after tomorrow, when the lady leaves the office and is near her home. The four hackums and the ruffler will be waiting in a coach in Well Close Square by her house. When she gets out, they boil out and grab her, all bob. Safe, that is to say."

"Good God. You're sure they'll be at that end and not outside Cantarell Shipping?"

"That's the last place they'd try it," Barlicorn said frankly. "There's a mort of rough fellows around there that knew old Cantarell and don't mind fighting. Even if they don't care about his daughter, they'd know you and Hawkins take an interest in her. They'd be on the bullies like dogs on butcher's meat. 'Sides, the street's busy with wagons and barrows. Easier and faster to drive away from a residential square."

How could he best protect Olivia? He could travel with her, with a couple of his men…He frowned. He couldn't simply thwart this attempt; he must insure there would be an end to the plan.

"Would you like some advice, Captain?"

He looked up at Barlicorn, whose voice and face were utterly neutral. "If you have any to give, I'll hear it. I have fought pirates, but this is out of my experience."

"Here, then. Your lady and her escort, who is one of her clerks, I believe, are in the habit of walking to Custom House Stairs to go downriver by wherry. They disembark at Hermitage Stairs and take a hackney from there—Little Hermitage Street to Artichoak Lane to Virginia Street, which leads to Neptune Street, the other side of the Ratcliff Highway, and into the square."

"You know a great deal," Easterday observed, thinking of the man's mention of Hawkins.

The archrogue shrugged. "You can't keep much secret in Little Barbary."

"Little Barbary?"

"Wapping." He sipped his coffee. "The architect of the kidnapping would have been happy not to divulge the plan. Alfred capped he would not send his crew into the job without he knew what was planned. He asked very particular how 'twould be done. Alfred vouches for the rogue having some experience, as he did not try to argue the men needed no advance instruction."

"I suppose a thieftaker would know something of planning an abduction."

Barlicorn barked a laugh. "The fellow was no thieftaker. Alfred wouldn't deal with one. No, he's a wrong 'un, says Alfred, though he never saw him before. Not a London lad, though he knew something of docks and wharves."

"Did Alfred describe him? It would be useful to be able to recognize him if I see him."

"Ay. He's taller than you but not as tall as me. Neither thin nor thick in body. Wears his own mud-brown hair. Eyes the same color. A few pock marks on his face. He might be from Plymouth or Bristol. Alfred's not clever at accents, but he's sure he doesn't come from Yorkshire or thereabouts. You can't mistake a tyke, he says. There's iron and stone in their voices."

Easterday's coffee was cooling. He drank it anyway.

"There's no chance they will spirit away Mistress Olivia between the office and the square?"

"While on the water? The river is busy with wherries, barges, lighters, and there's all the ships at anchor in the middle...no, the objections to grabbing her outside the office apply on the river, at Hermitage Stairs, and in the coach, until it reaches Virginia Street."

"Then..."

"As Virginia Street is wider than the others and less busy, it might be possible to ambush her hackney there. However, the only means of entering or leaving the street are Artichoak Lane at the southern end and Pennington Street and then Ratcliff Highway at the northern end. A handful of little lanes lead into and around the market gardens on either side of Virginia, but they don't emerge into any useful street. Well Close Square is reached by half a dozen streets or alleys.

"If it were I," Barlicorn went on, leaning back and gazing at the wall opposite, "I'd have men in the square, disguised as chimney sweeps, porters, and the like. I can supply the accoutrements for your own men, or I can supply the men, at a slightly greater cost, if yours cannot impersonate street vendors."

"Perhaps I should take Finley's place in the coach."

Barlicorn shook his head. "I advise against it. If one of the kidnapper's agents is watching the office, a change in routine might alert them. It would be a good thought to make sure Finley is armed, and you will wish to advise him of what is expected."

"And her, as well."

"Hmmm. From what I hear of the lady, she has nerve in plenty. Sensible to recognize that fact."

"I will be present with some of my own men."

"I understand. It's only to decide where and in what disguise."

"I am not quite easy about Virginia Street," Easterday said slowly. "I trust your...professional...opinion as to its unsuitability for the stopping of the hackney—"

"As I would yours, regarding the handling of a ship."

"—but can we be certain that the abductor is as well able to plan a kidnapping as you are?"

"A point. Alfred thought him knowledgeable, but not having met the man myself, it's hard to be sure. To make certain all happens as planned, Alfred's lads have instructions to refuse to go along if the blackguard tries to make changes at the last moment."

"Will they obey them if they're offered more money?"

John Barlicorn smiled. "No. I promised I'd pay them double to balk. That, and reluctance to disoblige me, will guarantee the attempt will take place in the square or not at all."

"Thank you. I'll reimburse you for whatever you pay out. But still…"

"As you wish to participate, why not wait in a wagon near the south end of Virginia? If there appears to be some weighty piece of freight aboard, the presence of several men would be explained. If the carter is examining the harness or wheel, no one would wonder about the halt. Once the hackney passes, your wagon could follow."

Easterday nodded. "Ay, that would do. I'll see to it, and speak with Finley and Mistress Olivia." What the devil made a man like Barlicorn live on the fringes of London's criminal class? He spoke like a gentleman much of the time and had the wits to succeed at anything he chose. One could not ask such a personal question. One could ask about motives.

"Why are you helping me, Barlicorn?"

Barlicorn turned the coffee bowl in his lean fingers. "It's pleasant to deal with a gentleman for once. Hawkins is a friend of mine, but while he is honest in his way, and began as a gentleman, he has—" He hesitated, searching for the correct words. "—grown away from his roots."

As the archrogue himself had?

His tone changed. "And it may be that sometime you will be in a position to do me a favor."

This was awkward. "If it is not dishonorable, I will do so gladly."

The man laughed. "I swear I will never ask you to perjure yourself to clear me of a crime or do anything else that would offend your principles."

"I believe you would not. Would you not find it more satisfactory to engage in some other business?"

"Ay. But we make choices, and then how is a man to go back? Though I contrive to avoid capital crimes. I don't rob the King's Mail." Barlicorn must have noted his curiosity. "I buy and sell odd lots, the goods of bankrupts or of dead men. Information, sometimes. My services in settling disputes." He set the bowl down. "You've arrangements to make, Captain, and I perceive someone is waiting to speak with me."

Easterday rose. "I thank you for your assistance. Ah...bene lightmans."

"A good day to you, as well," Barlicorn said, laughing. "Later in the day, it would be bene darkmans."

Easterday picked up his hat from the bench and wended his way among the tables and the hurrying waiters. A heavy-set ruffian and a thin, ferrety fellow stood up from a bench some distance away and bulled their way toward the table in the corner. Barlicorn's next appointment?

\*\*\*\*

Alderman Saltstall greeted him warmly. "Thank you for coming. I would have visited your office, but I know your business often requires you to be out and about rather than behind your desk—and we could not be as private there."

"Your message made it sound urgent."

Saltstall twisted a heavy carnelian ring on his finger. "Only in one sense. I know you well enough to be sure you still experience some guilt over my foolish daughter's elopement, even though it was not your fault. Indeed, as I believe I told you afterward, I am exceeding grateful you arranged matters as you did. Yet I feared your recent betrothal would make you feel awkward in my company. I want to assure you that there is no cause. On the contrary, I was heartily glad to hear you are to marry. You are betrothed to the heiress to a shipping and import company?"

"I realize it appears to be unseemly haste—"

Saltstall waved this away. "I understand completely. It's time you started your family. As Mistress Olivia is said to be past her first youth, she's unlikely to be flighty, and thus a good choice. Under the circumstances."

"You could not imagine anyone less flighty. She has been managing Cantarell Shipping since her father's death and was active in the business for years before."

"Shocking, of course, but proof she's sensible. May I hope there is more to it than a mere business merger?"

Easterday's face heated. "Ah...yes."

"I am glad to hear it. Love can be the devil at times but still be well worth having."

"So I've heard."

"Congratulations again. I am particularly pleased for you as I have some happy news of my own. My wife has written me—she has been in Bath to take the waters, as she has been in a lowered state of health ever since that embarrassing episode with Mariah and the Duke of Guysbridge—that we are expecting an addition to our family. After all these years!"

"Felicitations! I'm happy for you, sir."

"Thank you. But I asked you here for another reason. An acquaintance introduced someone to me recently. Whatever pretext he gave for requesting an introduction, he really wanted information about you."

"Did he? Who was it?"

"A Horace Ainslie. A gentleman, very well dressed, but…" The alderman gestured vaguely.

"A gentleman, so not a cit, but…?"

"Country gentry originally, I'd think, with pretensions. He was too fashionably dressed, trying to ape the beau monde. He began by saying he meant to ship a cargo and wondered about your reputation for reliability. I gather he had discovered that I know you."

"What cargo?"

"He did not say. It sounded like a cock and bull tale. He kept working around to you. He commented upon your betrothal. 'Quite a catch for the lady, the captain having a reputation for being flush of money,' was how he put it. I said neither yea nor nay, and eventually I escaped. But it seemed so strange to me that I made some inquiries about Mr. Ainslie. I cannot claim I understand the reason for his interest in you. All I learned was that he owns a heavily mortgaged property in Herefordshire and owes both for tradesmen's bills and for debts of honor here. Do you know anything of the fellow?" Saltstall rose and went to a side table which held several decanters and tumblers. "Brandy or claret?"

"Brandy, please. I know a little of Horace Ainslie, none of it good. What you've told me fills in a little more of the picture. However, as there are others involved and the matter is delicate, I cannot tell you. Not yet, at least."

They enjoyed a brandy together before Easterday took his leave, curiously lighthearted despite the looming kidnap attempt. Learning that his old friend was not offended at his engagement and was looking forward to the birth of a child—a more satisfactory one than Mariah, one hoped—contributed to his improved spirits. Confirmation that the elder Ainslie was probably behind the planned abduction helped. That his betrothal was doomed to end as his previous engagements had formed the only cloud in his sky. No, not quite as those betrothals had done, as Olivia would certainly not elope. He wished—he cut that thought off without completing it. He had arrangements to make.

Chapter 38

Willie gave made a convincing carter, squatting on his haunches to inspect the wheel for damage while Easterday and two of his old shipmates stood idly by. Willie's father had hauled freight, so he'd grown up around the trade. Sharp-eyed Davy cried, "There it comes!" as a coach turned from Artichoak Lane.

"Dan?" Easterday could not be sure; fifteen years ago, or even ten, his eyes had been nearly that keen.

"Ay. Dressed fine, that horse is, with red ribbon knots to its harness. Don't often see that on a hackney coach horse."

Olivia's hackney, then. As it drew nearer, Davy said, "I don't see nothing behind it. Ah, there's a wagon, one man up, but I'd lay you a half a crown it's naught but a farmer, 'cause if he's got anyone with him, they're lying flat in the wagon bed."

Easterday muttered, "We'll follow the coach. If by chance that wagon is the kidnapper's, he'll have to pass us. You've assured yourself the wheel is sound, Willie."

"Ay." He stood, gave the wheel an affectionate pat, and climbed up to the seat, and Easterday scrambled into the wagon bed, followed by Davy and Dan.

"There, the farm wagon's turned off," Davy reported.

Willie took his time adjusting the reins in his

hands, to let the coach pass them. When he did signal the horses to move and the wagon rolled forward, the hackney was sixty or seventy feet ahead.

This heightened awareness, increased heartbeat, and taut muscles were familiar from his seafaring days, when some danger hove into sight. Some men enjoyed the sensation. He did not. The actual fight never bothered him; once it began, he had no time to think about it.

Finally, they saw the Ratcliff Highway ahead. Easterday's linen shirt grew damp with sweat as they rattled toward it. The hackney turned into the highway. Willie, an aggressive wagoner, urged his horses forward to cross in front of a slow-moving dray, earning a spate of invective from its driver.

The hackney made a right turn into Neptune Street, with the wagon only thirty feet behind. Right again, by the courthouse on the corner of Neptune and past the public house, to draw to a stop before the Cantarell house, almost at the east end of the square. On the other side of the street, not quite opposite, stood a gentleman's coach, as evidenced by its glossy paint, sleek, well-fed horses, and a footman on the perch at the back. *He must be the one who hired Alfred's crew of ruffians.*

"This is the one. Willie, go past the hackney but slowly, as if we're looking for the right house."

The hackney driver climbed down to open the door and unfold the steps. Finley sprang down and turned to help Olivia out.

"That's the house," Easterday sang out. "Pull 'em up here, Willie. Lads, let's move this thing so's we can go home."

\*\*\*\*

"It will all go according to plan," Finley said. "That's the captain's wagon passing us."

He must think she was apprehensive. They had not spoken much since getting into the hackney near the Hermitage Stairs. The hackney driver had made no objection to the fastening of ribbon knots to his horse's harness, not once Finley had tipped him a small coin, though the man clearly thought them peculiar.

It was true, she was all on edge. Why she should be, when she had faced down Noakes without a qualm, was a mystery. However, she had not had to look ahead to that confrontation. The waiting was the difference. She clutched her reticule. It was a bit too elaborate to look right with her plain jacket and petticoat. Aunt Rachel had wondered that she should choose to carry it, most especially since she seldom carried any reticule, preferring to tuck her handkerchief, purse, and a tiny hussif with pins and sewing necessities into the pockets tied under her petticoat.

"Almost there," Finley remarked as they passed the brick courthouse that served as the seat of justice for the Tower Liberties.

Her heart pounded as the coach rolled to a halt outside her house and the coachman clambered down to open the door and let down the steps. Finley bolted out and spoke softly to the man, handing over a crown in addition to the regular fare, bidding him wait, no matter what.

Alarmed, the coachman echoed, "No matter what, sir?"

Finley helped her step down and replied, "Nothing to worry you, but if you stay it's a guinea to you."

"Ah, well, I will, then." He turned toward the front of the vehicle.

As she glanced up the street, a freight wagon bearing a great crate and men enough to move it by brute force pulled up at the last house before Ship Alley. She could not recognize any of the men, but two were sitting in the wagon bed with their backs to her.

Finley murmured, "A coach is standing on the other side of the street, opposite the next house. Are you ready?" His right hand slid into his coat's deep pocket.

Their coachman bent in a leisurely manner to inspect his horse's off front hoof. Olivia shook the creases out of her petticoat and made sure her reticule's strings were wound around her wrist. At the sound of footfalls on the cobbles, the coachman's head jerked up. Two men rushed past him toward Olivia and Finley.

" 'Ere," the hackney coachman shouted, laying hold of the horse's headstall as he was shouldered aside. A third man paused to say, "Get out o' 'ere while you can, and all's bob." The rattler driver swarmed up to his seat with the agility of a spider but did not signal the horse to move. The temptation of the riches he'd been promised if he waited was clearly stronger than his fear of a fight.

The first two men bracketed Finley. "Stand away from the mopsie, and I'll not spoil your face or your duds," said one. The other reached out to take Finley by the arm and pull him aside.

Heavy shoes thumped on the stones, but Olivia dared not look away from the tableau before her. The man to her left pivoted, distracted by the sound of someone approaching. Finley tapped the other briskly on the elbow with the cudgel he had been hiding behind a fold of his coat skirt. Knowing how it felt to bump one's elbow even rather gently, she was not surprised that Finley was able to follow it up with a punch to the jaw that sent the fellow reeling back.

The second villain wheeled and threw himself at Finley, knocking him down, while the first tried to pick himself up. A hatchet-faced footman—the source of the footfalls—edged around the struggling men to her side. Did Captain Easterday arrange for other rescuers as well as the freightmen? And where were they? The footman grabbed her by the left arm and pulled her away from the hackney. "Come along, Long Meg, don't give me trouble or—"

Olivia swung her little drawstring bag at his face. His nose took the brunt of it and spouted blood. He ignored the blood and lunged for her, crouching, and tipped her off her feet. Hanging head down over his shoulder, she had a moth's eye view of his shabby livery coat. It smelled musty. A moth had eaten a small hole in the cloth, invisible unless one were so close; the lining was the same green as the fabric. Someone was screaming shrilly.

Then the footman was running, Olivia jouncing painfully on his hard shoulder. Bracing her hands against his back, she levered herself up to look around. Her range of vision was limited, given her awkward position. She could not see Finley and his attacker, who were on the far side of the hackney coach. Where was the second man? Where were Easterday and his men? She glimpsed Kitty standing in the open doorway, hands to her mouth, still screaming.

"Scower! Constables a-coming from the court,"

someone called out, and she heard several sets of feet running.

She shrieked, "Help!" as the footman sprinted across the street. Arching her back to raise herself more, and bracing herself only with her left hand, she gave her reticule several twirls and struck back over her left shoulder. It connected with something; the footman broke stride and snarled a phrase she had never heard in her life. She spun her weapon again, as heavy shoes thudded someplace behind her.

The footman lurched to a halt before she could strike.

"You can't escape. My man's holding your driver at pistol point." Easterday's shout came from behind her.

Her captor dropped Olivia to her feet, twisting her around to face toward Easterday and a well-kept coach a few steps beyond him. The coachman, his gaze fixed on someone standing by the horses, sat frozen. She was motionless herself, except for her ragged breathing; the footman had one arm around her neck. She could feel the tension in his body.

If she had brought the dagger she kept in the desk at work…but she had not be able to work out a way of carrying it both concealed and accessible. In the present situation, her reticule was useless.

"Tell him to let the coach go once I'm inside with the woman. I'll turn her loose when we're well away."

Easterday stood relaxed, hands at his sides, face utterly calm. His air of authority was unmistakable, even in workman's clothing with smears of soot on his face and hands. "I don't know you, so I don't know whether I can trust you. In a bargain, both sides get something. If I let you take her, I may be left with nothing."

"I can snap her neck easy as kiss my hand. They can only hang me once."

"Then neither of us would have what we want. Not a good result, I think."

When the footman did not reply immediately, Easterday went on, "I want Mistress Olivia unharmed. What do you want?"

Pressed against the footman's body, she fancied she could feel his mind scrambling like a rat in a box, looking for a way out.

With a short, unamused laugh, he said, "I want to be out o' this curst disaster. But it's too late."

"Not if Olivia is unharmed. If you let her go and testify against the man who hired you to kidnap her, I'll see you safe out of this 'curst disaster.' I want him punished."

The footman laughed derisively. "Who're you to make such a promise?"

"Captain Marcus Easterday. Alderman Saltstall and the Duke of Guysbridge will both support me in this. Do you know who Ambrose Hawkins is? He is also interested in Olivia's welfare."

The man swore softly. Nothing moved. "I've heard of Hawkins."

"You can't escape if you kill her. The only way out for you is to let her go and testify against your employer."

"Rot those hacks!" the false footman burst out. "If they hadn't run…"

Easterday shrugged. "They're hirelings. They decided to save their own necks. Will you do the same?"

"Do you give me your word you'll get me off?"

"Ay."

The man holding her heaved an exasperated sigh, then his arm loosened around her neck and fell away. She threw herself toward Marcus, the only safety in the world, who had already started forward to meet her. Three men, including Finley, were moving to surround the footman. She could not spare a thought for them. Then the heel of one shoe slipped sideways on a cobble and she stumbled to her knees.

Easterday scooped her up in his arms as if she were a child. With a sigh of her own—but a contented one— she let her head rest against his shoulder and enjoyed the novel sensation of being cradled in a man's arms. The man who had been standing by the kidnapper's coach was now pointing his pistol not quite at the footman. The driver of the gentleman's carriage cracked his whip and coach wheels clattered as he realized he was no longer under guard.

"Where are you injured?" Easterday demanded, staring at her stomach. "You're bleeding."

Her arms encircled his neck. "My knees are bruised, and my ankle is turned, I think. The blood is his."

Easterday glanced away from her bosom to the footman. "A bloody nose?"

"I did that. With my purse." She felt quite proud of herself, now that she was safe. She nodded toward the little embroidered drawstring bag lying on her stomacher, the strings still looped around her wrist. "There's a lead ball inside."

He glanced down to where it lay. "How large a

lead ball?"

"About two inches across. It's a cannonball my father used as a paperweight. From his time sailing, you know."

"Ow."

Their own hackney coachman spoke up. "I'd like me guinea now, if it's all the same to you, sir."

"Take care of it, Finley. But we'll still need the coach for a while yet. I will see the lady safe in the house. Then we will go to the courthouse."

"Must you go? Someone said the constables were coming. Aren't they here yet?"

He gave a cough that she interpreted as a suppressed laugh. "The speaker must have been mistaken. There may be a constable in front of the court, watching. I do see a crowd outside the public house looking this way."

Kitty was still standing in the doorway, though she had stopped screaming, and Aunt Rachel was behind her, wringing her handkerchief. They both fell back at Easterday's approach.

"Please bring her into the parlor, Captain. Oh, Livvie, are you hurt? The blood—"

"It's not mine, Aunt. There's nothing wrong with me."

"I think she should rather be taken upstairs to her bedchamber," Easterday said. "Please show me the way. And send for a doctor. I must leave to deal with matters outside."

"It's not necessary," Olivia protested.

"If Captain Easterday thinks you should retire to bed and see a doctor, you must do so," her aunt said decisively. "He is naturally concerned for you."

She yielded, enjoying the strength of his arms and the intoxicatingly masculine scent of soap and sweat, spices and tobacco. *This must be why cats purr when cuddled.* The only thing better would be if he kissed her as Ambrose Hawkins had done.

"I won't drop you, I promise."

Alack, they reached her chamber far too soon.

How small and plain her chamber was. It needed painting. The furniture, new when her parents moved to Well Close Square, had never been fashionable or expensive. The bed hangings were faded and fraying. She had never needed anything better; unlike ladies of fashion, she was not in the habit of lolling in her chamber in the morning, or any other time. This was not the setting in which she wanted Marcus Easterday to see her. *The moon bed, with crimson hangings, in a pretty room with a view of a garden...*

He deposited her carefully on the edge of her bed. "She should change into a nightgown, Mistress Williams."

Easterday seemed not to notice their dreary surroundings. He was gazing at her with an expression she did not recognize, intent and warm at the same time. It made her feel warm, too, like sitting by a good fire on a winter evening, not hot with embarrassment.

*Will he kiss me?*

Evidently not, though he did clasp her hand. Disappointing but not surprising. He was a staid, sensible man, as a merchant must be. As she was. She could not really enjoy a kiss in the presence of her aunt and the maid in any case. Perhaps when he came back, if he were allowed to see her alone? To be alone with him in her bedchamber—and she in her bed—would be impossible, even if they were supposed to be betrothed. Her face must be flushing at the thought.

"I'll return as soon as may be, my love," he said.

*Oh, please do.*

"I hope you are not coming down with a fever, dear."

"I'm sure I am not, Aunt."

Chapter 39

When he returned to the group outside, the "footman" was lounging against the side of the hackney, with Finley, Willie, and Davy surrounding him, and Dan leaning against the door on the other side of the coach, in case the fellow should try to nip into the hackney and out the other side to get away.

"Captain," Finley said as he came up, "I would hazard a guess that this is the scoundrel that kidnapped Kit and threatened him. He resembles the boy's description. How many similar rogues can the uncle be employing, after all?"

The scoundrel snorted derisively. While waiting, he had made an effort to clean his face of the blood from his nose. Only a few streaks were left.

"I'm sure you're right. What's your name?"

"Swithin Fowler, if you must know."

"I don't suppose that's your right name. Mayhap John Barlicorn could set us straight."

"You know Barlicorn?"

"We've done business. Bene lightmans," he added with what he hoped was a sinister smile.

"I wish it might be. 'Tis shaping to be a bad 'un for me. Is he involved in this?"

"Interested, rather than involved."

"In the cod's-head that engaged me? Rot him."

"On my behalf, your victim being my intended

bride."

Fowler closed his eyes for a moment, as if the light hurt them.

Bidding their coachman still to wait, Easterday led them to the courthouse on the corner.

It would have been altogether easier to deal with the Bow Street Magistrate, Thomas de Veil, who was perspicacious and energetic. However, the crime had taken place within the Tower Hamlets rather than Westminster, making this the court with jurisdiction. The magistrate looked upon them without approval; Easterday had forgotten he was attired as a workman. Fortunately, his speech, together with his monogrammed card case containing both his personal visiting cards and the small trade cards he used for business, went far toward reassuring him. When Easterday said they wished to lay a criminal information regarding an attempted kidnapping, the magistrate nodded briskly.

"Already have the scum in charge, I see. Excellent."

After Easterday explained he was not charging the man they had in custody, who was willing to make a deposition against the actual instigator of the crime, the magistrate's expression soured again.

Swithin Fowler was no longer lounging. In fact, his expression and demeanor suggested that of a Presbyterian deacon.

The magistrate scowled at him, then subjected Easterday and Finley to intense scrutiny, as if he were having second thoughts about believing them.

"Alderman Saltstall will vouch for my character, sir."

"Hmmmf."

He could see the magistrate was torn. On the one hand, he had a perfectly satisfactory suspect before him who had been apprehended in the commission of a felony by an apparently respectable citizen. On the other, the respectable citizen—allegedly known to an alderman of the City of London—wanted the law to pursue some other person and ignore the actual agent of the crime, making for more work and complication.

"I should add that the lady who was to be kidnapped is my betrothed, and that the man who hired Fowler to abduct her has persecuted her previously. Earlier a boy in her employ was kidnapped and questioned by an as yet unidentified miscreant. Subsequently, the instigator, one Horace Ainslie, approached her directly in a threatening manner."

As perjury was—at least theoretically—a serious offense, he tacked around the truth and hoped the magistrate would fail to notice. Some were lazy; some were bribable. If necessary, he would pay out money to deliver on his promise to Fowler although he would never ordinarily corrupt a magistrate. Fortunately for his own conscience, Easterday was willing to wager this justice of the peace was lazy.

"How came you to catch this fellow in the act, Captain?"

"The docks and wharves are always rife with rumors, sir. It came to my ears that someone planned to hold Mistress Olivia Cantarell for ransom. I would have treated it seriously anyway, but the fact that Ainslie had harassed her earlier made it the more credible."

"What is the connection between them?"

Ah, the tricky part. "Mistress Olivia's late father

was the owner of Cantarell Shipping. A young man employed there recently is the nephew of Horace Ainslie and is the owner of an estate in Cumberland. Apparently, the uncle hoped to become Ainslie's guardian, although he already has a guardian in Scotland where he lived until coming to London."

"Do you know this of your personal knowledge?"

"No, sir. But another clerk at Cantarell Shipping, Finley here, who worked for me until he went to work for Cantarell, knows young Ainslie and his family and situation."

The magistrate raised his eyebrows. Apparently, this was turning into more effort than he had hoped.

"Your worship, my name is Jeremy Finley. I have known my fellow clerk, Matthias Ainslie, since boyhood, as my family lived within a mile of his family's manor, and I know that after his father's death, his mother took him and his brothers and sisters to Scotland. Ainslie's paternal uncle is a wastrel, and his mother feared he would gain guardianship over his brothers and sisters and Matthias."

Finley could only know the latter from talking with Ainslie, making it hearsay rather than something he knew of his own knowledge. Though perhaps he had also heard of it from his family. Or perhaps Finley was not quite clear on what constituted hearsay evidence. Easterday preferred not to inquire into it.

"You, fellow—Fowler, is it? How the devil did you dare try to abduct a lady? And is she available to bear witness?" he demanded of Easterday.

"She lives a few doors away, sir, but she was somewhat shaken by the event and I left her reclining on her bed in her aunt's care."

The man consulted his pocket watch and sighed. "The day is growing late. Let us be done with this quickly. What have you to say for yourself, Fowler?"

To give the rogue his due, he was glib. He spun a tale of making the acquaintance of a gentleman in a coffee house, who had bemoaned the unexpected failure of his suit for the hand of a lady.

"Fair beset, he was, not knowing why she would refuse an equal match, and she an old maid to boot. He had good birth and a manor but no ready rhino, and she had money from trade but no husband. I'm no hand with the women, myself, so I couldn't advise him. He hadn't much acquaintance in London, so as he needed a friendly ear, he invited me to dine with him at an ordinary. After a while, he says he don't think the lady dislikes him but maybe she is shy or only undecided. 'I could persuade her if I could get her alone for a bit,' he tells me."

"Meant to compromise her, I suppose," the magistrate grunted. "Far too common a practice in some circles."

"He swore he didn't mean to touch her, not being a young rakehell, only to take her into the country to see his property, thinking as seeing's believing. Not but what showing her a prime London house might impress her more, being London born, but he couldn't afford one, without her money."

"Ay, ay, get on with it."

"Then he asked if I might know anyone who might be willing to bring her along to him for a fee. Your worship, I was a footman to Sir Chesley Rodgers until three years ago. He'd no heir, and none of us had references from him, he having died sudden, making it hard to find a new place. I've got by, taking any job of work I could get. The temptation was too much for me, especially as he is a respectable gentleman, and his scheme seemed like it would benefit both him and the lady, as I said before."

It was a good story, considering Swithin Fowler could only have come up with it since they'd captured him. Plausible and hard to prove, given the length of time since his last supposed employment, and Chesley Rodgers's lack of family. It might be possible to disprove, if one placed an advertisement for the man's former servants, who could testify that Fowler had been one of their number—or not! Would any of them respond? Some might have moved away from London. Even assuming those still in town saw it, most if not all might well ignore such an appeal. Some would be fearful of becoming involved in any legal matter, even if they were offered a reward for coming forward. At the least, hunting for former servants of the baronet—if the law bothered to do so—would take time, during which Fowler might escape.

"This fellow's broken the law, and it's no use saying the one that hired him is worse," the magistrate grumbled. "He should be locked up."

"Sir, it's not uncommon that an accomplice who gives evidence against others may escape prosecution."

A sigh. "And you couldn't catch any of the rest?"

"My most pressing task was to prevent my future wife's abduction. When I and my men appeared, Fowler had Mistress Olivia over his shoulder and meant to throw her into a waiting coach. The others ran like rats. They will surely be arrested for something eventually."

"True enough. Who were your accomplices?" he barked at Fowler.

"Two of 'em I met in a dram shop in Wapping, and they brought the other two in. One of those two knew where to get a coach that'd belonged to a gentleman, so it wouldn't stand out."

"Their names?"

Fowler shook his head. "I misdoubt they'd not do you any good, your worship. 'Tis as likely one was christened Jack Smith and t'other Tom Brown as a hog is to fly. I never told them my true name, and I never heard the names of the others at all."

"There's a deal of this business I mislike. Had you not been a gentleman, sir," he stated, staring at Easterday, "I would lock the lot of you up overnight for disorderly conduct."

Easterday stared back at him.

"Before I proceed in this matter, I will question the alleged victim. As say you she is overcome by the event, I suppose we must wait for tomorrow to speak with her." He turned a basilisk-like gaze on Fowler. "As I do not intend that this fellow vanish like the dew on a warm morning, he will spend the night in our accommodations here." Meaning the cells.

Easterday sensed Swithin Fowler's twitch. "Sir, I am sure that if sent for, Mistress Olivia Cantarell will come immediately. Her aunt meant her to rest on her bed until a doctor could examine her ankle, though we believe it only a sprain, but Mistress Olivia is a lady of dauntless courage."

Fowler fingered his nose meditatively.

Easterday kept his amusement out of his voice. "I have no doubt she will insist on hastening the course of justice. Shall I send my clerk here to fetch her? A hackney coach is waiting outside her home, which would save time and further strain upon her ankle."

"Hmmm. You say she lives nearby. I would not wish to drag her out when a doctor has been sent for. As 'tis already time I was on my way home, I suppose I could betake myself to the lady to confirm the facts. I could return here in the hackney to take whatever steps are warranted while the coach waits. Make no mistake, Captain Easterday; I expect Fowler to be available to testify."

"I will undertake to make sure he is."

"Very well, then. Let us pay a call upon the lady."

Easterday sent Finley to alert Mistress Williams and Olivia to expect their arrival, while the magistrate issued a spate of instructions to his staff and his clerk packed a satchel with paper, pens, and ink. Easterday's men would remain with Fowler.

\*\*\*\*

Rachel Williams took them up to Olivia's chamber, twittering all the way.

"I was never more shocked in my life! If such a thing had ever happened to me, I must have swooned quite away and gone into strong hysterics when I came to myself again. My dear niece has amazing fortitude..."

Olivia was resting against several pillows on her bed, still dressed, although a blanket covered her to the waist. Easterday guessed she had permitted her shoes and stockings to be removed in anticipation of the doctor's arrival.

"When Dr. Robertson comes—he has been delayed, having been called to treat a sick baby—I will offer him tea if you are still with Olivia, but he is very busy and may not wish to wait," Rachel murmured. Easterday thought she would be the better for some composing draft, or perhaps a glass of brandy.

Unflustered, Olivia greeted the magistrate and thanked him for coming to her. She bit her lip when he asked in the tone used for addressing children and those of weak mind if she could tell him what had happened. Easterday hoped her teeth were not grinding audibly. He could not hear them, but then, he was standing back to make room for the magistrate and the clerk, who had requested a small table be provided for his use in writing down the witness's testimony.

Her account was concise, and like Easterday's was mostly the truth. The less truthful bits were not provable as lies. A young man calling himself Barlow had worked for Cantarell Shipping for a time, then left abruptly without notice. One of the office messengers had been detained by a man who questioned him about Barlow. A man claiming to be Barlow's uncle and guardian had confronted her and threatened her.

"He told me he made a bad enemy, and I now perceive he was correct," she said primly. *Admirable woman!*

"Did anyone else hear him make that statement?"

"Mr. Finley was present, as was one of the boys."

"The attack must have come as a severe shock to you, Mistress Olivia. In my experience, after such an event most ladies would be in a state of collapse."

*Most ladies are not Olivia.*

"Certainly, it would have been an alarming experience if Captain Easterday had not told me of the rumored abduction."

"He told you?" The magistrate glanced at Easterday, eyebrows raised.

"I believed Mistress Olivia would be less frightened if she knew of it in advance, rather than be taken by surprise."

"That is certainly an original notion. I would have thought the apprehension of it would quite overset any lady."

"I fear I lack delicacy of feeling," Olivia confessed mournfully. "My father, having been at sea and then engaged in the shipping trade, did not encourage missishness or megrims."

"I see." He asked several more questions and requested clarification on some points. Olivia remained composed, and at last the man was satisfied.

Easterday said, "I will accompany you back to the court to collect my people. Will you trust me to produce Swithin Fowler to testify at trial?"

"I suppose so." His clerk was already repacking his satchel.

As the magistrate stumped out followed by his minion, Easterday said, "I'll return again, if you have no objection?"

"None at all. I would not be able to sleep tonight without knowing what is going forward."

Chapter 40

Dr. Robertson came soon after and performed the most important of his services: calming Aunt Rachel. It was, after all, only a sprain. The young lady (the doctor was in his sixtieth year) should keep the foot elevated, and perhaps a hot compress would be soothing. She might walk on it if she felt inclined. He did not recommend laudanum. Here he levelled a satirical glance at her, having been her doctor since she was a child. He knew full well she would not keep to her bed a moment longer than necessary.

"Thank you, doctor. I expect it will be perfectly comfortable by tomorrow."

Aunt Rachel accompanied him downstairs, only to return in a matter of minutes. Her aunt's agitated voice in the corridor provided her first inkling of Easterday's return.

"...not quite proper even with your betrothal, and she should be resting," Aunt Rachel fretted. After two soft taps at her door, her aunt's voice inquired, "Livvie? Are you still awake?"

"Yes, Aunt." As though she could have fallen asleep in a matter of five minutes and so early in the evening, too.

"Captain Easterday is here again. If you wish to see him, I will bring him in."

"Please do."

Her aunt flitted in, with Easterday close behind. "You may move that chair a little closer to the bed if you wish, Captain. I shall sit on the bed."

He made Olivia a handsome bow and turned the straight chair from the dressing table to position it nearer, though Aunt Rachel being perched on the edge of the bed, he was still a good three feet away.

"Captain Easterday, thank you for taking the time to come back."

"How could I not assure myself that you were recovering from the shock? You do not appear to be prostrated, though knowing your mettle I did not expect that you would be. How is your ankle? Is it very painful?"

"No, only a bit stiff and sore when I walk on it, and somewhat swollen."

"You should keep to your bed for two or three days, with your foot elevated on a cushion, no matter what Dr. Robertson said," her aunt declared.

Olivia and Easterday exchanged a glance of total understanding.

"I will be up and around tomorrow and going to the office at the usual time."

"Livvie, really…"

"Captain, will you tell me what happened at the courthouse?"

"In brief, the magistrate was persuaded to release Swithin Fowler into my custody to insure that he is available to testify against the uncle, who will be arrested as soon as he can be found."

"Does Fowler not object?"

"He dared not, as he would otherwise have been lodged in a cell at the court. He will be more comfortable aboard my ship *Queen of the Sea* at anchor near the Tower, than he would be in a cell. Less likely to catch jail fever, too."

"Will he not have to incriminate himself to give evidence against Ainslie's uncle?"

"The magistrate decided prosecuting Ainslie was more important than hanging Fowler, who might have escaped serious consequences in any case, as he is a very facile liar. Also, I suggested that after the trial, Fowler might remove himself to one of the colonies at my expense."

"That seems a very satisfactory outcome."

"I am not sure Fowler would agree, though he may change his mind. When I parted from them, Finley was describing the delights of New York City: its port, its bustle, its many nationalities, the beauty of the women."

Olivia laughed.

"I cannot stay longer. Fowler gave directions to the cottage outside London where you were to be delivered to Ainslie. I've sent one of my people to the nearest livery stable to hire me a horse. I mean to secure Ainslie before he realizes the abduction has gone awry."

"But the magistrate will send constables to take him into custody, surely?" Aunt Rachel asked.

"Yes, but I am not sanguine that they will be quick enough about it. Considerable time has been lost already, but if I leave as soon as Willie brings me a horse, I believe I can be there before Ainslie realizes something has gone amiss. A horse will be faster than a coach, and Ainslie cannot be certain some delay did not occur in your leaving your office or in travelling to his lair."

"You do not mean to confront him, Marcus? If he chances to be armed—"

"I have a pistol. But does Horace Ainslie sound to you like a dangerous man?"

"At our one encounter, I accounted him a blusterer. 'All heat and no fire', as Ky described him."

"That's what I thought."

"Still, it would be better to wait for the constables."

"I do not mean to board the pirate ship all on my own. I will only act if he decides his scheme has failed and tries to escape. His capture is of greater concern to me than to the court; once he's away, the law will put little emphasis on finding him. Better to take him now."

The warmth in his eyes made her swallow hard.

Rising to take his leave, he approached the bed. Somehow he possessed himself of her hand although it, like the other, had been clutching the coverlet, and pressed a kiss upon it. His lips upon her hand in her office had seemed shockingly inappropriate. Here…she felt both hot and cold at once. Here it was more…more…intimate. Perhaps because they were in her bedchamber and her aunt was watching. Or perhaps she was recalling her feelings when Ambrose Hawkins had taken liberties with her in the house off Old Gravel Lane. Although less dangerously exciting, the kiss and the look in his eyes spoke to her. His hand clasped hers, warm and strong. How had she not realized earlier how very attractive Captain Marcus Easterday was? She hoped her eyes answered.

"I cannot bear the thought you might be hurt."

His smile widened. "I protest I am a cautious man, not some young hothead. I will call upon you midmorning tomorrow."

And he kissed her hand again.

Chapter 41

The cottage, though isolated, was not far outside London, and within a mile of a well-traveled road. A kidnapper could not be expected to transport his victim any great distance without risking some mischance leading to discovery or the victim's escape.

Twilight was dimming the road. He was lucky enough to get a good hired horse; he had made fair speed, given his late start. Fowler had told him, "Watch for a low, broken wall on the right," and here was a dilapidated stone wall. Someone should repair it. What was the sense of having a wall if it would not keep livestock in? It ended at a narrow track leading off toward a copse, and there, shining like a star, was the golden light of a candle. He walked the horse as far up the lane as he dared and tethered the nag to one of the trees. A small structure stood beyond the coppice, candlelight glowing in one window. Ainslie must still be waiting for his hirelings to bring Olivia to him.

He approached the side of the house carefully, through the trees. Ainslie probably was peering out the unshuttered window at intervals, hoping for the sight of coach lamps approaching. Someone on foot without a lantern should be invisible by now to a man staring into the dark from a lighted room. Passing the end of the cottage, he made out the shape of a large shed or barn as ill-kept as the wall. Presumably Ainslie's horse was within. Or a coach and horses? If the latter, there must be a coachman present in the house. Subduing two men would be more difficult, if it came to preventing Ainslie's leaving. As the constables had not arrived, Easterday was willing to wager a tidy sum they would not arrive before morning. *I should have thought of the possibility Ainslie would have brought a way to transport his prisoner. I was not made for a life of crime.*

How likely was it? No flicker of light showed through the shutters on the east side of the house. Except for the one window, none had been visible on the front side or the end wall he had passed. Anyone who was in the house must be in the front room. Would Ainslie be keeping company with his coachman? Likely a servant would be sent to the kitchen to wait, but not in the dark, surely.

And why would Ainslie risk moving Olivia from here, when there were no houses nearby? It would only create complications. Best, always, to keep things simple. He smiled at the thought. Why bother to watch the house? Instead he could watch the horse. Ainslie would not have marooned himself here without a means of transport.

Stepping carefully and hoping not to step on some cast-off implement which would make noise, he crossed the yard to the outbuilding, freezing at the sound of a creak. No cover was near enough to shelter behind unless he ran for it, which might alert a listener— particularly if he tripped over some debris. He chose to remain where he was. Another creak, then another which sounded exactly like the first he had heard. Picking his way carefully, he approached the double door and took a deep breath in relief. One side hung askew, the top hinge separated from the jamb, the latch missing. The door swung a few inches in the rising breeze.

He slipped inside and paused to take his bearings. The last light of evening fell through the open door. He did not really need it. He smelled hay and horse and heard a soft equine snort to his left. There would be nothing on the floor between the door and the stall, whatever obstacles there might be elsewhere. He glanced out at the back of the house. Still dark. He pushed the door open farther which gave enough light to make out an alcove to the left of the doors and several tie stalls of the simplest sort, with roughly constructed side walls. The alcove served as a tack room, with pegs for harness, a trestle holding a saddle, and several buckets and a keg or two. In the first stall, he could see a horse's hindquarters.

In line with the doors a small wagon stood, one wheel missing. The right side of the space was occupied by a wheelbarrow and a jumble of agricultural tools, with some barrels and kegs against the wall. None of the equipment looked to have been in recent use. An abandoned farm?

He selected a keg and rolled it over to the wagon. Positioned by the rear wheel on the side away from the stalls, it would make a seat. Ainslie was unlikely even to glance at anything but the stabling area. When he came in, Easterday would have him. If by some chance the minions of the law arrived, he was certain to hear their approach in the quiet country night.

Easterday wondered how soon Ainslie's nerve would break.

Sitting in the dark with nothing to do was strangely peaceful, not unlike some watches at sea when the weather was calm and warm. A man kept alert for changes and the approach of another vessel without thinking about them. He could recall what occupied his mind then: girls he hoped to bed and girls he might like to marry, his prospects for advancing his career.

Opportunities for reflection came less often now. Nor had he wanted to think about the shipwreck of his first betrothal. Dwelling upon the pain and humiliation would have been pointless. In retrospect, he had begun to wonder if 'twould have been better to pay as much attention to why Claudia had eloped with someone else as he would have given to some problem with a ship or cargo.

He knew the bare bones of why she had done it without considering it in depth. One, she had loved the other man or thought she did. Two, her papa had insisted she accept his own proposal, as Easterday was already successful. Claudia's other wooer had little to offer apart from a competence and a store of compliments and sighs. He also presented her with nosegays of violets out of season or one perfect rose accompanied by a poem comparing it to her complexion, to the rose's disadvantage.

Easterday thought he had complimented her though he could not recall on what. He had given her the kinds of little gifts considered unexceptionable from a single man to a lady: a fan, a book...Why would he have thought a book suitable? Claudia had not been at all bookish, he was fairly sure. He could not remember what they had talked about on the occasions they had been together. He could not call to mind anything about

Claudia's interests or her likes or dislikes apart from her partiality for overblown praise and romantical gestures.

Why had he ever thought her a suitable choice? Had he loved her?

If he had, he should be able to remember why. No, she had been suitable, and he had been ready to marry. She was very pretty, with golden hair and big blue eyes, she was docile, and she was the daughter of a banker with whom he had done business. He would have put far more thought into entering into a business partnership.

He blew out an exasperated breath. The horse snorted softly in reply. Well, he had been young, and many men married for reasons as slight. Probably such marriages sometimes worked out well. Given his experience with Claudia Dean, however, if he had thought about it afterward, he would never have offered for Mariah Saltstall. Mariah's qualifications as a potential wife were virtually identical to Claudia's, except that she was lively and spoiled. The latter made her a less suitable wife in his opinion, though some men apparently enjoyed catering to their wives' caprices.

Obviously, he was slow to learn from past mistakes. Unlike Claudia and Mariah, his mistresses had been selected with the care he used for his business dealings; all of them had been pleasant and sensible, none of them sulked or made demands. Their liaisons had been conducted on sound commercial principles; they were willing to accept what he was willing to pay, and in return they made their bodies available, did not entertain other men while he retained their services, and were pleasant companions. A truly shocking thought—

any of them would have been a better wife than Claudia or Mariah. *Good God!*

He was forgetting his current betrothed. Olivia was nothing like the first two. While not conventionally pretty, her face and form were elegant. She was intelligent. She had a sense of humor. Hawkins had compared her to a blade of Damascus steel, with nothing trumpery about her. For all the man's faults, he was exactly right about Olivia.

When he had carried her into the house last night, the feeling of her lithe body in his arms heated his blood. He would very much like to share that Chinese bed with her. Not only because he had been without a woman for too long, either. How strange that he knew her better than he had known Claudia or Mariah. It would not be difficult to imagine spending an evening in her company. Living with her. Having children with her. She had not seemed to dislike being carried up to her bed, either.

If she were willing...What would be a suitable wedding gift for a lady of taste with an interest in shipping? He could not attempt to find something Chinese to suit her, being too ignorant of the subject (unlike Hawkins, damn him). Unless he consulted Ah Fong, which he might consider. Jewelry? Easy to buy, but would she wear it? Then he almost laughed aloud. He had seen a painting of a Dutch timber ship by Samuel Scott, who apparently made a specialty of maritime scenes. Artists were always eager for commissions; could the fellow be induced to do a painting of ships in the Pool, perhaps with the Custom House in the background?

Then he heard footsteps and a horse's hooves

approaching. The magistrate had given orders for two men to apprehend Ainslie. Not the law, then, for a constable might go to the back door while his colleague took the front; he would not lead his horse to the stable. He rose from the keg to stand pressed against the wall to the right of the door, where he would not be seen until the intruder stepped across the threshold.

The door creaked open. The glow of a lantern cast faint illumination over the floor as the man entered. Was it possible Ainslie had gone outside and found Easterday's mount? He had left it at some distance from the house, making discovery unlikely unless Ainslie had walked down the lane toward the road, and even then only by luck. Might he have done so to look for the coming of the coach with his henchmen and victim?

Once he saw the horse's head, he knew by its height the nag was not the mount Willie had chosen. Easterday waited while the fellow led it into the second stall, murmuring to it, and busied himself removing the saddle and bridle. Rustles indicated he was rubbing the horse down with a handful of straw and filling the manger with hay.

"Ay, that's good. Have a bite to eat."

The groom, if that was what he was, made everything a great deal more difficult. He must have been sent on some errand. Easterday silently cursed himself. He should have known Ainslie would not travel without a servant.

The groom's presence made it impossible to wait until Ainslie panicked at the failure of his hirelings to arrive. The servant would be the one sent to saddle the horses when Ainslie was sure his scheme had failed unless Ainslie, wrought up to a high state of nerves, came out with him. Mayhap the heroes of drama and the more bombastic novels would not hesitate to take on two men at once; no prudent man, past youth's foolhardiness, would attempt it. He must capture the groom before he left the stable.

He heard the man sigh. "Off to the well, then, for a bucket of water, then off to bed—I hope!"

As the groom bent to pick up a bucket in the alcove, Easterday was upon him. Jerking him upright by his collar, he punched him in the side of the jaw. The man was short, bowlegged, wiry and taken by surprise. He must be strong to handle horses; he might have been a veteran of stableyard scuffles. In a sailors' brawl or fight with a boarding party, he was an infant. The fellow tried to elbow him in the stomach without doing more damage than a bruise. A blow to the chin which made Easterday's knuckles smart laid the fellow out. Definitely unconscious. Easterday wished he had thought to bring rope with him. He'd know better next time, he thought, grinning.

He took the lantern from its hook on the stall's end. By rights, a stable and barn should contain rope. A peg in the alcove yielded a coil of the useful stuff. He rolled his victim over and set about securing his hands and feet without bothering to cut it until he finished with several loops around the ankles. He was unfolding his penknife when some instinct—perhaps taking note of a sound he had not consciously heard—caused him to surge swiveling up from his crouch.

The brass lantern struck jarringly between neck and left shoulder rather than on his head. The blow was amazing painful. Ainslie—he assumed—was raising his arm for a second blow. If it hit his head with the same force, he was finished.

His left arm responded weakly, all but useless. His right acted by reflex, bringing up the penknife to ram into Ainslie's upper arm. Easterday lost his grip on the little knife's handle when the man jerked back in surprise. So much the better; it gave Easterday an opportunity to drive his fist into Ainslie's chin. He needed to render the scoundrel incapable, not merely prick him, for given the way his left shoulder was sagging, and the difficulty in moving that arm, a gouty old man would be a match for him. Ainslie, no matter how indolent, would be more than a match. Had he struck hard enough?

Easterday reached into his pocket to draw out his pistol as Ainslie fell back against the door jamb and slid to the ground. Then he slumped over onto his left side. Easterday silently thanked God.

Returning the pistol to the flapped pocket seemed out of the question for the moment. Was he going to be able to tie Ainslie up? To do so, he first had to retrieve the knife so he could cut the excess from the rope with which he'd bound the groom. In order to accomplish that feat, it would be necessary to do something about his arm, which hurt confoundedly. A broken collarbone, he suspected. He undid several of the buttons of his waistcoat, picked up his dangling left hand and succeeded in maneuvering the fingers into the opening. It was an improvement of sorts, if not as good as a sling.

Bending to heave Ainslie off his side was awkward; for a few moments, his own head swam unpleasantly. The thought he might faint like some tightly corseted lady steadied him, too ridiculous to contemplate. He took hold of Ainslie's waistcoat and tugged, dragging him to a sitting position against the door frame. Easterday leaned panting against the wall, chilled and shaky. *Best get him tied up before he stirs.* He bent once more and drew out the knife. Blood gushed over the toes of his boots, pooling beneath them.

*Hell!* He let the penknife fall, dropped to his knees, and pressed down at the point where the blood welled, stemming it. It needed to be bandaged. He could use Ainslie's neckcloth. To get it off, he would have to use his right hand, which would mean he could not apply pressure on the wound. Cautiously he released it. The blood flowed again, but more slowly. He scrabbled to free the cloth around Ainslie's throat. The task was too slow with one hand. Reluctantly, he removed his left hand from the support of his waistcoat and winced at the pain. He did not think he could stand leaning his weight on the hand, but using only his fingers to squeeze the cut seemed to work. His shoulder hurt fiercely, but he could tolerate it while he loosened and unwound the cloth.

Getting it wrapped tightly enough around Ainslie's arm cost him several painful attempts and some thought before it occurred to him to clench one end between his teeth to hold it taut while he wound the rest of the length around the upper arm. He tied a sloppy knot with the last few inches. Ainslie stirred and muttered something before quieting again.

He tucked his hand back into its improvised sling and picked up the knife. He almost closed it before realizing he would not be able to open it again one-handed. He stood up wearily, trying to marshal his thoughts. Instead he found himself staring numbly at the blood beneath his feet. He wore sailor's trousers as part of his disguise; the lower legs were now soaked and clung to his legs. How much blood had Ainslie lost?

The constables would not arrive now; it must be midnight or later, and they were London men. The countryside would not see them blundering around in the dark.

It was tempting to lie down and wait. *Get thee behind me, Satan.* He could not rest yet. Shipboard emergencies must be dealt with briskly, and he had found it a good rule on land also. Ainslie needed a doctor. Blood had not yet soaked through the binding, but he could not be certain the bleeding had actually stopped. He would have to go for help. How far was the nearest place he could expect to find a doctor—and preferably a magistrate, too?

Turning to take stock of his surroundings, his eyes met the groom's wide gaze.

"Do you know anything of the nearest village? What's there?"

The fellow swallowed several times before answering. "Ay, sir. I was there this evening. Mr. Ainslie sent me on an errand."

"What errand?"

"He wanted to know if friends of his had come—stopped for supper, mayhap, or if they'd gone through and missed their way coming here."

"The villains he set to kidnap a lady, you mean."

"I don't know nothing about that, sir."

"If he believed they might have stopped for a meal or a drink"—neither likely with Olivia in the coach—

"there must be an inn?" He did not remember seeing one, but then, he'd been watching for the landmarks.

"A small one. They wasn't there nor hadn't been."

*No, they wouldn't have been there.*

"If you don't mind me saying, sir, I think your collarbone's broke."

"I think the same." The candle was guttering in the groom's lantern hanging by the stall. The candle in the other had gone out when the lantern fell to the floor. Its translucent horn panes had not broken when Ainslie used the lantern as a club or in falling, far safer than one with glass panes for use in a stable. He picked it up and set it on the keg beside his pistol, which he fumbled awkwardly into his pocket after several attempts. He would replace the failing candle with Ainslie's almost unburned one.

"I intend to ride for help, but I'll leave you with light."

"Would ye be so good as to untie my legs, sir?"

"Why not? I'll cut the rope partway through and you can do the rest." He did not give a damn if the groom escaped. The fellow was likely not a knowing, or at least not a willing, accomplice.

Then he began trudging back to his horse.

Chapter 42

She would have sworn she had lain awake all night, turning from one side to the other, pushing back the blanket and pummeling her pillow to better support her head, except that each time she recalled fragments of uneasy dreams. Rising somewhat earlier than her custom, she found her ankle only a little stiff. She washed her face with the water left over from the night before, then unbraided and combed out her hair. She put it up in its usual tidy style, but her mirror told her she was pale and had dark smudges under her eyes.

When Kitty came with hot water, Olivia was already dressed and standing at the window, peering down at the street.

"Lawks, ma'am!"

"I woke early. You may as well take the water to my aunt. I am going downstairs now."

"Mistress Williams said you should rest your poor foot."

"I only turned it. I am able to walk."

"Cook won't have nothing ready for breakfast yet."

"I wouldn't expect her to, so early. After you've taken Aunt Rachel's water to her, please have Mistress Grissom make coffee. I would very much like to take a cup or two, while I go over some matters in the office."

She had nothing much to do in the little office and could not have settled to it if she had, but she felt at home there and could pretend to review the household accounts. In the parlor or dining room, she would have had nothing to occupy her, and in the latter, she would have felt she was making their cook nervous by seeming to await a meal that was not yet ready.

Which was ridiculous, except that Kitty would tell Cook, and Olivia knew the knowledge would make her fidgety, leading to over- or under-cooked eggs and burnt toast. She herself was nervous enough for the entire household.

What had happened since Marcus left? Had he found Ainslie and brought him back? Very likely he had. One could not expect that he would then hasten to her in the middle of the night. That would be the act of a romantical-minded man, when no urgency attended the matter. In a home like theirs, too, where he would have to rouse an elderly footman, Kitty, or the cook to admit him, it would be ridiculously noisy and inconvenient. He could have tossed pebbles at her window. They would certainly have waked her out of her light sleep if she had been asleep.

The idea of Marcus Easterday, the most responsible and composed of men, carrying on like a lovesick swain made her smile. No, she really could not have expected it of him. She had told him she would be at Cantarell Shipping today, and he would have taken her at her word. Ambrose Hawkins would have pounded at the door, waking the entire square, to let her know he had returned and to check on her—unless he had insisted on her taking a dose of laudanum before he left, to guarantee she slept. He would certainly not have wanted her to go to the office, this morning or any other.

Such extreme solicitude stirred something in her, perhaps because it indicated care for her, even love. Who could resist the pleasure of being loved? Not even she, although she did not mean to give in to it. She had already made up her mind about Hawkins long since. His love would wrap her in swaddling clothes, which she could not endure. He was also arbitrary, would expect to be the master of his house, and occasionally violent, if his treatment of poor Kit was any indication. She understood those traits, but she would not put up with them. He would take her business and her freedom as well.

If only Marcus…She cut that thought short. Their engagement was a sham and would soon be ended. Fortunately, as her mind treacherously pointed out how placid and rational life would be with a man like Marcus Easterday, Kitty came to announce that breakfast was ready and that her aunt was already in the dining room.

She would have left for Cantarell Shipping early but for the reflection that she should not be in the office before Finley. The captain was correct: being alone in that area was unsafe for a female. She would go in at the regular time. Her aunt was distressed at the thought of her going in to work at all. Had she insisted on going early, Aunt Rachel would have given way to a fit of the vapors, which would have delayed her departure.

In any event, her departure was delayed anyway, for Davant, who had taken over morning escort duty from Matthias Ainslie, failed to arrive with a hackney. She waited for near half an hour before sending Kitty out to fetch one. It was surprising that he should have failed to arrive but on reflection, it occurred to her that perhaps Finley—or Captain Easterday—had needed him to do something related to yesterday's abduction. Guard Swithin Fowler, their witness? Something else? It hardly mattered…probably. With Horace Ainslie thwarted, it should be safe enough to go to her office by hackney coach which would deliver her to the door. So she would not arrive before midmorning now, which was when Marcus had told her he would call on her. She only hoped he had not become concerned when she did not arrive and gone to Well Close Square in search of her. Would he have done so, or merely assumed that she had been too feeble to get up?

****

When she swept through the door, the air of tension and activity were palpable. Finley's and Davant's heads snapped up.

"Mistress Cantarell…" For once, Finley seemed at a loss for words.

"What's happened? Captain Easterday…?" She did not know what she meant to ask. Or was afraid to put it in words.

"He found the house and, er, captured Horace Ainslie and a servant. I apologize for keeping Davant from coming for you, but when I received the captain's message early this morning, I needed Davant to take a letter to the captain's office, and…er…"

"You supposed me so weak and womanly, I would not come in today."

"I thought you might need a little additional time this morning. I sent Kit to Well Close Square but told him to deliver the letter to the magistrate first. He must have missed you. I've sent Ky to hire a travelling coach. It will be here shortly. I need Davant to tend to

368

the office."

Clearly, he was nervous about her reaction, but Olivia took no time to reassure him.

"What has happened to Captain Easterday?"

"He was slightly injured. It's nothing to signify, but he will be more comfortable travelling by coach than riding and—"

Ky burst in. "It's here, Mr. Finley! Sorry, ma'am! Didn't know you was here."

Finley stood up hurriedly. "I'll be away, then."

"Why was a coach not hired where Captain Easterday is?" Was it because he was in no condition to arrange it?

"It's a tiny place. They have nothing for rent, barring a farm cart, mayhap. The constables meant to return with Ainslie and his fellow, but Ainslie's hurt, too—"

"No doubt there's room for the captain, Ainslie, and myself in the coach, even if Captain Easterday must lie down. You can ride on the box if necessary. Come, Mr. Finley, let's be on our way." Unless, dear Heaven, both Marcus and Ainslie needed to lie down. In which case, she would ride on the box, and Finley would have to ride with the constables.

"Ma'am..."

"If at least one of the rogues can ride, and the constables ride, there must surely be a spare seat inside. I am coming."

Finley looked as though he would like to protest; Davant appeared to approve of her decision.

"Come, Mr. Finley, am I an unreasonable employer?"

"No, indeed, ma'am." He opened the door and

ushered her out.

Neither of them spoke much in the coach. The journey seemed interminable to Olivia, with numerous delays in the crowded streets, although once out of London, they made good speed. She did question Finley further, but he had few details to give her. The captain's letter had mentioned he was slightly injured, though not how. Yes, the letter was in his own hand, which she found reassuring. He had also been able to give instructions about hiring a coach and sending messages to her, to the Well Close Square courthouse, and to his office. Presumably he was not badly hurt, but if he felt unable to ride, his injury could hardly be minor.

Finley dredged up a fresh piece of information. "He said a doctor had tended him."

****

The hamlet could not have seen so much excitement since...Olivia could not guess when. A festival atmosphere prevailed, with people loitering in front of the Sheep and Shrew (a small, unpretentious inn which probably did far more business in ale and cider than in rooms), children and dogs running back and forth, and a woman selling fresh-made buns—*Hot buns! Hot!*—from a board over a pair of trestles. The travelling coach caused a stir.

"If you will wait in the coach, Mistress Cantarell, I'll go in and tell the captain we've arrived."

"I'm coming in with you."

Finley did not persist. He was beginning to know her ways.

The door, standing open, led into a taproom. Olivia caught fragments of conversation before silence fell at the sight of them.

"...brought in for dead, he was."

*Not Easterday!* she hoped.

"...woke me in the middle o' the night when the London gentleman come pounding on the door, demanding a magistrate and a doctor and a wagon and men to guard a gang o' felons..."

"...what with rousing Thatcher and his old woman, and them waking the ostler and sending Bert for Sir John and the doctor, soon enough the constables woke, and them sent to arrest the ones the first fellow was talking about."

By then, Olivia and Finley were in the middle of the room. A thickset woman in a grubby apron started forward, wiping her hands on the said apron as she came.

"Mistress, where may we find Captain Easterday?"

"You'd be the folk he expected? Back this way."

She led them to a small room that served as a private parlor or dining room at need, not that the Sheep and Shrew seemed the sort of place the gentry would frequent. As the woman tapped at the door, Finley stood aside to let Olivia precede him. Fortunate for him he was courteous!—Olivia was prepared to push past him if necessary.

"Sir, this gentleman and lady..."

He was sitting in a high-backed old chair, left arm in a sling. He was unshaven, untidy, and his gray face bore lines of pain and exhaustion both.

"M—Captain." She swallowed. He was so much less...less composed than usual that her heart was wrung. Seeing her, he began to rise with an obvious effort, bracing his right hand on the arm of the chair.

She hurried forward. "Don't get up! You should be

resting on your bed."

He sank back but gave her a death's head grin, saying, "...not an invalid, only tired. Finished with the justice of the peace around five, then I had to write...there wasn't time..." His voice was hoarse. His eyes were slightly unfocused and tended to wander.

"When did you last eat?" Seeing him trying to search his memory, she said, "Never mind. Mistress Thatcher! We'll want tea and something to eat— whatever you have that's ready. Mr. Finley? Will you take tea or would you rather have ale?"

"Ale, if I might."

"Ay, ma'am and sirs. I've wiggs come out of the oven just now, which I wouldn't as a rule, but this has brought a mort of folk in and they all wants a morsel with their ale." She gave a brisk nod and marched out.

Olivia grabbed a rush-seated chair and dragged it over next to Easterday's before Finley could move to do it for her. "Marcus, Finley tells me you were attended by a doctor. Should you not engage a room here and rest before returning to London? "

Easterday gave himself a little shake and winced. "Ainslie needs to go by coach. Boards across the seats so he can lie down. Ostler knows. The medico cauterized it. Only a little cut, but it bled and bled."

"You shall tell me about it later. Finley, you'll tell the ostler to make the same arrangements for the captain. He cannot sit up all the way back to London."

"Yes, Mistress Cantarell."

Before he could leave the room, Mistress Thatcher brought in a tray. She set it down on a table near them and hovered, waiting for further instructions. "Shall I pour, ma'am?"

"I'll pour the tea, Mistress Thatcher. We need nothing more at the moment."

Finley helped himself to his tankard of ale and a bun. "I'll go out to the stable yard. Shall I say we will be leaving in about two hours, to give them time to make up a second bed in the coach? The horses and coachman will be wanting a drink, too, and the horses need a rest."

"That will do very well. We will not be travelling fast on our way back," she said before Easterday could speak. She was not sure he had even intended to reply; he was looking stretched very thin.

Olivia busied herself with the tea tray. She added sugar to Easterday's bowl though he ordinarily took only milk in his tea, as she had noticed during his visit to Well Close Square. She suspected he had not eaten since the previous midday. She looked for a place to set his cup, the table being a little too far from his chair and cluttered with the mismatched tea service, plates, and the cloth-covered basket holding the buns. A battered joint stool stood near the fireplace. She fetched it over and positioned it by Easterday's chair. The stool was low for a table, but it would serve. The seat was big enough to hold a tea bowl and a small plate.

The innkeeper's wife had provided both wiggs, redolent of caraway seeds, and diamond-shaped pieces of gingerbread. Olivia put one of each on a plate and deposited bowl and plate on the stool, convenient to the captain's right hand.

He raised the bowl shakily. She restrained the urge to take it from him and hold it to his lips. He managed unassisted, swallowed, and blinked. He took another long swallow and set the bowl down.

"Eat that lovely bun, Marcus. You would not want to hurt Mistress Thatcher's feelings."

He picked up the wigg and looked at it. "I must have been thirsty."

Three bowls of tea, two buns, and three pieces of gingerbread later, some color had returned to his face, though the dark smudges under his eyes testified to exhaustion. His attention focused on her in a manner she found unsettling. Bewildered? Stern? Doubtful? All of them at once? Unquestionably, the place for Captain Easterday was in bed.

Clearing his throat, he said, "You are a fine steel blade rather than a trashy bedizened dress sword." His face took on an inward look. "That doesn't sound right. Hawkins said it of you, but he put it more poetically."

She had raised a morsel of bun to her lips, having discovered she was hungry, too, having taken nothing but coffee and a slice of bread and butter earlier. Now she paused and stared at Easterday. "Hawkins has very insinuating ways. I take it as a great compliment to be compared to good steel. Poetical or not."

"You possess rare qualities. You are sensible. You do not collapse in adversity…"

"I fear you flatter me, sir." To cover her confusion, she sipped her tea. It had gone cold while she plied Easterday with tea and food.

"You have the heart of a lion—"

"In a crock, preserved in spirits of wine," she murmured, taking refuge from embarrassment in whimsy.

He smiled at her in a way that made her feel warm all over.

"I know you haven't been thinking of marriage…"

Oh, she had.

"We enjoy each other's company, and marriage would have advantages for both of us. Olivia, would you consider changing our bargain to a betrothal in earnest?"

"Oh, Marcus." She could only look at him mutely.

"I'm sorry! Please don't take offense. I wanted to do this better. I'm not good at expressing sentiment at my best. When I was younger, I could go without sleep for days without sounding like a babbling idiot." He tossed off the tea remaining in his cup in the manner of one fortifying himself for a challenge. "We can write in the marriage settlements that you retain your property and the right to manage it. On my honor, I will never treat you as chattel. Do we have a bargain?"

She chewed her lip. She wished...

"I hope you are not absolutely opposed to the wedded state?"

"I don't think I am. I could never have married Ambrose Hawkins because I could not endure having nothing to do beyond making and receiving calls, presiding over social events, and deciding what to wear. I agree to your terms. Shall we shake hands on it?" She swallowed hard, her eyes and heart aching with the tears she was holding back. There was nothing she wanted more, except what was missing from his offer.

How she wished it might be more than merely a sensible marriage.

"We should indeed shake hands," he said, rising more easily than at his attempt on her arrival. She began to believe he had only needed food and rest, and he could sleep in the coach.

He studied her face, his brow furrowing. "I should

say I love you. Which is true. Everything I've said is true. My God, I'm botching the most important negotiation of my life."

She stood so abruptly the cold tea almost splashed out of the tea bowl she was still holding. "You do?"

"We should kiss. This is more than a business transaction. Olivia, dull as I am, I will love you until I die."

"Marcus, you are not dull. You are a romantic."

He laughed ruefully. "Please don't tell anyone."

Olivia searched for words. "It's hard to say, even without being exhausted and injured...I love you, too, for your kindness and decency and courage and sense and oh, everything. Now I'm babbling."

She extended her hand.

He gripped it in his.

After a long moment, he drew her toward him, to kiss her lingeringly, though their clasped hands were between them.

Delightful, if rather more chaste than she would have preferred. She wanted to press against him. When the kiss finally ended, he looked down at her apologetically.

"Alas, my love, I have only one useful arm with which to hold you. Also, I fear I reek of sweat and stable. I'll do better once my curst collarbone is healed. I suppose a true romantic would ignore such a mundane concern."

"I am willing to forego pleasure now in favor of rapid healing and embraces in a month or so. At the moment, the place for you is in bed."

*And in a month or so.* Her unruly imagination brought a blush to her face.

"Ah, you are a romantic, too," Easterday said, and kissed her again.

## A word about the author…

Kathleen Buckley wanted to write almost as soon as she learned to read. Fast forward to college, where she read the entire 1,000,000+ words of Samuel Richard's 1747 novel *Clarissa* over one Christmas vacation. This is probably why she feels at home in the 1740s.

She enjoys sewing costumes and quilts, testing historic recipes like Chelsea buns and Portugal cakes, cooking with Hatch green chiles—which are excellent in apple pie and almost anything else—and learning traditional handicrafts.

She has worked at a variety of jobs (receptionist in a hospital financial services office, light bookkeeping in a commercial print shop, paralegal, security officer), and learned interesting things in all of them.

She is now retired and lives in Albuquerque, New Mexico, with a friend and several cats.

Visit her at:
kbuckley87110@gmail.com
https://www.facebook.com/anunsuitableduchess/
https://www.goodreads.com/author/show
/270998.Kathleen_Buckley